. . . And never to better effect than in this contemporary novel of a missing boy and his strangely disturbing family:

His father, August Baird—A scientific genius, now dead, he has left behind him a huge estate and a dangerous emotional legacy of love and jealousy.

His mother, Bella—Charming, selfish, and perverted, she is ruthless in pursuit of anything she wants.

His Uncle Bo—Bella's twin brother, he's a talented and cold-blooded artist who has devilish impulses and insights.

His stepfather, Tom—A publisher of scientific books, he is crippled with severe arthritis, struggling against amnesia, and searching desperately to find the missing Gabriel. Because he loves him—or because he feels intense guilt in connection with their first meeting?

His Grandmother Baird—She is the woman who understands better than anyone else Gabriel's deepest longings.

In these characters, innocence and knowledge, hope and despair, good and evil are so entwined that not until literally the last page are all the strange turnings of their fates—and Gabriel's—resolved.

Books by Joan Aiken

Beware of the Bouquet
A Cluster of Separate Sparks
The Crystal Crow
Dark Interval
The Fortune Hunters
Midnight Is a Place
The Silence of Herondale
Voices in an Empty House

Published by POCKET BOOKS

*Are there paperbound books you want
but cannot find in your retail stores?*

You can get any title in print in **POCKET BOOK** editions. Simply
send retail price, local sales tax, if any, plus 35¢ per book to
cover mailing and handling costs, to:

MAIL SERVICE DEPARTMENT
   POCKET BOOKS • A Division of Simon & Schuster, Inc.
   1 West 39th Street • New York, New York 10018

   Please send check or money order. We cannot be responsible
   for cash.   *Catalogue sent free on request.*

Titles in this series are also available at discounts in quantity
lots for industrial or sales-promotional use. For details write our
Special Projects Agency: The Benjamin Company, Inc., 485
Madison Avenue, New York, New York 10022.

Joan Aiken

VOICES IN AN EMPTY HOUSE

PUBLISHED BY POCKET BOOKS NEW YORK

VOICES IN AN EMPTY HOUSE

Doubleday edition published 1975

POCKET BOOK edition published December, 1976

*All of the characters in this book are fictitious, and
any resemblance to actual persons, living or dead, is
purely coincidental.*

This POCKET BOOK edition includes every word contained in
the original, higher-priced edition. It is printed from brand-
new plates made from completely reset, clear, easy-to-read type.
POCKET BOOK editions are published by
POCKET BOOKS,
a division of Simon & Schuster, Inc.,
A GULF+WESTERN COMPANY
630 Fifth Avenue,
New York, N.Y. 10020.
Trademarks registered in the United States
and other countries.

ISBN: 0-671-80795-1.
Library of Congress Catalog Card Number: 74-14376.
This POCKET BOOK edition is published by arrangement
with Doubleday & Company, Inc. Copyright, ©, 1975, by
Joan Aiken. All rights reserved. This book, or portions
thereof, may not be reproduced by any means without per-
mission of the original publisher: Doubleday & Company,
Inc., 245 Park Avenue, New York, New York 10017.
Cover illustration by Roger Kastel.

Printed in the U.S.A.

To Julius and Tenth Street

Printed in the U.S.A.

One

Having just realised that he had lost his memory *again*, the man in the taxi felt an accustomed feverish sweat of panic begin at his feet and surge uncontrollably all the way up his body to end somewhere above the hairline. Accustomed? Yes, he felt certain that this was by no means a new experience. It had the familiarity of recent occurrence; must have happened many times before, as well.

It's going to be a slow job getting through life at this pace, he thought, loosening his tightly interlocked fingers —they were acutely tender, they shot small spurts of warning pain up his arms—and shifting his feet, which had somehow been left twisted sideways at a very uncomfortable angle, up on the centre bump in the taxi floor.

Rather like living with an old person who has become senile. What time is it, dear? I told you ten minutes ago. It's half-past three. And what *day* is it?

He looked out of the taxi window. Summer, evidently. The girls on the sidewalk wore minimal skirts, the men, with shirts knotted over navels, carried their jackets on their arms. Everybody strolled slowly, many licked at ice-cream cones. And there, slicing into view on the left, was, unmistakably, the Flatiron Building, that sharp and witty architectural impertinence, an elegant card-house cocking a knife-edged snook at the spires and rectangles and sober elevations round about.

Blue mailboxes, yellow cabs. Fierce gouts of steam pouring from holes in the street, as if the taxi was making its way through a thermal area. WALK, don't walk. Donuts. Chock Full o' Nuts. Fifth Avenue, New York. Great to see you again, New York, he thought, remembering the President who used this hearty greeting on friends and strangers alike.

Do Presidents have friends?

1

Look, let's stop fooling around, shall we?

Turning his observation inwards, he noted that he was wearing a grey suit, summer weight. White shirt. Had with him two bags, one a canvas hold-all, the other a grey fibreglass, not new; both carried PanAm labels. Returning from a trip, then? Or over on a visit?

The labels on the bags bore the name Cook, and so, on investigation, did his passport. British, much used.

A faint voice came back to him—doctor? lawyer? friend?—"Well, old boy, just so long as these spells go on, the best thing you can do is always carry your passport around with you. Then people will easily be able to find out who you are."

But what's the good of other people knowing who I am if *I* don't know?

He opened the passport and saw the usual startled, bespectacled face with dark hair that looked too short— it felt much longer now, he must have grown several inches of it since that picture was taken. Mr. Thomas Cook.

Well, well. Fancy that. Let's go on a tour of Mr. Thomas Cook.

He could feel the muscles of his face begin to stiffen into a false smile, perfunctory social acknowledgment of a joke already wearily familiar. Frowning instead, he turned the page. Place and date of birth, borough of Rumbury, 1933.

Occupation, biologist.

Biologist, huh?

If you had a scientific training, chum, why can't you avoid getting into this kind of jam, answer me that?

The driver turned his head and made some brief inquiry through the hole in the bullet-proof screen.

"What did you say?"

"Which side?" the driver repeated patiently. "Fifth and Tenth, you said. Which side?"

Which side? Which side? *Which side?*

The man called Thomas Cook fell into a panic again.

"Oh—right-hand side," he said at last, after what seemed like five minutes of feverish, fruitless thought. The driver glanced back again, puzzled. But, after all, why do we expect our minds and bodies to work always at lightning speed, dashing off memoranda like people in the movies, whipping exactly the right change out of our pockets, adding up columns like computers, leaping nimbly in and out of taxis with our luggage (in spite of the fact that our arms and legs hurt like hell), not a thought nor a movement wasted? Animals don't function in this way, or not most of the time; animals conserve their energy, animals are slow and ruminant in their movements, except when pursued.

That's the difference, of course. We are being pursued.

We live in the jungle, we are being stalked, and must act accordingly.

But who *is* the stalker, the unknown factor, the enemy whose hot breath we can feel right there close behind, so that we don't dare turn round? Like one that on a lonesome road doth walk in fear and dread and having once turned round, walks on and turns no more his head, because he knows a frightful fiend doth close behind him tread.

There! That came out pat as a pill. Why not my name?

With a stylish swerve the driver swept his taxi in to the kerb. Thomas fumbled for coins and bills and dropped them into the slot. Taking them, on his side of the screen, the driver looked them over without joy, gave a brief nod in acknowledgment, and waited. Thomas levered himself out painfully with his bags, and stood on the corner at a loss. He longed for courage to say to the driver, who had not yet driven off, but was still observing him with curiosity, "What address did I give you when I got in?"

After all, people come down with slight touches of amnesia practically every day, there is nothing to be ashamed of, nothing uncommon about it. Go on, *ask* him. Don't be such a coward. But after another long, inquisitive stare the man turned, shot his yellow cab away on a long slant into the thick of the traffic, and sped off. There he goes, taking my address with him; now what the hell do I do?

However, Tenth Street, when at length he tentatively walked round the corner and surveyed it, seemed to present a vaguely familiar, vaguely comfortable atmosphere, an indefinable sense of welcome and homecoming, as if a shape, a stencil in his mind, had fallen into place over the external pattern of houses in various shades of soft ochre, red, and rose-colour, wrought-iron railings, trails of leafy creeper, garbage cans, parked cars. Plane trees, acacia trees, ailanthus trees.

I'll walk along very slowly, he thought. After all, anybody walks slowly when they are carrying two heavy bags, specially if their arms are aching the way mine do —I'll walk slowly along and perhaps something will suddenly strike me.

Wide, aged sidewalk, cracked and patched. Two or three people in the distance. Elegant nineteenth-century brownstones.

He stopped and stared aimlessly at a tiny green hedged-in grass patch on which a somnolent tabby lay fully extended in the sun like a towel spread to dry.

A birdcage hung above; the budgerigar in it seemed to eye him with the same alert, detached curiosity—not sympathetic—as that shown by the taxi-driver.

How calm I am; how amazingly calm. Well, there's a phone-booth at the end of the street; if I have remembered nothing by the time I get to the corner, I'll walk back and call up the first doctor I can find in the book.

The budgerigar suddenly let out two notes, shrill, derisive. Lost! Lost!

> I'll *drive the van, with our things in it*
> You *walk be'ind with the old cock-linnet*
> —*But I dillied and dallied*
> *Dallied and dillied*
> And I can't find my way 'ome.

It was the worst nightmare of childhood, the known unknown, the familiar turned strange. Christmas Eve— why does that make me think of coming home on Christmas Eve?

Another verse came into his head, from even farther back, even more frightening. That was about the poor old woman, coming home from market, who had fallen asleep by the wayside.

> *Home went the old woman, all in the dark,*
> *Out came her little dog and he began to bark:*
> *He began to bark, and she began to cry*
> *Lawk a mercy on me! This is none of I!*

It always used to make *me* cry, when she sang it. To come home and find everything turned strange; to come home and have nobody recognise you—which would be worse?

4

What a terrible thing to do, to take away a person's identity. The worst kind of theft.

Now here, thought Thomas Cook, pausing, here at last was something truly familiar: a set of battered garbage cans, untidily overflowing, a bent railing, a flight of cracked steps. Each crack fell neatly into place in his mind. Our feet, luckily, know where we are going, even when our minds are travelling on a different level.

As he climbed the steps, he was thinking of the story that Bo had told him—told it as a huge joke—of the man at the printing works, the man who wouldn't join the union, so the others had boycotted him, not only by ignoring him, but by an elaborate pretence that he didn't exist at all, removing his name from lists, looking straight through him—so that in the end the wretched fellow had a total breakdown, was afraid to go home, was picked up wandering on Battersea Embankment in the small hours, weeping that he was Little Bo Peep's black sheep and had lost his tail. How much of that story had been true, and how much fantastic invention? It was certainly the kind of trick that Bo himself would like to play, would be quite capable of thinking up and carrying out; there was a decided streak of sadism in Bo's nature.

He was clever, entertaining, but one could never truly think of him as a friend; I never really liked him. Certainly never trusted him; felt nothing but relief when the connection was cut. But how did that happen?

Slipping out of his brief spell of oblivion as quickly as he had slipped into it, Thomas Cook walked through the open outer house door, fumbled slowly through a largish bunch of keys, and selected the little one that opened the mailbox. This was jammed full with the accumulation of months: bills, brochures, advertising circulars. Impatiently he unzipped his canvas hold-all and stuffed the envelopes and papers on top of his clothes; no need to re-zip. A faint uneasiness pursued him as he selected the next key and opened the front door—something he'd been trying to remember a moment ago, what was it? Something important, connected with what, with whom? It had been right there in his mind, just before the recollection about Bo. Or just after?

Too often, now, this happened: an essential link slipped away from him just before it could be hooked into place.

As always, he checked the marble table in the lobby

for mail, but there was none for him. There he stood, facing himself in the hall mirror: thin, tired; bushy dark greyish hair. A professor, one might have said; some kind of scholar.

He began slowly climbing the first of the four flights of stairs. Each step sloped sideways, and his right-hand bag, the canvas grip, kept bumping against the rail; he had to compensate by hitching himself to the left. The air in the stairwell was solid with heat—old, well-preserved air, summer vintage, matured in wood. Old hot cracked wood, old dirt-ingrained paint. He was obliged to rest after the second flight and again after the third. The last flight was narrower still, the black-painted stairs were thick with dust. Few people had climbed as high as this during the last week or two. Didn't blame them.

Manoeuvring two bags in the narrow space proved, as it always had, too awkward; he left the canvas one at the foot and, with a lighter load, took the last twelve steps two at a time. Climbing made his knees hurt; get it over as fast as possible.

He still retained the keys in his hand, uncomfortably wedged under the suitcase handle; found the right pair and, with difficulty, undid the two locks, first the Yale, then the mortice. The apartment was further defended by a police lock, a rod which fastened into place on the back of the door and hooked into the floor, so that the door would not open beyond a certain point. He put his arm through the narrow space, reached round, and unlocked the rod. It cost him a painful twinge. Ahead, to his complete astonishment, he heard the sound of voices: several voices, male and female.

His heart gave a great leap. Gabriel, and who else? Never mind—whoever it was, Gabriel must surely be one of the party. He had never for a moment expected that Gabriel might be *here*. Relief, hope, joy flooded over him. Added to that was the sheer unwonted happiness of coming home to company, after several years of returning to an empty place. His whole being expanded with delight as he ran down the stairs to pick up the second bag.

Of course Gabriel would not dream of coming out to welcome him. They never did that, these offhand young. Gabriel would be squatting on the floor with his back turned, studiedly unconcerned—

6

The voices seemed to be rising to a quarrelsome climax, round the corner.

"Stop! I order you to stop this minute, d'you hear me?"

"Uncle! Uncle! Please!"

"I won't, I refuse, I haven't finished. You have destroyed my life!"

What the hell was going on in here? Thomas dumped the second bag in the tiny lobby, went back for the first. Picked up the police-lock rod and leaned it in its usual corner.

"I'm leaving this hell right now! I can't stand it any longer!" some woman shouted.

And a man cried, "My life is ruined. I could have been a Dostoyevsky! Oh, I'm talking rubbish, rubbish! Mother, I'm going mad!"

That certainly wasn't *Gabriel?*

Thomas strode past bedroom and bathroom doors, both open, round the corner into the open studio room.

"Hullo? I hadn't expected anyone—" he began, then broke off. Gabriel wasn't there. No one was there. The room was empty. A disc spun on the record player.

"Gabriel? Are you here?"

Completely puzzled, Thomas turned to check the small kitchen and bathroom, knowing before he did so that the search was futile. He had already passed the open doors. The rooms were visibly empty.

"Gabriel!" But calling was pointless, and he stopped at once, embarrassed by the sound of his voice. The recorded voices, ignoring him, continued their protestations. Nobody was here in the small apartment, nobody but himself.

Could the boy have slipped out somehow while Thomas undid the police lock? Could he have been hidden in the bathroom and darted past Thomas as he stepped forward? No; impossible. He had stood in the doorway as he unfastened the rod; and it was only another four steps on round the corner into the living-room.

Gabriel was not there. Eight months' dust covered floor, couch, table, bookshelves. The New York *Times* for last February lay on the table, yellow and ancient-looking as an Egyptian papyrus. Windows and skylight were shut and fastened—Thomas checked them—the air up here was stale as an old slice of toast, thick with heat, no flavour of humanity left in it at all.

7

You left us alone, declared the books, the furniture, the brittle, dusty, faded curtains. You shut us in, you abandoned us; we are not prepared to welcome you back.

Somebody said, "You must admit that his behaviour has been strange, to say the least."

Somebody else wailed, "Nurse! Nurse!"

The disc. Who had put that record on the player.

The third act of *Uncle Vanya* whirled to its frantic end, with revolver shots and screams and tears and re-criminations. Thomas pulled back the arm and took off the record. The catch had been hooked up, so that the record would automatically begin to play again, each time it finished. He took it off, absently wondering how many times the scene had been played in this room—in the world?—how often had Vanya and Sonya suffered their disillusionment, rejection, heartache. *What a pity she is so plain. Oh, I am talking rubbish, rubbish!* Poor Vanya was one of the most lovable characters ever created— while he is suffering his agony, people suffer with him in every corner of the world.

I had talent, I had courage, I had intelligence. But who loves me?

Who indeed? Or rather, who hates me? Enough to play a trick like that?

A cardboard slot on the sleeve announced that the record was the property of the New York public library; good; he could take it back tomorrow and discover who had borrowed it. Who had a key to this flat, who could come in and out at will, setting cultural booby-traps, leaving the dusty emptiness torn apart like the upholstery of a vandalised railway-carriage? Who has slipped in like a burglar and taken a chopper to my peace of mind? Don't I have troubles enough already? Could it have been Gabriel? But no, Gabriel, that gentle child, that shy considerate boy, would die, would go to the stake sooner than commit such an invasion of someone's privacy.

His thoughts ran coldly on that word, *die*, and slipped back to the past: Gabriel complaining, half in joke, half serious, about the church bells: It's a hideous noise! Nobody else is allowed to advertise at full pitch all over the town on Sunday morning. *I* don't play *my* radio in god's ear. And an earlier memory: Gabriel at age eleven on a drive down to Cornwall. Thomas, tired, had stopped for a short nap; when he woke, although rain was pouring down, Gabriel had not been in the car. It was fairly soon after they had met, fairly soon after his leg . . . Before Thomas had time to become anxious, however, the boy returned. He had been sheltering under a clump of yew trees farther along the road; he explained, hesitantly, "You were talking in your sleep. It felt too like eavesdropping to sit and listen, so I went for a walk." His hair and jacket were soaked, and Thomas, roughly scolding, finding a sweater, switching on the car heater, felt a total immersion of shame, as if his whole soul were suffused in a deep, scalding blush; because he could not help wondering *what* the boy had heard, and fearing to ask, and that engulfed him in even greater shame; and it made matters no better when Gabriel, giving him the ingenuous, confiding smile which was hardly more than a warmth of the eyes, added reassuringly:

"Don't worry, I left before you could come out with anything really bad!"

Pushing away memory—if his mind was going to mislay chunks of its own history, for Christ's sake, why could it not erase some of the more painful moments—there were plenty of *them*—which would then seem a logical behaviour-pattern at least—instead of subjecting him to these unnerving random blackouts? . . . Thomas walked into the hot little bathroom. By now his arms and back were beginning to hurt so acutely that all his function processes were channelled into the aim of speedily finding something to relieve the agony: Had he left any painkillers in the medicine-cabinet on his last visit? Or was he going to be obliged to stoop, to go down agonisingly on his knees, and delve with exquisitely tender hands in those tight and randomly packed bags?

To his huge relief he found an almost full bottle of Paracetamol tablets. Two large pale-brown roaches scuttled out as he opened the door of the wall-cabinet, but he could not be bothered about them; the bottle cap was tightly screwed on, anyway. He ran water into the basin till the first rusty gush had cleared, rinsed the dirty plastic beaker perfunctorily, and washed down a handful of tablets with a gulp of lukewarm water.

That was better. His mouth still tasted like a mudbank, his sweaty clothes clung to him, his shoes felt as if they were full of sand, but he was too exhausted to do anything about these details at the moment, or about the dusty confusion of the living-room. Indeed he found a kind of satisfaction in the feeling that everything matched, his circumstances were all of a piece, within and without. He need not feel guilty, as he stretched himself on the old brown-velvet couch, because his shoes were soiling it with transatlantic dirt; he sank gratefully into its fusty depths. Old dust, dry as snuff, burst in a cloud from the faded red cushions as he settled his head. Last December's faded *Times* crackled under his back, from which the pain was slowly ebbing; with luck, two hours of sleep or so might see him through to a period of moderate respite.

If not, hunting for Gabriel would hardly be difficult; merely impossible.

Just as he shut his eyes, the telephone rang.

Happy Noah, Thomas thought, as he struggled to push himself upright, trying to spare his throbbing hands; there was no phone on the Ark.

The telephone was on the window sill, at the other side of the room, half hidden behind worn rust-coloured hessian curtains. A table had been left in front, covered with dusty crockery; also a large wicker basket, piled full of books. There was no room to get by. Cursing, Thomas dragged and shoved these things out of his way. Haste made him clumsy; he knocked the phone off the narrow sill. It fell to the floor. His legs becoming too weak to support him, he sat down on the filthy boards and picked up the receiver.

"Hullo? Hullo, who is that? Gabriel, is that you?"

But there was no sound from the other end of the line. "Hullo? Gabriel?"

No answer. Perhaps, after all, the phone had been damaged. He replaced the receiver on its rest; then, after a moment, picked it up and listened. No, it seemed to be working all right; he could hear the dial tone.

A wrong number, perhaps. If not, whoever it was would ring again.

Just in case it *had* been Gabriel, he dragged the old couch across the room, with an effort that made his shoulders and back scream almost audibly, and lay down right beside the window sill, so that he could grab the phone at once if it rang.

It did not ring again, however, and his mind slipped gratefully towards dissolution. Sense goes first, he thought mistily; words leave last; isn't that strange; words begin to gallop and rattle meaninglessly inside the mind, like an unshackled anchor-chain, like an engine out

10

of gear; while I am evolving these more-or-less connected thought-processes in the basement of my brain, random language, an endless conveyor-belt of dissociated vocabulary, continues to race rattling overhead. Garbled audio, he remembered the old TV repairman in Sixth Avenue telling him; your set's got garbled audio. Garbled audio isn't the worst, Uncle Vanya; I've got garbled life, that's my trouble.

I wonder what Gabriel did hear, that time in the car? He sank deeper into the dusty brown velvet; he slept.

When he woke next, it was late afternoon. The rose and ochre façades across the street, bathed in brilliance by the westerly sun, threw a warm reflected light, yellowish pink, up onto his ceiling. Voices of children on their way home to supper floated faintly from the sidewalk. A helicopter puttered overhead, droning like a bee. All seemed calm, unmalevolent, and commonplace.

Thomas moved his head warily; then with extreme caution levered himself up on one elbow. No pain. For the moment the demon had retreated. He stood up, walked, raised his arms to his shoulders, bent forward. Still no pain.

This reprieve, which really did seem like the departure of some evil spirit, was so unexpected that he became filled with illogical cheerfulness.

I'll find Gabriel all right, he thought, standing under the shower, letting the blessed hot water soothe and relax him, letting it stream and stream over his shoulders and arms and back; it should be simple enough, why not? There must be any number of people to ask. I'll begin with old Mrs. Baird, she's only a block away. I could telephone, but it would be simpler just to walk round. Old ladies distrust the telephone.

Clean shirt—trousers—jacket—keys—money—and—I'm on my way.

He was hungry now, though; he stopped for a hamburger at Nick's Pie 'n Pizza, then walked up wide, shabby Sixth Avenue with its little stores, its launderettes, bookshops, cleaners, drugstores, past the liquor store, its windows still full of hideous china ornaments, and the newspaper shop, and the patisserie, and the little Greek restaurant that was always empty; perhaps it was really a Mafia headquarters.

Perhaps, he thought, I'll find Gabriel staying cosily and irreproachably with his grandmother.

11

But when he rang the bell of the beautiful little old brownstone on Twelfth Street and stood waiting, the unaccustomed optimism began to ebb away as irrationally as it had come. For a start, it took a discouragingly long time before anybody arrived to open the door.

Thomas fidgeted on the step, feeling exposed. He observed a tall, thin man with a mop of yellowish-white hair, who appeared to be trying to dissociate himself, while at the same time keeping a critical eye and a tight grip on its lead, from the activities of his equally lanky but more elegant Russian deerhound, which was slowly defecating in the gutter. The man glanced across the street and caught the eye of Thomas, watching him; his cold gaze detached itself instantly and he gave the dog's lead an impatient twitch. The dog, interrupted in the process of sniffing its own deposit, jerked away pettishly, and Thomas, feeling rebuked, hastily withdrew his eyes and turned back towards the door, from behind which, at the same moment, he caught the sound of footsteps. Finally, after a prolonged rattling, the door was pulled back.

Old Mrs. Baird stood there, leaning on a rosewood cane. My god, she looks ancient, he thought. Well, and so she must be; August was in his mid-seventies when he died, old Hannah's his mother, she must be at least in her mid-nineties. She could be a hundred: a tiny bent figure peering up at him, wrapped in a cardigan, snowwhite hair scraped back into a bun, skin wrinkled and freckled like some rain-soaked leaf trodden into the soil of an autumn wood. But the jutting angles of cheek, nose, and jaw still bore witness to intelligence and strength, even more plainly now that the roundness of youth no longer survived to mask them. Shrewd grey eyes, sunk far back in huge triangular violet-stained bony sockets, still observed Thomas with a clarity undiminished, so far as he could make out, since his last visit.

"Well? Who are *you?*" she said, holding the door with one freckled claw, poking her head forward like an aged seagull. He noticed the glint of white hairs over her cheek and jawbone. "Whoever you are, you ought to know that I don't receive callers in the afternoon; Hattie's at the market and I'm having my siesta. It's not convenient."

"I'd forgotten; please forgive me," said Thomas humbly, but at the same time relieved to hear that Hattie, who must be nearly as old as her mistress, had not yet died but was still functioning. "Do you remember me? Thomas Cook? I'm your son's publisher."

"Rubbish," said the old lady tartly. "My son *has* a publisher already. All his books have been brought out by a perfectly respectable firm. Crusoe and Selkirk. They have been publishing his work since World War One—as you would no doubt call it. *I* call it the Great War."

"Yes, Mrs. Baird; I'm the director of Crusoe and Selkirk. Do you remember, I came to see you last year about the illustrations for the *Collected Letters?* And the year before that about the biography?"

"Illustrations?" she said suspiciously. "No, I don't remember that. What should I have to do with illustrations? I'm not an artist. I know nothing about such things."

"Photographs; family photographs, which you kindly agreed to lend us. And, if you remember, at the time I came to see you about the biography, I was married to Bella—"

"Bella? Who is that?"

His spirits sank still further. Between her memory and mine, he thought, we should be able to forget the whole of the twentieth century without too much trouble.

However at this point something about his visual aspect seemed suddenly to make a connection in the old lady's mind, for she pulled the door wider, and remarked:

"Well, it's not at all good for me to stand on the doorstep in this draught, and there seems no reason why you should not come in; Hattie will be back soon and she will make us some tea."

"That's very kind of you, ma'am," he said, relieved.

She turned away, without looking to see what he did, and led the way at a slow, laborious, shuffling pace, helping herself with her stick, across the tiny hallway and into the double sitting-room, which ran from front to back of the house and had windows both ways, onto the street and onto a small, overgrown garden. The room was exactly as he remembered it: rather dark but not unfriendly. The arrangement of the crammed furniture suggested that nothing had been shifted or introduced during the last fifty years. There were braided rugs on the floor, worn basket-chairs, tables crowded higgledy-piggledy with Japanese netsuke, spectacle cases, papers, pamphlets, and yellowing postcards. Tarnished mirrors swallowed the light. The volumes on the shelves wore none of the bright-jacketed exuberance of contemporary book-production; they were solid and dowdily dressed, to wear, not to attract, with covers in the rough, tweedy textures favoured during the first twenty years of the century. The works of August Baird, filling one whole shelf, were the only exceptions; every one of these, every paperback, reprint, anthology, and translation was there, Thomas noted with a rapid eye, and they looked well-handled, as if they were in frequent use.

The pictures on the walls were all photographs, mostly of August himself, at every age. From dozens of different positions on the dark-grey-striped paper his calm, slightly accusing regard rested on Thomas, who seated himself nervously in a small creaking cane chair as soon as he had helped the old lady back into her rocker.

She gave Thomas another long, severe scrutiny—not unlike that of her son—and he looked back, thinking that she seemed like some landmark, left over from the twenties or thirties. The checked gingham shirt she wore, the long box-pleated tweed skirt coming to below calf-level recalled photographs of the Bloomsbury Group, snapped informally in the gardens of their weekend cottages with pipes and walking-sticks. For such a frail old lady, Mrs. Baird had remarkably stocky legs, unshaped, running straight up and down like those of a kitchen table, her stockings ribbed grey wool, and her shoes black laced oxfords; he wondered where in present-day New York she was able to find such clothes. Perhaps she wrote to London or Boston for them. Perhaps she still had a charge account at Harrods or the Army & Navy stores? Mrs. Baird, Edinburghborn, had moved to America when her son had a professorial position at Harvard; had found the American way of life congenial and remained there, planted, even after he returned to England.

"Well?" she said again, hooking her stick over the high brass fire-guard, which fenced off a dusty castor-oil plant in the fireless hearth. "Have you come back for some more photographs? For another biography, is that it? What was wrong with Bodoni's? Didn't it sell?"

She had a brisk, somewhat trenchant manner which, with the girlish checked cotton shirt, threw back a disarming reminder of what she must have been like in her forties, her thirties: a liberated woman before liberation was a catch-word, an equal spirit long before equality was thought desirable.

"No, Mrs. Baird, no, thank you, the photographs you lent us for those books were just what we needed; that business is all finished," said Thomas, noticing that the volume in question lay on the little piecrust table beside her chair, with another pair of glasses marking her place. "No, I've come to America on quite a different errand this time, I'm not working on one of August's books. I'm looking for Gabriel—I don't suppose you happen to know where he is at the moment by any chance?"

"Gabriel?" she said vaguely.

"Gabriel; your grandson. August's son. I wondered if you had seen him recently? If he had been to visit you? I understand he has been over here all this year."

"Gabriel," she murmured thoughtfully. "Now, let me think, who would his parents be? Have I met him?"

"Your grandson."

"My *grandson?* Have I got a grandson?"

"August's son," Thomas repeated. "As a matter of fact he's also my stepson."

"Who was his mother? Berengaria?"

"No, Mrs. Baird." Berengaria, August Baird's first wife, had died in 1930. Thomas felt that he was rapidly losing his grip on the conversation. And here also he came up against another complexity which he felt sure would only lead to more confusion if he pursued it. He said simply, "Gabriel's mother was August's second wife, Bella Farragut. You remember Bella?"

"Oh, *Bella*—why didn't you say so?" A sudden sparkle of pure malice came into the triangular, hooded eyes. "Dear me, yes, it's a long time since I've thought of poor Bella. Not quite a lady, that one, I always told August; I was rather surprised when he decided to marry her. Do you see what I mean? Why should he bother? There was something just slightly vulgar about her: like a hotel receptionist. A good hotel. But not out of the top drawer, as we used to say. Did you ever notice her shoes? Like a servant's. You can always tell. Oh dear me yes: Bella. She used to amuse me very much. Has she been in America lately?"

"I really don't know," said Thomas, slightly embarrassed. "But what I came here to ask—"

"I always thought of her as Bella the Bunny-girl," said old Mrs. Baird unexpectedly. "Did you ever see a rather vulgar magazine called *Playboy?* My son used to bring

15

me a copy from time to time; a very entertaining magazine. Yes, now, Bella; did she have any children?"

"There was Gabriel, do you remember? I wonder if by any—"

"Oh, *Gabriel*," she said, using exactly the same intonation as that in which she had previously referred to Bella. "Why didn't you say so? Dear little boy. Of course I'm very fond of Gabriel. I was looking at a photograph of him only a few minutes ago, just before you rang the doorbell. Now, what did I do with it? I know, it's probably marking my place in Wittgenstein. Just pass me the *Tractatus,* will you please?"

Every table in the room, Thomas observed, bore at least three books with markers in them; it seemed probable that the old lady moved from chair to chair and from book to book, varying her reading-matter according to mood or the time of day. He pulled the slip of card from Wittgenstein and saw Gabriel, aged twelve, standing with a worried expression, holding a tabby cat against his shoulder, in front of the door of No. 38, Wanborough Parkside, London S.E. 22.

The familiar combination of guilt and dread engulfed his heart at the sight of that young vulnerable face.

"Yes: there's Gabriel," said the old lady with satisfaction. "Isn't he an angelic little boy? Of course he's bigger now; let me see, how old was he on his last birthday?"

"Sixteen, that's why it's so important for me to find him. You haven't seen him lately, then, ma'am?"

She shook her head. "Not since August brought him last time he came; that would be about four years before he died. They were alone; Bella had gone off somewhere. Now, dear me, which year was that? Was it the same year he won his Nobel prize? I know Gabriel was just old enough to travel about on the subway by himself; which he very much enjoyed. I thought he was too young but August said he would be quite capable of looking after himself; and he was perfectly right."

"Does he write to you, Mrs. Baird? Do you get letters from him?" Thomas asked, without a great deal of hope.

"His own mother? Of course he does. What an absurd question," said Mrs. Baird with acerbity. "He writes every single week. Why, you should know; you published his letters yourself, last year."

"Not August, Mrs. Baird—Gabriel," said Thomas, thinking, thank heaven, at least she isn't deaf.

"Oh, Gabriel; why didn't you say so?" Her sharp old eyes softened. "Yes, he does write to me. He writes beautiful letters. I have a whole lot of them somewhere. I'll find them for you another day."

"If you could possibly lay your hands on the most recent ones now—or tell me where to look—" Thomas began, with a terrible hopeless feeling of time being wasted, of time pouring, bleeding away like the fluid of life itself, clotting, drying to dust, irretrievably lost.

"There was one from San Francisco that began, 'Only think Grannie, I'm writing this from an opium den,' and one written sitting on a rock by Niagara, and one from the Grand Canyon. Wonderfully funny, lively descriptive letters, often pages long. He's a very good boy, the way he writes to his old granny—"

The front door slammed.

"Who's that in there?" said another sharp old voice, New England this one, instead of Edinburgh, but Thomas noticed that, from long association no doubt, the two accents had grown alike and now overlapped. "Who's in there tiring Mrs. Baird?"

Hattie stomped into the room with a dour expression. She wore a startling toque of crocheted wool sewn over with large brown sequins, and carried two brown-paper bags full of groceries.

"Oh it's you," she said, recognizing Thomas instantly. "Well you can't come visiting now, the doctor's due in five minutes to lance her knees, and we have to get her upstairs and her stockings off before that, and anyway she ought to have been resting—"

"I'm terribly sorry," he said guiltily. "It's just that I'm so anxious to find Gabriel—"

"Well, you'll have to come back another day, she can't attend to you at present. Gabriel isn't here, at all events, you can see that. And any minute now Dr. Warmflash will be ringing the front doorbell—"

"You wouldn't know where she keeps Gabriel's letters?" murmured Thomas, elbowed into the little hallway. "She did say I could see them. This really is important, Hattie, it's about his heart condition—"

"They're probably all over the house," said Hattie grimly. "One in every book she's been reading for the last

17

six months. I'll have to hunt for them. I'll let you know. Where are you staying? Do you still keep that little place on Tenth Street that you rented when you were working on Mr. August's letters? I've got the number written down, I'll telephone you on Thursday or Friday when I've had a look around. Tomorrow's my cleaning day, and Wednesday I go to put flowers on my sister's grave at North Salem."

"Please, Hattie, this is really urgent. We've simply got to find Gabriel without loss of time. You remember about his heart condition?"

"Pish. He's only sixteen, he'll be all right," said Hattie robustly, pushing Thomas out of the door. "How old do you think *I* am? Eighty-nine, and lively as a jack-rabbit. What's a sixteen-year-old boy got to worry about?"

"That's just the—" he was beginning, but she briskly shut the door in his face; there was nothing for it but to retreat down the steps. A large, glossy, chauffeur-driven limousine was just pulling in to the kerb; Thomas hoped it was not that of Dr. Warmflash or his stock with Hattie would sink even lower.

As he walked towards Sixth Avenue, pain descended on him again like a bird of prey that had been waiting perched on some convenient cornice.

His one wish was to get back to the apartment and swallow a couple of Najdolene tablets; eight hours must certainly have elapsed since he took his last, so it would be all right to; but he had better lay in a few supplies, milk and coffee and soap and something to drink; the apartment's kitchen was destitute of any provisions save a few dusty packets of herbs.

Dusk had begun to fall: a mild New York dusk that seemed like a gentle benediction on the strollers loitering along the wide pavements. Soon it would be time to take cover, to make each for his own lair, to be on the alert for muggers and rapists, but not quite yet. At present the tender shabby light and the untidy street in its shirt sleeves were joined in reflective union. New York, Thomas thought, is like the country of the future in Wells's *Time Machine;* by day, sunlit exhilarating playland; while each night the tribes of cannibal Morlocks emerge from underground to roam across the city, pouncing at random on the charming little sun-people who think themselves so civilised.

Every luxury the heart can desire.

He walked along to Kormendi's, pleased to see that it still appeared to be thriving. And small wonder; it had a lavish stock of first-class foods from all over the world, at lavish prices. As he pushed through the glass doors and walked in, the air-conditioned atmosphere struck icy-chill on his wincing muscles; he found a wheeled basket and started quickly along the frozen-goods counter in search of milk, ignoring the piles of halvah, baclava, Earl Grey, Camembert, Bath Olivers, and other foreign luxuries.

He had just picked out a carton of fat-free Slim-Queen when he saw walking towards him, unaware of his proximity because all her attention was focused on the two 1-gallon packages of ice-cream, the pecan pie, and the bag of French pastries that she carried balanced in her arms, his ex-wife Bella Farragut. Bella Baird. Bella Cook.

He was so startled that he dropped his carton of milk. It bounced and buckled, but fortunately did not break.

"Bella! What the *hell* are you doing here? I thought you said that you couldn't get away from England for another three weeks?"

He was not at all pleased to see her, and made no effort to sound it.

Bella did look embarrassed, but more, he thought, at being discovered with all those carbohydrates in her arms than from any guilt at having been caught out in a piece of deception. Her baby-smooth skin turned slightly pink; her eyes locked with his in the straight stare of the confirmed liar. She began to speak instantly and rapidly, as if it was nothing out of the common that they should meet in a luxury food-market in Greenwich Village.

"Well, you see, old Charcraft said I'd better go—he knew how worried I was about Gabriel—and I managed to finish the design job for the coffee people much faster than I'd expected to, and old Pankhurst found somebody who wanted to rent the house on Parkside and move in right away—"

"When did you come?" he said, cutting her short.

"Well, yesterday, actually—a woman I know at the Wanborough Drama Group managed to wangle me onto a charter flight—she'd been planning to visit her sister in Detroit and couldn't get away—"

It was characteristic of Bella, he thought, always to have a friend conveniently placed who would oblige by fixing

19

some slightly under-the-counter scheme for her advantage. He said sharply:

"So I needn't have come at all. It was desperately inconvenient for me to come away just now, with the Frankfurt Book Fair only a few weeks ahead. Why didn't you telephone me and say that you were coming yourself?"

Her lips parted reproachfully; she opened her large blue eyes to their fullest extent. They were a strange iridescent shade, between slate and grey; very beautiful, he had once thought.

"But darling! I didn't know I was going to get the seat in the plane till the very last possible minute! And anyway you love Gabriel—didn't you *want* to come? Surely you must see how important it is to find him? Aren't you worried about him?"

"Of course I'm worried," he said irritably.

It was like Bella, too, invariably to slide the other party into a need for self-justification, to initiate a jockeying of moral claims and counter-claims. To set up a magnetic field where the particles flow violently north and south, where Bella, virtue embodied, attracted to herself every grain of right and justice.

"You're always so good with Gabriel," she was saying reproachfully, "because you have the ability to keep calm, you don't overwhelm him with too much anxiety and love, the way Bo and I do; I made sure you'd see the need for your being here. Of course if you don't *want* to stay and help find him and persuade him—"

"It's not a case of wanting," he snapped. "It's a case of necessity. Is it necessary or is it not?"

"You know it's necessary; it's vitally necessary!" Her voice rang; her eyes flashed; she looked like Joan of Arc. "Listen: that boy's going to *die* if we don't find him within the next six weeks and convince him that he's got to have this operation—don't you realise that? Perhaps the time is even less than six weeks. Doesn't it affect you at all? Haven't you a *grain* of compassion in your nature?"

"Yes, yes, I realise—for pete's sake, Bella! Cut out the histrionics!" He lowered his voice; two college girls and a woman with a basket full of frozen pizza were staring at them curiously. "Do you have all the stuff you came to buy? Well let's get out of here and find some place where we can talk quietly. And just keep calm, will you, kindly?"

"All right," she agreed, suddenly meek, and waited by the checkout point while he rapidly assembled eggs, butter, soap, and coffee. She stayed there until he joined her, before putting down her own purchases on the counter by the cash-register, and it was plain she hoped that he would pay for hers along with his, but he took a sour pleasure in frustrating her aim by returning to the centre aisle for bread, which he had forgotten, so that, urged on by the queue behind her, she was obliged to go through and pay for herself. He did not, he decided, intend to supply Bella with three weeks' ice-cream; specially when she had obliged him to come to America on what was almost certainly just another of her wild-goose chases.

"Right," he said, having caught up with her again by the main entrance, where she stood biting her lip, staring out through the big glass doors at the dusk-filled streets. "Where are you staying? Shall we go there?"

"Oh, no, I'm at Angie Wasserman's, in Fourteenth Street, no, that wouldn't be at all a good place to talk. What about you, are you with old Mrs. Baird?"

"Of course not; why should you think so?" Why should she indeed? Old Mrs. Baird never had visitors actually sleeping in her house unless they were members of her immediate family; Bella herself, even when married to August, had never, so far as he knew, been invited to stay there.

"I'm at the flat in Tenth Street," he said.

"Oh," she said artlessly, "do you still keep on that little place? I didn't know."

"Crusoe and Selkirk took it on a five-year lease. It's used from time to time by other office staff when they're visiting the New York branch."

"Well, shall we go and talk there?"

"No, it isn't worth it; there's not all that much to say." In fact he had a violent revulsion against the idea of Bella's visiting the flat; the objection to her seeing its dusty squalor and discomfort was only one of several factors contributing to this. "Besides," he added, "you wouldn't want to climb four flights of stairs with that load. We might as well go in here and have a coffee."

He walked ahead of her into Nick's Pie 'n Pizza.

"Oh, *Tom*—can't you think of anywhere better? This really is a cheesy little joint."

"It won't kill you."

Cheesy was one of Bella's words that always annoyed

him; she possessed a curious knack of hanging onto out-moded slang and using it inappropriately with the happy confidence of someone who feels thoroughly in the swim of dashing contemporary idiom.

"Anyhow I really ought to get back," she said plaintively. "My ice-cream will melt."

"Not in five minutes, for god's sake. Do you want tea or coffee?"

How like her it was to launch into high drama in front of a crowd of strangers about the urgency of finding Gabriel, and then five minutes later to begin back-pedalling and worrying about her ice-cream.

"Tea. No milk or sugar. I'm on my usual diet," she said primly, and slipped into one of the red-upholstered booths which gave the illusion of privacy.

When he returned with the two teas she had pulled a handful of transparencies from an envelope in her hand-bag; she passed them across the table to him.

"Look, these are the designs I did for the Coffee Centre. Do you like them? Old Charcraft was really bucked with them, he said they had a kind of Klee touch. What do you think?"

Thomas received them sceptically; for a start, he did not admire the work of Klee. Suppressing the comment that this seemed a curious time to ask his opinion of her work, he looked at the photographs, which were designs for fabrics—towels, tea-cloths, table napery, as well as kitchen wallpaper. There were also some plates and cups.

"Very good," he said at length, judicially. Her face brightened into the smile of a child, greedy for praise. He passed back the pictures. Her work always surprised him slightly, by being better than he expected; it had a fluid, easy charm. She could do little trees and houses and land-scapes, little plants and boats, birds and fishes, that, while not particularly original, contained a pleasing freshness and gaiety of their own. And every now and then, by accident it seemed, she was able to produce a design that appeared to be really original, out of the common run. Although incapable of real application or research, she had built up for herself quite a successful free-lance connection with half a dozen different firms, and could have trebled her income if she had wanted to work harder; but why should she? Gus had left her an annuity that saw her comfortably provided for. Sometimes Thomas wondered what were her motives in doing as much work as she did. To stay topsides with Bo, perhaps?

"And what are *you* doing now?" she asked magnanimously.

"Running Crusoe and Selkirk. Writing a book about molluscs. When I have time."

"Molluscs!" She shuddered. "How dreary! And what about your awful arthritis? How's that?"

"Not too good," he said briefly.

"You should take more care of yourself, you know. You don't want to get the way your mother ended up."

"You don't know anything about it," he said sharply.

"Only what you told me, darling," said Bella, lighting a cigarette and blowing smoke. She read him a lecture about acupuncture, Zen, and a diet consisting of apple-vinegar and honey.

"Let's get back to Gabriel, shall we?" he suggested.

"All right, darling. Where have you tried so far?"

"Nowhere, apart from old Hannah. For heaven's sake, Bella! I only arrived this morning."

"So you did. I keep forgetting."

I keep forgetting, Thomas thought, but he had no intention of letting Bella know about his flashes of amnesia, if he could help it. He would hate to put a weapon like that into her casual little spiteful hands.

He tried to look at her dispassionately. Gus had married her when she was twenty-five; she must have been enchantingly pretty then. For even now at—he did sums in his head—Gabriel was coming up to sixteen, so she must be forty-one or thereabouts—even now at forty-one she could easily have been taken for little over thirty. Her exquisite pink-and-white skin had the smoothness and glow that comes with health and a secure income and freedom from care; her little round face was poised like a cherry on its long stalk of neck; she wore her soft dark hair coiled in a very becoming chignon. She was dressed in a beautifully cut grey cotton dress with black piping here and there—anticipatory mourning? he thought uncharitably—and might, so far as appearance went, have stepped straight out of the pages of a Henry James novel. And in some other ways too.

"You look like a Persian cat," said Thomas, not meaning it as a compliment.

She took it as one, however.

"Sweet Thomas! It is so *lovely* to see you again!"

Hardly accords with what you said last time, baby, he thought, and remembered how she had screamed, Get out! And I don't care if I never see you again as long as I live. I hope you bloody well *die* of your stupid illness! Could she have forgotten that?

A sidelong, smiling glance from the slate-blue eyes assured him that she had not.

"Now; tell me all that you know about Gabriel," he said curtly.

"But, darling, nothing! Nothing more than I told you on the phone when I frantically rang and asked you to come over and try to locate him."

"Why did you ring me just then?"

"Because old Moncrieff said we must find him."

"When did he come to the States?"

"In January, after he had finished those language courses he was taking in London. He had a list of people to get in touch with over here, the Wassermans, and the Bradshaws, and old Moncrieff had given him the name of a heart specialist in New York to go to if he had the *least* trouble, a Dr. Tsihiffely, but *he* hasn't heard from him, and nor have any of the others—"

"And you—didn't you hear? Didn't he write to you?"

"Darling: I told you. Only this one, rather *strange* letter at the end of April, saying he had a lot of thinking to do and I wouldn't be hearing from him again for a long time."

"Have you got it?"

"No, I *lost* it, darling, I cannot think what can have become of it, it's too maddening," Bella said, glancing absently at her handsome black calf handbag. I'd say a fiver it's in there, Thomas thought. "I hunted for it high and *low* before I came over, but it never turned up. I think perhaps that naughty Bo must have put it in his pocket sometime when I was showing it to him, and you know what a ragbag he lives in. Anyway it didn't really *tell* anything—there was no address on it."

"Was it handwritten?"

"No, typed; quite well typed, too."

"Postmark?"

"San Francisco. But that was in April and here it is nearly September—he may be *any*where by now."

"Back in England, for instance."

"I *doubt* it, darling. He said he *liked* it in America and

24

he wanted to stay as long as he was able. Haven't you heard from him at all?" she asked innocently.

Thomas shook his head and a sparkle of triumph shot into the wide slate-blue eyes. She had always bitterly resented Gabriel's affection for his stepfather—those chess-walks for instance—how she did hate them! Soon after they were married, Thomas had realised that an infallible way to stimulate Bella's somewhat scanty and capricious maternal feeling was to make much of Gabriel himself; but this was a devious line of behaviour which he very much resented when he found himself, almost unconsciously, beginning to adopt it. After that he tried to steer a narrow course between the risk of exhibiting too much interest in Gabriel, thereby rousing Bella's antagonism, and erring in the other direction, assuming a brusqueness that might puzzle or hurt the boy.

"No, we don't correspond," he said. "But do you mean to say that you left it from April until now before you started to get anxious about him?"

"Well, darling, what could I *do?* After all, Gabriel's always been sensible, and I never thought but that he'd turn *up.* But then old Moncrieff wrote to me last month, to remind me that Gabriel's due for his teeny thing in October and telling me he'd booked a bed for him at the Cavendish Clinic—and he wanted Gabriel to go along and see him, around now, for a check-over, you know—then he rang me up—so then I really did begin to worry."

"Did Sir John Moncrieff know that Gabriel had gone to America?"

"Oh *yes,* he'd more or less suggested the trip. A summer roaming around getting fit was just what Gabriel needed, he said. He and old Manresa had a consultation about it all, and they took a lot of X-rays and decided that Gabriel would be perfectly okay till the autumn. After all, darling, you can't very well keep a sixteen-year-old boy in a *box.*"

"I daresay not," Thomas agreed, remembering how irrationally angry he used to get at Bella's habit of referring to anyone she knew above a certain social eminence as "old" so-and-so; the old Manresa in question was Lord Manresa of Keele, very likely the most skillful heart-surgeon in the world. Having been married to August Baird for ten years might have cured her, one would have thought, of such little social pretensions, but it had not.

For perhaps the ten thousandth time Thomas found himself wondering, Why did August ever marry her?

"Darling I must rush," she said, stubbing out her half-smoked cigarette. "Thanks for the deevy tea. Now we'll keep in touch, won't we? I'll try out all my contacts and you try yours, and if you have any brain-waves, let me know. Oh I got in touch with old Sam Schillenbach, did you ever meet him? He used to be a crony of Gus at Harvard and he's now head of NYBS, one of these huge networks, or owns it or something—he's going to have an SOS broadcast on telly and radio too, with me appearing in person and asking people to keep a lookout for Gabriel. Nobel prizewinner's son needed for urgent heart-surgery ought to get results, you'd think, wouldn't you? Sam said he'd offer a reward too, but *I* thought that would produce a lot of phoneys."

"Very likely," said Thomas, thinking, how vulgar, and how she is loving all this exploitation of the situation. He hoped that Gabriel would soon turn up, for the boy's own sake; he could not think of anyone who would more violently object to the kind of publicity that Bella seemed to be setting in motion.

She slipped the cigarettes and the envelope of transparencies back into her bag. Idly following the movements of her hands as she did so, Thomas chanced to catch her eye; he was surprised when she blushed a violent red, which, for a moment, made her look a much older woman.

"So long, then, sweetie, to the re-see," she said rapidly, fluttered her hands at him, and took her departure. Several men glanced after her with approval as she walked out. It occurred to Thomas, vaguely pondering over her unexpected confusion, that it might have been due to his catching a glimpse of a packet of Coconut Candy Cookies among the cosmetics, coins, keys, letters, and oddments in her capacious handbag. Was she ashamed of being caught out yet again in another lapse from her perennially self-imposed, perennially violated diet?

Then it struck him as odd that, if she had bought the cookies at Kormendi's—which seemed most likely, since there had been a large display-rack of this brand just around the corner from the check-out desk—the packet had been tucked into her handbag, instead of in the large brown-paper sack along with the rest of her purchases.

If the other articles were contributions to the housekeeping at Angela Wasserman's, perhaps greedy Bella had intended to keep the cookies separate, for private bedroom munching, and so stowed them where they would not come to light when the other things were unpacked?

Anyway, hell! Bella's little private greeds and stinginesses were no affair of his, these days, thank god. Let's forget about Bella, shall we? His feet, hands, back, arms, hurt more than he could bear; he paid for the tea and walked the couple of blocks back to Tenth Street.

This time the dusty black stairs seemed like a trailer from next week's showing of the Inferno. Hell might as well be up as down, he thought, toiling, toiling, not daring to stop because if he did the worst pain of all, the one just a step behind him down there like a pursuing fiend, that pain would catch him before he could climb to safety and swallow the two little red bullets that were going to set him free.

But suppose home wasn't at the top of those stairs after all, suppose he had come to the wrong house, suppose the staircase led only to some great and windy height, off which he would be unable to prevent himself sliding, launched helplessly over the edge into that ultimate terrifying descent which has no end? The worst part is not the crash at the foot, for that must be over in the hundredth part of a second; no, by far the worst part is the fall itself, and suppose we discover that death turns out to be a never-ending fall? Suppose the retreat from life is not sudden but a gradual, eternal diminution, a whirling away, an infinitely prolonged collapse into space?

But I am not going to die, he told himself, I have no intention of dying, other people have learned to live with pain at this degree, surely I have enough resolution to do so? Suppose I *haven't* enough resolution, though, or suppose it crumbles during one of those blank spells—suppose I return from one of those little trips into vacancy to find myself *in articulo mortis?* Suppose I get back to find myself endlessly falling, endlessly dying, trapped in eternal farewell? Suppose I fail Gabriel yet again by not being there to encourage him, to persuade him, to help him? I am not worth much, he acknowledged humbly, digging with his delicate fingers, each of which seemed to be an individual small howl of pain, into a pocket that was stuffed with sharp edges and jagged lumps of rock, I am not worth much more than the flaking bones that support me so inadequately and painfully, but Gabriel may well be worth something.

27

Only how can I pull him back from that brink if I am not capable of pulling myself back?

After several tries he got out his key and put it in the lock; its pressure on his fingers while he struggled to turn it was extreme agony, but on the other side of the door lay the little warm bathroom with its plastic tooth-mug and all the water in the world ready to come out of the tap, and the white cardboard container with its neat round cream-coloured plastic lid, and under that the miraculous red torpedoes, of which he must swallow no more than two because even two every eight hours came dangerously near to the top safety level beyond which there was no guarantee against undesirable side-effects—

But who is to judge, he thought, pushing open the front door and walking straight into the bathroom, who except I myself can possibly judge which is more undesirable, those hypothetical side-effects, or pain to the degree that I am feeling now? Spells of amnesia are certainly inconvenient, they are more than that, but what is this, a TV quiz, and the prize a trip to a desert island with Miss Lola Casanova? What sets off those blank spells anyway, not just pain, pain plus what?

He swallowed the two capsules, gulped another mugful of the warm, brackish water, kicked the front door shut behind him without looking back, and made straight for the sofa. It was too lumpy and sagging, though, the position it imposed on him was far too cramped for the pain that was now invading him; that pain wanted plenty of scope. He searched in a closet, found a dusty blanket, flung it on the floor with a cushion, and lay down, unfolding himself with as much care as if he had been a Dead Sea Scroll.

Thomas the Dead Sea Scroll, he thought, true Thomas returned from inside the hill, back home to tell what he has seen, and no one believes him because who would want to believe such a tale? It's not to their advantage. I am Lazarus, come back from the dead, come back to tell you all, I will tell you all.

But they said, That is not what I meant at all.

They said it's absurd to encourage that bird, so they smashed the old man of Whitehaven.

Suppose the phone rang now and it was Gabriel, what would I be able to say to him?

28

Listen, Gabriel, there is more to it than this. To the measure of the pain that I feel now, that you may feel in your turn, may already have felt, there is also joy, there is also amazement, there is also discovery; look back on your past, child, do you see nothing worth remembering there? You, of all children? And as the road leads back to a mysteriously beautiful distance, so it also leads forward, who knows where? How can you shut your eyes to the possibilities of that journey into unknown territory?

But if he says, no, I don't choose to be a pioneer, I do not choose to travel ahead, why should I be obliged to undertake this laborious and painful pilgrimage probably leading nowhere, what do I say to him then?

Listen, Gabriel. Do you know how to measure the height of the sun? You take a grassblade, you take a tree, you measure the angle from the grass to the top of the tree, you produce that line upwards, you cast it into the sky like a fishing-rod to hook the sun. Do you know how to draw a graph, Gabriel? You begin at the bottom left-hand corner, you make your graph spring on and upward like a chamoix from point to point, you can forecast the end from those beginnings. Surely you, above all, ought to be able to throw your mind ahead of you and guess what heights it may be within your power to climb?

If even I, wrapped as I am in clogging webs of pain, frustration, inadequacy, and deceit, can make some vague forecast of what might lie ahead for you, surely you with your clear and unimpeded vision could see enough of that landscape to make the trip worthwhile?

Why, the very first time I saw you—

A steely hysterical trill cut through his arguments; at first, confusedly, he mistook the stridency for a translation of his pain into terms of sound; then he realised that it must be the telephone.

Careful now; don't knock it down again.

Employing as much care as might be needed to manoeuvre a liner into dock, he raised himself to a kneeling position, propped against the window sill.

Let it be Gabriel this time, he thought, in the position of prayer. Just let it be Gabriel. Let me put the necessity of his return to him in a couple of well-chosen sentences, let him be convinced and agree to fly back to England with me tomorrow. We could have such a happy trip;

with Gabriel in the seat beside me to chatter and tell me his adventures, give his impressions of America, the pain would be bearable, we'd probably fall into one of those philosophical discussions that we used to have, coming back from our chess-walks. The little skinny, bony claw tucked so confidingly into mine: Uncle Tom? Are you very busy? Would you have time to come on a chess-walk? It was always Uncle Tom, never daddy or papa, though Bella tried hard to make him adopt one of those, he always rejected them with calm logic: But he isn't my father. Yet he seldom addressed August as father, Bella said; mostly called him Gus, right from the start, and August preferred it.

The old sense of deprivation returned to him, the swift immediate anguish and loss of watching water widen between the quayside and the boat that has sailed prematurely, the friend who left the rendezvous without waiting, the unique bargain that was taken ten minutes before you entered the shop.

When a great man suddenly dies whom you have waited all your life to meet, you feel a purely selfish sense of bereavement, as if providence had dealt you a special, spiteful blow. And whatever arduous method you adopt of sublimating, dissipating your childish rage, some of it will remain with you till your last breath.

With a careful, trembling hand he lifted the receiver and held it to his ear.

Gabriel? Is that you?

"Hullo?"

But again, on the other end of the line, there was nothing but silence, a black, breathing, waiting silence that seemed to greet him like a familiar. I know you, the silence muttered in his ear; I know you from a long way back; you and I have a bone to pick, my friend.

"Gabriel!" he shouted angrily. "Look, Gabriel, if this is you, will you grow up and stop playing these childish tricks? It isn't funny; it's disgustingly stupid and cruel. You ought to be ashamed of yourself. Please, will you tell me where you are? *Gabriel!*"

Nothing answered him but a ghostly click, rejecting his plea with mocking finality; the silence now had a different ring to it, metallic and empty.

He crashed back the mouthpiece onto its rest and let himself down onto his blanket again with a creak of agony,

30

muttering in weak hysterical rage. That boy—fucking—sodding—young lout—Yet, after all, why should he assume that it was Gabriel? There was no reason to suppose that Gabriel even knew he was in America. And if he did know, how could it conceivably be in Gabriel's character to play malicious tricks of this kind? Wasn't it much more likely that somebody else—the person who had been illicitly making use of the apartment, some complete unknown—was now phoning to check whether the owner was there? And now they knew, they would very likely leave him alone.

But now it did occur to Thomas that he had not locked the front door. With an angry groan he hoisted himself up once more, limped across the room, snecked the catch. Then, stumbling over his canvas grip, he remembered for the first time that he had thrust a bundle of mail into the open top, downstairs, when he first walked into the house.

What a fool. Perhaps there's a letter from Gabriel right there in that lot, and I never gave it a thought.

He pulled out the bundle and sorted hastily through the envelopes. Suzanne from the office was supposed to come periodically to clear out the mailbox, but evidently she had not done so for some time. They all contained publishers' promotion material—*Book News, Publishers Weekly*—there were leaflets from the Block Association, ads for local decorators and furniture-movers—invitations to long-extinct cocktail parties celebrating the publication of novels he had no wish to read—no personal mail, nothing hand-written. Yet—wait—there was a plain buff envelope, Thomas Cook, typed address, no postmark, delivered by hand. Bella said Gabriel had typed a letter to her.

The envelope was very flat. Nothing at all inside?

He tore it open.

A smallish, thinnish strip, off-white paper, the kind spewed out by a cash register as it lists all the purchases and then adds them—indeed on one side were faint violet figures adding up to seven dollars and eighty-five cents' worth of something. On the other side were typed words.

YOU TURD, YOU SHIT, YOU FILTHY DREG, WHAT
MAKES YOU THINK YOU HAVE A CHANCE TO FIND

31

Holding the slip in stiff fingers, he worked his way slowly back across the room to his blanket—it felt like a day's journey—and sank down into a kind of squatting position.

Was this what Gabriel had become in the course of eight months?

But it said *him,* not me. What company can Gabriel be keeping?

I have to sleep now. I'll study the implications of this tomorrow.

Who hates me so?

Why?

Useless tears, acid burning tears crept sideways across his face. Jan, what had I done? What did you have against me? And earlier still—she loved Christmas so, why did she have to die on Christmas Eve?

Two

Thomas 1967

Sharp, shameful tears kept welling from his eyes, blurring his vision. They stung like vinegar, they burned his cheeks. He could not wipe them away, he did not dare take even one hand from the wheel, as he drove down the dark, yellow-sodium-studded length of Wanborough High Street, because the night traffic, though not so thick as that of daytime, was travelling much faster, was crowding peevishly behind him, and the road surface was slippery as plastic, a thin layer of half-melted snow on top of a thicker layer of half-frozen rain. And rain, turning to snow as it fell, was ribboning down ahead of him, clinging soggily to his windscreen, clogging the wipers so that they creaked and jibbed, so that for seconds at a time, even when he blinked away the tears, his visibility became reduced to a dim square of orange-coloured glass. Even

32

when the wipers pushed past the frosty obstruction and resumed their sweep, all that he could see was two freckled cones of light, bored by his headlamps into the whirling mess before him.

Out of the congested centre of Wanborough at last, thank god. Past the ABC cinema's big red-and-blue neon, and the Wanborough Park Service Station's orange-illuminated scallop shell, and the Talbot Hotel that must once have been a coaching inn on the London to Dover road, but was now given over to business lunches and more dubious evening rendezvous. Not so much traffic now, longer spaces between the vehicles. But the road was glassier. Like driving in a salad bowl. Be glad you forgot to turn off down the new bypass, then, what used to be Coultershaw Lane, before they extended and widened it and sliced clean through mother's rockery and vegetable garden and half the lawn. Lucky she wasn't there to see. And now, the old man tells me, when I remember to call up for a chat, they call it Suicides' Mile, there are more crashes on it than on any other five-mile stretch of clearway in South London. So something will have to be done about the sharp curve where it joins back onto Wanborough Parkside, but nobody can think quite what.

Living beside a motorway must be like living by the Berlin Wall. Only noisier. Death if you try to cross. A man-made ligature that transforms the landscape, mutilates, amputates, cuts off circulation. How often have I been across, since Uncle Edward's printers moved their works to within a mile of father's front door, as the crow flies? I'm no crow. Perhaps twice. Other reasons for that, of course. The concrete steel-and-death barricade between adolescence and the grown-up world.

Meanwhile I have somehow to find a way across to the other side. Didn't they sink an underpass a bit farther on, using one of the roads that led across from Wanborough Common to the big cricket ground beyond Wansea Village? Anyway, why am I doing this crazy thing, the old man will have been asleep since nine o'clock and won't be in the least pleased to see me if I wake him. He'll come blinking out, dry, wizened, shrivelled, like some peevish old mummied Pharaoh in his Viyella pyjamas and Jaegar dressing-gown and sheepskin slippers, creaking, croaking, rubbing his skinny powdery hands together, making a dry unhumorous crack. This is an unexpected pleasure. To what do we owe the honour? Is your journey really necessary? And what do I say? Hello, Father, thought I'd come back to the old place and spend a night. Thought I'd like to have a look at mother's kitchen sink, where I've seen her so many times up to the elbows in soapsuds, saying cheerfully, "If there's one thing I really enjoy, it's doing a little wash." I thought a visit home would make a pleasant change. Well, yes, also I had a row with Jan; my girlfriend, you know, you did meet her once and thought she was a surprisingly nice girl for an actress—that was what you said: "Surprisingly nice girl—for an actress"; I've had a row with her, she won't let me into her flat, and somehow I don't fancy going back to my own place, which is quite remarkably empty. Some places are emptier than others, and that flat is at the moment, without a shadow of doubt, the emptiest spot in the northern hemisphere. So I thought I'd drop back for a touch of what you might call family atmosphere. Besides, to be honest, I couldn't think, just now, of anywhere else to drop. Except off some bridge. Or the printing works; I suppose I could always fall back on spending a constructive eight hours correcting the galleys of Austin Douglas's *Dictionary of Biology and Related Subjects* in four vols.

What did Jan and I quarrel about (not that you would be in the least likely to ask)? Well, Father, this is the curious thing, *I don't know.* You may think that singular, too, but it's the sober truth. Yes, and I *was* sober. And she, she was as sober as a judge. Justice MacArthur. Madam Justice Jan. Back from Portia at the Aldwych and still carrying the aura of it around her neck like a toga. "Let you in here? After what you did? Are you mad?" Wouldn't even answer her front doorbell at first, though I knew she was in behind there, motionless, alert, with her head cocked like some forest thing, a deer I suppose. So I went back down to the lobby and phoned her from the box there and she did answer then, but said no, I *couldn't* come in, no, *never;* but at last, because I was a bit pleading and frantic, she consented to come down to the hall and talk, standing just inside the glass doors, out of earshot of the porter, with the snow cascading down outside, though she said it was stupid because there was nothing to talk *about,* nothing more to discuss at all, everything was finished, kaput, totally, and furthermore she needed her sleep, she had a rehearsal of *Twelfth Night* tomorrow at half-past nine. But

34

Jan, I said, look girl, we've got to have this out, what is it all about? What did I do or say? So there she stood, very pale, wearing a dark sweater and trousers, with her face all covered in grease, some kind of nightcream that made her look, in that dim light, like a photograph of a Michelangelo statue, you know the concentrated responsible expression, mulling over some knotty problem before taking very decisive action. Look, Jan, I said again, what is this? *Why*, suddenly, won't you let me in? What's up? It's not like you to behave in such an arbitrary way. And she, transfixing me with her transparently truthful gaze—do you remember her eyes at all, Father, they are so clear you feel you might be able to see right through to the other side, it is sometimes almost a shock to rediscover what a good, just, intelligent, tolerant mind resides behind those eyes—she said, "Are you crazy? If you can't work it out for yourself, that's even more reason why we're not suited. You really expect me to go over it? After what you did? I said I'd come down because you sounded so queer I thought you might be ill, but you look all right now, so I'm going back to bed and I strongly advise *you* to go to your *own* bed. Please. I don't want an embarrassing fuss in the lobby here. Will you just *go?*" As she said this, she had been walking back to the lift, which was open, waiting; now she stepped in, pressed the botton, and went. So. Out into the snow. Never darken my doors again. Farewell forever, Rembrandt Court, Melville Road, N.W.3. And, quite simply, that's how it was, Father, that's why I happen to have popped in to see you at midnight on a fine winter's night. Slightly without a plan. When Jan says something like that, I reckon she means it.

If he's asleep, what do I do? Make myself a cosy pot of tea in the kitchen that is so imbued, every inch of it, with memories of mother even now, even after fifteen years? Curious how, even in a short time, some personalities imprint themselves on an environment so that however long after they are gone, however many other people have been there muddling about in the interim, you only feel, This was *her* place, where she used to stand peeling apples for jelly while she watched the nut-hatches outside on her bird-table. She was there only five years, but she loved that garden. It was worth the move. Of course it was.

Some people are like signposts in one's landscape, and she was one, and Jan was another, because although quite young, and, as you have so justly pointed out, Father, an actress, Jan nonetheless has *standards;* she seems to have a purpose and know where she is going. And where she is not going, apparently, is with me, though why this is so remains to be discovered. Therefore I shall have to find another signpost, or learn—which would be the better course, it goes without saying, the adult, serious, stand-on-your-own-feet, responsible course—to do without a signpost.

Some might find it curious, Father, they might think it shed a significant light on your and my relationship, that I was never able to regard you as a signpost. The only serious precept for living that I can ever remember your passing on to me was the principle you told me you had adopted in World War One, which was: Live completely in the present, never worry about tomorrow. An excellent rationale for life in the trenches, I'm sure, but not, perhaps, quite so well adapted for managing one's existence among fellow-citizens in a modern metropolis. Didn't stand even you in very good stead, actually. But who wants a precept, anyway, mother never handed out any precepts, and neither did Jan; they simply followed a clear path and dealt justly.

There is one other person whom I might have taken as a signpost, Father, while we are having this interesting conversation; did, in fact, to some extent, only, as misfortune would have it, he died last year in a plane crash; one of those really wasteful crashes disposing at a blow of about thirty scientists and philosophers on their way to a UNESCO conference in Lima, Peru. I read somewhere that if all the birds in the world took off simultaneously, the gravitational shift would be so great that we'd be deflected out of orbit. If all the greatest minds took off simultaneously—

Damn, wasn't that the underpass turning that I just overshot? Which means I shall have to go all the way down to the Dartford roundabout, because I'm pretty sure that the other roads going left are all culs-de-sac, and this is no weather for trying to make a U-turn, with visibility down to about six feet and the road surface like a wet glass plate.

Now comes the long black stretch on the right, Wanborough Common, once not more than about twelve minutes' walk from our front door. Wild deer off the common used to stray into Wansea Village sometimes; mother boasted that she had once looked out before dawn on an

April morning and seen an elegant young stag lean over the front palings, like an Edwardian dandy helping himself to a buttonhole, and take a mouthful of hyacinths from her flower-bed. God knows how you get from the house to the common now the motorway lies in between like the sword Excalibur; probably have to take a bus down to the roundabout and another bus back. But Father doesn't worry; never much of a one for walking at any time, and these days, tapping along with Judy and his lame leg and his stick, the letter-box at the corner is about his farthest extent. As for the deer, they live enclosed behind twelve-foot iron railings, and probably just as well, or there'd be even more fatalities along Suicides' Mile.

On the left, now, handsome large houses, mansions, mid-nineteenth-century merchants' dwellings, each standing in half an acre or more of garden; maybe a bit less, the motorway sliced all their rumps off, but still they come out of it better than the little houses on the north side. They have their pride and dignity left. Old, mature trees, solid brick front walls, wide double driveways, gravel sweeps, none of your cheap nasty concrete, fancy brickwork, Gothic pinnacles. You can hardly see them, set so far back, because of the snow—just from time to time, between blowing gusts, one of those crenellated brick bulks will loom out dimly; some have carriage lamps gleaming in their porches, but there are few other lights; the rich go early to bed. Or else they are all away in Morocco and on the ski-slopes.

And that's reminded me—returning to our conversation about signposts, Father—you probably never knew it, weren't the least interested I daresay, but somewhere along here—

Jesus, what a skid. Lucky the steering in this car had just been overhauled. Even so, that was the worst I've ever survived; I hope I never have another as bad. Funny how the adrenaline rushes all over you *after* the event; to combat the shaking, I suppose. Snow much thicker now; better get down to five miles an hour. Have to open the window and hang out to see where we are: Overbury Road, Leamington Road, Eliot Road. Left, and left again. Back to the main road. Zebra crossing. Orange beacons ahead. Just as well they have them, you couldn't see just black-and-white stripes in this, all covered with snow

37

and ice. Hands sweating on the wheel, take care, go slow, keep a sharp eye out for late-night pedestrians—

And—careful, watch it—yes, there—something lying right on the zebra crossing, half dusted over by snow already. Brake right down, a little at a time, no more skidding, creep to a stop. Looks like a sack, but more angular —not very big. Come to a halt, here, well back; illegal to park within ten yards of a crossing anyway. Get out and investigate.

Heart in mouth; know what that means, now.

He jumped out and ran forward; slipped in the treacherous mush; ought to have put on a raincoat; the snow was wet, sloppy, and thick, like porridge falling out of the sky.

Not a sack on the crossing; a small person, a boy, with snow powdered already all over his hair, face to the ground, one leg stuck out at a bad angle. Dead?

No, thank God, unconscious, breathing. Daren't move him though, leg almost certainly broken, might be internal injuries also. Tyre marks? Completely obliterated, if any, by snow. Probably impossible for anybody to say exactly how long the boy has been lying here, but not long, obviously; feels warm under jacket. Nobody in sight. How to get help? Run to nearest house, telephone? Terrified to leave him, in case of other careless drivers, but must get him shifted with all possible speed, otherwise possibility of pneumonia, as well, from shock and exposure. Move car closer? Rug, red triangle?

While he stood, indecisive—hardly an instant had passed, actually—a figure emerged sudden and ghostly, out of the streaming snow—a woman, grey-haired under scarf, red-faced, in gumboots, gloves, dark-purple raincoat.

"Oh, thank god," Thomas said in simple relief. "Look, there's a boy here, hurt, in the road. Can you go and phone for an ambulance, quickly, while I stay by him? I saw him lying there as I drove along—looks as if someone hit him and didn't stop—"

"Yes. Of course. I'll go right away." She had a deep voice, rough, like a man's. "Is that your car back there? The Renault?"

"Yes, it is. Please hurry!"

"I was only thinking, if you have a rug, better cover him."

Was that really why she had asked the question? Or had she wondered—natural enough—whether Thomas himself were the hit-and-run driver responsible for the accident? Well, if she had been walking along the Parkside, she must have seen him pull up, far back from the orange lights; she must realise that the boy had been lying there, injured already, at the moment when he stopped.

"Why not *this* house?" Thomas called after her, pointing to the nearest entrance.

"This one's mine—" Her voice floated back as she walked through the next gateway. "Shan't be a minute—"

That made sense, of course. It was obviously better to use her own phone than waste time ringing the doorbell of people who might be asleep, away, out of earshot, deaf, stupid, unhelpful. She seemed to have a head on her shoulders, more like a man, really: laconic, prompt to do what was asked, no fuss, no exclamations.

The boy still lay motionless; better if he stayed that way, probably, until help came, though it was frightening to see him flopped out there like a corpse with the snow steadily covering the zebra stripes of the crossing, piling on the folds of the rug. Thomas had gingerly tucked the warm Shetland plaid around him, leaving a gap just big enough to let him breathe. What age would he be? Children had not often come in Thomas's way. Nine or ten, perhaps? Dark soft hair, rounded ingenuous curve of cheek over which, just in view, could be seen one semicircle of dark eyelash. Eyes definitively shut. One small bony hand clenched, the other hidden beneath him. He wore some kind of parka. What had he been doing out so late for god's sake, in such weather? And why was nobody looking for him, you'd think his family would be concerned—at this time of year, of night—in an upper-class neighbourhood like this?

Now the woman was returning, scrunching along in her gum-boots. She carried a torch with her, this time, which she flashed, for an instant, blindingly, in Thomas's face, before turning it downwards on to the boy.

"The ambulance will be here in five minutes. I phoned the police as well," she reported briefly. Then she stooped —not too easily, for she seemed stout, and was heavily swaddled against the weather, and said:

"Oh dear, it's young Gabriel."

"Do you know him?" he asked foolishly.

"Yes, he's a neighbour. Lives just along there. Where I came from. A nice boy," she said with a judicious air. "I hope he's not seriously hurt."

39

"You know his family? Which is their house? Shouldn't I go and get somebody—tell them what's happened?"

The woman, however, shook her head in a very emphatic manner. It was made more emphatic by the massive size of her head, which seemed even larger because of the tightly frizzed grey hair, bulging like wire wool under the gaudy scarf she wore. Her eyes were small but exceedingly shrewd and piercing. The mouth, under the big fleshy nose, in the middle of the round, wet pink face, was small and set; very firm indeed. Butterfly-shaped diamanté spectacles added an incongruously modish touch to what was otherwise a somewhat dowdy appearance.

"No," she said with decision. "Better not go round there yet. His mother would be no help at all. In the first place she's a very silly woman—there'd be tears and high-strikes, she'd probably come rushing out in her nightgown, try to pick him up and carry him indoors herself —she's quite capable of dramatics like that—and do untold damage. And in the second place she's just recovering from flu, so she'd do herself no good either. No, we'd much better wait till the ambulance has taken him off, and *then* tell her."

"You're quite sure?" said Thomas doubtfully. "Mightn't she want to go with him?"

It seemed a large responsibility, to withhold the information. If the boy were hurt badly—if he were to die—If *he* had a son lying injured in the road, with god knows what injuries— Suppose he were to come round, suppose he wanted his parents? But this woman was a friend of the family, doubtless she knew best. A hysterical mother certainly was the last thing they needed just then.

"What about the father?"

"Died last year. There's only her and the boy. Which also contributes to her overwrought state."

"Oh Lord. Poor woman."

"Do you live round here?" she asked.

"No, in Kensington. My name's Thomas Cook. I'm a publisher," he said, wanting to establish some kind of respectable image.

"Really? I used to be an editor. Loraine Hartshorn."

If he was supposed to know the name he did not, but he said:

"Oh? How interesting. Do you know this woman—the boy's mother—well?"

What a strange, stilted conversation, standing here in the whirl of snow at the roadside, icy wet wind whipping their legs. The orange beacons winked and flashed. The big black trees on the far side of the road tossed and thrashed their boughs, appearing and vanishing between gusts.

Miss—Mrs?—Hartshorn made some reply that he did not fully catch, for it was drowned by the noise of an approaching motor. Had she said, "I clean their house"? He did not ask her to repeat her words, for a white police Jaguar slid to a stop beside them with a creak of snow-tyres on slush. Two uniformed men jumped out; one of them went directly to the boy and knelt down by him; the other, who seemed to be the senior, came up to Thomas and the woman.

"Was it you who called us? You're Miss Hartshorn?"

"Yes. And this is Mr. Cook, who found the boy. Where's the ambulance?" she inquired briskly

"It's on its way; it'll be here in a couple of minutes."

As the woman had done, the police officer instantly asked:

"Is that your car, sir?"

"Yes, it's mine."

"Would you mind telling me just what happened?"

While Thomas was hastily describing for the second time how he had found the boy, the junior police officer, having finished his quick examination of the boy and also made a survey, with measurements, of the snow-covered road, walked back without comment to Thomas's car and studied that. Presently he returned to the group at the crossing. Thomas observed him catch his companion's eye and shake his head briefly.

"No marks," he said, and went back to the police car, where he could be heard making a report on the radio.

Thomas, who had his cold wet hands stuffed into his pockets to warm them, unclenched the fingers, which were becoming increasingly painful. He said:

"Do you think the boy's badly hurt?"

"Can't be sure, yet, sir. Here's the ambulance now."

It arrived with lights flashing but no siren, and pulled up ahead of the Jaguar. Two attendants nipped out and expertly slid a stretcher under the oblivious boy. Thomas, meanwhile, kept as near as he could, watching all their movements with acute attention; it seemed to him that he could feel every jar, every jerk; his own arms and legs shrank in sympathy for the small, damaged bones. Longing to help, he could do nothing; he shook out and folded the tartan rug, took it and the red triangle back to his own car and stowed them away. When he came back the woman, Miss Hartshorn, was saying to the policemen:

"I'm a friend of the boy's mother. I live in that house there, number thirty-four. The mother is convalescing from flu—in fact I was just on my way back from making her a hot drink and settling her for the night when I saw this gentleman pull up. I had my corgi with me, so I took him indoors and came straight back. The boy knows me well, so I'll go along with him in the ambulance, shall I? In case he comes to?"

"If you would, ma'am, that would be helpful. Then you can give them at the hospital any information about him they may need. Which house does he come from?"

"That one along there, number thirty-eight. His name's Gabriel Baird."

Thomas felt a strong, wild, physical pressure, as if his heart, after swelling and swelling from some painful inflammation, had finally burst asunder inside him, doing unknown but vital damage, lacerating every part of him as the jagged fragments flew outwards. He cleared his throat and said:

"Baird? He wouldn't be the son of August Baird?"

"Was," the woman said. "August's dead. Died last year. Didn't you know? Look, I must go, they want to be off. Would you do two things for me—lock up my house—here's the key—and go with the police when they tell Mrs. Baird about the accident. Tell her I'll phone from the hospital as soon as there's any news. And will you kindly stay with her till I do phone? She definitely ought not to be alone and worrying in her present state. Say I'll come back to keep her company as soon as I can."

"Are you sure she'd want a total stranger?" Thomas asked doubtfully. "Isn't there some other neighbour or relative I could call?"

"Are you scared of the responsibility?" Miss Hartshorn asked, eyeing him sternly. "I thought you looked like an intelligent, sensible, reliable man."

"Well, I am, I suppose; I mean, I wouldn't rape her or

burgle your house," he said lamely. "I was thinking of her—"

"*She* won't mind; it'll give her a lift to see a new face. Take her out of herself. Which she needs, God knows. No, she has no other close friends round here. Tell her not to worry too much; the ambulance attendants think it may be just a broken leg and concussion. . . . I'll give the hospital his medical history, tell Bella—"

Thomas opened his mouth to make another objection, but giving him her emphatic nod, she climbed, nimbly for all her bulk, into the ambulance, and the doors closed behind her.

What a power-house of a woman. He could imagine her sitting behind a huge office desk, ordering her staff about. He had not quite liked her; although she had been helpful and efficient he felt there was something—what? arrogant? officious? a wish to impress her personality, a refusal to make any contact with his. Still he must admit that her intentions seemed wholly altruistic and benevolent. Off she went, in the ambulance, in her gumboots, at midnight—heaven only knew how or when she would get home to her corgi—laying this command on him, placing what seemed complete confidence in him. It was all very well to say he looked respectable, reliable—How did she know he was not a homicidal maniac, had not, in fact, been the author of the accident? *Why* had she asked him to do this? Surely it was not strictly necessary for him to go in—the police would tell Mrs. Baird what had happened, they were accustomed to breaking such lugubrious news. Would not the boy's mother think it very odd, pushing, intrusive, downright suspicious, really, that he, a complete stranger, should invade her privacy, when she was ill, furthermore—should suggest remaining with her till her friend came back? She might be appalled.

But if she was really ill, it was true that she ought not to be left alone, and in such circumstances too.

Not that Miss Hartshorn had sounded all that friendly towards Mrs. Baird, in a way? She had been very detached in her attitude. What was it, what were the words she had used in describing the woman—silly, hysterical, high-strikes? But no doubt she was one of those bluff characters who ride rough-shod over their friends and tell home truths that no one wishes to hear.

God knows, anyway, thought Thomas, moving with

43

reluctance after the two policemen, going into that house, of all houses, to inform that poor woman that her boy has been run over and hurt, is just about the last thing I want to do in this world.

He felt—now that he had time to think about it—rather sick; partly from wet and cold, partly from shock; a kind of disbelief in the last three hours, a refusal to accept that this could be happening to *him*, added a dreamlike, feverish, dislocated element to his physical nausea. His feet and hands ached with cold; his sodden jacket flapped uncomfortably against his hips, and his wet trousers clung to his legs. Not the most favourable circumstances, he thought dourly, for somebody with my particular complaint.

"Nasty night," one of the policemen remarked, looking after the dim flash of the ambulance as it sped off, receding between layers of blowing whiteness. "You live near here, sir?"

"No, Kensington. But I used to live near here as a boy, my father still does. I was on my way to visit him in Wansea Village."

"Would I know the gentleman, I wonder? I'm from Wansea myself."

"Mr. Samuel Cook."

"Oh yes, I know him," struck in the younger man. "We met at the dog-training school; I had one of his Alsatian puppies. He's a retired gentleman, isn't he, lives in Garibaldi Villas?"

"Yes, that's right," Thomas said.

The atmosphere warmed, insensibly. But then the first man remarked:

"You were coming rather a long way round, weren't you, sir? To get to the village?"

"The snow was so thick that I missed the first turn-off."

"Easy to do that," they agreed, passing between the big stone gateposts. "Do you know this boy's family, then, or does your father?"

"No. No, I don't know them at all." What an irony, Thomas thought, what a choice sample of fate's malicious timing. "Of course I've heard of them. I mean, of August Baird."

"Oh, him, yes. Well-known scientist, wasn't he?"

"Yes, writer—philosopher—"

"Didn't he get killed last year? In a plane crash?" put in the younger man.

They were walking up the curved drive to the house, which stood quite far back from the road, protected successively by a high central front wall, a belt of shrubbery, and a semicircular plat of lawn, in the centre of which grew a huge cedar. The tree was veiled in snow at present: nothing of it could be seen but the tips of its black-webbed branches; thrashing and sweeping in the wind, they came and went like mourning banners, like hands in the act of being wrung. On a clear day, Thomas knew, the great tree could be seen for miles around, was quite a famous landmark; he had heard somewhere that it could be identified from as far away as the Crystal Palace. He had tried, once or twice, to locate it from there himself, but could never be sure that he had the right tree.

They climbed three wide, shallow, circular steps. In addition to Thomas's other miseries, he now had an urgent need to empty his bladder. What a fool not to have had the presence of mind to step aside into the shrubbery.

A pale light showed behind the glass-paned front door.

"The other lady said just walk in, the door wasn't locked," said the senior policeman, after briefly pressing the bell-knob. He tried the handle gently. The door opened, letting out a waft of warm, woodsmoke-scented air.

They all moved softly inside, the two policemen with the quiet confidence of those who are working completely within their rights, carrying out a necessary duty, whereas Thomas felt all the furtiveness and anxiety of an illegal intruder. After passing through an inner porch containing rubber overshoes and milk bottles, they found themselves in a largish L-shaped hallway, with blue-painted walls, and five or six white doors, most of them shut. Round the corner to the right a wide flight of carpeted stairs led upwards. Worn but beautiful Persian rugs covered the polished wood floor. One painting, an abstract, predominantly red, black, blue, and white—the same colours as the rugs—hung on the end wall facing them.

The house had a singular aura of familiarity, Thomas thought: the rugs, the picture, the warm, waiting silence, the resin-scented air, all seemed to be saying something to him; he could have been a long-lost son, returning to the home of his childhood.

As the police walked, at their firm but measured pace through the hall, a woman came fast and silently out of a doorway that had been concealed from their first view, far over to the right behind the flight of stairs.

"*Oh!*—I thought it was Gabriel—" she exclaimed. Her hand flew to her mouth; over it large round apprehensive eyes stared guiltily at them. *She* might have been the interloper, not they; though she seemed less alarmed than disconcerted, as if she felt the need to apologise for her being downstairs.

"Mrs. Baird?" the senior policeman asked.

She nodded, swallowing; a slight, strangled murmur was her only reply.

She was still quite young, Thomas realised. Her youth was evidently a surprise to the policemen as well. She wore a floor-length white woollen dressing-gown, made like a monk's robe, with a cowl; it was belted round her waist by a cord. Her small feet were bare, in sandals.

The senior officer started on a low, calm, unhurried explanation of what had happened, while she listened in silence, watching him with large, frightened eyes, her hand still at her mouth.

As the man began to speak, Thomas realised, with shame, that neither his bladder nor his stomach could hold out any longer; by now his physical state was too acute to be borne. A rapid glance to the left as he closed the front door behind him had shown him what was almost certainly the entrance to the kind of little downstairs coat-closet-cum-lavatory frequently found in such large Victorian houses. Murmuring an apology, he slipped away from the group, hurriedly pushed another stained-glass door shut behind him, and, with a sense of assuagement that was almost ecstasy, relieved himself, first by emptying his bursting bladder, then by vomiting into the handbasin. He felt as if he were obliged to expel from his guts the whole of the day that had just passed. Sick, shaking and sweating, clasping his hands over his throbbing forehead, he leaned against the wall for a moment, then doubled against the basin and vomited again—nothing but a thin thread of green bile this time—with an effort that seemed to drag out every muscle in his body to its fullest extent. Then, feeling as if he had scoured the last dregs from his system, he rinsed his face with cold water, gargled and spat, and shakily made his way back. The hall was empty now, but, following the sound of voices, he walked through a door to the left of the red-and-blue abstract painting, and found himself in a large, cold, dim, book-lined room.

Mrs. Baird had seated herself, probably at the policemen's suggestion, in a polished wooden Windsor armchair that faced a massive desk in the middle of the room. The two men were standing. There was no other furniture in the room. The desk, Thomas noticed with a pang, held papers stacked in neat, orderly piles, which looked as if they had not been disturbed for a long time. The woman, though of average size, seemed somehow touchingly small and childlike, dwarfed by the wide polished expanse of mahogany, as she sat huddled together in her white robe, with her sandalled feet tucked behind a rung of the chair.

Thomas, nervously glancing sideways, noticed many book jackets that were very familiar to him on the shelves: biology, sociology, philosophy, poetry, fiction; he longed to look more closely but did not dare. He recognised a portrait of Darwin, hanging over the mantelpiece. Beneath it, gathering dust, lay a large round engraved plaque, apparently made of gold, and what appeared to be a chunk of rock.

"And this is the gentleman who found your son and asked Miss Hartshorn to call us," the senior officer said, shooting a keen glance at Thomas, who imagined that he must look ghastly enough after such a bout of vomiting; probably green as the hearth-rug.

"It was most terribly kind of you," Mrs. Baird said. "I can't tell you how grateful I am. Thank god you stopped. What a *horrible* thing to happen— Do you think whoever it was *knew* what he'd done—that he'd knocked Gabriel down—and just drove on, without caring?"

She spoke jerkily, with pauses between her words, in a soft, schoolgirlish voice that was high but breathy. It seemed, Thomas thought, quite different from the voice in which she had called out when they first arrived.

"I'm afraid that's very likely, ma'am," said the senior officer. "We get that sort of thing all the time. There are some real swine about on the roads these days. Belt along at eighty, no matter what the weather conditions, take any risks, to themselves *or* other people, and if they do any damage, nothing matters to them so long as *they* don't get involved and run in."

"It's disgusting," the other man said.

"So you were fortunate that someone like Mr. Cook came along soon after," said the first one. "Specially as he risked having it thought that he'd run over the boy himself. Plenty of people wouldn't have stopped."

"Luckily I've got Miss Hartshorn's word that I stopped before I got to the crossing," Thomas said. He spoke with an effort; his mouth still felt rough and harsh from vomit.

"Yes, it's a good thing for you she completely confirmed your story, sir," said the senior man heartily. "Now, I shouldn't worry too much, Mrs. Baird; the ambulance attendants are pretty experienced, and they seemed to think there were no signs of internal injuries. How old did you say the boy was?"

"Ten," she said with a hiccupping sob. "He's small for his age. He's all I have in the world, since—since his father died—"

"Now, now, don't you fret too much, madam—if it's just a broken leg, why that's nothing, nothing at all; he'll be hopping about on a crutch in three days, likely as not, and forgotten all about it in six weeks' time."

"Which hospital did you say they'd taken him to?"

"Can't be sure yet, ma'am, probably the Wanborough General. But if their emergency is full up, the ambulance may have to go on to the Riggs Memorial. Anyway the lady said she'd call you as soon as she has any news, and then maybe this gentleman can go along and fetch her back, so there's not a thing for you to do except relax and take things easy. A nice cup of tea's what you need. Would you like us to stop and make it for you?"

"No—no, thank you so much," she said hastily, blowing her nose. "You've been so kind—I—I've had such a lot of bad things happen to me lately, I wouldn't have thought I'd be able to take any more awful news. But I suppose god sends us strength as the occasion demands."

Both police looked a little embarrassed, but also relieved.

"Er—he does indeed, ma'am," said the senior. "Now I can see you're going to be all right. And this gentleman's kindly agreed to stay with you till Miss Hernshaw rings—"

"Hartshorn—"

"So we'd better be on our way. We'll be in touch with you, of course, if there are any further developments."

"You mean if you catch the beast who did it?"

"That's right," said the younger man. "Not that there's

much chance, in weather conditions like this. No tyre marks, you see. Nothing to go on. Still, we'll keep you informed."

"Thank you both, so much," she said again, raising huge blue-grey tear-filled eyes and giving them a faint smile.

"Now we'll say good night, ma'am. And good night to you too, Mr. Cook," said the senior police officer briskly. "Er—if I was you, sir, I'd move your car into the drive here."

"Oh, yes," said Thomas nervously. "Am I infringing parking regulations where I've left the car now?"

"Oh, no, sir, it's quite all right to leave it parked where it is, but it's not very sensible in this visibility, is it? You don't want some other careless fool to come along, not looking where he's going, and bash into it? Oh, by the way, sir, I notice that one of your rear lights is lacking its red shield; want to get that fixed, don't you?"

"Oh—oh, is it? I didn't know. I'll have it dealt with tomorrow. . . . I'll be back in a minute," he assured Mrs Baird, and followed the two police out, just in time to hear one of them say to the other:

"Well, you can never be sure, in a case like that, can you?"

Calling good night, they got into their Jaguar and drove off, leaving Thomas with the uncomfortable impression that they were not a hundred per cent convinced by his story. Still, what could he do about it? His driving record was clear and he had no other crimes logged against him. Sighing, he drove the forty yards to the Baird house from where he had left the car, and cautiously turned its nose in through the gateway, remembering with a wry shrug the hundreds of times that, at a younger age, he had hopefully imagined doing just this.

Had, in fact, when his father retired prematurely at sixty, been instrumental in persuading his parents to move out to this particular suburb, just in the hope that through some concatenation of local affairs, some chance meeting, some heaven-sent piece of luck, they might get to know August Baird. At the age of fourteen, such things seem possible. The encounter on the steps of the post-office: Excuse me, sir, did you drop this? Why yes, thank you, my dear boy, and now let me see, weren't you one of the prizewinners in the science division last week at the high school's founder's day celebrations? Or the lost Abyssinian cat, found and returned amid gratitude and arrangements for further meetings. The chess club—"Professor Baird, I'd like to introduce one of our most promising junior members"—the public library—"Why, what a coincidence, I see you're reading my *Man, Woman, and Survival*." Railway platform, supermarkets, motor-accidents, near-drownings in Wanborough Pond—no daydream had been too elaborate or preposterous for him to frame it.

Nothing of the kind had ever come about. Once, only, had he even so much as caught a glimpse of Professor Baird being driven along the High Street in a Riley by a dark, plain woman, presumably the first wife who died, Berengaria. The Bairds, it seemed, were much too busy to mix in local affairs. Professor Baird spent most of his time advising foreign governments, flying to the scenes of famines, sitting on commissions for technical aid to under-developed countries, making documentary films in various exotic parts of the world; presumably his books got written on the long plane journeys.

But he did lecture at London University. And then, just when the nineteen-year-old Thomas, still hoping, still worshipping, had triumphantly achieved a scholarship to University College, and thought at last he had a chance of coming to closer terms with his hero, Professor Baird had departed on a second three-year exchange with Harvard. The prospect again disappeared over the horizon. Thomas, though bitterly disappointed, still did not lose his confidence that some day they would meet. Providence just could not be so disobliging as to deprive him of this reward, after having arranged for them to be born into the same century, and the same hemisphere, speak the same language, and be interested in the same subjects. August Baird, Thomas felt from the moment when he first read *The Biology of Love and Pain*, was his spiritual father, his natural pastor. It was just a malign mischance, a kind of fourth-dimensional proof-reader's error that Fanny Purbeck had not married him, but had instead met and married Samuel Cook, that thin, dry unadventurous manager of a fountain-pen factory, who had done nothing of note in his whole life except have his hearing impaired by a minor rail accident when returning from Aylesbury to Marylebone, for which the Great Western Railway had grudgingly paid him a small sum of compensation. Although Samuel manufactured pens, he hardly ever, even after he retired, read anything beyond the newspaper; he was not interested in ideas. It had been Fanny, venturous and lively-minded taster of books in the public library, who always had an open volume propped against the dish-rack as she rolled pastry or podded peas, Fanny who had introduced her thirteen-year-old son to the writings of August Baird.

"Here's a book that'll interest you, darling; this man, who's an anthropologist, so he ought to know, says the most *sensible* things about society and social relationships, how we all need to crawl about on our stomachs, and feel the ground with our elbows, and give each other shocks, and learn where our bones are."

From that week Thomas combed all the reviews and publishers' advertisements for news of Baird's new publications; he tirelessly searched for, bought secondhand, or borrowed from libraries the books already published; he hunted through issues of *Nature* and the *New Scientist* for articles, he listened to radio talks, and watched alertly for Baird's rare television appearances. Nothing that Baird ever wrote or said gave him less than that first pure thrill of enlightenment and joy. Here was a mind, it seemed to him, that could not be slipshod or insincere or second-rate: a brilliant, humane intelligence, continually discovering new and important facts about human relationships, about man's place in his environment, and imparting them in a beautifully clear and precise style that also had the gift of wit.

Somewhere along amid his teens, Thomas's simple wish to meet August Baird, just to see and touch the hem of his professorial gown, had changed into a longing to be allowed to work with Baird. What a wonderful experience that must be, to work with such a man. But not impossible, after all; people did; he had assistants; he had mentioned them, warmly and gracefully, in several of the books; when they had made independent discoveries, praise had been unstinted.

Setting himself a rigorously high standard, in school and university, Thomas worked towards this secret goal, forbidding himself even to think of approaching Baird until his own opinion of his achievements should be high enough to justify such an ambition. . . . But perhaps, in his secret heart, he knew that his work would never be of sufficiently high calibre? At all events, if a graph had been kept of his hopes, it would presently have described a downward curve; circumstances began to pile up against him. Just as he had his Ph. D. and had been offered a minor but interesting research job in Cambridge that would have been a stepping-stone in the right direction, the widowed Mr. Cook became totally deaf and simultaneously lost a long, ill-judged, and expensive suit against the railway for more compensation. As a result of this reverse he had a slight stroke. He was now much less well-off and in need of full-time care. It would have been a practical solution for Thomas to live at home and take some job close at hand, but he knew that he would find this arrangement intolerable. Since his mother's death, home had become a place to visit as infrequently as possible, an empty, echoing, haunted husk of a house; the fact that Samuel, too, missed Fanny, on whom he had been pathetically dependent in every way, made no bond whatsoever between father and son. The only solution had been to engage a housekeeper, and no job in Thomas's own field at this stage in his career was going to be sufficiently well paid to cover her salary as well as a separate establishment for Thomas, however tiny, in London or Cambridge.

Help at this juncture came from Samuel's unmarried brother Edward Cook, who, solid, hardworking, more successful than his brother though no less dull, had a small but solvent publishing business which, founded on calendars, desk-diaries, and gift-verse, had flourished and extended its scope to include textbooks and atlases. Having no children of his own, Edward offered Thomas a place in the firm with later promise of a partnership if all went well. It would have been folly to refuse. The work was not uninteresting; Thomas received a thorough grounding in the publisher's trade, had a reasonably good relationship with his uncle, and was rewarded by being allowed to widen the field of the firm to include more and more works on biology, sociology, and general science, some of which received a moderate critical acclaim. During this period Thomas made a great effort to keep up his reading in his own subject and pursue small lines of research, in such spare time as he had; and although he suffered always from a kind of numbness, the bruising result of a life warped from its chosen course, he continued to be buoyed up by two private, only half-acknowledged hopes: the first, that his father would die fairly soon, so that he could return to biology before it was too late; the second, that August Baird would fall out with his own publishers, Crusoe and Selkirk, and, by another unlikely miracle, that Edward Cook and Co. might be offered the chance to bring out his next book.

Neither of these things had happened. Samuel Cook was still alive now, aged eighty-one; frail, but quite capable, so far as Thomas could judge, of living for ten more years yet. Samuel was still alive; August Baird had not quarrelled with his publishers. Instead he had died, killed in a wasteful plane-crash last year at the age of seventy-three.

His death had been the most bitter shock of Thomas's life, and it had come at a particularly bad time for Thomas, at a moment when some dismaying physical symptoms, that he had been hoping were merely psychosomatic reactions to his deflected career, proved to be the first premonitory onset of the painful and crippling affliction which had caused Fanny Cook to stagger and fall to her death in front of a Bakerloo Line train on Christmas Eve, fourteen years earlier. Thomas was in a bad way, and knew it, and felt a punch-drunk terror of what fate might have in store for him next, because it is not irony so much as a natural consequence that anybody staggering about in blind pain tends to fall into the path of more punishment.

So here comes the punishment now, he thought, uncomforted by this dry gulp of the past: a somewhat severe reprisal, surely, for having cherished romantic, adolescent aspirations, for having persuaded Samuel and Fanny to move from a comfortable lower-middle-class neighbourhood, where they knew everybody, to a chilly upper-middle-class suburb where they knew no one, for having failed to love Samuel or be any comfort to him in his sad solitude. The punishment for that list of surely venial sins lay in being obliged to drive through this gateway just a year too late. Or twenty years, Thomas thought, slamming the door of his car and locking it. Then he remembered that he had promised to lock up that woman's house—blast her, what was her name? Hartshorn—and he walked impatiently back along the road. Stupid not to put on his overcoat, but he was soaked anyway, it could make little difference. What he really needed was a boiling hot bath, but he could scarcely ask Mrs. Baird for the use of her bathroom.

He locked the door of number thirty-four, and hurried back to number thirty-eight, his only wish now to escape as quickly as possible from the freezing, pouring, windy dark.

Closing the front door behind him, he heard Mrs. Baird call:

"Is that you, Mr. Cook? I'm in the kitchen—do come through."

Her voice came from beyond the staircase; he went in and round to the right-hand door from which she had first emerged, and through it.

The kitchen was a big, well-lit, cheerful room, lacking the library's awe-inspiring, melancholy grandeur. The walls and floor were white, so was the round table in the middle. A large buttercup-yellow stove at the far end gave out a most grateful heat, a tabby cat slept in a rush basket, and Mrs. Baird in her white monk's robe came eagerly to meet him. She had a charming appearance, he decided now, though her features were not individually remarkable. The appeal lay in the combination of round serious grey-blue eyes, velvet-smooth skin, pale, but covered with a peachlike down, and the alert way she carried her small head poised on that long neck. She had a lively, but innocent air: Maria, from *Twelfth Night*.

Thomas had been a little disconcerted when August Baird married again, after his first wife's death, and a girl considerably younger than himself, at that. It was an undignified thing to do, Thomas felt, when he read about it in the papers, a first sign of human weakness and folly in his paladin. Still, how could he judge? The second marriage had been successful, so far as he knew; August Baird had a gift for almost total avoidance of publicity; even when awarded the Nobel prize, he had managed to escape without newspaper profiles or revelations as to his private life and habits. The marriage had been happy, apparently. It had been blessed by a son. Nothing was known by Thomas of his wife, save that he had married her. And then, poor girl, she had been widowed, at little more than thirty, it would seem; in the course of nature her husband must have died a good many years before her, but August was an exceptionally healthy man, by all accounts, lively in body as in mind; she must have depended on at least fifteen years more of his company, enough to see the boy through his adolescence. How she must *miss* him, Thomas thought with an almost physical pang of sympathy; it would be like having some great tree, some massive landmark removed, as if the cedar on the lawn had crashed down in a freak hurricane. Now she is left with the sole responsibility of his child.

August Baird's child.

And I have to be the one to come and tell her about this bloody accident. Suppose it is more than the leg? Suppose there is internal injury—permanent crippling—disfigurement—brain damage?

"Oh, you look so wretched," she said in her soft, rather childish voice. "My goodness, it must have been terrifying for you, finding Gabriel like that. You must have wondered whether he was dead. It was just so lucky that you came along when you did."

"I—I only hope that he hadn't been there very long," Thomas said lamely.

"No, he couldn't have been. He'd only gone out a few minutes before, to hunt for his cat."

"That one there?" Thomas looked with distaste at the sleeping occupant of the basket. He was not fond of cats; never had been; a result of his mother's passion for birds.

"Yes. You see my neighbour Loraine Hartshorn had come in to make me a hot drink, because I've been having flu. She brought her horrible little corgi with her, and it chased the cat out through its cat-door, it always does. Gabriel was very upset about the cat, because of the bad weather—the cat's old, you see—so he went out to hunt for it. I suppose he must have gone across onto the common. And of course, while he was out, the wretched cat came back in again through its cat-door. I'd made Loraine take bloody little Brownie home by that time. The stupid thing is that I didn't even want her hot drink in the first place."

"Oh, lord, yes," said Thomas, "you've been having flu, haven't you." No wonder she was so pale. "Should you be up like this? Shouldn't you go back to bed?"

"Oh no, I'm much better now, quite all right, really. Loraine just loves to come in and fuss about—it gives her an excuse, you see. She always longed for a chance to be allowed into this house freely, whenever she wanted to come, and August found her terribly boring; he didn't often take dislikes to people, but when he did, he was quite firm; so she could never come in a lot, or stay long, while he was alive. Now we're never rid of her. She practically lives here. Naturally, as soon as she discovered I had the flu, she was round like a shot, and she's been in every half-hour since. She adores feeling that she's indispensable."

"She seemed a very powerful personality," Thomas said.

"You're not kidding! She used to edit one of those big glossy women's magazines—*Mansion House*—do you know it? It's a domestic magazine for professional women with lots of stuff about investments and equal pay. She's like a steamroller in the house—after half an hour or so, one's quite flattened out, limp as a clout."

Mrs. Baird beamed at Thomas confidingly; she had a funny slapdash way of expressing herself, he thought; direct, like a child. In spite of the painful circumstances, he began to feel slightly more at ease.

"Well I hope she telephones fairly soon with some good news," he said.

"I expect she will; the police seemed to think it mightn't be too bad."

She seemed so calm that his own hope increased.

"Now look," she said, "do have something to eat while you're waiting. *I* was just going to—a shock always makes me feel hungry." She laughed ruefully, conspiratorially.

"Well—that's very kind of you—"

On the round white table, Thomas saw, she had assembled the makings of a feast. Quite an elaborate feast —could she have been expecting somebody? Could she really have put all this together while he was moving the car? Or had Loraine Whatshername arranged it—was this her notion of a nighttime snack to accompany the hot drink? There was a pot of caviare, some smoked salmon, a small bowl of homemade potato salad, a plate of lichees, a pan of hot rolls, the kind that are sold frozen ready to bake, a dish of grapes, and a jug of cream.

"Loraine brought the grapes," she said, laughing at his surprise. "The rest is all out of the store cupboard. We need to keep up our spirits while we wait. I was ravenous, actually—I haven't eaten for days. I never can when I have flu. Do tuck in. And can you open this— I'm still rather weak—"

From the refrigerator, which was large enough to hold a muskox, she brought a bottle of champagne.

"Do you think you ought?" he asked doubtfully. "Have you been on antibiotics?"—knowing also that he had much better not drink champagne himself. Dr. Liddy had warned strongly against wine or any acid-containing food, particularly while he was taking the course of Najdolene, and champagne came high on the proscribed list.

"My dear, it's the best possible thing! I must certainly ought, and so ought you. They *give* you champagne for gastric flu, anyway," she said with a knowledgeable air. "It's exactly what I need; I've been dreadfully low-spirited. And I haven't had any fizz since—oh, for ages. Come on—open it, do. It'll be good for you."

He uncorked the bottle over the stainless-steel sink. The sight of the wine frothing out exhilarated them both; Mrs. Baird skipped across the room, moving with the freedom of a dancer in her sandals and monk's robe on the white polished floor, and opened a huge wall cupboard to display glittering shelves of glass, china, and crystal.

"Which glasses shall we use? I know, these—" pulling out a pair of large, tulip-shaped goblets, slightly twisted in form, and decorated by a spiral green thread inside the glass, twirling down from the lip to the base of the stem. "August's lab assistants gave him this set when he won his Nobel; he thanked them, of course, he was always sweet about that sort of thing, but he never liked them, he thought they were a bit vulgar. *I* like them though, I think they're pretty, don't you?"

She wiped them rather perfunctorily with a tea-towel and poured in champagne.

"Cheer-cheer!" she said gaily, passing Thomas his glass and taking a sizable gulp from hers.

Oh well, he thought; I'm going to pay dearly enough for this evening anyway; one glass of champagne won't make all that difference. And I can hardly refuse now. And it will certainly help me to feel a bit better at the present moment.

"Cheers," he said with more formality. "Here's to your boy. I hope he'll be all right."

"Poor little Gabriel, poor lambie—yes. I hope old Lorry rings up soon. Now, do please help yourself to whatever you fancy."

She pulled up a chair to the white table.

The champagne had made Thomas feel instantly both warmer and lighter, as if he were an unbaked loaf, set to rise in front of the fire.

"Do you know what I'd really like?" he said. "If you don't think it a piece of gross impertinence?"

"No, what?" she said, round-eyed.

"Could I take a bath?"

"Oh, you poor thing!" She was all apology and solicitude at once; she jumped up and felt his jacket. "Yes —you're sopping! Of course you should have a bath. Why don't you hang that coat on the stove rail. You'll find a bathroom two flights up—first door on the right at the top of the second lot of stairs. Towels in the cupboard. And if you want some dry things to put on, August's dressing-room is the next door along the landing on the right; there are still some of his old clothes and I should think they'd fit you fairly well; he might have been a little taller than you but he was about the same build."

"Oh—I couldn't—that would seem too—"

"Why? *He* wouldn't mind. He'd be the *last* person. Go on—hurry before you catch rheumatic fever or something. You can eat when you come back. We'll take some things up to the sitting-room and have a picnic, if you like. Here—here another glass of bubbly to take with you."

She poured herself one at the same time and almost pushed him from the room; she seemed delighted to have him go upstairs.

He climbed the two long flights slowly—realising now that he was shockingly tired, that his legs were not quite steady and his head was buzzing—found a big, old-fashioned bathroom with a blue-carpeted floor, brass taps, and a mahogany-enclosed bath and toilet seat. It seemed like paradise.

Turning the taps on full tilt he stripped in clumsy haste, struggling with buttons, wrenching off his tie, kicking off his shoes—and almost fell into the bath. The blazing water was wonderful. Submerged in it he felt immeasurably better—relaxed, calm, even optimistic. In his legs and hands the pain abated.

Perhaps, he thought, towelling himself, this is going to be a turning-point in my life. Perhaps after all I have not arrived at this house too late but *just in time*. If, as Whatshisname says, there is no such thing as coincidence, perhaps I have somehow constructed this whole episode from the very roots, in order to teach myself some profound lesson?

What a solipsistic outlook, what about her, what about the boy?

He had intended to get back into his own trousers and shirt, but there were so cold, so sodden, so unappealing and clammy that his now warm and expanded flesh rebelled; he could not bear to drag them on. Instead he went next door, into an austere, almost empty room with a dark-brown carpet, a web-and-steel chair, a divan in one corner covered by a plaid rug, and a small bedside table on which lay two books: Plato's *Symposium* and Donne's sermons.

Here Thomas felt a strong desire to fall on his knees. But suppose she were to come up?

Look, he thought, just *forgive me*. Forgive me. That's all I ask. A chance of redemption. A chance to start again. I'll have to manage the rest somehow—I'll have to do better from now on. I've been weak, poor-spirited, mean, inadequate in every way—I've made such a shambles of my life I can't bear to contemplate it; oh, I don't believe a mind like yours can even imagine how often spinelessness and inertia have led me into wrong choices, how hopelessly astray from my proper course I've wandered; and I've lost Jan—through what exact fault I don't know, but it must stem from the rest; but now I'll change, I'll be purposeful and uninvolved and strong. If only you'll understand how it all was.

Did he address god, or August Baird? He hardly knew. The room listened quietly, it made no comment. He opened a closet, found a pair of old, soft corduroys and a black shetland sweater with darns under the arms, put them on. Taking his own wet clothes and the empty glass, he returned downstairs, barefoot. The dry warm clothes felt encouragingly light and comfortable against his bare skin.

"Oh!" cried Mrs. Baird. "How nice you look. Much better. That's right, put your shoes there and drape all your wet things over the stove. Now, have some more fizz and some food."

She must, Thomas noticed, have managed to open another bottle by herself while he was upstairs, for the one she helped him from was only a quarter empty, whereas they had almost finished the first one by the time he went to take his bath.

Furthermore she had made substantial progress with the caviare, the salmon, the salad, and the hot rolls. Poor thing, she must have been hollow, what with the shock and the flu.

"I don't, truly, think that I want anything to eat, thank you," he said. "That bath was wonderful, just what I needed; it really saved my life. Has Miss Hartshorn telephoned yet?"

"No, not yet. How about some grapes, then? Turkish delight? Coffee? Tell you what, if you're sure you don't want anything to eat, let's just take these things upstairs —it's comfier up there. Gabriel had built me a smashing fire just before he went out, poor angel. That's right, you bring the fruit. There's a phone extension up there, so we'll hear just as well when old Lorry rings. Can you turn out the lights?"

With expert speed she had assembled a coffeepot, cream, sugar, cups, and glasses on a tray. She went briskly off up the stairs ahead of him to the first landing, kicking her skirts out of the way. Thomas paused a moment, looking at the tabby cat which, as if aware of his scrutiny, rolled lazily over in the basket on to its back, extended its front and back legs in a long stretch, and then curled up on the other side.

If it weren't for you, Cat, Thomas thought, Gabriel would be sound asleep in his own bed now and I—where would I be? At father's house—across there, beyond the motorway? Or at the printers? Or driving on into Kent? To the cliffs of Dover?

How the presence of the dead does surround us: watching, beseeching, unspeaking, but unmerciful. Our own consciences, dressed out as ghosts.

I hope to god that bloody woman telephones fairly soon. This house gives me the willies. It's like falling into a tidal river. I can't tell which way the current is going to turn.

He switched out the kitchen lights and went slowly upstairs, to find his hostess established in what seemed to be a kind of all-purpose room. It was large, had probably been the main sitting-room of the house, but was now apparently also used as a studio, for on a raised section of the floor at one end stood an easel, and a table covered with paints and drawing materials. There was also a double bed in an alcove: freshly made, with pillows plumped and covers turned back, it looked irresistibly inviting and made Thomas realise again how deadly tired he was. Even the floor would be acceptable to lie on, he thought: warm, dry, and flat—what more could one ask? Images fizzed gently in his mind; the snow, like bubbles, the motorway, bright beads shooting both ways, drops of accelerated awareness; the huge presence of the cedar outside, keeping guard in its mourning draperies (he could hear the wind crashing among its branches); all these things swung and dangled in the forefront of his consciousness like baubles on a windscreen.

This room was restfully dim after the gleaming whiteness of the kitchen; small picture lamps and a huge, piled, glowing wood fire gave the only light. At right angles to the hearth stood a wide comfortable sofa piled with cushions among which Mrs. Baird was curled up, with the coffee things on a low table by her, supplemented by a bottle of brandy.

"Come and join me," she said. "I bet you're bushed. Isn't this a gorgeous fire—Gabriel has a real gift with fires."

"How old is he?"

"Ten, poor lamb. He misses his father terribly."

"He must . . . I was a tremendous admirer of your husband. I always longed to meet him—I was so sorry when he died," Thomas said jerkily. "I really do believe he was one of the greatest minds of this century."

"Oh," she said in her high soft childish voice, "thank you! That's very nice. Are you a scientist too, then?"

"I was meant to be," he said, "but things didn't work out that way. In fact I'm a publisher—scientific books, mostly."

"That's interesting."

"I think I've read every line your husband ever wrote."

"*Have* you? He *is* marvellous, isn't he?" She spoke about him, Thomas thought, in a rather endearingly proprietorial, confiding way, as if he were a sort of Santa Claus, almost as if he had been her own father, not the boy's. Well, she must have regarded him in the light of a father, to a certain extent.

"Do sit down," she said again.

"I was just looking at this picture." He glanced uneasily round. "Did you paint it?"

"Heavens, no! It's by my brother. Do you like it?"

Like, Thomas thought, was not a word that anyone would use, a sentiment they would feel, about the large canvas over the hearth.

It was a landscape, dramatically painted in sharp clear slashes and masses, predominantly grey and black, dashed with white and yellow. It showed a winding valley which at first glance seemed calm and even beautiful. But, looking closer, Thomas could see that the grey curving strip at the bottom of the valley was a dual road, a motorway in fact, and along the length of it, half of them going one way, half the other, sped little people, desperately fleeing from something, their mouths open in a rictus of terror, their faces contorted, their eyes bulging, staring crazily at the sky. They were trampling and mangling each other in their haste to escape, stabbing and clubbing each other; some, in cars, were bloodily forcing their way through the pedestrians; the scene was painted in tiny, grotesque, but realistic detail. Yet no reason was shown for this panic; up above the greenish-grey sides of the valley sloped empty and smooth, a few trees on the hillside were sculpted in severe lines of dark paint, the grey sky, flatly spread, seemed to hold no menace.

Like it? No, Thomas did not like it. Looking at it he felt very uncomfortable.

"It's a parable?" he said. "That's supposed to be mankind?"

"Oh no, I don't think so? He just said it was a picture of the view from our roof, looking across to Wansea Village. That's the motorway, you know, the Wansea Bypass that they built a couple of years ago—his idea of it, anyway."

"He's a good painter, I can see that," said Thomas. "What's his name?"

"Farragut, Bo Farragut," she said. "He's my twin, actually. Not that we're very alike."

"Farragut? I've heard of him, of course."

Had he heard that Baird's second wife was Farragut's sister? Surely he would have remembered that. There were some rather peculiar stories about Farragut—shooting a crossbow arrow through the altarpiece of a contemporary he disliked, spitting at the Queen when being decorated, getting drunk and making libellous remarks at a Royal Water Colour Society dinner. He was an *enfant terrible*. It was quite difficult to relate this girl to him. In spite of being August Baird's widow she seemed to fit into a completely different genre—simple, cosy, domestic, commonplace.

"That's a picture of Bo there," she said, nodding towards a photograph on the top of a bookshelf behind the sofa, to the side of the hearth. Thomas walked round to study it more closely. Farragut was dark, like his sister, but otherwise there seemed no resemblance: her face was round and smooth; his, concave, skull-shaped, hollow-cheeked, prematurely wrinkled; the dark hair had receded a long way, leaving him half bald, completing the skull effect; her teeth were small, like a child's first teeth, but his, glimpsed between slightly parted lips, appeared to be long, stained, and broken; her expression was ingenuous and solemn, whereas deep diagonals from nose to mouth gave him a kind of lugubrious, derisive sneer; his mouth was slightly drawn down at the corners. The chin was long and pointed, leading into a scraggy neck; the eyes glanced melancholy, mocking, sidelong. As the painting had, so the photograph imbued Thomas with immediate, instinctive dislike; he felt a strong impulse to turn it with its face to the wall. He longed to know how August Baird had got on with his brother-in-law, but it would be impossible to ask such a question. Glancing about for pictures of August himself, he realised that there were none in the room; perhaps she kept them in some special place? Or perhaps August had not liked to be photographed?

"Gus and Bo absolutely adored each other," she said, uncannily as if she had overheard his thought. "They really hit it off. They loved arguing with each other; they'd carry on great rambling serial arguments that lasted for days and weeks. I used to lose the thread and get bored and go away. Now Gus is dead, Bo hardly ever comes here, though his studio isn't far off; he has a funny old place on the common, just outside Wanborough, part of some old stables; it's pitch-dark but he doesn't notice that, he doesn't really care where he works, so long as people can't come bothering him. . . . I think he minded Gus dying even more than I did."

Thomas felt a curious, complicated pang. Jealousy? Of a dead man's relationships?

"Now do come and have your coffee. Do you take it black or white?"

Coffee was another thing he had recently been avoiding, not only on doctors' recommendations, but because he had been sleeping so badly. However she had already poured two cups, so he said he would take his white, and looked about for a chair.

There was none. He was repelled by the soft, squashy appearance and the lowness of the sofa, but lacking any alternative, after considering and rejecting the notion of sitting on the floor, he perched, rather upright, at the far end. She passed him the cup of coffee with cream in it, and a glass of brandy which, also without asking, she had already poured for him. Quietly resolving not to drink this, he put it on the low table.

"It's so *sad* that you and August didn't meet," she said thoughtfully. "If you are such an admirer. I do wish I'd known. Did you say you lived near here?"

"No, my father does. I'm in London. I was on my way to visit him when—" His voice tailed off. Visit Samuel? If I repeat that lie once more, he thought, the falsity will begin to blossom out on my skin, like leprosy.

"It's dreadfully quiet and dull round here," she said. "Gus liked it to come back to because he was always rushing round the world, and because of the common. I'd move back into town if it weren't for Gabriel. The air's better for him here—he's delicate—and of course he can go to Wansea School next year."

"Yes, I see."

"He misses August all the time," she said. "Of course, in fact, Gus was away from home a lot, but he had tremendous theories about how you should bring up children, what a lot you should try to put into them; when he was here, he simply poured his attention into Gabriel, as if he were filling a jug—I just can't hope to replace that kind of companionship. August believed that you can *create* personality like—like building a cathedral—that's what he was hoping to achieve with Gabriel. So his death has really been a tragedy for the poor boy."

She spoke simply, unresentfully, keeping her greyish blue eyes fixed steadily on Thomas.

64

"But you must miss August in the same way," Thomas said.

The eyes suddenly brimmed with tears. She nodded, without speaking, and turned to stare at the fire. There was a long pause, then, making a visible effort, she swallowed, and put down the coffee-cup which she had been holding with rigidly clenched fingers. I'm a crass, clodhopping fool, Thomas thought. Shouldn't have said that. But if she has no close friends round here—as that woman implied—perhaps she longs to talk about August; bereavement can swell and swell if it's unslaked. I know poor father has a permanent, painful need to ease his grief about Fanny by discussing her, even after so many years; again and again he tries to drag the conversation round to her, her life, her habits, her illness, her death; and I, I always meanly frustrate him if it's possible, I ignore his gambits and quickly close his openings because I won't participate in her death with him, I won't share the pain that is a whole part of me with this silly shred of a man. I can't be that magnanimous. But this poor girl's pain, which is probably torturing her at this very minute, choking her like some appalling growth—her pain it is both my duty and my privilege to relieve. If it took the rest of my life, I'd still owe it to his memory— and my gratitude—to do what I could. She is the embodiment of grief, he thought—like a frozen water-fall a fountain of ice, a snow-covered weeping willow. Melted by warmth and wine, his thoughts flowed in elegiac forms; he saw her as a mourning dove, a stringless lyre, an unfilled urn; mute, speechless, there she sat with drooping head, classically robed in widow's white, restrained and uncomplaining, while the vulture tore at her heart's core.

Hesitant at first, but gradually gathering momentun and urgency, he began to talk about what August Baird had meant to him: the philosophy, the principles, his writings, his theories, his place in the twentieth century, the absolute importance of his life. She listened quietly, unmoving, with her hands clasped in her lap. Astonished at his own fluency, Thomas described the history of his feelings about Baird, his devotion to the books, his deductions from them about the man.

As he went on talking her head slowly came up, her round eyes fixed on him. Unaffectedly, she pulled a crumpled handkerchief from the white cave of her woollen sleeve.

"Why," she said, blowing her nose, "I believe you loved him just as much as we do." She stared at Thomas over the handkerchief like a solemn twelve-year-old. "You must have felt *dreadful* when he was killed—that you had lost a father, almost."

"I believe I did." He was greatly touched at this evidence of her ability to put her own grief on one side and enter into that of a stranger. "I do wish—if it doesn't upset you too much—you could tell me a little about him. Just the personal side of him. Anything at all."

"The personal side?" She seemed slightly at a loss. "You mean, what he ate for breakfast—that kind of thing?"

"Anything," he repeated. "The sort of jokes he liked, things he said, what kind of music he listened to, what he enjoyed doing most, what upset him—if he ever got upset."

She wrinkled the soft skin of her forehead, perplexed. "Nothing upset him, really. He never used to get cross. He liked simple things. Shredded wheat was his favourite food for breakfast."

She seemed to be one of those people without any talent for description. Baird had been too large for her comprehension, perhaps; it was like asking a child to describe a whole metropolis. What can the child say? There were hundreds of windows, hundreds of chimneys—hundreds of doors, hundreds of people—but still you have learned nothing about the city's essence.

"Did he talk to you much about his work? What sort of things did you do together?" What did you talk about, Thomas wanted to know; only remember, only tell me one or two things he said. Ashamed of his own egotistical greed, he said, "No, never mind. . . . Did he work at home, here, much of the time?"

"He had one rule, that he mustn't be disturbed if he was working in the library with the door shut," she said. "And yet he didn't mind if one had to go in. He was never in a bad temper."

How many hundreds of evenings he must have spent here, sitting in this very room, Thomas thought. Yet what remains of him in here? Not even an echo, not even a whisper.

"He liked lamb stew, that was his favourite," she said. "He didn't mind how often we had it—every night would have been all right with him. Luckily Gabriel likes it too, if there are dumplings."

She fell silent, looking up at Thomas apologetically, as if conscious of her own deficiency, but unable to remedy it.

"You see—it's having so much gone," she said, her lip quivering. "I don't know where to begin."

"I shouldn't have asked." Thomas had to withstand a sudden extraordinary impulse to touch her, stroke her soft untidy dark hair, take her hand, put an arm round the small white-cowled shoulders. It seemed to be purely physical preoccupation, unprompted by sympathy or liking—though he felt both; the kind of half-conscious motivation that causes one to reach out an absent hand for a cigarette or kick shut a half-open door.

"It's all right, I'm just silly." She swallowed again, looked down, and then up, smiling, her eyes swimming with more tears. "Goodness knows, I ought to able to talk about him by now, it's nearly a year. And you're very kind to do this, I know you are doing it for my sake. I tell you what—I'll take you down and show you my memory place."

She uncurled herself from among the cushions and stood up. He jumped up too with a sense of relief, in spite of his fatigue; jumped up too quickly, as it turned out: momentary dizziness made him sway, and a familiar slight warning ache had invaded his arms and shoulders. But he was delighted to get away from the sofa. It was too low; he felt trapped down there. And it was too soft. He had been afraid that he might go to sleep, or topple forward and weep, with his face in her white woollen lap. The heaped glowing fire, the dim light, the womblike silence and seclusion of the room, the house, and her gentle forlorn grief and sympathy had seemed like dangerous luxuries; they terrified him; he felt as if he were inhaling some irresistible but deadly perfume.

"Your memory place?" he said. "What is that?"

The phrase had stirred some curtain in his mind. Between Wansea Village and the common there had been, fifteen years ago, a big eighteenth-century manor, Fynche Place, bought and converted by the local council into an old people's home. It had a magnificent garden, rarely visited by the aged inmates of the home, who could not walk so far, but thrown open to the public as a park. Far removed from the main town shopping area, the park was never crowded, was often, in fact, completely deserted. After Thomas had learned that it was important, if his mother were to hold her ground against the assaults of her illness, that she should take plenty of exercise, he had tried to make a point of coming home from college every weekend and taking her for walks in Fynche Park. No persuasion was needed; she loved the garden, which had a miniature lake and a cascade, and small wood full of rhododendrons and azaleas. But it had become a daunting distance from home for her to struggle on her own, and Samuel was no walker. Hours, Thomas had spent with her, strolling round the lake arm-in-arm, or climbing the moderate slopes at a slow pace suited to her disability. Sometimes now, when he was desperate for sleep, a method Thomas used for lulling his mind was to rewalk the garden, in memory following its vanished paths, stopping to smell the flowers in their familiar places. Last night—the recollection suddenly came back to him now—he had been dreaming about his mother in the Fynche Place gardens. But the lake was filled in with grey sand, the place was bare and changed, men were stacking up the plants in pots and removing the trees in trucks. "They were all borrowed, those things, didn't you know?" said Fanny, leaning on her stick. "The real owners want them back now, they have to go. Oh, what a scene of chaos!" she had said, half laughing, half in despair. Thomas was immediately flooded with guilt because, though he had indeed vaguely been aware that the plants and flowers were all on loan, he had hoped that nobody would ask for them, that he would not be obliged to return them. Why must the owners reclaim them *now?* They had, after all, managed without them all this time. Why lend anything at all, if they were going to ask for it back? But the worst of the dream was that Thomas, left in charge of the plants, had dismally failed to take proper care of them; they were withered, drooping; he picked up a draggled frond of fern and passed it to one of the apron-wearing movers' men, who looked at it with disgust. "Is this *all?*" the man asked. "Aren't there any others? What have you done with all the rest? You should have brought them back long ago." In the bushes somewhere a child had been crying miserably, some child to whom Thomas, without in the least intending it, had been too harsh; he was accountable, he knew, for all these troubles, but felt abused; he had not asked for the loan of the plants in the first place, he had not wanted any of this responsibility. "Oh, what chaos!" his mother cried again, her face contorted with grief. "Well, they might at least have thanked us for looking after the plants," Thomas woke himself by exclaiming indignantly.

Now the whole flavour of the dream came back to him as he stood up, swaying with fatigue, and said, "What is your memory place?"

"I'll show you." Luckily she had not noticed his weakness. "Come along."

"Did you ever go to Fynche Place gardens?" he asked, as she led the way downstairs. She glanced back, faintly surprised, and said:

"Why, yes. Gus had been a friend of old Sir Percy for years, before the old boy went gaga and finally popped off; Gus used to bring back rare plants for the Fynche Place greenhouses from his travels. So after the Council took over, they gave Gus a special key to the garden; nice, wasn't it? He used to go for walks there before breakfast. He always got up at six."

"Oh, I wish I'd known! I used to go there so often."

"But you wouldn't have met him," she said matter-of-factly. "The public aren't allowed in before nine, and Gus always came home long before the gates were opened."

"He must have been sad when the garden had to go."

"Yes, he said destroying a garden to make a motorway was like cutting off somebody's hands to prevent them picking their nose," she remarked absently, opening one of the doors in the downstairs hall to reveal a short passage and a flight of brick steps leading down, presumably to a cellar region.

"Gabriel doesn't like what I've done down here. He's a funny boy, he absolutely shies away from any form of emotion," she said, switching on a light. She walked down the steps and opened another door at the foot. It led into a small vaulted room whose brick walls and roof had been painted a sultry pinkish grey. A modern Venetian-glass chandelier, also pink, hung from the vault; it seemed rather too big and slightly incongruous in the cell-like enclosed place, which had no windows. The floor was cov-

69

ered in grey carpet, wall to wall; there was a tiny table and a grey-velvet hassock, and the room was lined with flowers; pots of cyclamen and pink azaleas were ranked along both walls and across the end. On the table stood a vase of roses and a silver-framed photograph of Professor Baird. His expression was abstracted, but indulgent and speculative, as if he were being offered some rather unpromising object, whose value he doubted, and with whose use he was unfamiliar, though he was prepared to give it dutiful attention. The table held also, Thomas noticed with slight dismay, a large darkbrown urn, elaborately shaped, made, apparently, of Bakelite.

Did it contain the professor's ashes? Had he been reassembled and cremated and brought back from that Andean crag where his life had ended?

As soon as she entered the room, Mrs. Baird's demeanour totally changed. Hitherto she had been calm, controlled, demure, with a certain dignity. But now, quite deliberately it seemed, she abandoned this discipline, completely threw it aside. Taking no further notice of Thomas, she ran forward, dropped onto her knees on the hassock, and, with her head bowed over her arms on the table, burst into a violent fit of sobbing. It appeared that she had only to come into this place for the tears to be released, as if by an act of will.

"Oh! Oh! Oh!" she cried, rocking herself to and fro. "Oh, Gus, oh, Gus! Come back, come back!"

Thomas, totally unprepared for such a change, could not help feeling embarrassed for her and uncomfortable for himself. What ought he to do? Stand watching this display of grief? Kneel also? At length, stiffly, reluctantly —kneeling was beginning to be difficult for him—he lowered himself onto the grey carpet, which was quite thick, fortunately, and stayed for a while in a respectful and devout posture, with his head slightly bent. He felt a fool, and also a hypocrite; as if he were dissembling a grief which ought, in any case, to have been allowed some quite different form of expression.

There could be no doubt as to the reality of *her* grief; it was bursting from her with the force of a geyser, she seemed rocked by a great natural power that, once unleashed, was quite beyond her ability to control. Despite his discomfort, Thomas felt that this must be right for her, he approved in theory such an abandonment of mourning. It was evidently a release for her, and could only do her good.

Yet somehow it seemed to bear no relation to the dead man.

Looking around, rather cautiously, after five minutes or so (not that Mrs. Baird would be likely to notice) Thomas was unnerved to meet the gaze of another portrait of August Baird, done in oils, this one, hanging on the right-hand side. Mrs. Baird had certainly done a thorough job of concentrating her memories all in one spot.

Both portraits were painted in a highly finished, realistic style, almost photgraphic, and both, he guessed, were the work of Bo Farragut; though the technique differed from that of the landscape upstairs, the painter had, possibly by accident, contrived in each case to give the sitter a touch of his own sardonically melancholy expression. Feeling pinned under the scrutiny of the two gloomily amused, regretfully ironic sages, Thomas rose painfully to his feet. The portraits reminded him irresistibly of two headmasters comparing wry notes over an unpromising batch of examination candidates. He tiptoed backwards out of the little room to the foot of the brick stairs. He was greatly tempted to return to the warm kitchen—suppose, for instance, that the telephone rang while they were down here?—but decided this would be discourteous, not to say unfeeling. He therefore sat down on the steps; really his legs would not hold him up any longer.

After another ten minutes, Thomas began to think that Mrs. Baird ought to pull herself together. The little vault was not particularly warm; the brick steps were decidedly chilly. He himself, with no underclothes on, was beginning to shiver. And she, though wearing the warm wool robe, was after all convalescing from flu; too much abandonment to such a degree of mourning would surely send her temperature up again. Moreover the place was beginning to give him a bad case of claustrophobia.

He stood up, once more, with difficulty, on his stiff leg—hesitated—then walked forward and laid a gentle hand on her shoulder.

"Mrs. Baird. Mrs. Baird! I do not really think it's time you came back upstairs into a warmer room. You shouldn't give way like this for too long at a time. It can't be good for you."

There was quite a long pause before she seemed to hear or take in the sense of what he had said. At last,

71

but not until after the third or fourth repetition, she lifted her face from her hands and turned it not towards him but forward and up, listening as if to a voice that came from somewhere in the vicinity of the chandelier. Then, very slowly, leaning heavily on the hand he placed under her elbow, she rose to her feet. She was a completely different person; she had lost her calm buoyancy and was limp, abstracted, drowned in grief, like a plant battered to the ground by rain, a tree that has been overwhelmed by a flood. Weakly, as if hardly able to move, she moved a few faltering steps towards the doorway, then stumbled over the edge of her long white robe and swayed sideways. Thomas caught hold of her elbow again and, as she leaned against him, put an arm around her.

He had become thoroughly chilled by now, but she, he found with some surprise, had remained perfectly warm, perhaps due to the violence of her sobbing. As she rested against him, still vibrating in the aftermath of her explosion of grief, he could not help being rather glad of the sheer animal comfort of her body pressed against his. It felt like acknowledgment, it felt like recognition.

She lifted her face; the eyes were closed again, the cheeks were shiny with tears, which were still sliding down; the face looked piteously like a death mask.

"You must try to stop crying now," he said gently. "You must try to be calm."

The eyes opened. Surprisingly close to his, they seemed glazed, unseeing, wild; their bluish grey was dark as slate. Like a newborn organism seeking nourishment, like a half-drowned creature demanding the kiss of life, she moved her mouth up to his.

He meant to kiss her gently—that was his intention, a gentle brotherly kiss—but she clung against him with totally unexpected violence; their lips, having once joined, seemed glued together, her teeth rattled on his, her droping tongue twined against his, which met it with a shock of recognition. Thomas, confused, almost incredulous, was swamped by a tidal wave of pure lust which, emanating from the two ends of his body, met in the middle with an erotic force that almost lifted him from the floor. His scalp prickled, his eyes burned, his mouth, which hers was still greedily exploring, ran salt and sweet at the same time. She slid up her hands and clasped them tight round the back of his neck. This movement upset their precarious balance and they toppled over together onto the soft grey carpet. Even the fall did not undo their joined mouths. Her hands, dislodged from his neck, clutched even more tightly round his back, under the loose black shetland sweater. She was shuddering now, and whispering; her body arched and shook against his.

"Darling—oh please, oh please! I must—I want you terribly—please, please—help me, please help me!"

Her mouth came back into his; he could not protest, even if he had intended to.

With one hand, disengaged from under the sweater, she had managed to unzip his trousers—August's trousers. She was gasping and crying:

"Oh quick, oh quick—do it, do it—"

Wholly carried by the power of her emotion, he was outside himself, a long way beyond awareness or misgiving. With a kind of anguish that was equally triumph, he rolled over and flung himself onto her, into her, under the mournful, ironic eyes of the two portraits; as he came in a series of shuddering gasps he heard her call out ecstatically, not with the high, soft voice of her conversation, but in a deep, hoarse cry that seemed drawn from her very spine:

"August! *August!*"

It was hardly the act of love. They were like two frantic, magnetised particles, hurled together by currents powerful enough to batter them to pieces. Yet, as when some great force goes whistling by, leaving an irreversible change behind it, and is gone almost before its imminence and its danger have been perceived, love seemed to have been in the room with them.

Three

Bo and Bella 1974

"Have you ever paused to wonder what August would think about all this?"

"August's *dead*," she said peevishly. "What's the point of bringing him up now?"

"How practical you always are, dear. Aquaplane over

73

the bumps. Make do with the circumstances you happen to be in. That's the way, isn't it? But didn't you love August at all?" he asked with real curiosity. "Doesn't his memory weigh with you; weigh *on* you ever?"

"Of course I loved him," she said in a goaded manner. "You ought to know. Didn't you love him, for that matter—how about his memory weighing on *you?* But he's dead. Like I said. And this was your scheme, not mine. What are you getting at? I don't understand you one little bit. First you plan things, and then you—and then you *poke about*—what's the big idea?" She broke off a thread with a resentful snap.

"Just interested, my love."

"In what?" she said sulkily.

"In you. As always."

There was a short pause. Then Bella, who seldom bore ill-feeling against her brother—or, consciously, against anybody at all for the matter of that—beyond the moment when something else distracted her—remarked:

"Boney, how can you possibly see to paint when it's nearly dark?"

She was sitting curled up in a basket-chair, shortening a skirt she had just bought by doubling over the hem and re-hemming along the fold. A small orange-shaded reading-lamp on a stool close beside her gave her just enough light for the task. The only garments she had on were black brushed-nylon briefs, frayed and draggled with age, a grubby slip that she had worn ever since leaving England, and a pair of soft, worn, green-velvet traveling slippers.

Bo, looking across the oblong room, could see her partly in outline from where he stood on the white piano. Orange light aureoled her shoulders and hair, spreading mistily like paint on wet paper. The tips of her knees shone, the skin on her body was clear, pale, and waxy like the white of a hard-boiled egg. She brought the skirt up to her face and bit off another thread; wound a new length round her finger and knotted it; held the needle up against the orange light and approached the thread to the needle's eye. She was humming to herself tunelessly. Bella never sang out loud when she was with anyone except her brother, because he had told her that she had no more voice than a grasshopper, and although she did not want to believe him, neither did she wish to take the risk of other people discovering that he had spoken the truth.

"What difference does it make whether I can see or not? That isn't the point."

He painted on.

"Where did you meet James?" she inquired presently, breaking off another thread.

"Morton Street pier. Nice and peaceful; nobody around."

"Where is he now?"

"Car was on a parking meter. He went to shift it."

"He probably won't get in touch again for six months," Bella said with spite. "I suppose it's his Russian blood coming out. I seem to remember last time he left his car on a meter and went to shift it, we heard of him next in Spain. And the time before it was the Hindu Kush, wasn't it?"

Bo made no answer. Agile and angular as a spider-monkey, he doubled his thin length and put one foot on the floor, dipped his brush into one of a row of jam-pots fille with paint, and then, making no apparent effort, swivelled round and hoisted himself back into a standing position on the grand piano. His feet, in dirty white sneakers, appeared to possess suction power comparable to those of flies. With his recharged brush he continued to paint, whistling between his teeth. A scatter of newspapers lay along by the wall to catch drips, but it was evident from the state of the Japanese matting and the piano that he did not greatly care where the splashes went.

"Thomas may be coming round," Bella said presently.

"Oh, Christ."

"Boney, when he comes, you will be sensible, won't you?" There was the faintest trace of anxiety in her dove-like tone.

"Oh sure, I'll be as sweet as a hummingbird's uvula," he snarled, scooping up a brushful of red paint and describing a rapid, intricate curve across the design he was executing on the wall.

"After all, if you start to act nasty, it could upset the whole applecart."

"Bull. You're overdramatising again. How you do love a little excitement. If Thomas falls apart, they'll just send over another trustee."

"That might take too long. Just be friendly to him. You *know* Thomas is funny and touchy; one can't tell what he'll do."

"You should tell me that?"

"It's the stuff he's taking, the Najdolene; he's on an intensive course again. I can tell from the look of the skin round his eyes. It makes him moody and forgetful. He's got great chunks missing from his memory. *That* makes him uneasy too," she said knowledgeably.

"Can't think why. Most people would be only too pleased to forget half the things they'd done."

"Boney, I honestly don't believe he remembers *any*thing about the *Hetaira*. It's just clean dropped out of his mind. He was on a high dosage just then too."

"And the show at the Waterlow? He's forgotten that too, I daresay?" Bo said sourly.

"Yes he has, I'm certain, Boney! Things that happen to him at those times are what he forgets. So you just keep quiet and calm; act as if nothing had ever happened."

"*All* right, all right. Don't fuss, ducks. . . . Anyway, I forgave him and put it all out of my mind years ago. Two years ago," Bo said smoothly. "Water under the bridge. It's just the taste of scotch I miss; in all other respects I'm as happy as a sandboy. What *is* a sandboy? I frequently ask myself. As hoppy as a sandbee. As hippy as a—"

"Shut up! Anyway it was *your* idea to get Thomas over here."

"Sure, sure. Very economical. Him being a director of Crusoe and a trustee of the August Baird Fund. Don't you worry your pretty head."

Dropping the completed skirt on the floor, Bella jumped up quickly, padded over to the door, and switched on an overhead light, revealing the huge, tangled fresco on which her brother was engaged. It was a Last Judgment, with no horror omitted.

The high, oblong room they were using was plainly and sparsely furnished; everything in it, apart from the white grand piano, being Japanese, made from wicker and bamboo and paper. The fresco seemed out of place, too lurid, too threatening. It overbalanced the flimsy furnishings.

"I wonder if Angie will *like* what you're doing to her livingroom?" Bella said pensively, taking up an English women's magazine from an untidy heap on the floor and flipping over the pages, stifling a yawn.

"To tell you the truth I don't care a fig whether she likes it or has it all painted out in flame-coloured emulsion the very next day. Her critical opinions are of absolutely minimal interest to me."

76

He twitched up the pot of white paint by the string round its neck, stood it on the piano, and began touching in some elaborate cloud effects right up at the top of the wall, whistling the same two bars of "Santa Lucia" over and over.

Bella became immersed in her reading. Easy silence filled the room; the silence of two people who have no need to keep up pretences with one another.

Presently Bella said, "Would you like to hear our horoscope?"

"Not particularly. Even less as it's probably last year's. Our Angie is a champion hoarder of old reading-matter. I found a *Maids', Wives' and Widows' Penny Magazine* for 1853 in the loo—"

"This issue is 1971," she said, turning to the front to check. "I always think that's more comfortable; then you don't have to worry, for it's all over and done with, whatever it was."

"I bet you'd live your life backwards if you could. Like you always read the last chapter of a book first, to make sure nothing nasty happens to the heroine."

"Of course! And then if something nasty does happen, I know not to read the book at all. It saves a lot of trouble. . . . Well our horoscope says, 'You may have a little difficulty with a colleague this month, but patience and tact should finally put over your point of view and bring matters out the way you want. An old love may suddenly come back into your life with unexpected results. Satisfactory outcome of money problems. Slight trouble with a young relative.' Really, Boney, that's practically on the bull's-eye. It's uncanny!"

"Oh, for heaven's sake. Grow up. They always phrase them so they fit anybody. Quite apart from the fact that piece of pulp is three years old. . . . And who is your old love? Thomas?"

She giggled. "Don't forget it's your horoscope too. I suppose *your* old love is James?"

Bo threw her a quick unfriendly look, but she did not see it.

"Here's a letter that says, 'Ought I to let my husband make love to me wearing his policeman's uniform? Somehow I feel that it seems disrespectful to the Queen.' "

Bo gave a snort of laughter.

"What do they advise?"

"Renting different costumes from a theatrical agency. They're quite broad-minded."

"There are plenty more interesting things he could dress up as."

"How funny, here's a kind of obituary piece about old Lorry. Beloved and respected colleague in journalism, for many years editor of the famous business woman's magazine *Mansion House*. Loraine Hartshorn combined editorial acumen with a warm heart and outgoing personality, trum, trum, trum—'"

"Poor old cow." He stared with half-closed eyes at the edge of his bank of clouds, then rapidly scalloped them with black. "She was a bit of a pain, Christ knows, but I quite miss her squelching in on wet afternoons with a hunk of some uneatable delicacy, and staying to smoke those crappy cigarettes of hers."

"I never could see what you saw in her. She gave me the sick," said Bella, yawning again. She dropped the magazine and lay back in her basket-chair.

"She did all your housekeeping for the sheer love of it. For years."

"She adored it; gave her a chance to name-drop. She could boast all up and down the town about Gus's sacred memory. Anyway it was hell having her creaking around the house, day in, day out."

"So why didn't you tell her to quit?" She did not reply. "I'll tell you; because it gratified your sense of vanity to have her there. You were her vicarious life; she was your built-in exclaimer."

"Saved me a lot of work," Bella said.

Bo levered himself to the floor and lit a cigarette. Then he squatted down to do some hell-scenes at knee-level. He painted at great speed, his thin Pierrot's mouth pursed together, with the cigarette dangling from one corner, and the long, Egyptian eyelids drooped over his melancholy eyes to keep out the smoke.

"Want a scotch-and-ginger ale?" said Bella presently.

"Without the ginger. Scotch-and-ginger is a skivvy's drink."

"Then I'm a skivvy."

"You're a beloved and respected colleague, original creator of many well-known textile, wallpaper, and houseware designs—"

"Flattery will get you nowhere, my boy," she said, but

she looked gratified as she went off to the kitchen, missing the narrow-eyed glance Bo sent after her.

The apartment consisted of four rooms linked by doors, the end rooms L-shaped and each opening onto either end of a narrow hallway. The kitchen, which looked out onto Fourteenth Street, was decidedly grubby and archaic in its fittings; it had a diminutive bathroom partitioned off in one corner. The room in which Bo was painting his mural was at the opposite end of the apartment and looked down over a row of shabby backyards and a car-park. A battered but elegant ailanthus tree dangled sooty leaves in the yard below their window; Bo had incorporated its shape into his picture, setting the judgment throne at the base of the tree.

On the throne sat a crocodile, cross-legged.

"Why—that's *ma*," said Bella, padding back with the drinks, and leaning easily against her brother's shoulder while she studied what he had done. "Bo! Poor Sadie! I don't think you ought to have done that with her, Boney."

She sounded really shocked. The figure that had caught her eye was that of a little woman, her face contorted with shrieking, who was being carried off to hell upside down, with her clothes dishevelled and torn, by a devil-sized cockroach with vaguely human features.

"Don't be sloppy-minded. What possible difference could it make to ma?"

"I'm sure it would upset her *very much*. She wouldn't like to think you regarded her in that way," Bella said primly.

"Well, as she won't ever see it, what you think she might think about what I think about her is irrelevant."

With two tiny dots of white he gave the cockroach protruding fangs.

"Anyway for all we know to the contrary, she's dead by now, and already installed in Beelzebub's lap."

He began to sing, in a thin, nasal falsetto:

Oh, Sadie,
You was never a lady,
But definitely shady
Always in the sack with some chap
Giving him a dose of clap;
Heydee, misery me. lackaday-dee

Now you're clean off the map
A-sitting in Beelzebub's lap.

He paused, squinted at what he had done, and stuck his brush in the opposite corner of his mouth from the cigarette, while he scraped off a fleck of paint with an extremely long, dirty fingernail. "Gilly and Sully would be proud of me. I could go on, but the only rhymes left are lewd and would bring a blush to your shell-like ear." He removed the brush and, still keeping the cigarette in his mouth, planted a sideways kiss on her neck.

"Ma was so sure she had a heart of gold."

"Whereas under all that ebullience and larkiness there was a mean and narrow streak."

"Streak? It was as wide as the main runway at Heathrow. She loathed anything she couldn't understand. Wouldn't have it."

"Like poor pa's classical music."

" 'I know!' I can remember her yelling at him. 'You think the place for me is the street! You've made that perfectly plain, plenty of times. Telling the kids their mother's no better than a tart. Well I think the place for your classical tosh is the street too, and that's where it's going.' "

"Her very words. And picked up his poor little radio, that he'd had ever since he was in the Gunners, and hove it out the window into Addison Gardens. A final hosanna came floating up and then there was a crash from somebody's windscreen."

They were both laughing. Bo had settled beside her on the newspapers, and was making one of them a cocked hat.

"It's funny, isn't it," said Bella, "how much better we remember those times when we're together. When I'm not with you I don't think about our childhood at all."

"How sad for you, ducky. When we know you're just longing to ramble down memory lane."

"No, but you know what I mean."

"Our memories are interchangeable," he said. "Like our dreams. We can get inside each others' minds."

"It's a spooky thought, Boney."

"True, though." He gripped her nose with his fingers and thumb and stared into her eyes. The whites of his

80

own were very yellow. *"Everything* that's in there I can see—it's like a well from which one knows one can endlessly dip."

The four slate-blue eyes exchanged their messages.

"Careful—you're hurting." She freed her nose from his grip and rubbed it. "Ma did have some good points though; at least she must have, surely. At least we didn't grow up with puritanical hang-ups. We've that to be thankful for."

"Oh sure," he said *"And* she gave us pennies to go and get an ice-cream cone when her boy-friends arrived and she wanted us out of the way. Probably accounts for your ice-cream mania now. And why I can't stand the stuff."

"Sometimes she was quite kind."

"Once a month or so; when nothing else was on hand. I can't recall her ever exactly overwhelming us with maternal devotion and solicitude."

"I remember her giving me a piece of advice once."

"What was it?" he asked with interest.

"Always take your rings off before you make pastry or do your hair."

"A really useful basic maxim. I hope you followed it."

"I think that was all the advice she ever did give me."

"She never told you about the facts of life?"

"Not she. I picked them up at school. Well, you know. And of course there was Uncle Hugh."

"Of course there was. Old existential Uncle Hugh. What a treat it was to come home from boarding-school and find *him* installed."

"I suppose I'd sort of got used to him by the time you came home."

"Yes, Uncle Hugh certainly taught us all a thing or two. Like those bath-times."

"Thursday evenings. Those larky bath-times. Yes. I didn't dig it much at first but in the end I got accustomed."

"I daresay people in the Inquisition did too. It's all a matter of adaptation. He thought it all such fun, didn't he; starting off by getting undressed and coming in the bath with us."

"Nursery high jinks. It's funny to look back on," said Bella.

"Hilarious."

"No, but why didn't we find it odder? Surely I must have thought it rather peculiar, in the beginning?"

"You have such a placid, accepting nature, my angel. And I daresay kids do mainly just accept adults' eccentricities. After all, Uncle Hugh was such a jolly joking kind of chap," Bo drawled in a high, fatigued voice, and added, "Where the hell was ma at those times, anyway?"

"Out, having her hair done. She always had her hair done on Thursday evenings, after hours, at her pal Yvonne's salon in the Earl's Court Road."

"Wonder what she would have thought of those bathroom gambols?"

"Oh, who knows? Maybe she'd have thought nothing at all. But actually I'm certain she never knew anything. Old Hugh always took care to have the floor dried and us bundled off to bed long before she got home."

"Of course he did."

"Getting into bed ought to have been a relief, but it wasn't. I can remember the exact feeling—lying curled up in a knot, all sore and trembling, in the dark; I always used to have horrible dreams on those nights, and it took ages to get off to sleep, too."

"Yes," Bo agreed tonelessly, and added, "I wonder what ever happened to Uncle Hugh?"

"Oh, he drifted out of the picture when we were eleven or twelve; you were back at some school or other I expect. Hugh's business failed, whatever it was—I think perhaps he was a book-maker?—and they began to have rows, and she kicked him out. I remember he came back once—he looked terrible, with his nose all purple and his cheeks somehow fallen in, as if he had very badly fitting dentures on—"

"Christ yes, I'd forgotten the dentures. He always used to take them out, didn't he, and put them on the little glass shelf, as soon as he'd locked the bathroom door, and he put the key up there too, out of reach. And then he'd say, 'Now for our little thpot of Thurthday thatithfaction—' "

"Thlap-and-tickle—"

"What did Sadie do when he reappeared?" Bo inquired.

"Oh well, the next one, Uncle Mischa, was installed by then—"

"Never could stand *him*. He used all that hair cream and wouldn't let me do jigsaws on the living-room floor and made such a thing of being dashing and Russian—"

"Like your dear friend James. Sadie thought he was the bee's knees. I remember her once telling her friend Stephanie that he was so *distinguished*."

"He really hated us, didn't he. Whenever we appeared he just used to say, 'Go away'; didn't make the slightest pretence about it. I suppose that was honest, at least. We ate all our meals in the kitchen."

"Anyway, Sadie was highly embarrassed to find old Hugh on the doorstep asking for a loan or a meal or a bed for the night when Mischa was lolling on the sofa shouting out to know why the borscht wasn't ready. So she said, 'Go away, go away, I can't possibly talk to you now,' all flustered, and he turned to me—I'd answered the door in the first place, and was hanging about to see what would happen—and said, 'Bella will invite me in, I'm sure. Little Bella hasn't forgotten her Uncle Hugh,' in a sort of shaky, joking way, and I just stared at my feet, and after a minute or two he turned round and went away."

"I daresay he's dead long ago," Bo said after a pause.

"I expect so."

"It would really be a good thing if the past could be reopened from time to time," Bo muttered, more to himself than to Bella. He stood up, stiffly, and walked into the kitchen, returned carrying the whiskey bottle and a plastic ice-bucket, and poured himself another drink. Glass in hand, he stood studying his mural. "The point is that in order to keep running smoothly, we definitely require to have a new and more favourable aspect of ourselves disclosed every now and then. We use ourselves like machines, we ought to be able to be serviced in the same way. Wipe the mileage off the speedometer."

"I don't know what you're talking about, Boney!"

He sighed again, soundlessly, and began applying dabs of paint here and there to his picture in what seemed a random manner. After a while he remarked:

"Uncle Hugh was the first person I met who convinced me that human nature is evil right through. There was absolutely nothing to be said in his favour."

"Oh I don't know; I expect he was rather pathetic really."

"You can't sincerely mean that. You're only saying it to establish yourself in a sympathic light, in your own opinion presumably, because you know you can't alter mine. Hugh was no more pathetic than a tick or a leech or a rat. They simply take what they need and so did he. After living with Uncle Hugh it was not possible to believe that a truly disinterested person could exist."

He was suddenly assailed by a flash of memory: standing with his hands tied to the chrome towel rail, waiting for Uncle Hugh to pull the plug; he pushed it aside. But the voice lingered: *"Now, who'th for a little chathithment? Who firtht?"*

"Oh, come on!" protested Bella in her soft, dulcet coo. "You mustn't be so naughty, Boney. That's a dreadful thing to say about anybody."

"And *you* mustn't be a sanctimonious prig, my angel. Name me one disinterested person."

"Well, what about Gus? God knows, you're always going on about him."

"Yes," he conceded after a pause. "Yes, there is Gus. I suppose you could say that about him."

He fell silent, remembering his first encounter with Gus.

The Boeing was on its flight back from Sydney. He had been in New Zealand for six months painting volcanoes and thermal landscapes. After changing planes at Sydney he had glanced round the embarkation point with gloom and natural pessimism, wondering who was going to be his flight companion for the next thirty-six hours. Not much chance of getting three seats to himself at this season. Luckily, what fate presented when they were allowed onto the plane didn't look too bad: a medium-height, thin man, considerably older than himself, with a gentle, long-nosed, rather pointed face and a shock of white hair like an egret's plume. Thank god for that. Not some executive Australian built out of solid beef, or some terrible woman who would want to talk the whole way, and bore him rigid with her life history, and go hysterical over the Australian desert, or the Red Sea.

This man, in fact, showed no disposition to talk whatsoever; he had immersed himself instantly in absorbed study of a thick, typed, loose-leaf file which he had pulled from his briefcase even before they took off; and it was Bo, who, later on, after three hours' continuous flight over desert, had broken the silence by remarking:

"Quite impressive, wouldn't you say?"

The desert was, in the main, a rich dark ochre, wrinkled and creased, baked and crannied and gullied, serrated and creviced and seamed and ridged and cracked, with shadows of indigo and violet; the old, tired, dry skin of the world that has been alternately grilled and frozen for millions and millions of years. On and on the plane crept, trailing its tiny shadow behind, with brutal sun burning down on its roof, the heat on the metal, even at that altitude and with air-conditioning, distinctly to be felt. But now, suddenly, they glided into a great purple-black bank of cloud; the desert below darkened from rust to brown to bitter chocolate and then disappeared in gulps; a zigzag of lightning paralleled the jagged silhouette of the mountainy horizon and the plane leapt and staggered across a series of air pockets.

"One of nature's more extravagant manifestations," Bo's neighbour agreed. "There would be a certain satisfaction in crashing here—at all events it would be better than falling into a field of Dutch cabbages, or someone's swimming-pool in a Los Angeles suburb."

"And absolutely no chance of rescue."

"I understand from the stewardess that there is only minimal danger; they often do get electrical storms on this leg of the journey."

They fell into talk and exchanged names: Baird, Farragut. They discussed their respective occupations. They played chess, on a pocket set that Bo always carried with him. At one point on the trip, some hours later, as the plane droned on and on, through seemingly interminable hours of darkness, a respectful air-hostess had arrived with the captain's compliments and the news, which he had just heard over the radio, that Professor Baird had been awarded the Nobel prize. A bottle of champagne and congratulations had accompanied the message. Baird had seemed not so much pleased as irritated and embarrassed.

"Had you known already?" Bo asked.

"Oh yes, somebody did mention it. It had slipped my mind. I do hope there won't be a tedious fuss at Heathrow."

"Aren't there advantages to compensate for the fuss? Quite a substantial cash prize, for instance?"

"I get all the cash I can use in my research from a couple of governments already. Maybe I'll give the money back. I can't really think what to do with it."

"Marry my sister," Bo suggested. "She could use a bit of security."

They had both laughed. Bo ordered another bottle of champagne. The plane crept on, among stars big as cactus flowers in this desert of endless night; night in Darwin, night in Singapore, night in Delhi, night on the Indian Ocean, at Bahrain, with oil flares to the west like smoky reflections of the stars, night over the Red Sea.

Only when they reached the Mediterranean did a sunrise which seemed as if it must be a compound and retroactive dawn for the past three days gradually enkindle the mountains on their righthand side. Now they turned west and Europe seemed rushing at them with feverish speed: Rome, the Apennines, Corsica, the Alps. Bo felt depressed: he had left nothing but the debts behind, several unsatisfactory relationships, a couple of pending court actions, a number of angry demands from the Inland Revenue, and a hostile landlord who had been threatening to impound all his possessions. New Zealand had been peaceful and green and Arcadian, the landscape had stimulated him to do a great deal of work. True, the people had been uninteresting and the atmosphere repressive; in many ways he was not sorry to leave, and the paintings he was carrying back with him might solve some of his practical problems, but there would be new complications.

If only people would leave him alone to get on with his own life.

Complications, he thought. Foremost among these was Bella. It was time, time long overdue, to adopt some firm line about Bella. She took up too much room.

James. I'm off to Spain. Picked up his camera and keys, the way he did when about to move his car down the road to a new spot. But this time it was bloody Spain.

"Well, he'll come back, won't he?" said Bella. "What's so final about Spain? Why should he be jealous if you see your own sister? Specially when she's not well?"

Bella had been frighteningly thin at that time, all her velvety kittenish charm quite gone; her skin was shiny and yellowish and unhealthy-looking, the slate-coloured eyes stared like a starved cat's in huge crumpled sockets; her clothes hung on her with no more shape than washing on a line. Her lips were peeling and dry, her ankles, never Bella's best point, were hollow and bony, looked like those of some old lady tottering from her tiny cottage to the off-licence on the corner for two ounces of tea and a small bottle of Gordon's. What taste Bella had (little at the best of times he must admit) completely deserted her when she was feeling low. She resembled a betrayed slut. Bo, although not fastidious himself, could hardly bear the sight of her; she was a mote, a beam in his eye. "Look, here's fifty pounds, for Christ's sake go and stay at one of those health farms for a week, *do* something with yourself, fly to Ibiza and lie in the sun."

"How can I go to Ibiza on fifty pounds?" she said tearfully.

"Well it's all I have. Do the best you can with it, buy oranges and cod-liver oil."

Off in New Zealand, out of reach, he had felt bad about her, and sent her postcards of Mount Ruapehu and Lake Taupo; he had thought about her, painfully, as the warm rain spattered down on the warm strange green leaves, as he jolted his rented Volkswagen over dirt roads in beautiful little remote pastoral valleys set about with acacias and elegant gum trees. But he tried hard to forget her. She did not write, even to his poste restante address; he had no letter from her during the whole six months he was in New Zealand.

The doorbell rang, bringing him back from the other side of the world.

"That must be Thomas," said Bella, hauling the skirt over her head. It was a silvery pink corduroy. "Press the buzzer, will you, Boney." She wriggled into a thin blue-grey blouse with a high Victorian collar, and was all at once a different person, older, more responsible, more dignified.

"I'll just go and do my hair and put on some shoes. Will you let him in when he gets up here?"

She disappeared into the middle room, closing the door behind her.

"Wash your face!" Bo shouted through the closed door. "You've got paint on the end of your nose."

Four

Men were busy with poles and planks, erecting a criss-cross of scaffolding round a large old brown-brick office building in the Bowery, elaborately parcelling it up in a network of metal tubes, preparatory to knocking it all down. One or two passers-by shook their heads in disapproval of this destruction, for the building was handsome in a florid nineteenth-century fashion, with ornamental Ionic columns all the way up its façade and bas-reliefs across the elaborate tympanum on top. The neighbourhood in which the building stood was very run-down, however; the lot on one side, vacant already, was covered with a remarkable variety of rubbish, not small articles only, but objects which it must have taken considerable strength or ingenuity to transport there: several massive remnants of machinery, a derelict motor launch, a bundle of full-sized withered palm trees, and twenty defunct gas cookers.

The men at work on the scaffolding were combining the task with calling reminders through the windows to the illegal occupants of the building that the whole place was coming down on Monday and they had better find themselves other quarters before then.

One workman, glancing through a window as he buckled two bits of steel together, thought at first that the room inside was unoccupied, then was startled to discover that it was not. A boy lay stretched on a shabby old daybed immediately inside the window; he lay so still, and was so close under the inner sill, that the man's eye had travelled straight over him into the dim, dusty recesses of the room beyond.

"Hey, you kid, you better get outa here, you know that? This whole building's gonna come down."

The window had no glass in it, and the boy was only

a couple of feet away, but at first the workman wondered whether the kid had heard what he said. Maybe he didn't speak English?

"House coming down—kaput—all gone." He made a dispersing gesture with his hands.

"When?"

The boy did not move. His dark blue eyes gazed up calmly into the man's face.

The dirty old bed was covered with a rust-coloured velveteen spread, much faded. On top of this the boy had laid a large piece of plyboard, almost the same size as the bed. He lay extended on the plyboard, completely relaxed, with his arms clasped behind his head. The watching man received an impression of total passivity and total receptiveness. The man did not consciously reflect on the boy's clothes but felt that the kid looked somehow different from the usual blue-jeaned lot; maybe he wore things that had been handed down to him. He had on a pair of aged, baggy, dark-grey flannel trousers, a white cotton shirt, clean but ragged, a hand-knitted sleeveless pullover with a V-neck, and a pair of old-fashioned sandals with solid toe-pieces and a T-strap running up the middle of the instep.

"Demolition starts Monday," the man said.

"How long will it take?"

"Two—three weeks—a month, maybe."

"I could stay on a bit longer, then?" To himself, not the man, he murmured, "That might last my time?"

"No, kid, you gotta leave. It'll be dangerous, see? They got a big crane with a weight, they swing it against the building, they really slam it in, it all starts to fall apart, see? Nobody ain't allowed in. Anyways, this side's due to come down first."

"Oh." In spite of this, the boy did not seem too perturbed. He lay relaxed, gravely observant of the man. "Well, thanks for the warning," he said.

"That's okay. Hope you find yourself another place."

The man moved on. Funny kid, he thought. Kind of solemn. Acted more like a middle-aged man than a— what would he be—fifteen-, sixteen-year-old? Polite. Not like most of 'em nowadays.

After the man had gone Gabriel did not move but continued to lie in the same position. He heard the warning called through their window to the family in the next room and their shrill, indignant, squawking expostulation. They were a large clan of Puerto Ricans who sounded like outraged starlings—their exclamatory protests had the same high-pitched but gargling note. Although they must have been aware for some time that this moment was on its way, they sounded as full of affront and astonishment as if they had expected to bring up their children to maturity and end their days in the derelict building. Gabriel often wondered how many children there were; he had met at least six different ones on the stair, coming in or going out, but he did not think that was the total; from the sound, there could easily have been more.

His relationship with the family was confined to smiles, since he spoke no Spanish. Unfamiliar but appetising smells of cooking came at all times from their quarters, and they seemed to spend their entire days and nights in running, jumping, playing on drums, and listening to loud rock music. He liked them as neighbours; he enjoyed the sense of all this active, cheerful life going on so close to him, purposeful and voluble, in which he had no part.

I shall die in a foreign land, he thought sometimes, and the idea came with a slight strange chill. Yet to a rational mind, after all, what difference should it make where one's body fertilises the ground? The process of decay will be exactly the same here as in England—a bit faster perhaps—and I certainly don't want people coming to weep over my grave; so what does it matter where I am put? Why do people have these feelings about graves? It's very primitive. I suppose it is because of haunting, he thought. Perhaps the spirit really does hang around for a few months in the neighbourhood where its capsule of skin and bone finally disintegrated; like a scent; after all, why not? Spirit is a property of matter. Even then, why should I mind where I lie? I'm sure Gus didn't object, if his spirit suddenly found itself floating round some rocky cliff in the Cordillera Occidental— he'd look at the local fauna and learn all he could. Why should mine find fault with the streets of Manhattan? And he smiled faintly, imagining his ghost slowly drifting along Broadway looking into shop windows. Watches, Catches, Patches, Jewelry and INCENSE. Everything in this Store, 88¢. *Te Amo.* Would anyone see me? I doubt it. The old Indian woman in black, kneeling on the sidewalk so rigidly motionless, her curled feet in black sneakers crossed behind her, a bundle of yellow pencils in her clasped hands, her proud head, in fur headdress, raised in contemplation, ignoring the passers-by who walked on either side without regarding her any more than if she had been a fire-hydrant. The sidewalk slabs are full of ground-up slivers of oyster-shell—didn't she feel them in her bony old knees, through her thin black stockings? People will walk past my ghost in the same way, and I haven't even a bundle of yellow pencils to offer, he thought, assailed by a pang of homesickness, sharp and wistful, for the mere physical smell and objects of home, his old bedroom and the square of sunlight on the carpet, the shelves of books, the view past the big cedar out over Wanborough Common, the corner of the garden terrace where Fred the cat slept on sunny June mornings, the streets and paths where Gus took me for walks when I was little. Would I prefer to be buried in a corner of the garden as we buried old Fred when he died? I remember Thomas saying, "He'll be able to hear our voices as we walk by," and I was comforted and thought not too unhappily of him lying there week after week, warm underground, slowly turning into the roots of plants. Why should the process of decay disgust us? Why should the smell of dung, or rotting meat, or vomit, or maggots, or any broken-down matter make us feel sick? What's the purpose of that disgust? Is it a warning, like pain? Is it a feeling we are born with, that we inherit, or is it simply trained into us when we are children? Maybe it is only conditioning? After all, some primitive tribes enjoy rotten meat and maggots as delicacies; people eat Stilton when it is absolutely crawling; animals don't appear to have any objections to their own turds, dogs even seem to admire them. So why has the human race become so fussy about its leavings? Because the sight of disintegration reminds us of death? We love things that are growing and prospering, but we can't stand the sight of them in decay or decline. And yet that is just as much a part of our existence. Is that, he wondered, why people are liable to be overtaken by sudden frantic destructive impulses? Because the natural slow decay that ought to be going on visibly all around them is concealed and denied? Even art, he thought, when you get down to it is a kind of denial. The tapestries, those heavenly unicorn tapestries, are a contradiction of reality, with flowers of every season together, sprinkled thicker than you would ever find them in nature. (And the fact that I used the word heavenly as a description for them is significant in itself.) The Brandenburg concertos, trying to persuade us that they will last forever. Well, but perhaps they will? Even after we have run out of fuel and frozen to death, some undying echo of the Brandenburgs will still be circling out farther and farther among the galaxies. We shan't hear it. And this suppressed awareness that we are all slowly crumbling to bits but not allowed to admit it or try to console each other, is that the reason why people keep falling prey to the urge to stab each other and destroy whole cities with bombs or bulldozers? Just to show they are not fooled, just to hurry up the inescapable process?

Oh Gus, he thought, for the thousandth time, I wish you were here, so that I could ask you questions and talk over my unformed ideas and have you pour spirit into them and pull them into shape. Why did you have to die so soon? I wasn't ready for your death and I still can't accept it. And I know that's a self-centered way to think.

Becoming restless, he sat up and stared out of the window. He was small for sixteen, but compact and firmly built; his soft dark hair, cut fairly short, lay like a cap over his squarish head. His eyes were set wide, under strongly marked brows. His skin was pale, as he had spent most of the summer indoors; nevertheless he looked healthy enough, and his lips were unusually red. People meeting him found his face a pleasant one, open-featured and unremarkable; save for a certain clouded air which could be mistaken for aloofness or a tendency to sulk; though in fact it was merely preoccupation, a struggle to embrace the whole of the experience he was receiving, or expected to receive.

He tucked his feet under him, leaned forward over the filthy sill, rested his chin on his arms, and breathed in the warm rusty smell of New York, with its sudden overtones of hot laundry-steam and broiling hamburger. He looked across with affection, as he always did, at the row of calm primitive stone lions upholding the portico of the building on the opposite side of the street, and wondered whose inspiration they had been; what nineteenth-century architect had decided they were the final necessary feature to

92

complete that worthy but otherwise unremarkable office building? There are so many beautiful things to look at in New York, he thought; in every short street I see things that give me a warm feeling of happiness and discovery. I could walk about this town for twenty years, I daresay, if I had twenty years, and then be ready to start again. Perhaps all towns are like this if you get to know them really well? Everybody should be issued with two lives, or two personalities, one for doing and one for looking.

The afternoon sky was dissolving to the tender blue of dusk: blue with a touch of lavender. But the skyline still remained sharp and clear, a mad serrated silhouette of chimneys and roof-heights shooting up and down between a hundred storey and three—brick pinnacles, stone spikes, penthouses, triangular skylights, flat rectangular dominoes of concrete. What Gabriel liked best were the water-tanks on the rooftops: cylindrical, pointed, tethered in position by pylon-shaped skeletal iron girders, they seemed to him like so many rockets ready to take off into the sky. He imagined them all suddenly launched into the blue by some subterranean upheaval, dragging the whole structure of New York after them, rumpled as a lumpy carpet, leaving Manhattan Island bare once more, just a black rock in the Hudson River, waiting for birds to come and fertilise it, seeds to take root, grass to sprout, trees and bushes to grow. It will really be better when we are all gone, he thought. Nothing in the whole universe, ever, can have made such a hideous mess as we have done, in proportion to our size. We are like those starfish eating away at the Great Barrier Reef, eating our own house, tossing away the rinds and bones and seeds of life itself as we munch. *The Magic Flute,* the Taj Mahal, the *Ode to a Nightingale*—bits of indigestible rind. Mozart was dying; he was terrified of death when he wrote *The Magic Flute,* he wrote it to distract himself. Could one have guessed that? Chatterton made an elaborate joke of death, and then rushed at it. Now I, he thought, I am not afraid of death, no I am not; but I shall be sorry when I can't sit looking out at this amazing New York sky any more. I shall be sorry when I can't hear the Puerto Rican family squabbling over their paella of whatever garlicky food it is they are eating in there.

I'll be sorry to leave this room. He swivelled round on his sheet of plyboard to take a survey of it. I've become fond of this peaceful dusty place. It would have been a good room to die in, a friendly room but a dispassionate one; not a place where emotional associations clutch like tentacles.

Apart from the bed and two wooden crates it was unfurnished. A door led to an even smaller, equally empty room and a w.c. The smaller room had a number of canvases stacked against one wall which an artist, who had once rented the place for a studio, had apparently discarded as not being worth the trouble and expense of shifting when he left. Gabriel generally had one of them out, so that he could study it: today's picture was about six feet square, and bore a vague resemblance to onions, painted in muddy lavenders and greens and black. He was trying to decide what common factor the paintings possessed which had impelled their creator to discard them. They were all mildly coloured, based on natural patterns like skin whorls or wood grain or the ripples of sand; Gabriel felt a protective affection for them and, if he had known where to find the artist, might have pleaded with him to reconsider his rejecting verdict.

Along with the canvases the painter had left a few books in a corner: Nietzsche and a German dictionary, *Huck Finn, Paradise Lost,* and Emerson; enough to be going on with. And a moulting straw broom and a few rags. Gabriel kept the room swept, even enjoyed washing the wooden floor once in a while. If it were only a case of washing floors, he thought, accommodating oneself to natural objects and caring for them, how easy it would be to live. It's people that create the difficulty, people with their vortices and undercurrents. I suppose—I know—that my need to have everything bare and tidy round me is in reaction to Bella; therefore no more sensible or rational than her untidiness, but how much more rational it feels! I like so much to see things cared for and put to rights: the old man out on the sidewalk in the sun, leaning against the doorpost of his barber's shop and slowly, slowly, carefully combing out the blond wig, carefully setting its waves into position while he enjoyed the sunshine; how I liked that! It gave me a good feeling right down to my toes.

I suppose the feeling of horror that Duessa calls up in me—has for the last six years—really originated a long way further back, when I was tiny: I can remember when I was very young, four or five, how disgusted I was, how I used to hate it when she cleaned my face with spit dabbed on a handkerchief, the sweet nauseating smell of it. And her own odour—the whiff, warm, sharp, rank, pungent as a raw potato that she gave off—it was all mixed up in my mind with roundness and softness and motherhood. I could always tell when she had been in the bathroom or lavatory before me, it was like a taint on the air, made me feel slightly sick and sometimes I couldn't bear to stay in the room but had to go downstairs to the other one, or even out into the garden, into the fresh air, holding my breath till I got well away. It was like the smell of milk or a young, damp baby—acid, curdy, horrible—I couldn't bear to think that I was drawing it into my nostrils. I couldn't bear to touch her slithery underclothes, lying on a chair, or to lick a spoon that she had used. Her skin was too downy and too soft; if you pressed it, the dent would stay for a minute, like dough. Some words, too, associated with her, always vaguely upset and disgusted me—breast, belly, bosom, buttock—words beginning with a B?

The first time I knew clearly and consciously how I felt about her was that day when I ran back from the walk with Gus because it was cold and I'd forgotten my gloves, I'd left them in his study while I waited for him to address and stamp a letter, and he told me to race home and get them, he'd wait for me by the letterbox. . . .

He vaulted over the five-barred white front gate because it was such a sparkling clear cold day and because a walk with Gus was so precious that not a moment must be wasted. If he hurried, they might get as far as the windmill. Gus was off again at the end of the week to another of his scientific conferences, this one in Lima, Peru, and would not be back for two months.

Pushing open the front door—the latch hadn't quite caught because they had left the house with such silent care—he ran fast but on tiptoe across the porch and through the hall. Bella had stayed behind with one of her headaches, hence the silence: she was resting upstairs in her bedroom, she had asked them to be as quiet as possible and stay out a good long time and she might get off to sleep.

He entered the library with his usual feeling of slight awe. In general he did not go in unless Gus was there. Bella, ever since he could walk, had laid such stress on its sacred privacy and importance; over and over again she had said, "You mustn't *ever* go in there without asking Gus first; nobody must; and you must *never* touch his papers or move them. After all you wouldn't want anybody poking among your private things or reading your books, would you? And Gus is pretty special."

Even without her warning he would have stayed out of the library, which, without the human benevolence of Gus to warm it, was a slightly formidable room. So he was astonished now—more than astonished, devastated—to see Bella, not stretched out on her bed with a towel on her head as they had left her five minutes before, but instead upright, nonchalant, sitting at her ease behind Gus's desk, absorbed in reading his letters, turning over papers with one hand while in the other hand she held a thick slice of bread and marmalade, from which, every now and then, without raising her eyes from the document she was reading, she took a mouth-stretching bite. Then, still without looking up, she laid the slice of bread in a wire basket full of more papers, in order, apparently, to be able to pick her nose, which she did thoughtfully with her right forefinger: first one nostril, then the other, a long, probing, rummaging excavation; wiped off the resulting glob of snot on the blotter, *licked her finger,* picked up the bread again, and took another bite.

The discovery of Bella—his own mother—like this was the greatest shock that he had sustained in the course of his whole life. It made him feel physically sick, as if he had received a violent blow on the diaphragm and had had all the breath knocked out of him. His lungs collapsed, his heart raced.

He was terrified at the thought of the start she would give if she looked up and saw him there. What would she do? His imagination simply stopped short at that point; he could not conceive the next scene.

Now, looking back from the greater experience of sixteen years, he could be more detached about it, he could even laugh at himself in pity; while sympathising, he could see the comic side of his nine-year-old shock and revulsion. Because you see your mother picking her nose, your whole life is not disrupted, for heaven's sake? Worse things than that happen to people and they survive. Worse things, in fact, had happened to him since; but he could not recall any event of which the instant impact had been so horrific. It was not so much the nose-picking in itself that made me feel sick, he thought (though now I wonder why she bothered to tell me so often that *nobody* in polite society *ever* picked their nose? perhaps it was in deference to Gus?); nor the fact that she was in his private precinct, reading his sacred papers; nor the fact that she was up and evidently perfectly well when she had pretended to be in agony from a torturing migraine; nor the almost spiteful lack of care with which she dropped her jammy crust into his filing-basket while she picked her nose. It wasn't any of those things singly. It was the total contradiction of all my previous experience. It was her expression, her attitude, her whole demeanour, so completely at odds from anything I had ever seen before. It was the combination of all those things, so suddenly exhibiting her as someone *I didn't know*—as a stranger, a person wholly different from the one I thought I had known all my life. Bella the mother-person, so feminine, soft-spoken, smooth, gentle, deferent to Gus's lightest opinion—where was *she?* What had become of *her?* It terrified me. Who was this? There she sat in her crumpled unfresh nightgown, with her tangled hair hanging down her back, completely oblivious to everything except what she was reading; now she picked up a diary and began looking through that, eyebrows raised. The house was utterly silent; my heart, thumping in terror, was so deafening to me that I thought she must hear it. *Who was this woman?*

If she looked up and saw him, her eyes would turn him to stone. She was Medusa, she was Medea, who chopped up her own children, she was the witch of the ginger-bread cottage. Holding his breath, trying to subdue his thunderous heartbeats, he stole backwards out of sight and then, at frantic speed, back across the hall and out through the front door, which he softly pulled and pulled until it clicked. The library window looked onto the front garden, so he raced away diagonally from the house, across the grass, past the cedar tree, and pushed through the shrubbery and climbed over the wall, rather than run the risk of have her look up and see him go through the gate.

Blank, terrified, his mind empty of thought, he ran stumblingly along the sidewalk to where Gus waited by the red pillar-box. All he had was a sense of horror, as if he had pulled off a sticking-plaster and uncovered a wound full of writhing worms. As if he had opened a drawer and discovered a severed hand.

"Hey!" said Gus, catching his arm. "Where are you off

to? You were running right past me." Looking down more closely he added, "You've scratched your face. Are you all right? Did something upset you?"

"No—I'm all right." Gabriel was in a panic, for how could he explain what was the matter?

"And you *still* haven't got your gloves!"

"I—I couldn't see them." It was the first time he had ever lied to Gus. He hung his head, bitterly ashamed. And what would Gus think when he got back to the library and saw the gloves there on the corner of his desk, in plain sight? Perhaps it would be possible to get in there first—if Bella were gone—and take them away?

A whole web of deceit unfolded in front of him, complicated, nightmarish.

"Well never mind," said Gus equably. "You can share mine. A glove each."

Gabriel put his hand into the large comfortable leather glove, lined with wool. It was roomy and flexible, still kept the warmth of his father's hand.

They walked on.

Gus had been explaining about whirlpools, and he went back methodically to the point where he had left off, describing how they were formed, their relationship to similar circular formations in the air, typhoons and hurricanes; he told tales of great whirlpools, went into the theories of Archimedes, quoted descriptions of the Maelstrom, Corryvreckan, the Swilkie, the Well of Swona. Ordinarily Gabriel would have been completely absorbed by the words of Gus on such a topic. But today, although his attention did not wander, it was divided. Whirlpools, he thought, can be studied. You can make a model of a whirlpool, take a picture. You can chart its movements, find out when it closes in, when it spreads out, what affects it. You can predict in advance what a whirlpool will do.

"Papa," he said presently, when whirlpools had been fully discussed, "how can you tell what a person is really like? Inside?"

Gus answered, echoing his thought, "People aren't by any means as simple as whirlpools. You can study and study them, and still they surprise you."

"How do you study them?"

"Why, by watching them and making notes. You can ask questions too, but you have to take the answers with a pinch of salt. Even if people believe what they say about themselves and each other, they may not know the whole truth."

"*Is* there a whole truth?"

"How do you mean, Gabriel?"

"Can you *ever* find out what a person is *really* like?"

"Ah, that's a different question. In answer to the first, you see, yes, of course there is always a whole truth. About anything. The whole truth is what things are made of, every atom and molecule, and how they are put together, and how they work, and the complete history of what has happened to them, not only back to their own beginnings, back to the beginnings of what began them. Do you follow me?"

"Yes, but that would be the history of the whole world!"

"Right. And we can never know it all. Our minds aren't large enough. But it is there, just the same. It exists. Just as the world exists, though we have to take it on trust, since we can't see it all at once."

"But about people?"

"People have their history too: each one his own. And psychology tells us that the result of things happening to them when they are young—like you, talking to me, now— affects the way they are when they are older. But that isn't all. To know a person thoroughly, you'd have to know not only the history of his whole life, every minute of it, but his heredity too—the genes already in him that give him red hair, or a tendency to rheumatism, or bad temper, or mathematical ability. And even if you knew all that, you still might not be able to predict how he would behave in a given set of circumstances, because you wouldn't know all the associations and connections that were going on in his mind. If you saw a black cat racing across the road, for instance, you'd react differently from the way your friend Catriona would, because the cat would remind you of your old Furry, whereas Catriona keeps guinea pigs and has no associations with cats."

"So really you can never discover what a person is like underneath?"

"Only up to a point. People vary their behaviour in different company, too," Gus said, looking at Gabriel acutely. "You, for instance, would talk in a different way to me from the way in which you talk to Catriona. You'd

99

talk about different things, express yourself differently."

"Is that wrong?"

"Of course not. Conversation is an exchange. You give what the other person needs. It's no use giving him an apple if what he wants is a new vest. But the part of you that is in contact with other people is only the external aspect of you. The older you grow, the more you will find that there is a core inside you, of personality, of *you*-ness, which will change less and less. At least I hope so."

"Everybody has one?"

"Everybody has one. But some more than others."

"So the time to study a person to find out what they are really like would be after they are quite grown up, when they are alone?"

"Perhaps. But that's difficult to achieve. Because as soon as they know you are studying them, they won't be alone, will they? And that will start to affect their behaviour."

"You could secretly film them with a movie camera?"

"You think they wouldn't notice a movie camera?" Gus said, laughing. He turned Gabriel with a hand on his shoulder. "It's time we started for home. Look at the sun, it's like a great red golf ball, just going to drop behind the eighteenth green. Well, perhaps when you are grown *you* will discover a means of studying people that no one has thought of yet. It's complicated, though, because it gets all involved with violation of privacy, and privacy is one of the most important things that we have; it should never be invaded without permission."

"Like reading people's letters?"

"Or listening at keyholes. Come along—let's run; that other hand of yours feels cold. We'll buy some crumpets on the way home, and toast them, and if Bella is better we can all have tea in her room and play Scrabble."

So, during the following year, Gabriel had studied Bella. He spied on her. Doggedly, unceasingly, obsessionally, he learned how to observe everything she did, her habits around the house, in her bedroom, in the kitchen, with friends, with neighbours, with himself. He rapidly brought his technique for keeping her under observation to a fine degree of efficiency. And it was not easy. Watching her took plenty of skill. For Bella, not from any suspicion, but simply out of a native wariness, a set of

100

inborn defences, had the caution of a squirrel, the alertness of a deer, the cunning of a fox. Gabriel, however, throwing himself into the occupation with slightly mad intensity, was soon able to outmanoeuvre her. He watched her through cracks, in mirrors, through keyholes, through windows. He climbed trees, he made long devious detours in order to come on her from unexpected angles. He got up early, he stayed up late. He missed meals, he neglected his home-work, he abandoned his friends, he played truant from classes, he let trains and buses go without him and spent hours in freezing cold, in cramped positions.

At the school he attended they were deeply worried about him. But they put down this drastic change in him to the sudden tragic loss of his father. All they could do was treat him kindly and hope that he would work his way through the strange metamorphosis, and ultimately turn back into the happy-tempered open-hearted boy that he had been before.

During that year he learned more about Bella than he would ever know about any other single human being in the whole of his life. As M. Paul Emmanuel did of Zélie St. Pierre, he could have said, "You know her partially, but *I* know her *thoroughly.*"

Sometimes he felt guilty, remembering what Gus had said about violation of privacy. But he told himself angrily, *she* invaded *his* privacy. Gus never gave her permission to read his letters or his diary. And now he is dead, he has no privacy at all; she pokes about into everything he did and takes possession of it.

It did not occur to Gabriel for quite a long time that the dead really have the last laugh on the living in that respect.

Before, when he was younger, he had realised in odd disconcerting flashes that Bella could be highly evasive and disingenuous, that she was often insincere with outsiders, concealed facts, even from Gus, or overdramatised them and embroidered the truth to suit her own fancy or fit in with some story she had made up. But *now* he knew also that she was greedy, spiteful, thieving, fraudulent; that she was incapable of a straightforward relationship with anybody; that the Bella he had believed to be his mother bore as little relation to the Bella he saw when she thought she was alone as a chimpanzee does to

Piero's "Madonna della Misericordia"; that she could be totally ruthless and unscrupulous when in pursuit of something she wanted. It was during this period that in his thoughts he began calling her Duessa.

She seemed, too, he discovered, to be wholly lacking in any sense of human scale; everything had equal value or no value. He had seen her devote as much care and thought to getting a biscuit out of the tin or stealing a shampoo from a Woolworth's counter without being observed as she might to defrauding the Inland Revenue or persuading Bo that she was ill and needed a holiday in Greece. Did she love Bo? Perhaps. Had she loved Gus? Perhaps—in a vague, heedless, childish way, for the treats and comforts that he represented, for the security of his company.

There could be no doubt that she was stricken at his loss. The nine-and-a-half-year-old Gabriel was appalled by the savage self-absorption, the unbridled indecency of her mourning, which she made not the least attempt to conceal or moderate for the child's sake. She spent whole days on end crying in an unmade bed, she abandoned any care of the house or him, bought no food, stopped washing herself or combing her hair or even brushing her teeth.

Finally, in desperation, Gabriel went round to Loraine Hartshorn, who had often made it plain that she would be glad to come in and help; since her premature retirement because of severe asthma she had been overendowed with spare time.

Gabriel found it difficult to describe the situation at home. He just said, "Bella's not well."

Loraine gave him a shrewd look.

"Fretting for your father, is she? We'll have to see what we can do."

She was delighted at the chance to take command. Her own opulent, ugly house was empty and immaculate; there was nothing further for her to do there. She piled groceries into a basket and marched round at her ponderous flatfooted pace. From that day, her hand was over the Baird house. She wasn't a bad old thing—pretty good cook, too, cordon bleu standard. And had never had children of her own, so she enjoyed baking huge indigestible cakes for Gabriel, so long as he would eat them. Moreover she developed a funny proprietorial affection for

Bella—not maternal, exactly, the old girl was too tough to be considered motherly—but as if she'd constructed Bella herself, cut her out of cloth and sewed her together. Hours and hours she spent, persuading Bella to look at fashion magazines, buy new clothes, get her hair done, pull herself together. Odd really, because Loraine didn't give a rap what she looked like herself; her own clothes, those hideous floral nylon housedresses she wore, all her things, the ugly flat shoes and the mauve coats and hats—she had a decided fondness for mauve—they were invariably well-worn and shabby if not downright grubby. The only touch of frivolity about her appearance at any time was the inevitable diamanté spectacles, of which she must have had a least a dozen pairs in different colours and designs. Up to the appropriation of Bella, her only hobby seemed to have been cookery, collecting spectacles, and the maintenance of her horrible house in a condition like something out of her own magazine.

By degrees, Bella, although irritated, scoffing, ungrateful, petulant, began, slowly and reluctantly, to respond to all this attention and cossetting. She complained that Loraine's food was vulgar, disgusting, gross, fattening— but she ate it. She allowed Loraine to bully her into taking an interest in her appearance again. There was always an odd, opposing balance between them—as if each saw through the other's pretences, and yet agreed to abide by them.

Just occasionally Bella could be honest.

"Do you pay Loraine anything?" Gabriel asked one day.

"No, why should I? She thinks it's the world's treat to be allowed to shoe-horn her way into Gus's house and boss us around. She boasts about it all over Wanborough. She lets on she was his dearest friend—in spite of the fact that he only spoke to her about twice. He thought she was the bore to end all bores. You know she loves coming here; she ought to pay *us,* really." Glancing up at his grave face—she was lying in bed, reading the newspaper, waiting for Loraine to come up with a plate of home-made croissants for her breakfast—she said, "Don't be such a prig," and poked him in the stomach with her elbow. "Pass me the comb, will you, sweetheart, old Lorry will give me hell if she comes up and I haven't done my hair. Oh, there's a letter from Uncle Bo, want to read it?

He's still in Spain with James. Thinks he might come home in three months. Lucky old stinker."

He found her the comb and left. Looking back through the crack of the door he saw her break a tooth out of the comb—after she had given her hair a perfunctory scrape —use it to pick a shred of food from between her teeth.

It was shortly after this that he gave up watching Bella.

Though his last and worst discovery about her had not been made, and still lay several years ahead.

In the kitchen he found Loraine shovelling tablespoonfuls of sugar into a bowl of mayonnaise.

"I thought mummy was trying to keep sugar out of her diet?"

"Lot of bunkum. What the eye doesn't see the heart doesn't grieve over," Loraine said, stirring with spiteful vigour. "That's a ridiculous faddy diet she's set herself; if I weren't here to keep an eye on her she'd end up far too thin, without any stamina. Much better if she has a little more weight and a little more gumption."

"Uncle Bo is thin."

"Yes, but he's got his career and other things to keep him going. It'll be better when she has too. I've been looking at the drawings your mother used to do before she was married to your pa, and I can get her a job, easy as pull off your shoe, the minute she's back on her feet."

Gabriel could not think that this would be a solution. Inarticulately, he felt that Bella would never happily immerse herself in designing wallpaper, or whatever Loraine had in mind. He said doubtfully:

"Didn't she tell you she doesn't need to take a job? Gus left her quite a bit of money."

"Rubbish. She doesn't know what's good for her. She's just a silly girl. She ought to get out again. Meet people."

Loraine, underneath her numerous pretensions—the vanity, the intellectual snobbery that made her a most boring name-dropper when she started talking about the people she had known while editing her magazine; her food-and-drink snobbery, her house-and-furniture snobbery—had a certain rock-bottom, granite common sense.

It was to Loraine that Gabriel turned again after he came out of hospital with his leg in a cast. In that strange time. He had not thought it would be possible to feel more wretched than he had directly after Gus's death, but this was far worse. He had not finished grieving for Gus, and felt, besides, utterly disoriented, rootless, drifting. There was nobody of his own age with whom he could talk. His great friend and playmate Catriona had recently gone back to America with her parents, and he had abandoned all his friendships at school.

"You look terrible," Loraine said, podding peas in the kitchen. "What's the trouble? Leg bothering you? Or is it something about Thomas?"

Her shrewd eye ranked him.

"No. Thomas is okay."

"What, then?" Loraine poured the peas into a saucepan.

He looked at her warily. They were not on moderately confidential terms; her trip into hospital with him in the ambulance had suddenly advanced their acquaintance by several stages; she had been at his bedside when he recovered consciousness and had been calmly reassuring and instructive. Accordingly he felt grateful and at ease with the queer old girl; but his anxiety was a terribly basic one, tunnelling below the roots of his whole relationship with Bella, with Gus, with himself. He had lost every point of reference. And Loraine, though she had sagacity, was limited, and earth-bound; he did not see how she could help him here.

"Come on, duck," she said. "Spit it out. What's the big worry? It never does any good to brood. Here, have one of these." She pushed over a tray of cooling gingerbreads. "Now, what's on your mind?"

"Well," he said slowly, "it was something that happened when I was in hospital. The nurses used to tease me because I've got everything back to front. My heart and things are all on the opposite side from most people's. Did you know that?"

"No," Loraine said thoughtfully. "No, I didn't know that about you."

"And the nurses told me this meant I must be half of a pair of identical twins, because that's the way twins are, sometimes. . . . Here's a funny thing: when I was little, I often used to dream that I had a twin, I had quite distinct dreams about him. I can still remember his face. I called him Milo. Once, when I was six or seven, I asked Bella if I'd ever had a twin and she said no, of course not. She was quite cross about it."

"Perhaps," said Loraine, picking her way cautiously,

"the other twin died at birth and she didn't want to be reminded of it."

They both knew that Bella might have lied for any one of an infinite number of reasons.

"And then I heard a bit of conversation between two of the sisters," Gabriel went on. "They were outside my door, they didn't think I could hear. One said, 'You'd think his mother would come in,' and the other said, 'She's not his real mother, you know. I remember him from when I used to be at the Infant Welfare Clinic, because of the heart thing.' I was pretty sure they were talking about me."

Loraine looked at him for some time without replying.

Then she said, "But Bo and Bella are twins. Twins run in families. Doesn't that make it seem likely that you are her child?"

"Not necessarily. They're not identical. So she wouldn't have been more likely to have identical twins than any other person. I looked it all up."

"I can see you did."

Loraine went on looking at him, with her small fish's mouth pursed up in a silent whistle. She was standing at the round white kitchen table, rolling out pastry. Her hands were floury; she rested them on the table and leaned forward on her thick forearms, with a bulldog look of concentration: brow creased, her eyes thoughtful behind the thick lenses.

Then she marched flatfooted over to the door, to the foot of the stairs beyond, and yelled up them:

"Bella!"

"What?" a distant voice replied.

"What are you doing?"

"Washing my hair."

"Well, wrap a towel round it and come down here a minute."

"I can't. I want to get it done before Thomas comes home."

"Something important has come up."

"Oh . . . !"

In a few minutes Bella came down. She was wearing her old white monk's robe and, turbaned with a towel as well, looked like some fairy-tale *Arabian Nights* prince. But her expression was irritable.

"Well? What is it?" she said impatiently. "You're always *telling* me to wash my hair. It'll be too dry for the setting-lotion if you don't hurry up."

"Never mind. You can wet it again. This boy wants to know if he's your child or not."

Gabriel was startled at hearing the question put quite so flatly into words. And Bella's mouth fell open; her eyes widened, then shot sideways, first to Loraine, then to Gabriel.

Loraine went on, "They told him at the hospital that he's one of a pair of identical twins. You told him he wasn't, it seems. But you must have been giving him wrong information; *they* wouldn't make a mistake about a thing like that. Hadn't you better tell him the whole truth?"

For Gabriel these words rang a mournful chime. The whole truth . . . is what things are made of, every atom and molecule. He thought of whirlpools, of hurricanes, the Moskoe Strom, the Well of Swona.

"Oh, *heavens!*" said Bella. "Honestly, what a moment to choose—"

She looked put upon, abused, beleaguered.

"Things left to themselves generally do choose awkward moments," Loraine remarked in an even tone, going back to her pastry-rolling. "Anyway, now he's asking, you'll have to tell him. And he's old enough to have the plain truth."

"Well, yes, then, darling, you were adopted," Bella said with great haste, as if telling the thing quickly would somehow minimise its importance. "You see Gus wanted a son and he was infertile, some men are, and a friend of mine had had a baby and its father died, and then *she* died—you were her baby—so we adopted you."

"Did she tell you about my being one of a pair of twins?"

"Well, she was ill, you see; she wasn't able to tell me very much. Could I have forgotten? Would I forget? No, I don't *think* so." Bella pressed a distracted hand to her towelled head, as if playing for time.

"Couldn't you go to Somerset House or somewhere and find out a thing like that?" Loraine suggested.

"I suppose we could," said Bella, harassed. "But you see Alice was in Greece at the time Gabriel was born—Alice was her name, Alice Myers—she was a doctor—of course you were registered as a British citizen, that's all in order—but I don't even know the name of the place. Is it really so important? What difference does it make? Wait—maybe she did tell me you were a twin, and that the other twin had died. Yes, I think she might have said that. . . . I hadn't planned to tell you all this until you were much older. It was a perfectly legal adoption. Gus took care of all that, he wanted everything properly organised, and gave you his name, and you are his legal heir, or will be when you're twenty-one."

"What about Gus?" Gabriel tried to stiffen his voice; nonetheless, the words came out shamefully thin and wavering.

"How do you mean, what about Gus?" Bella said, preoccupied; she hunted in her robe pocket for a cigarette, got up, roamed about the room for a match, and then made a long business of lighting up.

"When did he plan to tell me that I was adopted? That I was a twin?"

"Oh," she said vaguely, waving smoke about, "very likely he thought you knew already. Don't you see, it didn't seem important to him. Whether you were born to us or adopted wouldn't make any difference to Gus."

Loraine said, "That's true, you know."

But she had not known Gus. Gabriel took no notice.

Bella went on, "All Gus wanted was a child, a son to try out his educational theories on. Anyway, you've got no call to complain. He loved you, didn't he? You know that. What's all the fuss about?"

"The boy's not fussing, Bella," Loraine grunted. "He just wants to know where he stands. Probably wants to know what his real mother was like. Anyone would."

In fact, Gabriel did not want to know anything of the kind. He did not want to know anything more just then. His real mother seemed as remote a concept as the square root of minus one. He left them and ran limping up the stairs, hoisting his plaster cast, up, up, to the attic bedroom, into which he had moved all his things after Bella and Thomas had got married.

He threw himself on his bed and stared up at the sky above, seen through the skylight, and felt the house sway below him, as if he were on the masthead of a ship, as if all his moorings had been cut loose and now there was nothing left to stop him floating away out to sea with the tide.

Presently he heard the slam of the front door. Thomas, home from his publishing.

It was too high up here to catch any words of conversation downstairs, but Gabriel could feel a vibration, a concerned murmur.

After a while, Thomas came up the attic stairs and tapped on his door.

"May I come in? It's Thomas."

"Yes." Gabriel's voice was muffled. He heard the door open but he had turned his head away into the pillow. Thomas came in and sat on his bed.

"Bella tells me she just told you that you were adopted," he said without preamble.

"Did *you* know that I was?" Gabriel got out, after a moment or two.

"No I didn't. Funnily enough, I've often thought that you looked like Bella. . . . Did it upset you very much, finding out?"

Gabriel thought, then nodded. "You see," he said presently, managing his voice with care, "I didn't like finding out that I'm not his. Not Gus's."

"Now look, Gabriel." It was the firm tone that Thomas used sometimes with the printers, when he rang them up from home in some crisis. "You've got to think intelligently about this. Do I have to say all the conventional things to you? Surely you can use your mind? Perhaps you were not *born* Gus's son, but believe me, that didn't make a scrap of difference. I've seen letters he wrote Bella about you when he was off at conferences. He was just as proud and happy about you as if you were his own. You *were* his own, don't you see? He'd chosen you to be his, and he just poured all his love and wisdom into you from then on. Didn't he? Isn't that the truth? Did he ever act as if he didn't feel like your father?"

"But why didn't he *tell* me?" Gabriel's voice was half stifled; he was lying with his face in the pillow.

"I think it's very likely that he just didn't consider it at all important—he simply forgot about it, once you were established as his child. Don't you think that might be so?"

After a pause Gabriel nodded again, into the pillow.

"Or," Thomas went on more cautiously, "he may have been leaving it to Bella to judge the right moment. Maybe he thought that hadn't come yet. Or maybe he thought she had told you and it was all understood and forgotten. It wasn't important. He loved you, that was the main thing. He was proud of you. And look at it this way.

Think what an unsurpassable piece of luck you had, out of the whole population of the globe, to be adopted by August Baird. Think of the people who might have taken you on and brought you up: dull, boring, stupid people. Unkind, narrow, snobbish people. Cruel people. Fascists, criminals. Religious bigots or cranks. Instead of which, you were chosen by just about the wisest man in the world—who happened to be married to one of the prettiest women. If *I'd* been allowed to choose my parents I'd rather have had ten years of Gus for a father than —than thirty of Newton or sixty of Churchill or seventy of Shaw. Think about that. Whom would you have chosen if not Gus? Can you think of anyone you'd rather have had? Maybe he couldn't put in as much time with you as some fathers could have, because he worked so hard, had so many things going on, but think what use he made of the time with you he did have!"

Gabriel wasn't talking any more just then, but he did not resist when Thomas took his hand; he let it remain in Thomas's comforting grip.

"Just you go on thinking about what I've said," Thomas told him after a minute, and went away downstairs.

A good man, Thomas, in his way; a kind, well-intentioned step-father.

All the same, Gabriel had not mentioned, and Thomas had not dissipated, the residual haunting doubt that still remained with him and always would remain. Perhaps after all he really *was* Bella's son? There was nothing to prevent a fraternal twin giving birth to an identical twin. And people did sometimes adopt their own children— their illegitimate children—after they got married.

But in that case, who was his father? He would never know. It would be absolutely no use asking Bella; he was certain of that. He would never get the truth from her. And perhaps it was better not to know.

Why had Gus ever married her? What wild, quixotic impulse had ever brought that about?

The door opened, letting in a wave of Puerto Rican voices and a waft of Puerto Rican cookery. A panel of light, thrown onto the wall from the hall outside, fleetingly illuminated a poster that had been tacked up, a reproduction of one of the unicorn tapestries: the Lady holding the morror, the Unicorn gazing confidingly at

110

his own image with his large, thoughtful, ingenuous eye. Gabriel had been twice to the exhibition of French tapestries at the Metropolitan Museum, and had been so bewitched by that particular one that he had returned a third time and bought the poster.

The door closed again. It was quite dark by now. But he knew who had come in. He could hear her strike a match; the faint glimmer of a candle flickered and grew. He could hear her stepping about lightly, putting a paper bag of groceries down on one of the wooden boxes. More unexpectedly he heard her murmur some soft remark in the next room, not to him. There came the sound of the tap running, then a subdued lapping noise.

He walked to the door and looked through.

Catriona had filled a foil pie pan with water and put it down on the floor for a dog, which was drinking thirstily.

The dog was tall, plumy, creamy, the colour of a slightly wilted chrysanthemum. Its long pointed face pushed the pan clumsily about the floor.

"He's rather a stupid pooch, I'm afraid," she said mildly, looking down with tolerance at his inefficiency.

As she observed the dog, her face wore exactly the same rather sad, sceptical, resigned, yet indulgent look which the Lady bestows on the Unicorn. She was a small, pale, flaxen-haired girl, with a strong resemblance to the Lady at all times; that was why he had bought the poster. He thought that she and the Lady probably shared the same disposition too: thoughtful, charitable, piercingly intelligent. Practical, sober, and clear-headed.

"Where did you pick up the dog?" he asked.

She began to laugh. "Don't worry, he's not here for keeps! It might be different if he were a guinea pig. There's a man who has come in for a hamburger several times lately; the dog's his."

"Why are you looking after him?"

"Well, it was rather funny; you know there's a bus stop just across from the lunchroom? Today this guy was in eating his hamburger when he looked out the window and suddenly gave a shout and said there was an old friend of his that he hadn't seen in years waiting for a bus; so he went haring across the road and just then the bus came, and I suppose his friend got on and he must have got on too, and the bus started. That was about six, and when he hadn't come back by eight, I offered to

111

take the dog home for the night when I went off, because Mr. Vanucci didn't want it staying in the restaurant. I expect the guy will come back for him tomorrow. He's quite a well-behaved dog; he won't be any trouble. Mr. Vanucci gave me a bit of hamburger for him."

"Did the man pay his bill?" Gabriel's voice was neutral, neither approving nor condemning.

"Oh, he's not that sort of person. No, he didn't, as a matter of fact. But he didn't finish his dinner either. He's quite an okay guy: he has white hair, and he's generally reading *The Virginia Quarterly*, or some big thick book; he'll be back I'm sure. He wouldn't just abandon his dog."

"That's all right then." Gabriel accepted the situation, and the dog, and thought no more about it. He went back and sat on the bed, looking out.

When she had unpacked the food she came to sit beside him, and they wrapped their arms tightly round one another. They had not much longer together now.

Nevertheless, when he said, "Do you mind if I do a little writing before we eat?" she nodded and detached herself from him instantly.

"I want to sash my jeans. I'll do that first."

She went back into the other room and began running the tap again. He rolled over onto his stomach, drew the candle near, pulled a half-completed page from his black leather folder—which was worn and shiny from being constantly carried about—and began to write with steady concentration. He did not notice when the girl came back into the room wearing only her smock and carrying her dripping jeans, which she hung up on an improvised clothesline.

Having done so, she sat down on a pile of newspapers, propping her elbows on her knees and her small grave face on her clenched fists. She would have liked to watch Gabriel, to study him, to memorise him, but feared that this might impinge on his concentration of deflect it. She therefore kept her haze resolutely on the window square of red-tinged night sky.

But inwardly she felt as if she were exploring his contours with her hands, learning his outline with her heart.

As if she were making a death mask.

Gabriel wrote on and on, page after page.

Slowly, by an effort of will, she withdrew her attention

from him, and turned it inwards to the sonata by Giuliani that she was studying. She could perceive the piece of music in three different ways simultaneously—as in the written score, in physical form as played on her flute, and as a pattern of inaudible sound. Gradually she became calm.

The plumy pale dog lay modestly in a corner, looking down its sharp white aristocratic nose. Its expression was as meek and self-effacing as a Madonna. But every now and then it broke into a smile, and a long tongue came sliding out over the yellow teeth and the speckled gums.

Five

Thomas 1967

He woke to a strange calm, and a strange terror. Even while his eyes were still shut, before he was truly awake, he knew by the light through his lids, and from the unwonted quality of the silence, that he was not in his own bed. So where? Not at Jan's, for she always woke first and did her yoga, accompanied by thumps on the bare floorboards. Not at his father's little house in Wansea Village where the hum of the traffic made an incessant background, night and day. Where, then?

He opened his eyes. A baleful pure light, snow-light, lay reflected on the white ceiling. By moving his head a little he could see the window, and one great drooping fringe of cedar-branch, thick-iced with snow, like a detail from a Japanese print.

Jesus. Now it all came back—Jan, the snow, the boy, the house. Her.

His first uncontrollable start of withdrawal took him to the edge of the double bed. Fly. Escape. Only harm can come of this.

But the sudden movement woke her. And in any case he knew while he was moving that it was already twelve hours too late. Impossible to withdraw now with honour. Impossible to withdraw at all. And as he accepted the

113

fact, the defeat, his calm returned to him, even with a kind of exhilaration. He had already crossed the frontier; all he could do now was observe this different landscape, survey its contours, and take what measures seemed best to meet the new demands that lay ahead.

She moved lazily towards him in the bed and stretched out a hand.

"Hello, darling!"—yawning and smiling; he caught a glimpse of slate-blue from under the half-closed lids. "I forgot to wind the clock; what does your watch say?"

It said nine o'clock; a pang of guilt assailed him. "I'll call up the hospital, shall I, and ask how he's getting on? I meant to do it at eight."

"What difference does it make? Let's hope the poor lamb's still asleep. Pass me the phone. I'll do it."

While she was getting through and making preliminary inquiries, he heard, to his dismay, footsteps downstairs, the clink of china and the roar of the dishwasher. His own clothes were still drying down in the kitchen; he gathered up August Baird's things and was preparing to retreat hastily to the upstairs bathroom when Bella, still with her ear to the receiver, beckoned him back.

"Where are you off to?"

"Getting dressed. I can hear your char downstairs," he said in a low voice.

"Oh that won't be the char. *She* doesn't come till twelve. It'll be old Loraine. Stay here. Don't you want to hear what they say about Gabriel? Yes, I'm still waiting," she said into the telephone.

"Of course. But won't Loraine be shocked to find me here?"

"So what?" Bella raised her brows. She seemed surprised. "What business is it of hers? She chooses to come to the house— Oh, good, thank you very much. Yes. Yes. Thank you. . . . They say he's going on well, the broken leg and a bit of concussion was all, and he's had a good night's sleep. He can probably come home in a few days. And we can visit him at any time, old Lorry seems to have very efficiently fixed him in a private room. One thing, the name of Baird ensures red-carpet treatment anywhere round here," she said with satisfaction.

"Oh, that's marvellous. Excellent news." Relief warned his blood like alcohol. "I'll drive you along to see him, then, shall I, as soon as you've had some breakfast?"

"Oh, my darling. Thank you, but I'm not sure that I'm up to going to a hospital. Those visits are always pretty gruelling. And it was a pretty short night."

Loraine had telephoned from the hospital at 2 A.M. with interim news. By then they had drunk several more bottles of champagne, for Bella kept insisting that she could not stand the suspense without some fortification.

Loraine had also, to Thomas's great relief, announced her intention of returning home by taxi; she said there was no point in his turning out again, it was still snowing hard, and she had a taxi already bespoken that was waiting for her. This seemed just as well, for he would not have been confident of his ability to drive her safely by that time. She had advised them both to get to bed as soon as possible and promised to come round in the morning.

In fact they had been in bed when she telephoned. But they had not gone to sleep for some time.

"Don't you think Gabriel will be wanting you?" Thomas said, slightly disconcerted.

"Well, poor angel, he knows I've got flu and that he can't really expect me to come. I feel definitely worse this morning; I'm so hoarse I can hardly croak. Fetch me the thermometer, there's a love; it's in the wall-cupboard in the bathroom. I'm sure I've got a temperature again; can't think why!" She gave Thomas a faint, conspiratorial grin.

A small bathroom opened out of her sleeping-alcove. It was wildly untidy, talcum everywhere, the floor a scented pool, towels and underwear draped over the bath, while the shelves and cupboard were a tangle of dusty cosmetics, gadgets of every kind from curling-tongs to water-picks, hair combings, and rusty razor blades. Slightly repelled—but after all she had been ill with flu —Thomas delved into this confusion and finally found a thermometer; then, after he had given it to Bella, withdrew circumspectly to the upstairs bathroom to shave and dress.

When he came down to the first floor again he saw that Bella's door was half closed; from behind it came the murmur of female voices. So he continued on quietly down the stairs into the kitchen, which was now in a state of ostentatious tidiness, all its horizontal surfaces scrubbed and damp, dish-towels washed and hung up to dry, every door and drawer shut. Not a trace of last night's feast, nor, indeed, or any food at all. Feeling like an interloper, he looked around for breakfast provisions. What did Bella usually have? He should have asked her, but felt reluctant to go back to her room if Loraine was in there. Coffee, toast? All he could fancy himself was a bowl of cornflakes or a bit of bread, but the place seemed wholly deficient in such homely staples.

There was an electric coffee-grinder the size of a barrel-organ, but he could find no coffee-beans. Opening various mahogany-finished drawers and cupboards he discovered a four-pound Dundee cake in a tin, its outer cellophane intact; unopened packets of Bath Olivers and cream crackers; a hare, hanging stiffly in its fur; a gallon can of olive oil; a string of French onions; another large un-opened tin of Peak Frean's mixed biscuits; and four shelves of herbs and spices, seasonings, molasses, may-onnaise, chutneys, and condiments. But nothing so com-monplace as a simple loaf of bread or a jar of instant coffee.

Perhaps they kept these things in the refrigerator? He pulled open its massive door and found some more cham-pagne, a few slices of black bread, very stale, four jars of olives, a lemon, a large bowl of boiled fish—for the cat?—and a number of varying-sized lumps swathed in silver foil which, when investigated, proved to be the re-mains of last night's meal—the salmon, the caviare, a small portion of potato salad—and various little pots con-taining dripping and pâté. No butter, no eggs, not even an apple or a half-pint of milk.

Well, there was a large wooden, lead-lined box con-taining smokey-smelling tea, probably Lapsang. Not his favourite, but he could make lemon tea and take her a cup. He filled a kettle and put it on the yellow stove.

More snow had fallen in the night. Looking out of the window while he waited for the kettle to boil he saw that all the branches and bushes in the big garden were blurred and veiled in heavy white. A cold, watchful sky palely re-flected the brilliance from below and flung light into every corner of the kitchen; Thomas, uneasy and conspicuous under so much daylight, flinched as if he were a specimen pinned out for observation on a slide. The nervous resolu-tion with which he had woken did not falter, but he felt it subject to ironic appraisal. By whom, by what? The house? He was very conscious of it, silent and dignified around him, the large cold empty place, impregnated still with the personality of its former owner. Like a microcosm of the sceptical world outside, it appeared to weigh his fragile desperate intention and his doubtful ability to sustain it.

"You *will* stay with me, won't you?" Bella had sobbed into his shoulder in the fractured night. "You'll look after me? They all went off and left me, they were scared of my unhappiness. I'm so terribly alone."

How easy it had been to promise. How inevitable.

The sun came out, and at the same moment the kettle boiled, filling the window end of the room with clouds of dazzling steam. As Thomas stepped forward to make the tea, he heard slow, padding footsteps and turned to see Loraine Hartshorn come into the room.

Her appearance this morning was built up of incongruities: the elaborately waved frizzy grey hair, jewelled glasses, and floral silk dress looked totally out of place in a kitchen setting and hardly accorded with the large bundle of dirty laundry she carried; the cigarette dangling from her mouth reminded him of some old charwoman, and contrasted oddly with the expensive, careful makeup that had been applied to her round pink face; the gold-and-pigskin handbag slung over her arm seemed grossly at variance with the trodden-down rubber-soled canvas house-shoes that she wore. And the homely roundness and pinkness, the good-natured shape of her face, were belied by the cold granite grey of the large observant eyes behind thick pebble lenses.

"Good morning!" she said without shifting the cigarette from her mouth. She dumped her bundle on top of the Bendix and dragged out a massive container of liquid detergent from a broom cupboard. She appeared so at home in the place that Thomas felt more than ever *de trop*.

"Do you want some breakfast?" Loraine asked, without stopping what she was doing. "I took a tray up to Bella's room; there'd be plenty for you too. I brought round half a dozen croissants I'd made. And there's coffee. All you need to take up is a coffee-cup."

She seemed so calm about his presence that he felt a little easier. Indeed, after tipping detergent into the machine, she gave him a curiously measuring, almost proprietorial survey, as if she had personally chosen him for a post and was congratulating herself on her acumen.

"How is B—Mrs. Baird this morning, do you think?"

"Oh, she's a bit feverish. Took her temperature. Says it's a hundred and one. She gets thrown off balance easily since August died. Psychosomatic upsets all the time. Best to keep her in bed a few more days. She said you'd kindly promised to go and see young Gabriel. Why don't you go straight along there, after you've had a bit of breakfast? Do you know where the Riggs Memorial Hospital is? Other side of Fynche Park."

"Yes, I know," he said. "Well, I really don't need to bother with breakfast. If you've looked after Mrs. Baird, I'll just put on my own things and go along."

He was uncomfortably certain that the sheets she was about to wash had come off last night's bed.

"Have a word with Bella first, though, won't you?" Loraine said, laconic, raising her brows and tilting her head sideways to avoid the smoke from her cigarette. "No doubt she wants to send some message to the boy."

"Yes, of course." He put back the kettle, which he had been holding all this time in a nervous uncertain grip, onto the stove, took his dry clothes from the rail, and left the room with all speed. He could feel her thoughtful gaze follow him as he climbed the stairs stumbling on the thick carpet.

While he had been downstairs, Bellas's living- and sleeping-room had been subjected to the same vigorous tidying process as the kitchen. The bed was newly made with clean sheets. Against a mound of plumped-up pillows Bella lay wrapped in a white woolly shawl, with a tray in front of her. She looked wan, frail, and cherished. Her hair had been brushed till it shone, and was tied back with a yellow ribbon. She gave him a warm but wistful smile and stretched out a hand to him.

"Lorry says I've a temperature of a hundred and two. So no hospital trip for me. She's like a Hitler in the house. Give my best love to Gabriel, my *best* love, and tell him I'll be there as soon as I *possibly* can. Will you do that for me?"

"Of course I will." He picked up the hand and kissed it, feeling guiltily relieved. The puritan streak in him had been dreading a recurrence of the overwhelming sexual force that she had generated last night. But this morning it was switched off. He felt not a trace of it. So much the better.

118

"Is there anything you'd like me to take him?"

"Oh, Lorry will see to all that. She said she'd put pyjamas and things in a case."

"What about books—games—is there any hobby—anything he specially likes to do? I could buy him something on the way, as I go through Wanborough centre."

She looked vague. "I suppose you could take along his pocket chess set. He spends hours brooding over that. And his recorder. Some books from his room maybe. Now, my darling, I'm going to have a nap. I feel like a washed-out *rag*. Can't imagine why!" She flashed him a swift smile, settled back, and closed her eyes.

"Shall I take away your tray?"

No answer but a murmur. He picked it up and carried it out to the table on the large landing. There was half a cup of coffee left in the pot, which he poured and drank standing; otherwise the tray contained only empty plates, a grapefruit rind, crumbs, and a few grape pips.

Thomas changed back into his own clothes in the upstairs bathroom, then came down to search for Gabriel's room. He encountered Loraine, slowly completing the ascent of the first flight of stairs; for a woman of her short stature she was substantially overweight.

"Hm," she said, taking stock of the empty tray. "I daresay she'll live. Or did you eat it all?"

He shook his head, embarrassed, and quickly asked:

"Can you tell me which is Gabriel's room? I said I'd take along some of his books. And Mrs. Baird said he had a pocket chess set."

"In here." She opened a door and trailed cigarette smoke ahead of him. "You choose the books, I'll pack up his toilet things."

It was a demure, tidy boy's room, furnished, he guessed, much on the austere model of the room upstairs. A telescope stood on the window sill, a half-finished Meccano model occupied the worktable, which also had a framed newspaper photograph of August Baird, vigorously addressing some public meeting. His hair was wild, his hands were making a diagrammatic gesture, his eyes were urgent with the importance of what he was saying. Thomas, hastily withdrawing his eyes from those of the photograph, looked round the walls. Two prints, "The Peaceable Kingdom," and le Douanier Rousseau's "Sleeping Gipsy." Several shelves of books. He walked across

119

and studied the titles. Which to take? Hardly Poe's *Tales* or restoration drama, or Ambrose Bierce, for hospital reading. Surely the boy was rather advanced in his literary tastes—but that was to be expected of course. Here were more conventional children's books, Kipling, *Black Beauty*, Mark Twain, *Kidnapped* and *Catriona*, Forester, Thurber—and here were several of August Baird's own books in familiar paperback covers. Thomas felt a deep nostalgic pang at sight of *The Biology of Love and Pain;* he could not have been a lot older than Gabriel when he read it for the first time.

Opening it he saw the inscription on the flyleaf: "For my dear Gabriel who will one day find out all these things for himself—and who knows how much more? with love from Father."

The snow-light blinked on the ceiling as a bird outside the window hopped from branch to sill. Loraine Hartshorn was pottering about behind him opening drawers and cupboards. Thomas turned the page and read:

"We can do no better than dedicate our lives to the pursuit of a vision; in this way alone is it possible for us to rise above the humble origins from which we sprang, and from the limitations and frailty of our abilities. We may never achieve our goal; indeed, how can we? But the hope of improving our legacy, and passing on to our heirs and successors a world that is a freer and a nobler place must be sufficient for us."

Pain above a certain degree of intensity sometimes carries its own anaesthesia; the page swam in front of Thomas's vision for a few moments; he heard Loraine mutter something to herself and leave the room; her heavy padding step receded along the passage. Now the room was quite silent, except for the bird expostulating softly outside on the snowy sill. Perhaps Gabriel usually put food out for them there?

A shabby armchair stood near the window; Thomas crossed the room and sat in it. For a moment he had felt that he might die, standing there by the bookshelf. But after resting for a short time he began to wonder how often in the past August Baird would have come to sit here for a bedtime chat. He stood up again, quickly found the recorder and chess set, and chose a mixed batch of reading-matter: Wordsworth's poems, which seemed well-used and full of bookmarks; O. Henry's collected stories; for its thickness, a history of the ancient world, which had lain open on the bedside table, and several of August's own books. He packed all these things into the case which Loraine had left open on the bed.

Then he went downstairs and found her in the kitchen putting on her coat. The Bendix hummed and throbbed. She looked at Thomas sharply.

"You're sure *you're* all right? You seem to have come over rather green. Not coming down with a touch of Bella's flu?"

He shook his head.

"I have arthritis. It gives me a twinge now and then."

"Oh, is that it? Well, that's better than flu." She nodded her head rapidly. "Can be a nasty thing though."

Strange woman; she seemed really relieved. Through the bulging lenses she gave him again that odd properitorial stare, and said, "You'll come back, by and by, for a meal won't you? It's the least you can do. I mean"— for the first time she seemed a little self-conscious, uncertain—"it's the least you can do after going off without any breakfast. Besides, she'll want to hear about the boy."

"Well—"

"You're good for Bella, you know. I thought I'd find her much worse this morning. But she's taken a great shine to you. And she badly needs someone to cheer her up; she hasn't by any means got over Professor Baird's death."

"You seem to be playing pretty much of a supportive role."

"Oh me!" She gave a short gruff laugh. "I'm just good for a dog's-body. Bella needs someone with *spiritual* qualities. I can see you have those. I'm just an old, practical friend."

Extraordinary woman; what could she possibly have at the back of her mind? It occurred to Thomas to wonder whether she were a Lesbian. But in that case why— As if parrying the thought, she said, not in direct relevance to what had gone before:

"I was married once but my husband was a poor stick; a real fool of a man. No one could possibly lean on *him*. Haven't seen him in years. Went back to my maiden name. But—unfortunately as it turned out—Bella was very much used to depending on August in every way; she's not easily going to get over that loss."

121

"No, of course not."

"Come back to lunch. I'll make a quiche."

"Oh, no thanks," he said, alarmed by her intensity and abruptness, the strange force of her persona. "I can't possibly, though it's kind of you; I do have an office, you know; they'll be wondering what's happened to me. I ought to have called them by now. I'll have to go along there, after I've visited the hospital, and see that everything's going on all right."

"Well, then, come back to dinner this evening. Stay the night again, why don't you. Bella really shouldn't be on her own too much, and I have to give a lecture over in Dulwich and shan't get back till late."

He agreed to this; he could hardly do otherwise.

If he had had a desperate notion of calling up Jan— just once, just to say sorry, to say good-bye—he abolished it. She wouldn't want to hear from him again; she had made that plain enough.

"Tell you what," said Loraine, giving him another of her sharp myopic glances, "run me along to Wanborough centre now, and while you're visiting Gabriel I'll buy some things for your and Bella's evening meal, anyway, but this will be quicker, and it'll save me having to carry things back on my two feet."

And it will ensure my coming back as well, Thomas thought. But it was a perfectly reasonable suggestion, and he agreed.

"Is it all right to leave Bella alone in the house?"

"Oh heavens, yes. She'll sleep for hours."

They set off, the car slipping and crunching in the new snow as he ran it out of the driveway.

"Bella's a very sweet person," observed Loraine dogmatically as they passed the pedestrian crossing. By now snow-ploughs and traffic had churned the snow along Wanborough Parkside into a black mess, but on the common it still extended celestially white and sparkling. "She's a sweet person. But she's childish. Know what I mean? It's hard for her, left all alone, responsible for the boy too."

"And what a responsibility." Thomas never took his cautious attention from the road, but felt it incumbent on him to make some reply. "August Baird's son."

She gave a curious sniff at this, as if her personal opinion of August Baird had not been so high, but said:

"Yes. There's that too," in a dry tone. "Gabriel's no genius though. He's just a nice boy. . . . But I'm glad he wasn't killed. Don't like to think what *that* would have done to Bella. She'd really have gone sky high. She can certainly think herself lucky *you* arrived on the scene."

Strange woman; all her remarks sounded ironic, double-edged. Whom was she denigrating, Thomas or Bella? Or August Baird? And yet there seemed little doubt of her goodwill. Thomas felt relieved, though, when they arrived at Wanborough centre. He said:

"I'll leave the car in the hospital forecourt, shall I; I'd like to walk along to Smiths and get a few magazines and things for the boy. Where are you planning to shop? Can I drop you anywhere on the way?"

"The forecourt will do fine for me. As we're here, I'll just drop in and say a word to Gabriel. I'll tell him you're on your way."

She marched into the hospital with her ponderous flat-footed gait.

Shopping for suitable offerings, Thomas had time to run the gamut of all his capacity for anxiety, apprehension, inadequacy, and guilt. What could he possibly say to Gabriel? I greatly admired your father, I have come straight from the bed of your mother, whom I never laid eyes on before last night. I am very sorry for you both in your irreparable loss. What words could cover such a situation?

Back at the hospital he met Loraine again, on her way out.

"He's expecting you," she said nodding. "It's Ward B, room number thirteen."

"Wait—" Thomas wanted to detain her. "What about— Shouldn't I— Did you— Ought I to— Have you mentioned—"

But she was gone, trudging off at a brisk pace with her basket over her arm.

Thomas walked along to room number thirteen.

In response to his knock a clear, childish voice called, "Come in!"

Finding himself rather breathless, Thomas pushed open the door. From the entrance he could not see the occupant of the bed because of the crane suspending the injured leg. He walked round the bed-end, put the case on the floor, and the magazines on the window sill.

"Hullo!" he said then, holding out his hand. "I'm Thomas Cook. I hope Miss Hartshorn told you about me."

There was a pause. Then the boy in the bed said, "I'm sorry, I can't shake hands. Both of mine are bandaged up at the moment. How do you do. It was nice of you to come and see me. Please sit down, won't you?"

Thomas sat, cursing himself for a fool. A falsely hearty, thick-skinned, blundering, hypocritical, unimaginative fool.

"I—I hadn't realised that your hands were hurt too?" he said clearing his throat. "Not badly I do hope?"

"No, not badly. Only grazed, they say. I suppose I fell on them."

Another pause. Before Thomas could ask his prepared questions, Gabriel said:

"Do you know—is Fred—is my cat all right? I didn't like to ask Loraine because she's allergic to cats. She's so shortsighted that she always trips over him, too, so he keeps out of the way when she's in the house."

And it was her dog that chased him out, Thomas thought. He cursed himself again. What a fool not to have looked to see if the wretched cat was there this morning. Why hadn't he thought that this would be the first thing the boy would want to know? But he could truthfully say, and did, that the cat had been asleep in its basket last night.

"Oh he'll be all right, then," the boy said, sounding relieved. "I got him some fish yesterday and cooked it, so my mother can feed him. I'm afraid all the trouble you've had over me was his fault really. Well, mine too, of course. I was carrying him back home from the common—he panicked and got away from me and dashed out and I tried to grab hold of him, but I slipped, I suppose. One couldn't see anything coming in all that snow. It must have been terribly frightening for you."

"Finding you? Yes, at first I thought you'd been killed. Never mind. You're the one who came off worst. And you'll be all right in a few weeks, won't you?"

"Oh yes. They say it's not a bad break."

"It's lucky you weren't lying out in the snow for long. That I came along as soon as I did."

After a minute Gabriel said, "Yes. I'm very grateful to you. . . . Is my mother all right, do you think?"

"She's fine. She sent her love. She has a little flu still. I expect Miss Hartshorn told you she has a temperature."

Gabriel nodded and winced. He had a bandage attached to the side of his head by tapes, and a graze on one cheek. A slight crease between his dark brows gave him a puzzled air, but the dark-blue eyes he raised to Thomas were wonderfully clear and direct. His face was round, and rather pale, with a sprinkle of freckles on nose and cheekbones. The blue eyes and the softness of his dark hair and the freckles and very red lips lent him an Irish look; he could, Thomas thought, have stepped from some illuminated manuscript, wearing a yellow kit, carrying a sling or a hawk on his wrist.

"She won't like being alone in the house," he said. "She gets nervous. I suppose she could go and stay with Loraine."

He sighed; he wore an adult, pondering expression. Thomas, who at first had thought him a rather ordinary-looking boy, engaging, but bearing little visible evidence of his heredity, began to recast his opinion. There was something deliberate about this child: shy, but far from uncertain.

Gabriel might be no genius, as Loraine had said; but he was no fool either.

Thomas, who had been hesitating, came to a decision. "Listen, Gabriel," he said. "I've something fairly extraordinary to tell you, for our first five minutes of acquaintance. But I hate keeping things concealed. And I hope that in a way this may ease your mind. . . . You'll think it pretty wild, I'm afraid, when we hardly know each other at all, but the fact is that your mother and I have fallen in love with each other—I went and stayed with her in the house, you know, last night, after the police had told her about the accident and Miss Hartshorn had gone off with you in the ambulance—and I've asked her to marry me and she's said yes."

The startled, yet expectant look that Gabriel had turned on him when he began to speak did not diminish at the close of his statement but it deepened in some unfathomable way; it became inturned and wondering.

After a minute or two he repeated Thomas's words, "You've asked my mother to marry you?" in a bewildered tone, as if he had expected something quite different.

"Yes." Thomas wondered uneasily what disastrous Oedipal conflicts this rash announcement was bound to stir up. "So now I'll be able to look after her, I hope.

125

And I hope you'll let me look after you, too, a bit. And at least that you'll feel able to stop worrying about her."

"I see." Gabriel fell silent again. The dark lashes lowered; Thomas was not able to see his eyes. After another longish pause he said:

"You hadn't ever—didn't know her before?"

"No, I met her for the first time when I went in to tell her about—about your accident, last night."

Gabriel said, and there was no mistaking the note of deep anxiety in his voice, "Are you marrying her because of what—because of this accident? My leg? Because she was so upset?"

"Oh, my dear boy." Thomas was greatly moved, and disturbed; he wondered what nature of scene the boy had imagined. Plainly the question was not prompted by childish self-importance; far from it. Trying to speak without regard to Gabriel's age, but as to an equal, he said, "You know how, sometimes, if you are thrown together with somebody in a crisis, you come to know them much faster than you would in the ordinary way? Has this ever happened to you? . . . It was like that with your mother and me."

The troubled dark-blue eyes lifted to his again. Gabriel said, "Yes—I see. But are you sure you really know each other?"

"I think so, Gabriel—enough. How well do most people really know each other? I've seen your mother at a time of great grief and shock, and tried to help her; that's the kind of occasion when people see each other at a fairly basic level. And, you see, I was lucky enough to know a great deal about your father too. I never met him, but I've read all his books and he's always been someone whom I admired immensely. So, as well as believing that I know your mother, I know what she has lost. And what you have lost too. You must miss him all the time. . . . Well, what I would like to do is not try to replace him— no one could do that—but, as it were, join the family. Do you see?"

Gabriel's mouth quivered. Suddenly he looked several years younger—no more than seven or eight—poignantly forlorn and vulnerable. He blinked, moved a bandaged hand towards his face, then impatiently thrust it back under the sheet.

"You see," he said slowly, doggedly, "my mother's very

126

—very unrealistic. Not very mature? I don't really see how you can know that yet? She likes to pretend. A lot of her life is a kind of—of play-acting. She makes up something and pretends that it is real. Specially since he died. Do you understand?"

His words were an odd reminder of something that Loraine had said earlier. Thomas felt a deep tremor begin somewhere under his breastbone. Laughter? Or a hysterical burst of tears? It felt as if there were a loose, dangerous thing in there, liable to dash itself to pieces, do terrible damage inside him. He tried to breathe deeply and calmly.

"Don't worry too much, Gabriel. Maybe I do know what you mean. But we all have to indulge in a bit of play-acting at times."

"It's just that my mother—I wouldn't want—"

"Hush! Don't upset yourself. Keep your strength for getting better. It'll all work out, you'll see. Try to think that this happening may have advantages for all of us. I do hope that you and I will become good friends. I'm sure we'll find lots of things to talk about. I used to be a sort of scientist—biology—as well as being a publisher, which is how I make my living now."

A faint light of interest showed in Gabriel's face. "What kind of books do you publish?"

"All kinds. Mostly scientific. I'm hoping—"

Gabriel said, sounding more like an ordinary child now in his self-absorption, and with a comic echo, too, of a common adult reaction when meeting a publisher:

"I've sometimes thought that I might become a writer."

"Maybe you will. Your father's written plenty of books. What kind of thing do you think you might write?"

The boy frowned, concentrating, so that the bumps on his forehead showed white; his mouth set in an unexpectedly firm line of maturity and suffering.

"I'd like to write about the importance of truth."

Thomas felt the loose bearing in his chest flutter dangerously again; it ached, it hurt him. But he said gently:

"Don't you think that perhaps you worry a bit too much about the truth? Everyone has his own. For instance your mother's play-acting, as you call it, may be necessary for her; it may be a kind of truth for her. Isn't there a bit in the Bible about truth being like leaven? You can only take so much at a time."

Gabriel's creased brow suggested that he would have liked to question this assertion. But he said nothing and Thomas went on:

"Don't forget that your father loved her. *He* must have understood her. I hope I shall, too, and I hope that you and I will understand each other. Don't forget, too, how much we all vary in different circumstances. Each of us can be childish at one time or another. But then, when we have to, we behave like adults. You do, I daresay, more than many people who are older. I know you feel anxious and responsible about your mother, but believe me, she's a grown-up person and can look after herself. And I am—part of the time anyway—and I plan to take care of her. So you stop worrying and get on with your own growing up."

A nurse wheeled a trolley into the room. She was followed by a blue-uniformed sister. Gabriel eyed the glittering implements in the trays apprehensively, but the sister said:

"It's all right, we're only going to change your dressings."

"I'd better make myself scarce, then," Thomas said. "I'm sure we've talked enough. I'll come back this evening, perhaps, shall I; we might play some chess; would you like that?"

"Yes, that would be great," Gabriel said politely.

"I brought a few of your books; shall I put them here where you can reach them? And these magazines. Are there any others, or books, that you'd like? I'm driving on into London, to my office, I could get you anything that you want to read."

"Could you get me a book about Leonardo da Vinci?" Thomas promised that he would.

"Is your car quite all right, then?"

"My car? Yes, it's all right. Why?"

Gabriel looked puzzled. "It didn't get dented?"

"No," Thomas said carefully. "Nothing's wrong with my car. Why should it be?"

"But wasn't it you who knocked me down?"

The nurse glanced up from the packet of dressings that she was slitting open; the sister paused in her neat meticulous writing on a report-sheet.

"I think perhaps you've got the wrong end of the

stick?" Thomas said. "Maybe Miss Hartshorn accidentally misled you?"

"You—I thought—that's why—" Gabriel swallowed and looked straight at Thomas, and said, "It wasn't you then? Who hit me?"

"No, Gabriel," said Thomas quietly. "All I did was pick you up."

He walked out into the hospital yard. Sun was melting the snow fast; the tyre marks were black and glittering with water in the dazzling white; trees dripped and shone, gutters gurgled. We've got some trouble here unless we're careful, thought Thomas. Will he always suspect this of me? Can he learn to believe that I am not that sort of person?

All I have to do is show him, convincingly, and for the rest of his childhood, that I am a responsible and caring adult; that I have the best of intentions towards him. Which god knows I have. But, as August might ask, which is more important, the intention or the performance?

His car spun out into the motorway. Traffic streamed by. His windscreen became covered instantly by a fine spray by melting snow and grit thrown up by faster-moving vehicles. He started his wipers. Over to the left lay the snowy slopes, the wooded gardens of the big houses on Wanborough Parkside—Baird's house somewhere among them. On his right were the smaller cluttered roofs of Wansea Village, and the gasworks and cricket pavilion. I never got to see father after all, he thought; not that he'd know or greatly care. It's nothing but an irritation to us both if I do go there: an upsetting reminder for him and a painful frustration for me, stumbling among the dead paraphernalia of a lost happy time that has become bleached and sterile, like a moon landscape.

Then he thought, But perhaps, with Gabriel, I might be able to cross that boundary again. Back into the lost land, the closed world of childhood.

Six

The Alleyn Club had recently modernised its nineteenth-century kitchen and extended the members' dining-room. Now, to the disgust of the older inhabitants, it had thrown open its membership to include women, provided they were of professional and executive status, and was celebrating this concession by a cocktail evening, ended by a buffet supper served informally in the new kitchens.

It was the kind of occasion that Thomas detested. A large crowd of distinguished and well-known figures surged to and fro between the cocktail bar and the lavishly spread counters in the kitchen. To the satirical eye, it was a prize display of well-bred greed and stylish rapacity; quite probably none of the people there had ever lacked a meal in the whole of their affluent lives, but they fought to get at the roast beef and lobster salad as if there were no other food to be had in London. And after the food, what then? An extension of purpose: the urge to be seen conversing with somebody more important than oneself. The need to show off, to make an impression.

Bella was in her element. This was the first really large party she had been to since she and Thomas were married and she beamed at everyone she met, sparkling, burnished like a pigeon in spring plumage, extracting the utmost gratification from all her encounters: friends and associates of August Baird, who of course came to honour his memory by being kind to Bella, and then there were all Thomas's publishing acquaintances, and even Bo was there and introduced her to some painters, so the evening was undiluted success. It could only have been enhanced by the presence of Loraine, who had seen her into her new silver wool dress with grunts of approval.

"Good thing you followed my advice and had them alter the collar. It sits much better now. You look stunning. But don't overtire yourself, remember. Tell Thomas to bring you back before you start going blue round the edges."

"Why don't you come along too, Lorry?"

"Who, me?" Loraine's tone was dry. "Not likely. My party days are done. Who d'you think I am, Cinderella? Besides, I'm not a member."

"You could be. Ex-editor of *Mansion*. Anyway you could come as our guest."

"Not me. Thanks all the same. Too old for parties. Too hard on the feet. I'll hear all about it tomorrow."

Bo roamed into the kitchen; he had no car and was driving into London with Thomas and Bella. He had put on an ancient dark-blue velvet jacket in which he looked like some distinguished roué—the Old Pretender, perhaps, or one of the Medmenham Abbey set. Nobody, as Bella often said, would have guessed that they were the same age. He crossed the room with his loping slouch and gave Loraine a hug, winking over the top of her head at his sister.

"Loraine the divine. Loraine, Loraine, Loree. Have you ever read that spirited poem, Loraine my angel? I always think you are just like the heroine. I can just see you in the title role, riding the horse to a standstill, bursting your brave heart in the act—or whatever it was precisely that she did. Here, this is for you—I know chocolate and cheese would lay you dead on the floor because of your anti-phobic medicaments, but turrón doesn't come into those categories—somewhere between the two—so I brought you a box."

"What nonsense you talk, Bo. You know I never eat sweet things," Loraine said gruffly, but put the little box in her overall pocket. Bella's eye followed the presentation jealously.

"None for me, Boney?"

"You're going to a party where you'll overeat outrageously. Loraine needs consolation. Besides, what do you ever give me? Whereas she is my ever-loving angel, bringing me delicious things to my studio every week. . . . Where's Thomas?"

"Just coming. Helping Gabriel with his maths homework."

"It was such luck that you should marry *another* scientist. What can they see in you? How did a little addlepate like you ever bring it off?"

"Don't you start teasing her, Bo," Loraine said tartly. "Thomas and I have just got her thoroughly back on her feet again, we don't want you coming home from Spain upsetting her and undoing all our good work."

"No, of *course* we don't. But Bella knows it's all clean honest fun, don't you, my nightingale?"

Bo went to lean by his sister against the big stove, turned her head to him with both hands, and gave her a loud sucking kiss, mouth to mouth.

There were sounds of laughter from upstairs, and running footsteps.

A voice shouted, "Yoicks! I got to fourth base," and steps catapulted down the stairs. Gabriel appeared in the doorway. His hair was tousled and he was out of breath. Seeing who was in the room, however, he sobered down instantly, and said, "Thomas is just putting on his tie. He said he'd be down in two shakes."

"It hardly sounded that way," Bella said acidly. She turned to Bo. "They play this endless game they call indoor baseball, with a shuttlecock. I sometimes think Thomas is reverting to second childhood."

"But how charming." Bo raised his brows. "Or can Gabriel be reverting to first childhood?"

"Come here," Bella said to her son, "your collar's half in and half out, and your hair is a mess."

He submitted to her tidying him up, his face perfectly blank. She said scoldingly:

"You've got dandruff all over your collar *again*. I can't think why you keep getting this terrible dandruff."

"I can't help it. I'm always washing my hair. Whenever I take a shower."

"It's infectious," Loraine said. "Perhaps he picks it up at school. But you get it badly yourself, Bella, whenever you're run down."

"You've been using your mother's hairbrush, you naughty, naughty boy," Bo said. "*Both* heredity *and* environment—how can he help having dandruff?"

Gabriel without comment turned to leave the room. But Loraine said, "Aren't you going to admire your mother in her new dress?"

"It's great," Gabriel said expressionlessly. "I hope you have a good time at the party."

"And me," said Bo. "Don't you hope that I have a good time?"

"Of course," Gabriel said. But his eyes avoided those of Bo.

Thomas came into the room. "Sorry I'm late," he said. "There's just a chance that Tom Maulever of Edinburgh Press will be at the Alleyn and I wanted to find a letter I'd like to show him—"

Noticing the slightly loaded silence he glanced round inquiringly. "Anything wrong?"

"Not a thing," said Bella coldly. "Please feel free to take just as long as you like. What does it matter if we're late."

"Good night, my old cocksparrow," Thomas said to his stepson, rumpling up the hair that Bella had just smoothed down. "Have a good orgy of telly. Watch the Leeds match so you can tell me about it." Turning back to Bella he said, "We shan't be late. There's no traffic into town at this time of the evening; it won't take us more than fifteen minutes."

"And we all know, don't we," said Bo, "what an utterly safe and reliable driver our Thomas is."

This time he winked at Loraine; Thomas, with back turned, was helping Bella into her fur coat, which was Gus's last present remodelled; Thomas could not afford to give his wife fur coats.

"Well, I'm off home," said Loraine into the gap. "I made a pizza for your supper, Gabriel, it's in the oven. Come round to my house if there's anything you need."

"Thank you, Loraine. But I'm sure there won't be."

At the party Bella said to her brother, "What was the crack about Thomas's driving? He *is* a good driver. That's a thing one *can* say for him."

"Oh, just my fun," Bo said airily. "There's nothing wrong with old Thomas. Not a thing. One of nature's noblemen. Heart as big as all outdoors. I've taken to him like a duck to water."

They were standing by a wide counter which was covered all over with oysters on the half-shell. Bella, equipped with a tooth-pick, was eating the oysters at steady speed; Bo, watching her with an indulgent smile, impeded the attempts of other people to dislodge her from her advantageous position. In the hubbub of the crowd they talked to each other as if they were on a desert island.

"Anyway, *you* seemed just the tiniest bit acerbic with Thomas yourself, my sweet pincushion. What's the matter, he's not screwing you so capably?"

"It's hopeless, just hopeless," she said, short and vehement, spearing two oysters on her toothpick.

"Well, come on, have a heart, give him time, you've only been married a couple of years. The first seven are the worst. No, seriously, why don't you read aloud the Khama Sutra, or something? It's not like you to be at a loss, ducky. You want to work at it. Old Thomas isn't so bad—steady, kind-hearted, reliable; you could have done a hell of a lot worse; and now he's got himself a partnership in Crusoe and Selkirk and a seat on the board, there's the money angle too; he can keep an eye on Gus's books and see they stay in print, and he's automatically a trustee of the estate; as a professional man, Thomas is not to be despised. Honestly, my angel, it would just be an act of *criminal lunacy* to give old Thomas the push just because you don't hit it off a hundred per cent in bed."

She looked up quickly and caught the warning in his expression. "Well, I wish you'd talk to him," she said, half sulky, half pleading.

"My darling cuckoo! I am not a marriage guidance counsellor nor yet Evelyn Home's column. What's the trouble, is he impotent?"

"Not *exactly;* but he gets a lot of pain from his arthritis. Says he feels rotten half the time. *I* think it's psychological really. You know Gus was always a sort of God the Father to Thomas—and I believe he thinks he's sort of *profaning* me—"

Bo gave a snort of laughter. "Excuse me! Don't look so hurt, Sarsaparilla. But when I think— Well, never mind. Poor old Thomas. If only *he* could loosen up himself— have a little fling with somebody—like that handsome piece he's talking to now—it might do you both all the good in the world. Relieve tension at home—with young Gabriel too—what is there about you that's bugging *him* these days?—ease things up in every direction—"

Disregarding the malicious reference to Gabriel, which normally she would have pounced on, Bella swung round, and demanded, "Who is she? That girl Thomas is talking to?"

"Don't you remember? We saw her do Portia at the Aldwych a couple of years ago. And she was in some TV serial. Jan somebody. Wonder how Thomas comes to know her. He's a dark horse, old Thomas; you want to keep an eye on him. Well, my love, *you*'ve eaten enough oysters to sink the *Ark Royal,* and *I* want to circulate, so I'll see you later."

He was gone, into the shifting crowd.

Bella began to make her way with determination towards her husband. But halfway across the room she was brought up short by a hand on her arm.

"Bella! Long time no see! By Jove, you're looking marvelous! What have you been doing with yourself?"

She turned to face a short, spruce-looking man whose neatly trimmed dark beard gave him a vaguely naval appearance; as also did the blazer he wore. A handkerchief folded into a triangle was tucked with exact symmetry into his breast pocket and his cuffs dazzled; a telescope under his arm would have completed the ensemble. But the large puffy pouches under his pale-grey eyes had probably not come from staring at marine horizons.

"Oh, hullo Arthur," Bella said without warmth. "How are you?"

He went on holding her arm, looking her up and down. "What a transformation. Yum yum! Good enough to eat. Little Bella! I was just thinking of you the other day, saying to old Peter, 'I wonder how little Bella's getting on? Ought to look her up.' Remember those jolly afternoons we used to have, the three of us? Ah," he sighed reminiscently, "those were the days. I've missed your cheery little presence, d'you know that? Missed you a whole lot."

"Oh what rubbish, Arthur," she said coldly. "I bet you've been doing very well for yourself. You certainly look it." And she returned his warm, assessing gaze with a chill and measured stare.

"Nope. Nope. I've missed you. And so has Peter. Often wished we could have a tiny reunion. Often said so."

"Well, you had only to pick up the phone," she said, offhand. "I don't remember your being so eager and helpful to come round just after Gus died, however."

Avoiding her eye he said hastily, "Oh well, you were in

a bad way just then, weren't you? It wouldn't have been the best of taste, would it? Not the time for fun and games. . . . Old Pete felt the same way. Very sorry for you and all that, of course. But I mean, when somebody's bereaved—"

"When somebody's bereaved is just the time they can do with a bit of company and comfort."

"Well, that's the time for the family to step in, isn't it, old thing? And you had the boy—how *is* he, by the way, all right?—and you had your brother. I see *he's* still got his Russian friend James Whosis. Kuriakin. Just like Hector and the faithful Whatshisname, aren't they, that pair?"

Bella followed his eye to a corner of the room where Bo, leaning against he wall, cigarette dangling, talked to a cadaverous man with a shock of white-gold hair who appeared to be lecturing him with one hand grasping his blue-velvet lapel.

"Ah, he's a character, that brother of yours," said Arthur, tolerant. "A clever one, mind you. But too deep for me. Most of what he says passes right over *my* head. Well, it takes all sorts, as I always say. Live and let live. One man's mate is another man's pass-on. But now listen—hey, Bella, are you attending?"

Bella brought her expressionless gaze back to his face.

"What say we all three get together again one afternoon quite soon? How'd that be, eh? Why not? I can answer for old Peter, he'll be raring to go as soon as I tell him I've seen you; we could have a bite of lunch, at Rules, say, and I've got a new automobile that I think you'll approve, a Crespina, the '70 model with the aerodynamic spoiler and the rev counter. Yellow, with grey tweed—Hey? What d'you say? Shall I tell old Peter to get out his brace and tackle?"

"Not Rules," she said. "My husband sometimes lunches there. . . . Perhaps. I'll think about it. I'll call you. I've got to go and talk to my husband now, goodbye."

"Which one is he? Over there, talking to the telly gal? Not a bad-looking chap. Did quite well for yourself, eh? Hey!" he said, overtaken by a further notion. "You don't suppose *he'd* fancy joining us? Is he one for larks?"

"No," said Bella shortly, and walked away through the crowd, which was beginning to thin out.

Coming up to Thomas she slid a hand under his arm.

She was aware of the violent start he gave when she touched him, almost as if she had woken him out of deep sleep, out of some profound, involving dream. The face he turned to her was very pale, though he smiled and said:

"Hullo, darling. Are you having a good time? What a lot of people you seem to know. Jan, let me introduce my wife," he said to the girl. "Bella. Miss Jan MacArthur."

"Oh yes of course," Bella said cordially. "I saw you in *The Merchant of Venice*. My brother took me. We both thought you were marvellous."

"Thank you," the girl said.

A slightly blank silence fell which Thomas filled by saying something about the production. Conversation, rather stilted, began to flow again. Bella meanwhile took covert stock of the girl. How could anyone, she thought, be an actress when they looked so uncompromisingly Scotch? Those freckles, those cheekbones! A face that might have been carved from some bit of wood that had paled and weathered on a Highland moor, where her ancestors probably assembled to sing hymns and read the Bible aloud in pouring rain. She'd be all right cast as Lady Macbeth, Bella thought, and it was true she wasn't bad as hair-splitting Portia, but I can't exactly see her in a Nöel Coward comedy. Striking-looking, yes, she is in a way, but much too tall of course; there must be lots of men who won't play opposite her. Taller than Thomas, a bit. . . . At least she has the sense to wear plain black. I wonder if she's always so pale?

"Thomas darling, I truly think it's time we went home, don't you? That's what I really came to say. I'm beginning to wilt on my feet. It's been so nice meeting you," she said to the girl. "I hope we see you again in something soon. Are you in a part at the moment? Oh no, of course not, or you wouldn't be here, would you, how silly I am. Well, we must look out for you. . . . I'll meet you in the hall in five minutes, then, darling; I'll tell Bo we're leaving."

Nodding to the girl, she went off to the ladies' to collect her coat.

When she emerged into the hall she found Bo there anchored against the stair rail amidst the drift of departing guests.

"Hullo," he greeted Bella. "Thomas has gone to fetch

his car; he'll be back in minute. He asked me to tell you."

"Thoughtful of him," she said mechanically. "I'll be glad to get off my feet, won't you? Bo, that girl, that Jan MacArthur, what do you know about her—"

A voice, so close by her ear that it made her jump said, "Bye-bye, Bella my sweet. See you next week or the week after. I'll give you a ring. Tootle-tootle."

Bo, glancing with concentrated dislike after Arthur's retreating back, said, "If you take up with that creep again, my girl, you'll be making a very big mistake; I'm telling you. Thomas wouldn't stand for that sort of nonsense. He's a tolerant, broad-minded, easy-going fellow, but he's not *that* tolerant."

"Oh don't be so silly," Bella said irritably. "Besides, there's no need for him to know."

"Thomas is no fool."

"Anyway, what business is it of yours, pray?"

"My dear girl, all I'm saying is, I won't guarantee to pull you out of any more messes. It isn't my life-work to prop you up."

"No, sometimes it's the reverse," she retorted bitterly. "Anyway you were saying yourself, not an hour ago, that it would do Thomas good to have a little fling. What's the difference . . . ?"

"We know that once you get off the rails, my lamb-chop, you make anything Thomas might do look like a glass of lemonade and a game of tiddleywinks with the Mother Superior. Do I have to spend all our time together warning you? It's so boring."

He looked down at her under his eyelids.

"*Oh*—" She flipped and unflipped the catch of her evening bag, exasperated, uncertain, but aware of the threat in his tone.

"Bo? Are you ready?" The tall, pale-haired man came up behind Bo and tapped him on the shoulder. "Hullo, Bella," he said. "We haven't had a word all evening." He spoke with a very faint foreign accent.

"Nor we have," she said coolly. "How are you, James?"

"Fine. And you?"

"Fine."

"I hear you are married again; congratulations. I haven't met your husband—"

"I don't think you'd have anything in common."

138

"Oh come, sweetie," Bo said mildly. "James is a chemist; Thomas is a biologist; they would probably chatter on for hours. Don't be so dogmatic."

Nobody seemed to have anything to add. James said to Bo:

"Okay, my dear? Shall we take our departure?"

"Bo?" Bella said. "Aren't you coming back with us?"

"No, I'm going on to a porno film with James: *Candle at Both Ends*. Say good night to Thomas for me and thanks for the ride." Over his shoulder as they walked towards the entrance, Bo said, "Maybe you should take *him* to a few porno movies."

Bella was silent for the first half of the drive back to Wanborough with Thomas. Then she said:

"When did you know that girl?"

He waited a moment or two, then answered in a colourless tone, "Before I knew you."

"Were you in love with her?"

In the same tone he replied, "I thought so at the time, yes."

"When did you break up?"

"Before I met you," Thomas repeated.

"Why? What happened?"

He said slowly, "Well, it was a bit of a muddle. It's never been quite clear to me really. You see I was having one of my first really bad attacks just then, and Liddy had put me on a high dosage of Najdolene for the first time. I'd never taken it before. It affects some people's behaviour very much—particularly at first—and apparently it did mine. Made me alternately moody and euphoric."

"And couldn't she take it?" Bella's interest was caught, in spite of her dislike for the girl; her tone was a degree more lively.

"Well apparently I did something she couldn't forgive —the odd thing is, I've never been able to remember what it was, exactly, that precipitated the bust-up."

"You mean to say you didn't *ask* her, this evening? Was it the first time you've met, since?" she inquired sharply.

"It was, yes."

"Well, I should certainly have asked her, like a shot."

"I couldn't. You see she was telling me that her mother, of whom she was very fond, had recently died. Her mother was blind for years, and had a flat in the

139

same block as Jan; at one time there was a suggestion they should live together but apparently Mrs. MacArthur said she didn't want to be a drag on Jan. Well, she finally fell off the fire-escape; the verdict was 'accidental.' But Jan thinks otherwise. I've sometimes wondered if whatever it was—whatever I did that Jan couldn't forgive—was anything to do with old Mrs. MacArthur. Jan wasn't one to be touchy on her own account."

"Well she seems to have forgiven you now. She seemed quite friendly."

"Yes."

Bella remarked in a light, brisk voice, "So, in a way, your bust-up was all a mistake, what a pity. What a shame you can't go back to her now."

"Quite apart from my own commitments," he said, "it would be out of the question. She wouldn't have me now."

"Why not, pray?"

"Various reasons. One is that her eyesight's going. She was telling me. She's got the same thing her mother had, they've discovered."

Bella said with explosive impatience, feeling this was all a bit *much*, "So what? Aren't there parts for blind actresses?"

"Some, I suppose. And there's always radio. She'll manage. She's very proud and independent, like her mother. She'll make out."

"Poor Thomas," Bella said spitefully. "Yet another lame duck you'd like to rescue and cherish as a way of buying your way into somebody's affection. It's too bad you're stuck already with me."

There was silence between them as he drove down the long straight of Wanborough Parkside. Bella felt rage building up inside her; she looked out at the passing streetlamps, at the long stretches of dark wooded common; she would have liked to smash her knuckles against the window glass. Rage against what, against whom? Against all of them, the fools! She suddenly thought of Sadie, throwing the battery radio through the window into Addison Gardens, and burst out laughing.

"What's so funny?" said Thomas, startled. They were just passing the zebra crossing with its winking orange lights; he looked at her in perplexity.

"Oh, nothing!" she snapped, thinking, as he drove through the gateway, how boring and undistinguished his profile was compared with that of Gus. *He*'d done all right for himself, had Thomas, marrying her, picking up all her interesting and distinguished connections. "Nothing that *you*'d think funny. Just something I remembered. Gus might have appreciated it. Oh god," she exclaimed, geting out of the car, "oh *god*, how I wish Gus was here now."

"So do I," said Thomas quietly. He locked the car and followed her indoors.

From upstairs, inappropriately cheerful, came the sound of Gabriel's television.

Seven

Gabriel 1974

He woke in the night, lonely for Catriona. They had decided some weeks ago to stop making love because she said, "It might kill you sooner, and I'd so much rather have you alive as long as possible." But her absence felt as if part of him had died already.

"It's going to happen sooner or later. You'll have to get used to the idea."

"I know. What's going to happen about your body? Bodies are such awkward, undisposable things. Even worse than old mattresses. Like old clothes that you can't quite bear to throw away. You love them, but there's nothing you can do with them."

"I used to feel that way about dead hedgehogs; do you remember what a lot we used to find along Wanborough Parkside and how miserable they used to make us? There's terribly little you can do with a dead hedgehog, except bury it."

"Well, that's one thing you can say for New York; not many dead hedgehogs in the streets."

This conversation had left him thinking, and he had telephoned the science faculty at Harvard and, after a little initial misunderstanding, had arranged to leave them his body, and added a clause to that effect onto his will (already written out on a printed will form obtained from a stationer's before he left England). He now wore a disc on his wrist which, in his careful italic handwriting, said, "This body belongs to Harvard Science Dept." with a telephone number. The will, signed and witnessed, had been posted to the New York office of Crusoe and Selkirk, with a polite request that they should keep the envelope for him, unopened, until he came to claim it, or they had other instructions.

"So that's all taken care of," he said to Catriona.

"Is a will valid before you're eighteen?"

"I'm not sure; the man I called up at Harvard said I ought to do it properly through a lawyer. But I didn't want to do that because I'd have to give him my address. But anyway they're bound to respect the body bit. So you won't have to worry about that. You just phone Harvard and they'll come and fetch it. It's rather good. Makes me feel free; like taking off shoes and going barefoot. I'd like to be free of everything possible."

"Even love?"

"Even love, in the end."

"I don't think I'm going to like their going off with your body," she said.

"Well, you can put a wreath of daisies round my neck first."

"Comb the dandruff out of your hair for the last time. Wash the neck." And she had looked him over thoughtfully, her small face unsmiling. Catriona rarely smiled, though many of her remarks were tinged with a certain sardonic dryness.

He turned over restlessly, longing for the comfort of her wiry, skinny little arms round his neck, her thin leg hooked over his; they had been accustomed to lie as closely entangled as nasturtium stems and, lacking the physical closeness and companionship, his dreams, he remembered, had all been of wide, lonely places—a little wooden hut, its floor green with weed from the high tide, on the edge of some huge reedy marsh where the sea came and went. "Look, Thomas, those are bulrushes." "So they are; and the others are matador-rushes." "How do you know?" "Because we are in the Camargue." "How do you know?" "Because of the flamingoes; you can hear them having a Camargument over there." Crazy logic of sleep, that seems so rational at the time.

"I had such a silly dream, Catriona." But of course she was not there; have to get used to that though.

The grave's a fine and private place, but none, I think, do there embrace. Or, on the other hand, There some pair of lovers lies, Who thought by this device to make a stay, and meet again at the last, busie day? It would be comfortable to believe that, but I don't. I wonder if it will be *lonely?* I never used to think so; always looked on death as the last, most comfortable rest; but lately I've begun to wonder. Perhaps one could somehow leave messages for oneself—a series of signposts, charting the way into the void? I'll tie this bit of string on to a tree in Washington Square; or perhaps the tree itself will do for a message.

I wonder why it is that I always wake so happy from my dreams? I always know that I have come from beautiful places full of light: landscapes in radiant clear colours, or old, friendly houses, well-known to me though none exactly corresponds to the real house of memory—and so many people always—countless warm-hearted friends who affectionately accompany me from one dream to another—who can all these kindly companions be, far more than I've ever known in my life, where have they all come from?

Are they the people whom I would have known if I had lived out the rest of my life?

He could hear a snuffle, and a whimper, as the dog woke, stretched, uncurled, and stood, and padded round in a circle, it's toenails clicking on the bare boards, before settling to sleep again. The dog was a kind of company.

Living with another person instead of being on your own, he thought, his mind going back to Catriona, takes a different adjustment from what one would expect. You have to learn to be more selfish instead of less. When you are alone, you constantly study the other people in the world, you spend immense amounts of time and energy in performing services for other people, remembering trivial facts about them and turning them to account; but once you have a companion, all that is put aside, living becomes more self-oriented and faster-paced. That's wrong, really.

It will be good for me to be alone again. Those two months travelling from west to east taught me something important. You need to be alone to grow.

"You'll be just fine on your own." That was the father talking to his little boy, overheard when we'd been for the walk to Battery Park and were waiting to cross the

143

road. "You'll go to granny's by *one* subway and you'll come home by a *different* subway. Won't that be exciting?" And the boy was looking wholly unconvinced, and I thought, the difficulty that parents have in persuading their children about any new experience is now complicated by the fact that they have to compete with commerical advertising. That father is making his voice as full of false cheer and enthusiasm as the man who says his insurance company will look after you like a mother, and the boy's used to ignoring them both. I suppose twenty years ago the father could just have said, It'll be all right, you'll see. Maybe the son wouldn't have beieved him even then. But now he knows not to expect the truth from anybody. However agreeable.

What can one tell children? It's just as well I shan't have any. If I'm really Bella's child, that's no sort of heredity to pass on. And everything points to my being her child: this peculiar flakiness of our scalp-skin seems too similar to be a coincidence; much more likely to be hereditary. I've been away from her now for nine months and I still have it. How I used to hate it after Gus's death where she wouldn't wash her hair for months on end and just let it hang down her back in a scurfy tangle, and cried whenever his name was mentioned; I felt she'd destroyed my memories of him, overlaid them with her vulgarised, dramatised ones.

She wanted to make him into a kind of saint, a hero; he wasn't that; just a wise man.

If only Thomas and I—

Thomas and Catriona would have got on all right. I wonder what she'd think of him? She and Thomas do the same things with words, they can take off from the ground in the same way. Bella never could stand that. "What do you *mean*?" she was always demanding irritably, she couldn't bear it when we were fooling around with puns and spoonerisms. "Really Thomas, how silly can you get," she said angrily when he came home announcing that he was going on that six-month cruise. The Faction, the Miological Fin-bonding Fashion, the Facto-started fooling around with the Fishological Mind-buying Biological Fact-finding Mission, he called it, and we logical Boy-minding Fission.

I wasn't sure if her anger was directed at our fooling or the fact that he was going away.

We were in the garden, I was sweeping up leaves from the walnut tree into barrow-loads and taking them to the bonfire, going and coming. It was one of those windy, clear September days.

"Having bought your way into Crusoe and Selkirk I should have thought the least you could do was to stay and keep an eye on it," she said. And he said:

"Crusoe and Selkirk are back on an even keel. John Voynitch is doing a very good job, as I thought he would, and everything will run perfectly smoothly for six months. Don't begrudge me this trip, Bella. It's something I've wanted to do all my life."

"All you're really doing is imitating Gus. Trying to imitate him. It's all you ever do. You've pushed your way into his house, and into his bed, and you fiddle about with publishing his books, and now you want to pretend to do the same kind of research."

I thought how odd it was that the things she said should have such an appearance of blunt mind-speaking, and yet be so false in essence. Thomas looked deeply hurt but kept calm as he always did.

"No, really, it's quite different, Bella," he began to explain in a patient voice, and then I went off with my barrowful of leaves, and when I came back next he was saying:

"I wish you wouldn't speak to me in that tone, Bella. I've done as good a job as I can."

"You call it a good job going off and leaving me for six months?" she cried out.

"As I said before, why don't you come too? I think you'd enjoy it, I really do."

"Pottering down the African coast, putting in at every smelly little port, hanging around while you dredge up old shells and plants? No thank *you*." And she added, "Besides, who'd look after Gabriel?"

I said, "I could board at school," which I'd always wanted to try, but she said that was a ridiculous idea, quite out of the question, they wouldn't know how to take care of me properly. Thomas began to look tired, as he always does when she uses my health as a lever in their arguments, and said:

"He's fourteen, Bella, and very sensible. I don't think there'd be any problem. And he could fly out and join us at Christmas. You'd quite enjoy that, wouldn't you, Gabriel?"

I said, "Yes, I'd like to see Africa," and Thomas went on cajolingly:

"Wouldn't *you* like to see it, Bella? You could do all sorts of drawings of palm trees and tropical birds. Wouldn't you like to draw from nature for once in a way? I should have thought it would be just your cup of tea."

"Oh don't be so idiotic. How can I possibly get away? There's the house to look after, and what about all my commissioned jobs?"

"Loraine would look after the house, and you could do your jobs just as well on the boat. Very likely better."

Bo came wandering round the house. That was in the days when he and Thomas were still quite friendly and he often used to drop in on a Saturday evening to watch football on our TV; it was the time he was painting his weird football pictures.

"I'm trying to persuade Bella to come on the cruise," Thomas said.

Bo had flopped down in a deckchair. He was wearing his dirty old khaki pants, covered in paint, and the thin black sweater that he always had on, winter or summer; the sun was really warm and he seemed half asleep. But when Thomas said that, he opened his eyes and said, "What a wizard idea!" in the old boys'-magazine language he uses a lot. "Absolutely top-hole. Bang on! Spiffing! You'll go, of course, Bella?"

"Are you crazy?" she said, sounding more disgruntled than ever.

"It would be like a second honeymoon," Bo said, rolling his eyes about with a kind of lovesick simper, and he began to sing:

> *I'll love you more, I'll love you most*
> *a-sailing down the Ivory Coast*
> *I'll never be unkind or selfish*
> *if you will come and hunt for shellfish*
> *we'll stroll the deck from dawn to dark*
> *and toss a crust to every shark*
> *on tropic sands we'll copulate*
> *if you will come and be my mate!*

146

and, either really enthusiastic, or pretending to be, he jumped up, shouting, "Avast there! Belay the main brace!" and started tossing handfuls of leaves about, scattering all the ones I'd just swept up.

"Oh, don't be so stupid, Boney," Bella said. "You don't really think it's a good idea, do you?"

"I think it's such a magnificent idea," he said, "that if you don't go with Thomas, *I* probably shall."

"You're not serious?"

"Serious? I'm as serious as the Sermon on the Mount. I'm as serious as the Declaration of Human Rights. I'm as serious as the UNESCO Constitution." And he darted off indoors—when Bo runs, which he doesn't more than about once a year, he's so skinny that he can go like the wind—declaiming, "Since war begins in the minds of men, it is on the minds of men that we must drop our biggest bombs. Come on Thomas, or you'll be late for the kick-off."

That man we saw last week on the Morton Street pier, the drunk man far off in the distance, he could easily have been Bo: tall and skinny, either drunk or high on something, doing a grave solitary dance all the way down the middle of the wide, wooden expanse, skipping, bowing, and curtsying to an imaginary partner. I suddenly had a feeling of grief and affection for Bo; I wished I could have been nicer to him. I could remember the exact tone of his voice, thin, high, and exasperated, saying:

"I'm in love with you, you stupid little fool, don't you see?"

And my reaction, a mixture of alarm and a tired feeling that I just couldn't manage this scene; like being presented with a big, awkward fragile expensive gift that I couldn't use and didn't want.

Poor Bo. I wonder where he is now. Maybe the man was him. Just to be on the safe side I went away fast; though I don't know what *he*'d be doing over here. When I went to see the unicorn tapestries last winter I wished that Bo could have been there too; though perhaps he would have poked fun at them, as he does at everything?

I'd like to have those tapestries to live with. Like to have seen them again.

Stupid. No use plaguing oneself with that kind of useless wish.

Catriona would say, Well, we could plague ourselves just a *little*, half-shutting her eyes in the way she does at something that would make another person smile. Gus used to tease her; he used to say she had an expression like a cat collecting spit before it starts washing. It's funny she doesn't remember him very well; she remembers places and things, not people. She just remembers that she liked him; the feeling she had about him. "He was golden, like bread and honey."

Practical, she always is.

"Look, there's a whole box of brandy glasses someone's throwing out," I said one day outside our house. There they were on the sidewalk in a carton—big balloon glasses, dusty, some broken but quite a few in good shape. "Shall we take them in?"

"What would we do with them?"

"Well, if we had a big mansion in California they'd be just right for drinking brandy."

"I don't want a big mansion in California," she said.

"Well then we'll have to drink Coke out of the glasses."

"Perhaps we'd better just leave them here."

Next time we went out they were gone. Catriona says you could furnish a whole house from the New York pavements and I guess she's right. Watch the streets long enough, you'll find anything you need. Or you can get rid of anything you want to jettison. I wish I could just put my body out there for someone to take. I'm sure death is really very good—like taking off your hot sweaty clothes and being free and cool at last, weightless and strong, like those dreams of swimming, of flying. That story where her dead husband came back to the window and held out his hand. "Don't be afraid. When I say *now*, just jump." It used to fascinate me. I don't really fear the prospect of death, itself, at all. It's just the awkwardness of the process. That python in the London Zoo, lying on a branch, scraping, scraping, scraping off its old skin, like somebody without hands trying to take off an all-over stocking. It was a terribly long, exhausting job. I stood there for over two hours, watching, longing to help. At last it was done, a snake and a ghost-snake were both twined in the tree. The real snake seemed just as dead as the skin, tired out. If death is as tiring as that, what happens when we recover from it?

It's not knowing *when* that fidgets me. Like that game, Old Witch, where you wait, trembling, for somebody to steal up and grab you from behind. I used to play it with Thomas, in the garden, and once he quoted me the bit from *The Ancient Mariner* about the man who turns no more his head, because he knows a frightful fiend doth close behind him tread.

I wish that Thomas and I—

Cockroach running over my hand. Cockroaches here are getting very large and venturesome. That was a real old bull-roach. Like Archy. I wonder if they know something is going to happen? Like rats on sinking ship? I wonder whether we have made cockroaches feel *guilt?* If not, why are they always in such a frantic, furtive hurry when spotted? I've read somewhere that we managed to put guilt into dogs and cats. Doesn't seem something to be proud of. Doesn't help them lead better, more constructive lives. What would be a constructive life for a cockroach, though? What do cockroaches do? Build nests, have communities, spin webs? Gus would know. Or do they just run about and lay their eggs and mind their own business? I suppose they are scavengers. More useful than us, really. We make a mess, cockroaches clear it up. But not fast enough; we need bigger and better roaches. I read that in Australia they have no insects to clear up the cattle-dung; no cattle in Australia till two hundred years ago, no dung beetles. So cow pats baked hard as granite are piling up and up. They brought some dung beetles from Africa, but toads ate them. God must get very fed up with our meddling.

The hot summer night pressed on him like a cushion. He remembered summer nights long ago, sleeping out under the walnut tree on an air-bed.

And that summer when Gus and I came over here and stayed with grannie; a man called Tom Thum lent Gus his mill and we spent a couple of weeks in it.

I always remembered the man's name because he was a big simple friendly giant, not a bit what I'd expected.

He came and showed us how to work the pump and light the oil-stove, then we didn't see him again the whole time we were there.

I wonder where Bella was that summer? Perhaps she'd gone off somewhere with Bo?

A man came by with a truck full of his own fruit that he'd brought all the way from California; we bought huge red apples and pink grapefruit and plums as bit as cricket balls and a crate of oranges and just lived on fruit. There was a beautiful stream with a mill-race, and a millpond just big enough to swim in, and Gus let me swim by moonlight every night. That was the best time in my life. I wonder where that place was? I'd love to go back there. . . . I spent the whole of every day playing and swimming in the stream, building dams, and islands, flating nut-shell boats, making harbours for them, getting back into the pool and swimming again. I was six.

Gus wanted to write something; he stayed up in the lofts of the mill, he said it was an excellent place to work. I had expected he'd be with me more, and was a little disappointed at first, but he said it was too good an opportunity to waste, and the stream was such company for me that I wasn't in the least lonely; anyway Gus used to come down at lunchtime and again in the evening to look at all I'd been doing and make suggestions, so I was happy all day long in the expectation of his arrival. And then when he came it was every bit as good as good as I'd expected. I wonder what he was writing that summer?

I can still remember every inch of that place, the rocks by the stream, and the black walnut tree and the big straggly grove of wild plum, and the locusts and little oaks and birches, and the chickadees that we fed until they were so tame they would sit on Gus's head, and the chipmunks, not so tame, and the day I went to sleep on the grass and woke to find a big snake fast asleep beside me; I left the ground all in one piece, as if I'd been thrown up by an earth-tremor, and the snake shot off, probably even more frightened than I was.

I wonder if that mill is still there?

A pallor was creeping into the window-square of sky. He sat up and pulled his black portfolio towards him, found a piece of unused paper, and wrote,

Down the broad flood of light
birds scatter loose their songs, pent up by night;
daunted by solitude and hush they cry
all their small story of knowledge to the sky

Eight

Thomas 1974

Thomas sat in the hot little dusty bathroom. In his ear still buzzed, like a menacing hornet, the tones, gritty, rasping, slightly foreign, of the voice issuing its cold instructions. He was trembling so violently that he thought, I shan't be able to hear the phone if it rings again. He was sweating, too, like a horse, his heart thumped, his blood throbbed in his ears. His bowels had turned to slime. It's lucky they didn't tell me to do anything today, observed the wry inward monitor that stood apart and dispassionately observed all these manifestations of rage and terror. Pretty useless I should be.

But the voice had said, Do nothing until we get in touch with you again. Just get the money ready. Tell nobody. In any case, who could I tell? The police? Probably disastrous. Bella? God knows what idiotic public hue-and-cry she'd initiate: her TV and radio appeals have been bad enough. Lucky she's only done a couple so far. I'll have to warn her to lay off those?

What about old Hannah? Ought she to be told?

I'd get more sensible advice from her than I would from Bella, but one couldn't burden her with it anyway, not the way she is now. Not the way she was this afternoon.

The old face looking up from the pillow. White skin transparent as tissue, huge hollow eye-sockets, like some death mask, but still activated by a spirit inside, which seemed as disengaged from its bony casket as the genie from the bottle. The spirit still made the eyes turn and focus, the voice formulate words, even fetched up a ghostly chuckle as she contemplated her own disabilities.

151

"I look a proper shambles, don't I? Oh, dear, dear, old age is a ludicrous condition. I'm often thankful for my son August that he avoided it; at least he escaped with his dignity intact. If, as some of my grandson's friends assert, we are all going to be reincarnated, I shall tell Gus, next time we meet, that he got off very lightly. . . ."

The change in her was shocking; it made Thomas realise afresh that, narrow as is the division between health and incapacity at any time, in old age it is literally no more than the distance between one breath and the next.

"Knocked down in the street," Hattie told him bitterly "Mugged by some big lout who wanted cash for his next fix. Took her purse. Eight dollars; if that. She got a bash that would have cracked anyone else's head like an egg. I will say for Mrs. Baird, she's tough; hobbled back home and she's not even concussed. But she's real sick; I guess when Dr. Warmflash comes he'll want to get her to the hospital, but she said she wanted to see you first."

In spite of her physical frailty, in spite of the great black bruise down the side of her face, the old lady seemed just as much in command of her faculties as on the last occasion when he had seen her, two weeks ago. More so, indeed. It was as if all the remaining powers had been concentrated into a single glowing point.

"Mr. Cook," the blue lips whispered. "Come quite close, I want to be sure it's you. You need not be afraid that I am going to assault you,"—drily—"Besides we have Hattie here for a chaperon."

"Don't you fret yourself now, Mrs. Baird. Dr. Warmflash said take it easy till he came. Oh, I could *shake* you, going out like that by yourself—I'd have done any errand for you, you know you had only to ask—"

"Don't be absurd, Hattie—and don't interrupt. I went to warn the little girl. And you couldn't have done that, because you were out both times she came here and you don't know what she looks like. Gabriel brought her to see me once," Mrs. Baird said to Thomas, "and once I went round with him to have lunch at the place where she works. Rather noisy music, I remember thinking, but otherwise not at all disagreeable. Quite clean and pleasant. The only time, to my recollection, that I have ever attempted to eat a *hero sandwich*. . . . I suspect they are not really intended for humans to eat. Boa constrictors, possibly. You need the kind of jaw that unhinges at will."

Thomas felt a little unhinged himself. "Mrs. Baird? You mentioned a little girl. Would that be some friend of Gabriel's, who might know where he is?"

In total dark even a tiny spark seems like brilliant illumination; he felt his whole being suddenly irradiated with hope.

"Such a nice child," whispered Mrs. Baird. "Daughter of a colleague of Gus who worked with him at University College back in the sixties. Family stayed in England for five years. The gal went to the American school over there; she and Gabriel made great friends. Catriona Vanaken; her father is a physicist. When he came over here he got in touch with her. Going to music school. Plays the flute."

"Where does she live?" Thomas tried to compress his impatience within bearable limits. "Do you think she might know where Gabriel has got to?"

"Now look here," whispered Mrs. Baird. "The reason why I wanted to find that nice little gal was for *her* sake. Nothing to do with Gabriel. I happened to notice when she left the house after bringing me the note that a man seemed to be *following* her. So it was my plain duty to warn her. Fairly sure I'd be able to recognise the restaurant where she worked, you see, if I saw it again; it was somewhere down south of Washington Square, not very far—"

"Did you find it? Did you warn her?"

"*No,* my dear man; that's the most aggravating part of the whole affair. That fool had to go and knock me down before I got there, and broke my long-distance glasses; of course I knew that without my glasses I'd never recognise the place. It was hopeless. Indeed I found it quite a problem even to grope my way home, but on the *whole* people were helpful—"

"Who knocked you down? This man who was following the girl?"

"No, *no;* just some big stupid boy who ran off with my purse; he could have had it without bashing me into the bargain. He's of no consequence; he ran off and I doubt if I'd recognise him. But the man, I think I *should* know again; I've seen him in this neighbourhood once or twice. Tall, with a face like a Welsh collie. And white hair."

The description stirred a vague recollection in Thomas

153

from way back, but he was concerned with more urgent matters.

"Mrs. Baird, you say this is Catriona—"

"Such a suitable name." The chuckle came again; Mrs. Baird's teeth, much discoloured by age, but large, firm, and all her own, showed in a reminiscent smile of pure affectionate pleasure. "When Gabriel first brought her he said, 'Grannie, I want to introduce you to someone straight out of one of your favourite novels.' He was quite right. Stevenson could have invented her. 'Steel-true and blade-straight,' as they used to say of heroines in my young days, 'with eyes of grey glass.' "

Thomas felt an exquisite thrill of pure grief touch his heart. So one might have spoken of Jan. . . . But it was no use remembering Jan. His duty was to the boy.

"You say she brought you a note? Was it from Gabriel?"

"Do you know—as I grow older—" Mrs. Baird was off at a tangent again. "Everything I see becomes *more and more beautiful*. Isn't that an excellent arrangement? Oh, physical discomfort, of course, there's that to put up with, but that can be tolerated. Tolerated, you see, because of this *mysterious beauty* in absolutely everything all around. Why, I can lie in this bed *perfectly* contented, looking at the beautiful shadows on the ceiling and in the corners of the room for hours together. And the view of Twelfth Street from my window! I sit there in the armchair— The houses are so elegantly proportioned, and the trees and light are so completely satisfactory, that I *constantly* think how lucky I am to be here. That was how I came to be looking out when I saw the man following her."

"Catriona?"

"You should pronounce it Catrina," she corrected him. "That is a mistake no Scot would make. I understand that her forebears were Scotch and Dutch. Of course a good many Stuart supporters did escape to the Netherlands. . . ."

"The note she brought . . . ?"

"And that pair—Gabriel and Catriona—do you know, they seem to me to move in a *golden cloud* of youth and integrity and grace. Grace from on high, I mean, of course; even the most partial observer would have to admit that Gabriel is physically clumsy. And rather plain. But such a dear little boy always, I was so *pleased* when he told me that he had been adopted—a thing it had never occurred to Gus to mention needless to say—because that precluded the least necessity for trying to find any resemblance to that mother of his. Of whom the less said the better. 'Don't you mind at all, Grannie,' he said, 'that I'm not your true grandson?' 'My dearest child,' I said, 'you are my spiritual grandson, which is a much better bond.' "

"When— You have seen Gabriel this summer, then?"

She looked up at Thomas, frowning vaguely. "Did I say I had not? No doubt I wasn't sure at first whether to trust you. Oh dear yes, he was in and out quite a bit at the beginning of the summer. Now I have to trust you because I have a message for you. Mr. Cook—Thomas —that boy must be *left alone*."

"But, Mrs. Baird—"

"Hattie, where did you put the note?"

Hattie, who had been sitting grimly at her mistress's left hand, pushed her metal-rimmed spectacles up her nose and opened a cedar-wood box on the bedside table.

"Shall I give it to Mr. Cook?" she said, taking out a letter.

"Yes, do; he may just as well read it all."

Gabriel's handwriting was a firm, black, upright script, which he had deliberately modelled on medieval calligraphy. Although it looked elaborate it was clear to read and surprisingly rapid in execution; Thomas remembered seeing Gabriel write school essays with astonishing speed, covering page after page with the black crabbed symbols almost as fast as if he were using shorthand. Gus had written in the same script; there were notebooks in the library full of it.

My darling Grannie:
   i am afraid i may not have a chance to see you again. you were so very understanding about my choosing not to live that i am sure you will be equally so about this. i do so very much want to finish the thing that i am writing, and i do not know how much time is left me but probably not a lot, so i have to use it in writing. i'm sad not to see you but please don't you be sad. actually i think you are too sensible! you know that you are one of my two favourite people in the world and even if i don't come to see

you you're the one i respect most of all because you
have truly high standards of behaviour and i've never
seen you slip from them even for a minute. well, if
our friend indira is right we may all meet again as
doves or something in another incarnation. and if we
don't, i can hear you saying that the important thing
is that we loved each other in this one. although
you're over ninety and i'm only just sixteen it's surprising how often our views coincide. you don't think
that individuals, as such, are necessarily important.
and nor do i. some are, of course, like gus, but one
of him was enough. and i would never be like him.
i just want to say one thing, and when i have said it,
i would really rather leave; i do not think it is worth
a lot of money and other people's trouble to keep me
in an environment where i feel such a square peg.
almost everything that happens seems to me so false
and wrong and contrary to good sense that it is like
living in a kind of mad cartoon. nobody means harm,
perhaps—but the harm they do! i've been thinking
about thomas. i'm afraid he will mind my dying because he was fond of me, but will you please ask him
to think very hard about it and perhaps he can learn
some lesson from it. i don't think bella will mind very
much, i don't honestly think she was too fond of me,
but please try to discourage her from making a terrible fuss. she will be all right for money. i know because i went to see worters and cholmondelay before
i left england and they said she goes on getting an
income from father's money as long as she lives. after i die all the rest of the estate goes to scientific
and sociological research which is much the best use
for it.

i suppose it is possible that thomas might want me
to change my mind and have the operation—i know
he thinks life is important—so to save you trouble,
grannie, i'm not putting my address on this. in any
case i'm just going to move.

i love you a lot and if we meet again in the elysian
fields what fun we shall have. we'll be able to play
bezique like we used to and have more talks.

love gabriel

Oh, the little wretch, the little prig! was Thomas's first conscious reaction. To put such a thing on his old grandmother! How could he? But then, looking at the face which had been studying his as he read, he realised that she was perfectly equal to it. Ninety-five years, carefully spent, can be a sound investment.

"Now, my dear Thomas, I want you to be sensible about this, if you please! For a start, no histrionics, they tire me out. What a mercy that egregious ass, Bella, is on the other side of the Atlantic."

"But she isn't. She's here," Thomas incautiously put in, and then regretted that he had done so.

"Here?"

"Staying in the flat of some friends on Fourteenth Street."

"Oh. Well you'll just have to tell her to go back to England. She can do nothing here. Nothing. The boy wants no part of her. I shall tell Hattie not to admit her if she comes here, I'm sure Gabriel was right, I don't think she was ever more than passively acceptant of him, but no doubt she'll make all the conventional to-do. And of course it's in her interest to keep him alive."

"Why?"

"My dear man! Because of the money! And don't tell me that Bella isn't what you, no doubt, would call a rapacious little go-getter, because I saw through her the very first minute I laid eyes on her. 'You've certainly picked a tough customer there,' I said to August, and he laughed like Little Audrey. 'I know, Mama,' he said, 'but there's something endearingly greedy about her, like a child. She's really very sweet.' "

Much interested though he was in this sidelight on Gus's feelings towards Bella, as to which he had often speculated, Thomas went back to the main point.

"What about the money?"

"Why—you must know about this—don't you see: if Gabriel lived to twenty-one he would inherit the estate. I daresay Bella might have some notion that she could then persuade him to let her have a part of the capital instead of just a life-interest. Though I'm willing to bet she'd be wrong. . . . However, the question won't arise. Gabriel has made up his mind."

"But Mrs. Baird—" Thomas began, and then stopped. Her face had grown even whiter as they talked; it was

157

transparent now, blue-white, the colour of skim-milk. She was dangerously exhausted. And, in any case, what use to argue with her? Gabriel had not given her his address. He didn't want her bothered. Why should Thomas be less considerate? Besides, there was much to think over in that letter; the juxtaposition of two sentences, especially, burned and ached in his side; that bullet was lodged between his ribs and would be hard to extract. . . .

"You are to leave the boy alone," she repeated. The hooded lids lifted, the grey eyes flashed at him momentarily, like arc-lamps. "Just because you feel guilty or because Bella is a greedy woman is no reason why Gabriel should be deprived of the dignity of choice. He has a right to his own death. Is that understood?"

"Yes, Mrs. Baird."

The front doorbell rang. Hattie went downstairs, and presently returned with Dr. Warmflash.

Thomas had not liked to leave the old woman alone until they came back. But she did not speak again; she lay breathing in painful asthmatic gasps; her old narrow chest heaved and her hands trembled. Thomas dared do no more than press her hand briefly before he left the room.

Dr. Warmflash, a stocky little man with a fleshy face and bright intelligent dark eyes under eyebrows like thick commas, took one look at her and said:

"Hospital for you, sweetheart. I'll have the ambulance here before you can say Popocatepetl."

"Oh no you won't, Toby! I'm staying right here in my own bed. You can get in a nurse, if you like, to help Hattie, but I am not going to end up in an institution, being treated like a parcel by a lot of strangers."

Thomas slipped away and left them arguing. He was willing to bet that Mrs. Baird would get her way. . . . He beckoned Hattie outside the door.

"Hattie, you're sure you don't know where that girl works? Catriona whatshername?"

She shook her head at him. "Now, Mr. Cook, you heard what she said in there. You're not to go plaguing Gabriel. I'm not worrying about him, but I don't want *her* upset."

"But if she wants to warn the girl about this man she thinks was following her——"

"Shucks, any girl of that age, working in a village lunchroom knows how to take care of herself. And if not, it's no affair of ours," Hattie said stubbornly. "Besides. I *don't* know where she works. Or where Gabriel is. Now you let yourself out, Mr. Cook, I've got to get back to her."

Thomas let himself out and walked along Twelfth Street, struggling with his moral dilemma.

"Is that understood?" Mrs. Baird had said, and he had said, "Yes." But he had not actually given her a promise. And he honestly believed that she was wrong in her attitude. At the age of ninety-five, life, seen foreshortened from a viewpoint so near its close, may appear short and trivial, hardly worth preserving. But it does not seem so at the age of forty-one. And what can sixteen know about it?

Surely there would be no harm in at least trying to find this girl?

A lunchroom somewhere south of Washington Square, not too far. A place with loud music, but quite clean and pleasant, where they served hero sandwiches.

There might be fifty, or a hundred. It was like hunting for one tree in a whole forest. Still, the name Catrina Vanaken was not so common; if he kept walking into places and asking, he might get word of her. All he had to do was quarter the area methodically.

Then it occurred to him that this was going about the business in a needlessly roundabout way. Perhaps her family lived in New York and were in the telephone book.

He hurried back to Tenth Street and almost ran up the four flights of stairs.

Half an hour later he was not so optimistic. Of the six Vanakens in the Manhattan directory, only three had answered their phones, and all three disclaimed any relationship with a music student named Catriona. But it was—he looked at his watch—only six-thirty. The other three might be on their way home from work; he would try again in half an hour. And how about the music schools? But it was summer; vacation time; probably none of the regular staff would be there. But it might be possible to get hold of registers giving names and addresses of students?

Meanwhile the pain was getting very bad again; mercifully it was time to swallow another capsule. And then he would put his feet up for a few minutes. . . .

It had been a long, hard day. He had spent the morning at the Madison Avenue office of Crusoe and Selkirk, discussing a full programme of activities, among them a new uniform edition of August Baird's collected works, which, all told, still sold a steady hundred thousand copies a year. Old Mrs. Baird was certainly a shrewd one; she had been ahead of him there; well though he knew Bella, it simply had not occurred to him that of course she had her sights fixed far ahead on that day when Gabriel was due to inherit the whole estate.

And there was the Nobel prize-money too. Gus had wanted a trust set up to provide money for students from minority groups. But the terms had been so general that lawyers were still arguing about it. And meantime, the money was accumulating interest. That would buy a good few cartons of ice-cream, if the trust plan fell through . . . or a good few fur coats. . . .

He was coming home, loaded with Christmas presents. Buying gifts for his mother was so easy: it wasn't that she had poor taste or was pleased by trash, but she had such a boundless capacity for all kinds of enjoyment. So many different books would fill her with delight; or scarves in the colours she loved, rusty reds, greenish blues, brown-and-gold; or bird-food for her bird-table, or reproductions of Impressionist paintings, a lamp so that she could read in bed, a green glass Venetian butter dish, shaped like a leaf—knitting-wool, paints, a warm quilted jacket. The difficulty was to know where to stop. But the real difficulty was to match this abundance of gifts to her with an equal number for his father, so that the disparity of affection would not be too apparent. For Samuel, in complete contrast to Fanny, was almost impossible to please. He did not read, he had no hobbies; his tastes in food were not adventurous, he ate merely to keep nourished. He moved around so little that he never seemed to wear out his clothes, and took, in any case, no interest in new ones. "Don't waste your money buying *me* presents," he said irritably. "I want nothing." But Thomas, filled with guilt, would spend hours on the fruitless task, ending, usually, with the same box of peppermint creams, a tie that would never be worn, a pair of socks that would go unused to the back of some drawer. If he did venture to get Samuel anything more elaborate, a dressing-gown, a winking red light so that he would know when the telephone was ringing—there always proved to be something unsatisfactory about it, the neck was not the kind that Samuel liked, the colour was too bright, the position was wrong—and it would have to be changed, or he complained about it bitterly and persistently for months afterwards. It was as if he guessed that the gifts were an act of penance, not

160

of love, and wanted to make sure the penance was sufficiently severe.

—The gifts were overloading his car, which did not seem to be steering properly; the wheel would not turn, a bulky leather case containing Samuel's present impeded its action. The case contained a hearing-aid, a large, enormously complicated piece of machinery which had cost five hundred pounds. But still, if it connected Samuel to the world again, it would be worth every penny. Wrenching the wheel, he must somehow have disturbed the mechanism, for the hearing-aid began giving off a menacing buzz—

He was now within sight of home, driving up the little short street, and there as always, was Fanny, who must have been on the lookout for him; she was wearing her favourite rust-brown skirt and the grey- and rust-speckled jersey with the angora collar; he had bought it for her himself at Liberty's last year and she loved it, she wore it all the time. She saw him from the doorway and her face lit up in welcome she ran out to welcome him she ran into the street and all of a sudden her ankle gave way under her she must have twisted it she fell off the kerb she fell straight under his wheel—

Thomas woke himself by screaming, "Stop! Stop!"

He was half off the couch, on the floor, still trying to turn the wheel, except that there was no wheel.

Where am I? Who am I? What is all this about?

My name is Thomas Cook and I am here in the flat in Tenth Street; I am staying in New York because I have to find my stepson—my ex-stepson, Gabriel Baird. Who is in urgent need of heart-surgery.

He remembered his outrage when Bella had first told him about Gabriel's heart.

The night of the reception at the Alleyn Club. She was in a funny mood in the car all the way home, and very annoyed with Gabriel when they got back to the house and found him still up.

"You *know* that with your heart condition you are supposed to go to bed early and get plenty of rest."

Obedient, without a word or argument, the boy turned off the replay of the Leeds match that he had been watching and walked off up the attic stairs to bed.

"Good night, Thomas. Good night, Mother."

"What do you mean, with his heart condition? What

161

heart condition?" Thomas asked, as soon as he was out of earshot.

"Surely you knew?"

"No, I've never heard it mentioned. What's the matter with his heart?"

So then she told him, in her most melodramatic manner, eyes widened until they were as big and pale as gulls' eggs and fixed on his in the way she did when she was trying to put over some lie or half-truth; at first he was so angry that he could not, would not, believe her; she was doing it on purpose to upset him, to arouse his feelings of guilt and responsibility, because she was jealous of his previous relationship with Jan, because her nose had been put out of joint by Bo going off like that with his Russian friend, whom she apparently detested. . . .

The news came as such a shock. Gabriel, after all, had seemed a normal, equable, likeable boy; quiet, certainly, introspective one might say; there was something not all it should be about his relationship with his mother, but any reserve there might be accounted for by her disingenuity over the fact that he had been adopted; the boy had evidently taken that very much to heart. Yes, he was quiet; he seemed to study the adults round him very intently; one received the impression sometimes that he compared them unfavourably with Gus—and hardly surprising if so; but he was always perfectly polite, frank, open, friendly—or had seemed so; Thomas had thought that he was on the way to building up a really good relationship with the boy.

And then to learn from Bella that Gabriel had this macabre shadow hanging over him, and had never even mentioned it, never so much as breathed a hint.

This on top of the profoundly disturbing shock of meeting Jan for the first time since that night——He had better not think about it.

"When does he have to have the operation?"

"Some time not more than eight months after his sixteenth birthday. It's not a *big* operation, but a very skilled one," Bella told him, her eyes fixed all the time unwaveringly on his. "Old Manresa is going to operate —you know, Sir Joshua—he's the only person in the country who's competent to do it. The only person in the world, really."

Thomas's rage would have been less if he had not felt certain that she was delighted to be able to show him he did not yet know all there was to be known about Gabriel; and that she was relishing to the full the somewhat macabre prestige that she, as his mother, would derive from the boy's situation.

Not a doubt but she was envisaging full press publicity for the operation: Nobel prizewinner's son, famous heart-surgeon, pictures of the boy's beautiful mother, a little thin, a little wan of course, from anxiety, but such a wonderful skin, such bone-structure, you wouldn't think she was a day over thirty.

"This heart-fault"—he cut roughly into her technicalities—"does it have anything to do with the last accident—when he was knocked down? Did—did that cause it?"

"Oh, good heavens, *no*," Bella said loftily—and he felt a huge relief, though nettled at her tone, which conveyed tolerant superiority and patient acceptance of his ignorance, "this is a thing he had from birth, poor lamb. Gus knew all about it. Of course, it did mean that I was extra *worried* about him at the time of the accident. Naturally. But he's really very strong—I've always made sure that he got plenty of vitamins and fresh air. . . ."

No wonder he seems a bit removed from everyday matters, Thomas thought. Who wouldn't be, if they knew that adult life was not going to be theirs by right, but had to be bought through the means of an experience, delicate, fiddling operation? An operation which, for nine boys out of ten—boys in low income-groups, in under-privileged countries—would be quite out of the question? And Gabriel had a very humble, modest sense of his own identity; Thomas had often felt this about him, that he judged his own value very low, presumably in contrast to Gus, or perhaps because Bella had never valued him very high.

"Time for bed, don't you think?" she said yawning. "After all those hours at the party, aren't you aching to get horizontal? I am." And moving behind the sofa, where he had sunk while assimilating this news, she leaned forward over his shoulder, nibbling gently at the lobe of his ear and at the same time running a hand slowly up the inside of his thigh. He resisted a strong impulse to slap her off as if she had been a mosquito. But honestly! The grotesque, unbelievable crassness of making a sexual invitation at a moment when he was troubled over such a piece of news.

163

But that was characteristic of Bella. Sex formed part of her daily life in a way which at first startled and excited him, later made him profoundly uneasy, and finally became intolerable to him. Since rapport of any other kind between them, never extensive, had dwindled to a depressed certainty on his part that he could see through most of her manoeuvres, his reluctance to be reminded of their physical relationship had grown stronger and stronger. Her hand on his leg aroused mingled feelings of lust, shame, and profound antipathy. He had a momentary recollection of noticing her earlier in the evening at the Alleyn Club party, talking to that bearded man; he had seen her over Jan's shoulder and the contrast had been a sudden revelatory shock: it was the absorbed expressions on the two faces, identical, interjacent—like castling at chess he had vaguely thought—and the man's proprietorial hand on her arm, in a gesture conveying old habit; he had received the instant conviction that some long-accustomed sexual bargain was being struck.

But if accustomed . . . that must mean that while she was married to August . . .

He struggled to his aching feet and walked straight out of the sitting-room door without a single backward look at her.

He limped to the telephone, which was ringing, and picked it up. The sound must have woken him, transmuted into the stuff of his dream, the gigantic hearing-aid.

"Hello?"

"Oh, Mr. Cook? Cornelius Vanaken again here. I said I'd call you again when I'd spoken to my brother in Los Angeles, if he had my niece's address—"

"Eh? I'm sorry, I didn't quite catch, what was that . . . ?"

"This is Mr. Cook? You called me an hour ago, asking if I had the address of my niece Catrina Vanaken, and I said she hadn't been in touch with us since she came to New York but I was planning to talk to my brother in California later on this evening and would be glad to ask him—"

"Oh, yes? That's kind of you," Thomas's tongue replied with automatic politeness, but his mind remained completely blank. He looked down at the massive Man-

164

hattan directory which he had left by the telephone, open at the page of V's. Three names crossed out, three with small red o's beside them.

"Well, Mr. Cook, I'm afraid my brother was *not* able to give me Catrian's address: it seems she just moved from a condemned building in Broome Street where she was squatting, living with some other kids, you know how that generation are—and she didn't send them her new address yet; all they've got for her is an address care of a girl called Pattie Lloyd who's one of her classmates. I can give you that. And there's also a teacher at her music school whom she visits quite a bit, Professor Foligno, who might be able to put you in touch with her—"

"Thank you so much, Mr. Vanaken." Thomas mechanically scribbled down the two addresses. "I do appreciate your trouble—"

"Oh, no trouble; that's quite okay. You said you were anxious to find your stepson; matter of fact we heard his mother on the radio, too; sorry I can't be of more help at present, but if Catrina should get in touch we'll let you know. So long now."

Thomas looked down at the phone book again, and then at his watch. Eleven-fifty. He had been asleep for over five hours. Or had he?

"You called me about an hour ago," Cornelius Vanaken had said. But the last time Thomas had any recollection of calling Cornelius Vanaken, marked "atty" in the book, attorney presumably, was at six-thirty; there were two numbers for him, one marked residence, the other office, and neither had answered; it seemed reasonable to assume that he was in transit between them. Thomas had intended to try again at seven-thirty; instead he had fallen asleep.

Did I call him again? An hour ago? I've absolutely no recollection of it. Would I be so inconsiderate as to call a total stranger at nearly eleven o'clock in the evening? Did I call him in my sleep?

It might be possible. I know that when I was on that intensive Najdolene course two summers ago I did some things which later on I couldn't remember at all. I accepted that awful Masters book on race and genetics that got us into such trouble; I said something to John Voynitch that he's never forgiven, and I've never discovered what it was; the things I did seemed to be frighteningly uncharacteristic of my normal behaviour patterns —like saying those terrible things to poor Jan's mother. Did I call up this lawyer again?

One way to check, of course, would be to ring up the other two names marked o, and ask if I had called them also. And if they recognise my voice. But at midnight that would seem pretty odd, pretty drastic.

Better leave them till tomorrow.

He looked at the names he had written in the directory margin.

Professor Giuseppe Foligno. Pattie Loyd. Professors need their sleep, but Pattie, a classmate at music school, might not object to being called at midnight; the young keep late hours.

He dialled the number.

"Hello?" A young, high voice.

"Is that Pattie Lloyd? I apologise for disturbing you. I was calling to ask if you can give me the address of a friend of yours, Catriona Vanaken."

"Oh, gee, I'm sorry," the young voice said—and truly sounded it, "I'm sorry, I can't. Trina just moved from where she was living and I don't have her new address."

Then, belatedly, caution overtook her and she added, "Who is this calling?"

"My name is Cook, Thomas Cook; I'm not looking for Catriona, primarily, but for an English boy, Gabriel Baird, who's a friend of hers; I hoped she might be able to tell me where he is. I'm his stepfather."

He wished that *stepfather* had not such an immediately wicked connotation: Mr. Murdstone, Claudius . . . but then, to Pattie's generation, parents, along with step parents, were no doubt equally suspect.

However, perhaps reassured by his English accent, she said, "Well, I don't have her new address yet, but I can tell you where she's working, or was; she had a job at a lunchroom in the Village, called the Stake-Out; it's in West Fourth Street—"

"Bless you, Miss Lloyd," Thomas said, from the heart. "I'm so grateful to you—and I'm sorry to have called you so late."

"Oh, that's okay. We were just practising." And indeed in the background he could hear the sounds of several instruments apparently tuning up. "Good night Mr.

166

Cook." There was a click as she rang off and he put his own receiver back.

The Stake-Out. I'll go there first thing in the morning. Surely there's a good chance that she'll know—But will she *say?*

The phone rang again.

Cornelius Vanaken? With another suggestion? Or some other body whom I called while in a slight state of amnesia?

He picked up the receiver.

"Is that Thomas Cook?"

"Cook here."

"Right. Listen carefully, Mr. Cook. I have a message about your stepson, Gabriel Baird."

A man's voice: slight, clipped accent—South African, Rhodesian?

His heart bounded up; fell, sickeningly.

"We have Gabriel with us, Mr. Cook."

"Where? Where are you phoning from?"

"We have no intention of telling you that."

"Who are you? Who is this calling?"

"Just listen, and don't interrupt, or you'll do yourself no good and Gabriel a lot of harm. We have Gabriel in a place that you could not possibly find. There isn't the least use in hunting for him. We shan't hurt him unless you try to find him. If you do that, or call in the police, we shall kill him."

"But the boy is in urgent need of heart-surgery—"

"Then you had better stop interrupting and do as we say, hadn't you?"

He said nothing more; he would not have been able to. His tongue seemed clamped by suction against the roof of his dry mouth.

"Now: if you do exactly what we tell you, the boy will be handed over, within thirty-six hours of that time, to the Cardiac Unit of the Cambridge Pectoral Research Clinic. Have you got that?"

The voice was not menacing, but cold and measured, colourless in tone like that of an announcer giving out some piece of information over a public-address system.

"During the next twenty-four hours you will have to get hold of three-quarters of a million dollars in five- ten- and twenty-dollar bills. Seven hundred and fifty thousand dollars. Random serial numbers, please."

167

Thomas found himself madly jotting in the margin of the Manhattan directory.

RANDOM SERIAL.

"Three-quarters of a m—but—"

"You will have the money ready in two suitcases, and the cases inside black plastic garbage disposal sacks. And have a car ready; you will have to drive out of New York."

"How can I possibly get hold of that amount of money?"

"Don't be stupid, Mr. Cook. Crusoe and Selkirk is a wealthy firm. Do you need me to tell you what they average yearly on sales of August Baird's books alone? It was in last month's *Publishers Weekly*. You can easily get hold of the money."

"What proof do I have that you have really got Gabriel?"

"Twenty-four hours from now I shall call up his mother and play a tape-recording of his voice. She should have no difficulty in recognising it. In the meantime, I repeat: don't call the police or we shall kill the boy immediately."

"But his mother has already asked the police to help find him because of the operation he needs."

"We have told his mother to abandon her publicity campaign and instruct the police to call off their search."

Thomas's smouldering suspicions began to flicker more brightly. Was this all some elaborate scheme of Bella's? But surely, even she would not stoop quite so low as a fake kidnap message—that seemed out of her league. Bella was capable of any number of minor deceits, petty evasions—but not criminality on such a professional scale.

"We have instructed his mother to return to England. Is all that quite clear, Mr. Cook? Repeat your instructions."

Mechanically he repeated what the voice had said.

"Good. That's all." There was a click. No more voice.

Thomas put back the receiver and stumbled as far as the bathroom where he was violently sick. The spaghetti that he had eaten at Nick's place—when?—some time earlier in the evening, uncounted hours ago—turned to poisonous sludge in his intestines and was frantically rejected. He leaned against the basin, sobbing and gasping.

Let's face it, Cook. You're not equipped to be the hero of melodrama. If the truth must be told, you're a sodden

168

mess. And to think that wretched boy depends on you. God help him.

He vomited again. Then ran the cold tap till the water came out cool, shovelled in all his ice cubes, and drank long, shuddering beakerfuls of the freezing, burning cold. Better. What time is it now? Getting on for 1 A.M.; 6 A.M. in England. Can't call the London office for another four hours.

I wonder if the Stake-Out is a twenty-four-hour place.

Despite the voice's warning, he had not quite abandoned his hope of finding Gabriel. It was too tantalising to be in possession of this lead.

He sat down, weakly, on the toilet seat, to try and debate the pros and cons of continuing the search.

There wouldn't be any harm in locating the girl. She might give helpful information as to where Gabriel had been living. And some clue as to his state of mind.

But if the threat was serious? If they kill him?

Think of having to live with that for the rest of your life.

But he's going to die in any case if he doesn't have the operation. Wants to die.

The radiator in the hot little bathroom fizzed, warbled, and spluttered. Water rushed to and fro in the cistern. And his own heart pounded, his digestive system heaved and seethed inside him like the pool at the foot of Niagara.

Should I be able to hear the phone if it rings again?

Though who would call at this hour of night, anyway?

Is this kidnapping connected in any way with the Uncle Vanya record, or was that just a random bit of terrorism on somebody's part?

But it's in her best interests to keep the boy alive until his majority, not to let him die. Three-quarters of a million in the hand is worth much less than a whole lifetime of sponging off one's adopted son. Let alone the power, the pleasure to be got from devious manipulation, which would be lost for ever if once she allowed Gabriel to slip away; and furthermore Bella could not bear to be left; look how she clung to Bo with jealous tenacity. The fact that her abandonment was due to somebody's death by no means mitigated the offense; her devastating grief at the loss of Baird was infused, Thomas had very soon discovered, by a very large admixture of simple resentment at

169

his lack of consideration in dying and leaving her a widow. How did *I* ever manage to get away? Thomas wondered. It was because Bella herself made the break; after that, her pride wouldn't let her withdraw.

How can I cope with this situation when my mind is full of holes?

The phone rang.

Nine

Thomas 1974

Thomas had been talking to Bella for ten minutes before Bo even turned round. He was doing something minute and fiddling to his mural with a razor blade; Thomas could not be sure whether he was putting paint on or taking it off. He crouched, like a grasshopper, head thrust forward, elbows on knees, and seemed completely unaware of the other two people in the room. His hair, Thomas noticed, was now peppered with white, and he was skeletally thin, far thinner than he had been on the last occasion they met, which had been—when?—two years ago, three? Uneasily Thomas realised that he could not recall the occasion; it must have fallen into another of those frightening gaps in his memory, the black holes, he was beginning to call them, those sinister areas of compressed but opaque consciousness, inaccessible to ordinary memory. They were like the strange black spots in space—August had had a lot of theories about them too —patches of the universe so dramatically condensed by some aeons-old galactic upheaval that no light-ray could even pass near them, so dense that one of them the size of your fist would exert a gravitational pull equal to that of the earth: solid darkness, pulling a contiguous dark into itself—space-whirlpools, space cephalopods.

It was the Najdolene that caused them. But what can you do? You have a choice: you can suffer constant pain at such an excruciating, unremitting pitch that it prevents your doing any useful work or leading a normal life, turns you into a whimpering, incapable parasite; or you can take the drug and lay yourself open to acquiring these potholes of black in your mental fabric.

Pull yourself together, Cook; can't have a pothole in fabric.

But suppose, he said to himself, suppose I forget what is happening now? Suppose I collect that three-quarter million dollars and then leave it on a bench in Washington Square and wander off? How can I be sure of acquitting myself adequately enough, rationally enough, to help Gabriel? For that matter, how much longer shall I be able to go on running Crusoe and Selkirk, keeping my own life on an even keel? *Is* it on an even keel?

Familiar questions.

"What are we going to *do?*" Bella kept saying.

She had taken down a large oval mirror from some wall, and propped it on top of two boxes. Across the surface of the glass she had scattered a bag of milliners' feathers—black, white, coloured, straight, curled, fluffy, large, small—and, all the while they talked, she fretfully, jerkily distracted herself by arranging them in random patterns, and then sketching the results, with the reflections, in ink and wash; dozens of sheets of drawing paper lay round her on the floor. Thomas found her occupation fidgety and irritating; he wished she would stop; but he realised that she did it to calm herself, and so forebore to criticise.

One of the reasons why he had agreed to come round immediately in response to her call was because he had still felt it possible that the kidnap message was some ploy in which she had had a hand.

But seeing her had changed his opinion. She was genuinely distressed and frightened; her hands shook, her voice was tearful, and she cast glances full of resentment at Bo as he squatted unheeding, scratching away with his razor blade, sometimes whistling softly to himself. Watching Bo and Bella, Thomas was aware, as on so many previous occasions, of two simultaneous layers of mental performance in himself: one, soothed, lulled, but stimulated too, by their presence and activities; the other apart, articulate, critical, feeling their complete disengagement from him. They were like members of a different species.

"It's the most monstrous thing ever!" Bella wept. "If they hadn't heard on the television how important it was for him to have his heart-surgery, they'd never have thought of it. Oh god, I was so frightened when that man with the awful voice telephoned, I thought I was going to die. If Bo hadn't been here—"

And whose fault was it that they knew about Gabriel's condition? said Thomas inwardly. If you hadn't given way as always to your love of self-dramatisation, we'd have only one problem now, not two. Maybe not even one, if I can get hold of that girl.

Bo, still facing the wall, muttered as if to himself, "Whose bloody silly fault was it that they knew? What did you expect?"

"It's just the most vicious blackmail!"

"That's blackmail," he said.

The word fell between them like some unpleasant lump of garbage, sooty, smutty, smelly, quite out of place in the clean, warm, white-and-yellow kitchen.

Loraine blinked at him through her thick lenses—today's pair were studded with presumably imitation sapphires round the rims. Her pink, powdered face—its colour between lavender and sweet pea—did not change at all, retained an expression of good-natured but dogged intensity.

"What a very strange notion you have of blackmail," she replied. "A blackmailer is someone who extorts money or concessions for himself, but what do *I* stand to gain? I find all this quite difficult, I assure you. I don't like disagreeables. I far prefer everything pleasant and friendly."

"God knows *what* you stand to gain," Thomas said wearily. He found her, as always, completely enigmatic. His feelings towards her remained confused; he did not even particularly dislike her.

She wiped her hands—they were floury, as usual—and moved a suacepan, which was bubbling and suddenly let out a jet of steam, to the side of the stove.

"You see," she went on in a mild conversational tone, "I'm very concerned about you and Bella. Bella's not herself these days. She's not happy any more. And it's such a shame. Everything seemed to be going along so nicely. She'd got over that terrible sickness of grieving for August. And with you taking on Crusoe and Selkirk so that you were really involved with August's memory and her affairs, your relationship ought to have worked out

172

so well; of course I didn't realise that it was all founded on a misconception, that it was all so precarious—"

Not precarious if you don't meddle with what's no concern of yours, you fat bundle of neurosis, he suddenly longed to shout. He felt like pushing a palm of his hand into the round pink face, so concerned, so censorious.

"It is not founded on a misconception," he said, looking coldly into the short-sighted grey eyes that stared into his. "I have Bella's and Gabriel's interests truly at heart. I am very fond of them both and want to do my best by them. If you could just leave us in peace to work out our own problems, I think we would manage quite satisfactorily."

"Bella worries about you so much, you know," Loraine pursued, disregarding what he had just said, keeping her myopic eyes fixed on his. "She feels so uncertain of you at times. For instance, at that party you all went to last month at the Club, she became terribly upset because you spent such a long time talking to some girl with whom you were once involved."

"She had absolutely no need to worry. The girl and I had parted—by mutual agreement—before I ever laid eyes on Bella. That was completely over and done with. I hadn't seen her since. I told Bella so. Of course Jan and I had friends in common to discuss, of course we talked. . . . I really don't see why I should have to justify myself to you about this. If I managed to reassure Bella there seems no need for you to be concerned." His voice shook with anger but he kept it down.

"Ah, but *did* you reassure her? Oh, I know you think I'm an interfering old fuss-pot," Loraine replied imperturbably. "But I'm so fond of Bella that I'm quite prepared to rush in where angels fear to tread. She had such a terribly insecure childhood that she needs more than just reassurance."

"In that case she might do well to consider the effect of her own behaviour—" Thomas rashly began, and then stopped. He saw again in his mind's eye Bella at the Alleyn Club party, absorbed in low-voiced conversation with that hungry-eyed, bearded man who looked like a dyspeptic D. H. Lawrence. At one point their heads had been so near together that Thomas, glancing over Jan's shoulder, had caught the strangely identical expressions on each face. He had observed before that, when two people know each other really well over a long period of time, they are prone to pick up expressions and mannerisms from each other; and Bella was particularly given to this. A number of her more uncharacteristic looks and gestures, he was sure, must be unconscious parrotings from Gus: a casual, relaxed way of throwing herself back and laughing, a trick of sitting very straight with her chin pulled in to deliver herself of some strongly held opinion. And many of her tones of voice and tricks of speech came straight from Bo. But a few brisker, more clipped inflections, to be heard when she made a particularly acid or cynical remark, seemed to stem from neither of these origins, yet not to be her own; seeing the bearded man with his sharp, foxy look, catching occasionally across the room the yap of his rather shrill yet grating voice, Thomas felt sure that he was the source. When had Bella known him? He had not asked her.

"Bella's such a child in many ways," Loraine went on, ignoring his last remark. "As I said, if she were to find out—if she had the remotest *notion,* that her relationship with you was balanced on—on what we've been discussing —or, of course, if Gabriel were to find out; Gabriel's such an ultra-sensitive boy—he has such a *thing* about absolute integrity—truth is just the be-all and end-all so far as he is concerned—"

"I see absolutely no reason why he should find out," said Thomas, goaded. "I have thought about this most carefully, I assure you; I've come to the conclusion that it would do nobody any good. There are times when relationships can only be upset by digging up a lot of past history and this is certainly one of those. Bella and I get on all right and shall get on better; I take this marriage and this household very much to heart, I need hardly say; and of course I regard Gabriel as particularly my responsibility."

"Well; good; I'm delighted to hear it," Loraine's voice was dry; she peered at him, frowning, compressing her small mouth, as if in spite of the thick lenses she could not see him very clearly; he returned her inspection with as bold and steady a look as he could muster.

"And *I'll* be delighted," he said, "if you don't discuss any of this with Bella. Or, most especially, with Gabriel. There's plenty of time for him to learn that people aren't all what they seem on the surface—that everybody has some secret hidden away."

174

"Who has some secret hidden away?" called Bella's gay voice.

She came through the back door, dragging Bo by the hand. Bo hung back, blinking, dazzled by the radiance of the kitchen strip-lights, covering his eyes with his hands. So many of Bo's gestures were catlike that Thomas would not have been surprised to see his pupils turn to vertical slits in the sudden light.

Bella's fur coat and hood were frosted all over with moisture; both their faces had the brilliance, the dark shine about the eyes, that comes from running at night. Gabriel followed them in a moment or two, also shielding his eyes.

"We've been badger-watching on the common," Bella said. "I picked up Gabriel from choir practise and we dragged Bo out of his studio; he didn't want to come a bit because he was waiting for a phone call from silly old James and he was cross with us but he enjoyed it, didn't you, Boney?"

She peered teasingly into his face; he did not reply but walked straight over to the drinks cupboard, found the whisky, and poured himself half a tumblerful. Holding it, he went to the wall telephone and began dialing.

"What were you and Loraine saying about guilty secrets?" Bella pursued.

"Oh I was just arguing that everyone has something—some past event or action in their lives—that they don't want made public," Thomas answered rather lamely.

With an intention to divert the conversation so obvious that it failed in its effect, Loraine asked Gabriel, "Did you see any badgers?"

He shook his head, keeping his eyes fixed on Thomas.

"That's all rubbish! Speak for yourself!" Bella said. *"I* certainly haven't any black secrets hidden away—and I'm sure Loraine hasn't, have you Lorry?—and angel-Gabriel hasn't, so there's three who don't for a start." She pulled off her fur coat and threw it over a chair; it fell to the floor and Thomas moved with automatic fastidious-ness to pick it up. Into his mind shot with strange clarity a vision of the first night he had spent with Bella: the almost bacchic frenzy they had fallen into, tangling, grappling together, driving at each other as if they needed to break down their separate boundaries and be incorpo-rated into some dual identity that contained them both; *duel* would be a better word, he thought, remembering the nonstop ferocity with which they had coupled, biting, clenching, wrapped round each other, crescendo after crescendo, letting go only to grab again, keeping every possible inch of surface in contact, as if any physical chink between their enmeshed bodies might have let in the thought of August Baird, wandering loose in the dark universe, or of Gabriel, hurt and bewildered and alone in a hospital bed.

How could they have done it? Was that the worst act in my life? he wondered, and was inclined to think it must have been; acts must be judged not solely with regard to their effect on other people—for considered by such criteria that night did nobody else any specific harm and might therefore be reckoned blameless enough; no, but it was the effect on the protagonists that was so ineradicable. It has permanently shattered my self-respect. And what about Bella? What did it do to her? He caught her round dark eye and wondered if she was recalling the same thing, but she merely looked nervous and feverish, as if determined to provoke somebody.

"Oh, don't bother about the bloody coat!" she said irritably. Thomas brushed some flour from the collar. She went on:

"Of course I daresay you and Bo are just bulging with naughty private affairs you don't tell us about; males are much more double-faced and secretive than females, everybody knows *that*."

Bo clashed the receiver back on its rest, having failed to get through. He said to his sister with calculated venom:

"Will you stop chattering rubbish like a magpie and talk some sense for a change? Do you remember the name of the club in Manette Street where you and I went with James that night after the Phoenix show?"

"Nope; I don't," she said, twirling on her heel. "And it isn't rubbish. What about *your* murky private life? Oh, ho, ho, if I were to tell all I know! And I daresay old Thomas, puritan though he be, has got a thing or two tucked up his sleeve."

Bo, really angry, crossed the room to his sister and shook her by the shoulders. "Will you shut up? I'd hardly think you'd want your own affairs laid out for public inspection?"

"Let go of me, you hurt me, you beast!" Pulling away she slapped at his face. He caught her arm, deflecting the blow.

Bella burst into tears. Her face turned cherry-red, her mouth opened in a square, like a child's. Tears spurted from her eyes and splashed onto the tilted floor.

"*You* aren't any help!" she said furiously to Thomas and, snatching the fur coat from him, she ran sobbing from the room.

"Now look what you've done; you've thoroughly upset her," Loraine said to Bo.

He gave an elaborate shrug, raising his hands palm outwards, but said nothing.

Gabriel, looking miserable, sat down at the white table and opened a book, which he had been carrying under his arm.

"I'd better go and soothe her down."

Loraine left the room at a slightly more bustling pace than her usual ponderous amble. Thomas moved to stop her, but Bo said languidly:

"I should leave them alone, if I were you. Loraine loves to feel she's indispensable. Bella will cry and carry on, and Loraine will tell her she's a poor hurt wonderful abused darling and presently she'll feel better and Loraine will feel important. They both need the emotional outlet."

Gabriel raised his eyes from his book and said, "Why do they?"

"Ah, there you have me, my dear nephew. There indeed you have me. Perhaps they don't get enough reality in their lives. Women love to indulge in these little spots of drama. Take Loraine now; take that horrible house of hers full of glittering bad taste and gadgets; what could you do with it but burn it down? What can she do but come round here and shampoo our lawn with carpet soap and wax the floor into a death trap and prune the roses so they won't flower till Bastille Day in the year 2000? . . . Well, be seeing you."

He drank off another half glass of whisky and walked out of the back door.

Little spots of drama.

"We'll have to pay the money they're asking. We'll just have to! After all, it's Gabriel's *life* that's at stake!" Bella said.

Outside the window a police-car siren, speeding along Fourteenth Street, rose to a maniac pitch, wailing, twitching, warbling, then dwindled away in the distance. It was extremely late—or very early, depending on how you chose to think. The traffic sounds through the city had diminished to a steady, muted sigh, like the distant sea. Red tapestry of sky hung outside the window.

"What exactly did they say to you on the phone?" Thomas asked Bella patiently.

"That we should raise three-quarters of a million dollars and have it ready, that they'd got Gabriel, that they'd call again with instructions about where it was to be delivered."

"What kind of voice?"

Bo turned from his painting at last; he stood, stretched, came over to Bella's collection of plumes, picked up a couple, and blew them meditatively into the air.

"Nothing special about the voice," Bella said. "Just a man's voice."

"English?"

"I'm not sure." Thomas saw Bo glance at her quickly. "Why—was yours English?"

"No. I don't think so."

"Stop fussing on about the voice," Bo cut in. "Can you raise the cash? is the main question. Will Crusoe and Selkirk come through?"

"I called old Alexander at his home," Thomas said. "It was a bit of a shock to him, of course, at six in the morning. But he said he'd cable instructions to the National and Mercantile Bank over here. We ought to be able to get it by noon."

"Well isn't that great," said Bo.

He did look greatly relieved; he went so far as to give Thomas a quick, twitching smile, though his high, fatigued voice kept its usual edge of irony as he added, *"What* a lucky thing, isn't it, Bella, that our Thomas had the foresight to marry his way into Crusoe and Selkirk? Such a convenience now."

"He didn't marry in; he bought a partnership," she said sulkily.

"Of course he did. It was you, wasn't it, my love, who married for money."

"We'll leave my marriages out of this conversation, if you don't mind," Bella said. Her angry glance at Bo seemed to subdue him a little, Thomas was interested to observe; his eyes fell before hers; he moved away without

178

answering, picked up some of her fallen plumes, and put them back on the looking-glass, lightly patting her wrist as he did so; she brushed his hand aside sharply.

"Did James leave his number when he called?" Bo asked Bella with seeming irrelevancy.

"No; why?" she said, curt.

"I was only thinking that his car might come in handy for delivering the ransom."

Faint suspicion stirred in Thomas again. He had considered telling them about the possible lead through Catriona Vanaken, but now, for some reason, he changed his mind; best pursue that thread by himself.

"Well, I'll leave you now," he said, "since there's nothing else we can do for the moment. Let me know if they phone you again, won't you? And I'll tell you if they get on to me, of course. And I'll be in touch later in the day."

He rose stiffly and painfully, from the uncomfortable basket-chair in which he had been sitting.

"Oh, don't go yet!" Bella cried anxiously. She jumped up, switched on the overhead light. "Wouldn't you—wouldn't you like—a drink? Something to eat?"

"I don't think so, thanks. It seems too late, or too early."

She seemed bent on keeping him, and caught his arm.

"Hadn't you better stay here, in case they phone again?"

"Don't detain our sweet Thomas if he wants to split, Bella," Bo said suavely. Thomas had the feeling, very familiar from the past, that they were using him as a sparring-object, bidding against each other for his favour, but also both in league against him.

"Or would you pause and take a glass of beer, Thomas, dear Thomas?" Bo added, as if a sudden thought had struck him. "I know at *one* time you went off beer, but perhaps you have recovered your taste for it now?" He spoke in a peculiar manner, without meeting Thomas's eye; Thomas felt certain that his words contained a veiled meaning but could not pick up the allusion, though it stirred a curtain far down in some gallery of his mind.

"Of course Thomas doesn't want any beer, stupid!" cried Bella. "How about coffee, though? I'll have some made in a jiffy."

She darted into the kitchen before Thomas could refuse. What was that about beer? he wondered. Did I have a quarrel with Bo sometime? Did beer come into it?

Gone, all gone. Bella clinked cups and pots in the kitchen, splashily ran a tap.

"How long have you been over here?" Thomas asked Bo.

"Oh—a while," Bo said vaguely.

"Do I gather your friend James is here too?"

"He lives in Washington these days. Teaches there. Hates it. He's going back to England."

"Perhaps!" called Bella from the kitchen. "You know how darling James never keeps a plan the same from one minute to the next."

"You don't know James particularly well, my angel," Bo observed mildly. "He never came to Wanborough."

"Just as well! Not at all a suitable person for Gabriel to meet," Bella said primly, coming in with two cups of instant coffee.

"Oh, come," said Thomas, who had not met James either. "Surely Gabriel has enough sense to judge for himself?"

"Which is quite fortunate, is it not," said Bo, "in view of the fact that none of *our* efforts to love and cherish him seem to have met with roaring success." His eye raked Thomas, and he added, "I always felt that your efforts fell off *signally,* Thomas, once you had learned that Gabriel was not August's own chick."

With a great effort Thomas suppressed his bitter hurt and anger at these words, which seemed to him completely unfair. What's making Bo so furious? he wondered. He's trying to keep it down but it's there all the time underneath.

Out of the blue he remembered a man in the packing department at Crusoe telling him about a house he had been thinking of buying.

"Seemed a bargain really, had the house surveyed, nothing wrong there. But luckily one o' the neighbours tipped us off—the *garden* was on fire. The actual soil was inflammable, an' it had caught right down underground; they couldn't put it out. Fast as they got one spot under control, another bit started up. Did you ever hear anything like it? A whole garden, just burning away quietly, month after month, looked all right on the surface, save

180

that all the trees and shrubs were dying, an' if you put your foot on the ground—hot!"

Was that what Bo was like?

Sipping at the hot coffee, which he did not want at all, Thomas turned to look at Bo's picture. Like all Bo's work, it made him feel very uncomfortable. Even more unnerving, he could feel Bo's ironic eye on him as he stared at it, trying to think of some safe, suitable comment.

"Do you like it?" inquired Bo graciously.

"Very striking," said Thomas. "Was it a commission?"

"Oh dear me no. I daresay our good-natured if boring hostess will be startled out of her sweet life when she comes back and finds it. But if she doesn't like it she can always sublet to the Met and charge for admission. Tell me, though, do you think it needs anything more done to it?"

"I wouldn't have thought so," said Thomas vaguely. Every inch of wall seemed thick with paint.

"Perhaps you think there is too much already? Or would you like a can of spray-paint to touch it up, like the subway graffiti-workers—or those enthusiasts who doodled in red on "Guernica" and the "Mona Lisa"? Or how about a nice pot of oven-spray? A bit of corrosive might add just the right satanic touch, what do you think? I'm sure Bella has some and would oblige, haven't you, sweetie?"

"Will you be quiet, Bo?"

Thomas was really startled at the ferocity in Bella's tone. Some coffee slopped out of her cup onto the rush matting as she almost ran across to stare Bo stormily in the face.

"All right, all right, don't give yourself a rupture," he said amiably. "I was only——"

"Well, don't! We're tired, we don't want your stupid spiteful jokes."

"Thomas doesn't mind, Thomas and I understand one another, don't we, Thomas?"

Thomas felt that he almost did. There was something about oven-spray—what was it? Something down there in the same hidden hole in his mind, along with the beer——

The telephone rang.

Bo got there first and said, "Yes?" guardedly into the receiver. Then his face cleared.

181

"Oh it's you, Jem. Good. Good. Right. Right. Sure. Fine. Okay, I'll be there. See you. 'Bye."

He put back the receiver, walked to the door, paused to say, "That was James. I'll ask about the car. See you later," and was gone, before Bella could do more than cry:

"Wait, Boney!"

The outer door slammed behind him, and they heard his feet rattle down the stairs; five seconds later the distant bang of the front door reverberated up the stairwell.

"Damn him!" said Bella furiously. "Really sometimes Bo is the *end*—"

"Three in the morning seems an odd time to meet."

"Oh, that James is a night-bird. He never goes to bed at all; or only between nine and noon. Or—"

She fell silent, frowning, nibbling the quill of one of her feathers.

"I must go too," Thomas said. *"We* need sleep, even if they don't. Try to get some rest; you have to, to take the strain of all this."

"Oh, don't go, just for a minute; I need someone to talk to." She looked forlorn, rather distracted; he thought, as he had so many times in the past, that she resembled a kitten: apparently furry and soft, but really hard, a mass of tiny tough wiry bones and tendons under the deceptive downiness; erratic and sudden in movement; and with the strange, blank, wide-eyed gaze.

"It's a pity Loraine isn't here," she said with a faint smile. "The old girl would be fussing round with cups of tea and tranquillisers like billy-o."

"You must miss her."

"Yes—yes I do." She sounded surprised about it, and faintly aggrieved.

"When did she die?"

"Don't you remember?" She gave him an odd look. "It was two years ago; around the time we were getting divorced."

"I don't remember." He was too tired to pretend about it, though he could feel her avid, inquisitive gaze boring into him.

"Thomas—do you really not remember things?"

"What things?" he fenced warily.

"Well—that, for one. Poor old Lorry doing herself in. I'd have thought you'd remember it, there was enough hoo-ha. And have you forgotten all about the *Hetaira* cruise?"

"What about it? Of course I remember it." But did he? He could remember the embarkation, and hot days aboard, and hot days ashore; isolated incidents collecting specimens. But did not his memories then taper off into cloudy vagueness?

He moved his head uneasily, to avoid her eyes, and said again, "I really must go."

"Thomas." She came close up to him and grasped his lapels. Wouldn't you rather spend the rest of the night here? It's pouring with rain—you really shouldn't go out when it's so wet. Why not stay? You could have Bo's bed. . . . Or mine, if you prefer?"

Looking up, she smiled at him—the old familiar come-hither smile.

"Don't you think it would be more sensible to stay here with me where we can help keep each other calm than go back up your seventy-seven stairs to that dusty little hole?"

The invitation was unmistakable. But he preferred to bypass it. That was one mistake he need not make twice.

"It's sweet of you. But I'd better not stay. For one thing my arms are hurting like hell," he lied. They were hurting, but not unbearably. Her face fell. "I have to go back and take some more of my stuff. Anyway, Bo wouldn't be best pleased if he got back and found me occupying his bed."

"Oh, Bo!" she said spitefully. "He's probably in James's bed by now. He'd be delighted to find you in *my* bed. He always thought our divorce was the most frightful mistake.

She gazed up at him solemnly. The look on her face was open, candid, pleading. Anyone who didn't know her, thought Thomas, would believe that she was as innocent and vulnerable as—as Gabriel. But vulnerability is not necessarily accompanied by innocence.

Rather unkindly, he inquired, "What happened to Arthur Bellamy?"

"Arthur? Oh good heavens, I lost sight of him ages ago."

"I thought you were going to marry him?"

"Arthur? Good god no. His tastes turned out to be much too kinky. He was a ghastly little monster, really. Thomas! Couldn't we—"

"Look, it's stopped raining," he said quickly. "I really had better go. I'll phone you later in the day, as soon as I've got the money. And you let me know if you hear anything more. We'll keep in touch. Try not to worry too much. Get some sleep. . . . How did you know my phone number, by the way, it's not listed?"

"Oh," she said vaguely, "I got it from that sour old bitch, Hannah's housekeeper. Do you know, Thomas, she actually wouldn't let me set foot in the house? Practically slammed the door in my face."

"Well, old Hannah's very ill," he said. "I expect she's worried stiff. Good-bye now. Take care."

And he walked swiftly through to the front door, before she could think of any further excuses to delay him.

As he passed Bo's picture he gave it another hasty, troubled look. Where had he seen some other paintings of Bo's—plants, flowers, jungle scenes; he could hear Bo's voice saying, "Hybrid Flemish. Le Douanier Bosch." When was that—where?

No good. Out of reach.

He shut the door behind him and ran down the stairs. He wanted to be by himself and think.

For a start, was Bo's presence in New York suspicious? Had Bella perhaps summoned him? The cat-and-dog relationship between them made this open to question; though on occasion they could seem very devoted. There was at all times a strange bond between them. Once or twice, during his marriage to Bella, Thomas had speculated uneasily about it. What old, atrocious subterranean secrets lay buried and rotting beneath the roots of their relationship, preventing either one from ever becoming wholly committed to any outside person?

True, Bo had a real attachment to Gabriel; an attachment which Bella had always watched with uneasy, jealous distrust. Was there some real cause for her distrust? Or was it just another manifestation of Bella's inability to tolerate any closeness between two other people from which she felt herself excluded? . . . It did seem possible that Bo might have come to New York in order to help Gabriel; or, of course, because his friend James had invited him.

Bo was a curious, uncomfortable, twisted character; was it at all conceivable that he had any hand in this kidnapping and ransom demand? Could he have done such a thing to his own nephew?

Certainly there had been a very peculiar undercurrent in that interview; though Bo had seemed amiable enough on the surface, Thomas had sensed something strong and bitter as brimstone underneath. It had the taste of antipathy.

Is Bo the person who hates me? Did he play the trick with the Uncle Vanya record? It could have been Bo; the library had no record of a borrower; someone had simply walked out with it; Bo's studio used to be stacked with stolen library books. But if so, why? Surely not because Bella and I split up?

My mind, Thomas thought, is like an unfinished bit of tapestry: half a picture in the middle, ragged ends sticking out all round. What about Loraine Hartshorn's death, for instance? Loraine was an interfering old ass, a meddlesome dangerous bore, easily put out of mind once out of sight, but we saw her all the time; it's strange that I don't remember any of the circumstances, specially if she committed suicide. Why did she? Too often frustrated in her urge for domination? Too lonely at last? Did Bella snub her once too often?

He had been walking along Fourteenth Street and now turned, at random, up Fifth Avenue. It was still very early in the morning. The city traffic had hardly begun, and the spacious sidewalks were empty of people, though littered with the night's detritus of broken glass and beer cans, cardboard boxes, six-pack tops, and huge brown-paper bags. City cleaning trucks rumbled slowly along, all driven by paid-up Mafia members no doubt.

The exaggerated skyline, ragged as a parrot tulip, blackly fringed a spectacular morning sky: rain had ceased for the moment, but there was more to come; great fronds and swags of black cloud were flung in wild shapes over the silvery pale blue of the sky, which was tinted with faint, shining rose towards the east; the wet, untidy, gleaming heaven above matched the wet, untidy shining street beneath.

Walking northwards up Fifth Avenue he gazed sleepily at the windows of export stores and admired the displays in them: crazily ornate Tiffany lamps, huge gilded rococo ornaments, objects that were almost sublime in their vulgarity: who would buy a glass table supported by a naked kneeling gold mermaid? Perhaps Bo would if he had a thousand dollars? Or a two-foot china cavalier wearing a tricorne, tails, and glasses, mounted on a china goat, also wearing glasses?

His mind, freshened by vigorous exercise and the cool damp morning breeze began to clear and settle; the black sediment of the night, the uneasy prickling emotions, the troubled anxieties conjured by the company of Bo and Bella slowly subsided and sank. Faint tinglings of constructive thought began to make themselves felt, like returning circulation. And, for once, pain had retreated completely; its absence made him feel unnaturally well.

I'll walk up to Central Park, he thought, Nobody will be stirring yet for two hours at least. No one will be likely to phone. I don't suppose it would be any use going to the Stake-Out before eight o'clock or so.

I'll take a walk in the park to brighten my wits. And then I'll get a bus down to the Village and have breakfast at the Stake-Out.

He thought: There's something about those two, when they are together, that I can only define as evil; no other word seems to fit. It's like a chemical reaction. Separately they may be harmless enough; I don't know. What is it they do to each other? The shockwaves set up by the opposing forces of their wills go bounding out with the incalculable deadliness of ricocheting bullets.

What harm may they have done Gabriel when he was a child? But Gabriel had Gus to protect and watch over him; Gus like a sheltering tree, a great cliff at his back. And, queer, perverted, bent as those two are, yet they did each have some kind of love, even reverence, for August Baird, which you'd think would be reflected in their feelings towards Gabriel. Even if Gabriel is not the child of August's flesh, he is the child of his intentions, of his spirit.

We all had our own reverence for Gus. Why not? He was a genius. The spatial adjustment theory, his work on human hibernation, the random continuum idea, the theory about the black holes that he called the cloverleaf system; he was a genius.

But did he do us all harm, just the same?

Filled with doubts he walked on. It was chilly. He was hungry, and tired.

Somebody had cast out a rent and gashed chaise-longue onto Fifth Avenue. There it stood, waiting for someone to move it. And meanwhile an old lady, was taking her ease on it, reclining luxuriously against the end; she was engaged in rolling down her stockings to the knee and examining her legs for possible varicose veins. Having done so and decided that all was well for the time, she leaned back and looked at the morning sky; then, Thomas happening to pass just at that moment, she gave him such a wide happy smile that the climate of 'his thoughts changed yet again, and he began to believe that, after all, he might be able to find Gabriel before it was too late.

Ten

Gabriel 1974

The park was bare and peaceful. Under the luminous clear sky of steel-blue and tattered black its empty spaces lay filled with light: a sourceless light that flowed round corners and shone reflected on the lower sides of leaves, and trickled into nooks of trees and crevices of rocks. A whole night's rain had sunk into the bone-dry ground, leaving it hardly moist. Still, the leaves had been refreshed, the defeated brown grass breathed out briefly a damp reminder of the days when it had been green and growing. Trees each held a lungful of mist, which would evaporate as the sun climbed. All tracks had been erased from the patches of bald ground, leaving only the freckled pattern of the rain. Among the taller trees a single bird let out from time to time one keen shrill melancholy cry.

The plumy biscuit-coloured dog ran ahead of them across the empty space, at a sedate and jogging lope that made his frills flap in a slightly ludicrous manner.

"He's like an Edwardian lady in all her boas and motorveils," Gabriel said.

"His trousers are so long they trail on the ground behind him; he doesn't leave any footprints," said Catriona.

"*We* do; we've left a terrific trail."

They turned to admire their tracks across the bare brown earth; each footprint held a saucerful of black grainy shadow from the rising sun.

"Crusoe and Friday."

"If anybody was tracking us they'd have it made."

"Some primitive tribes believe that you can magic a person by using his footprints."

"I wonder how? Do you stab them or dig them up? I can see the connection; footprints do seem like hair or nail-clippings. Some part of you left behind."

"A kind of possession. Maybe kings' footprints used to be valuable. . . . What are you thinking?"

"That it would be a good thing to throw them away Along with one's shoes."

"The boy without footprints. You'd have to throw away your feet too."

"Yes."

Catriona made no answer to this, but looked at him gravely and sadly. His eyes were fixed on the skyline of roofs beyond the park; he was thinking dreamily that they resembled the right-hand edge of a printed page with lines of irregular length. For perhaps the thousandth time Catriona meditated on the paradox of Gabriel. Everything about him conveyed warmth: his smile, his voice, his handshake, his whole habit of accepting events complete and making the best of them; and yet he was embarked on a process of folding himself away, closing up, raising a barricade round himself; all this he was doing with calm, deliberate intent; how could he do it? Wasn't it a cowardly thing to do? Cowardly? *Gabriel?* The bravest person she knew? How could she bear to let him? How could she bear to keep silent while it happened. And yet she knew that he would do it and she would bear it, she must; the simple keystone of their relationship was their mutual respect, their absolute abstention from any interference or pressure on each other.

"Like two rivers running side by side," he had said once, with his head on her breast, listening to her heart beat.

"Mesopotamia. The Garden of Eden."

It was queer, Catriona thought, and rather frightening, but sustaining too, this vision she had, they both had, of what lay ahead. It's a kind of spiritual headway we are making, and once the process has begun, there's no stopping or reversing it; as soon as we have learned something, as soon as one stage is passed, we can't help advancing to the next; we know that we shall undergo these changes, whatever pain, whatever sacrifice they entail.

The plumy dog circled and came back to them hopefully; Catriona picked up a stick and threw it for him. He galloped off after it, his banners flying.

Gabriel said, "Gus told me once that towards the end of his life he intended to get rid of more and more belongings, so as to end up with hardly anything. Even relationships with other people are a kind of burden, he said. And self-love is a ball-and-chain."

"I wonder," Catriona said reflectively, "if he was so wise——"

"You *know* he was wise."

"I was too small. I don't remember the wisdom. Only that he was warm and beautiful—like a big bonfire. But if he was so wise, why did he let himself be taken in by operators like Bella?"

"I don't think he was taken; he just let people use him because they needed to, like a tree allowing birds to nest in it."

"The tree can't stop the birds if it wanted to," Catriona said tartly. "You want to watch out for your similes."

He nodded, accepting her correction. "Did you know that the trees in Central Park are all dying because the ground is impacted? Too many people walk on it; their roots don't get enough air. I read they are spending six million dollars a year trying to save them."

A man strode out from under the doomed trees; he walked in a wild, veering, tacking manner, very fast; not as if he had no objective, but as if his objective continually altered. He was tall and plump; wore a black knitted cap and a long, European-looking overcoat which came down to his calves and flapped open as he walked; when he came nearer they saw that it was threadbare and torn.

"Just the same you'd think he'd find it rather too hot," Gabriel murmured thoughtfully.

"I expect it's his security. Like small children's comfort-blankets."

A white dove kept the man company in his erratic progress, occasionally perching on his shoulder, at other times flying round his head. He planted himself in front of them, and they saw that, although his mouth smiled, his eyes were wide with misery, staring at remembered horrors.

189

"There are too many fires!" he told them. "Too many. Too many. *Too many!*"

"I know," Catriona said gently. "There are." Her little pale face was filled with compassion.

"Listen—you don't *listen!* There are too many fires. Too many. Too many!"

"What can we do for him?" said Gabriel, troubled.

"Nothing. Just listen."

"I wish we could help him."

"There are too many fires. There are too many fires," he cried at them heartbrokenly. "Too many, I tell you!"

He swung round and strode off.

"New York's full of poor nuts like him," said Catriona. "Lots of them seem to ride in the buses, where they get a kind of audience when they talk."

"There's something pinned on the back of his coat—a bit of paper."

"Too far away now to read what it says."

His pace was so rapid that he was already twenty-five yards off, with the bird blowing round his head like another sheet of paper.

"Maybe he'll come back," said Catriona.

"That's the second bird we've met today."

The first, a pigeon, had arrived as Catriona came home from night work; it had flown through the glassless window and then panicked in the enclosed place and dashed itself against the walls and ceiling, scattering feathers and terrifying the dog, until Gabriel managed to entangle it in his shirt.

Even after it was liberated the room had seemed so full of fright and hysteria that they had decided to go up to the park and watch the sun rise.

"That man with his bird reminds me of a time when Thomas took me on an outing to St. Paul's," Gabriel said. "A swallow had flown into the catheral. There were crowds of people inside wandering about, but no one took any notice or seemed to be trying to do anything about the swallow, and it flew round and round, right up in the dome. I thought it was dreadful. One of the reasons no one paid any attention to it was because they were all staring at a fat man who had come in—he was grotesquely fat, mountainously. He must have weighed at least four hundred pounds. He waddled in with a coachload of tourists and made straight for a row of seats, and sat down as if he would never walk again. He couldn't possibly have gone round even the ground-floor of St. Paul's, let alone up those spiral stairs. I couldn't understand even how he could have got into the excursion coach; he must have taken up at least four seats. I wondered what possible pleasure he could have got from the trip; he seemed so exhausted; perhaps he just did it because he couldn't bear to stay at home. All the people were staring at him and grinning and nudging each other, and the swallow was flying desperately round and round up above. Both the things together made me so miserable that I asked Thomas if we could go home, although we'd only just come and had been planning to go up into the lantern and then on to the Tower of London. Thomas always tried to do all the things for me that he thought Gus would have done."

"But it wasn't the same?"

"Not the same. I could always feel him worriedly wondering if he was doing the right thing. It wasn't his fault —not those times. He tried his very best. But everything Gus did had—had a kind of brightness about it. After Gus had gone and I knew for certain that he was dead, was never coming back—and I took a long, long time to believe that—because, after all, he might have walked through those South American jungles for years and finally turned up at last—anyway, when I'd at last accepted that he was really dead, all the things he'd ever sent or given me grew to have a kind of sacred importance. Even oddments—like a grey plastic carrier bag from Orly airport that had had French cheese in it—envelopes addressed to me in his handwriting—a little scribbled drawing of a fern that he had done when he was explaining something to me—things like that, I couldn't bear to throw away. I had a whole cupboard full of stuff."

"What did you do with them when you left home?"

"Oh, I'd got rid of them before that. After I'd been watching *her* for a while—Duessa. The way she mourned him was so disgusting. So—so exhibitionist. It made me feel sick. Setting up a shrine for him in the cellar. It seemed to throw all my memories of him out of focus and I couldn't bear to do anything that seemed as childish as what she was doing. So in the end I took all my odds and ends and the presents he'd given me that I'd grown too old for—not the books of course—and burned them in the garden and buried the ashes."

"Did you feel sad?"

"Yes. But it taught me that you can get free from anything if you want to."

"Love, too?" She stopped a moment to tighten her short plaits, which she had brought forward and spliced together on top of her head, like the Unicorn Lady's.

"I expect so. Once you take the first step away it's like breaking through a barrier; after that it's just a case of putting distance between you and it. Nothing's ever so bad again."

He looked up at the sky and said, "More rain on the way."

"Lucky we picked up that umbrella."

A jet threaded the sky, leaving its white skein among the gathering rain-clouds, and Gabriel said, "All the nitrogen oxide they leave behind is going to reduce the ozone layer so that people will start getting skin cancer, and there's going to be so much sulphur dioxide up there soon that it will permanently change the climate."

"What a mess. Maybe this rain is dilute sulphuric acid."

"And what he took for H_2O was H_2SO_4. . . . Rain in the park makes me remember hearing about Gus's death."

"How did you hear?"

"I was out with Bo. Walking along Piccadilly. He'd taken me to the Apsley House museum. And we got ices and walked along eating them. And then we saw evening papers with the headline about Gus and the air-crash being sold outside Green Park tube station. Bo bought one and we read it standing there on the pavement. We walked into the park and I saw that Bo was crying. *I* didn't cry— he did. I was terribly shocked because he looked so devastated—his face just came to pieces like a paper bag in the rain. Real rain began to fall—it poured down and soaked my ice-cream cone and I threw it away. When I was little I used to believe that you could make it rain by crying out of doors—I suppose I'd done it once and it had. We walked across the park and down to Victoria Station and got a bus home, and Bo was crying all the way, not making any pretence about it, terrible great convulsing sobs that sounded like pure agony—like a person having a baby. When we got home Bella wasn't there, I don't know where she had gone; the house was empty. I've never known it to feel so empty. We switched on the six o'clock news and the radio said the same thing, that the plane had crashed and everyone was killed. I couldn't really believe it, but I began to shiver, I felt terribly cold, and Bo said I'd better go to bed and he'd bring me up some hot milk. So I did and he did, and we both drank a bit of it. And then he sat by me on my pillow and put his arm round me and guided my hand to hold onto his cock, which had all of a sudden sprouted up quite large, and he undid his pants, and we went on talking about Gus, and all the time he held my hand round his thing, and we talked and talked and he cried and I shivered with cold, I just couldn't get warm. In the end he got into bed with me."

"What did *you* feel? Surprised?"

"Not surprised; no. After Gus died I felt so terribly sad that nothing surprised me for months; I was just *tired* out with sadness. It was such hard work learning that I'd never see him again. The whole world seemed to be the wrong shape—as if it had ruptured its outer casing, like a slit bicycle tyre, and the inner bits were bulging out, so that all sorts of deformed shapes were to be expected."

Catriona looked at him thoughtfully. She had not been in the habit of using her mind to think about people. She thought constantly in terms of music: its patterns, its landscapes. Her mental processes were occupied in following the outlines of existing musical statements or creating new ones. Until the reappearance of her playmate Gabriel she had placed other people simply in two groups: those who knew more about music than she did and those who knew less. Because Catriona had been a politely brought-up child, the ones in the second group, which included her parents, were treated with civility, but avoided wherever possible, and escaped from at the earliest opportunity. Time spent with them counted as time wasted. The ones in the first group were accorded respectful attention until or unless they progressed to the second group, when they were quietly abandoned.

But now, with the return of Gabriel, her habit had changed. Quietly and continuously she studied him. The questions she put to him were almost the first she had ever asked about anything other than music. Until she began to wonder what had happened to Gabriel during the six years that separated them, the idea had never entered her head that human beings had past lives which affected them as much as their visible circumstances.

She said, "What did you think about Bo? When that happened?"

He pondered, watching a squirrel which had scampered across the grass and struck a heraldic pose and now seemed to be hoping that somebody would admire it.

"I felt he was reduced. Before, I'd looked up to him —he was quite well-known, then, with his paintings—"

"Yes, I remember—"

"He'd met the Queen—and was a friend of Gus—and he can be very funny and intelligent too; then to find that *he* needed *me* seemed to bring him down to a lower level. Instead of being larger than me he was the same size, and somehow soft and defenceless like an oyster without its shell."

"Did you mind?"

"It was a kind of loss," he said, frowning, still studying the squirrel. "I'd hoped he would comfort *me,* and instead I was having to help him."

"No, I mean did you mind what he did to you?"

"Oh no," he said in surprise. "That hadn't got anything to do with me really. I thought it was rather silly. If you'd been there at that time, I expect we'd have joked about it."

"You must have been lonely then."

"Yes I was lonely. I used to cry walking home from school. It was so horrible getting back to the house."

"I wish I hadn't gone back to California."

"Umm. But then I began watching Duessa and that gave me something to think about."

"Did she know about Bo and you?"

"No I'm sure she didn't," he said, and frowned again at another memory. "She was—is—terribly unobservant about other people. There were absolutely basic things she never knew about Thomas. Anyway she and Bo had a big row soon after Gus died and he went to Spain with somebody and didn't come back for months and by the time he did she'd married Thomas."

"How did Thomas and Bo get on?"

"All right. Till the cruise. And Bo's show. I told you

194

about that. Then Bo stopped painting and got very crabby."

She nodded and said after a while, "Was that the worst day of your life? When Gus died?"

"Yes. Yes it was." Gabriel was silent for a few minutes and then burst out, "The trouble was that he put too *much* into me. Like when you water a plant in a dry pot. You should trickle in the water a little at a time, so the earth has a chance to soak it up. He didn't do that. He *flooded* me. When he was gone, it was all spilling out, I felt I couldn't keep it, I can't keep him, he's gone. Trying to hang onto it was the most terrible struggle—like holding up a huge weight—"

"Maybe he wasn't really very bright about rearing kids."

"No. I just wasn't equal to what he wanted to do. If I'd been his real son— But he did love me."

"Was it that? Or did he want to put all of himself somewhere? To make a legacy of himself?"

"No, he wanted to be received, to be heard."

"He shouldn't have. When you write music, you don't think, Who is going to listen to this?"

"Music is just sound. It doesn't have meaning."

They had thrown themselves down under a tree opposite the open-air theatre. The dog was thirstily lapping water from the pond. Farther away in the distance, sounds of the city lay in layers like atmosphere: traffic, motor-horns, police sirens, the wail of a ship, the stutter of a helicopter.

"Not like those sounds," he said.

"That's just bullshit," Catriona told him kindly. "Shows how little you know. Music has plenty of meaning. It's a different kind, that's all. . . . Anyway, Gus shouldn't have done that to you. He was trying to force you."

"Not by his standards." Gabriel took off the faded blue sleeveless pullover, which had been knitted for him by Loraine, and unbuttoned his white cotton shirt to the waist. "It's hot. Even with the rain."

"Why don't you take your shirt right off?"

"Because I don't want a lot of people looking at my bare stomach."

"Prissy. There are about ten people in the park."

"Ten too many."

"People shouldn't leave things to their children," Ca-

195

triona said, lying back and gazing up at the limp, damp, late-summer leaves dangling overhead. "Children should be allowed to start free."

"They can't. How can they? They've got their legacy before they're even born. You have in you—I have in me—all the battles our parents ever fought."

"Did Gus and Bella fight?"

"Not on the surface. She pretended to do everything his way. But really she did what she wanted—deceived him the whole time I'm sure. Only he wasn't deceived. I hate," said Gabriel, propping his elbows on his knees and pressing his chin into his hands, "I absolutely *hate* to think I may be her child."

"What makes you think you are?"

"People who didn't know I was supposed to be adopted said I look like her. And in some ways I feel like her. The same shape. I've got the same urge to embroider things instead of leaving them bare. Only I try not to do it, whereas she does it all the time. She'd told me so many lies about my birth, I sometimes wonder if she's forgotten the real truth. First she told me Gus was sterile. But he wasn't, I know; Bo told me the main reason for his marrying again was that he wanted a child. His first wife had a baby but it died. So he was sad when he and Bella couldn't produce one and that was why they adopted me."

"Why couldn't they have one?"

"Bo told me that too. She'd had a—her womb taken out—"

"Hysterectomy—"

"Right—before she married Gus. She didn't tell him till afterwards. Then I suppose he was disappointed but it was too late."

"Wonder why she had the hysterectomy?"

"To save trouble perhaps? She didn't like looking after kids."

"Then why adopt you?"

"He made her."

"I guess. Do you suppose—if you are her son—that Gus knew? Guessed?"

"Probably," Gabriel said. "I'm sure Gus could see right through her. She's like those water-beetles that are all transparent. You can see the works inside. Now I bet she wants me to stay alive because, when I'm twenty-one she'll be able to wheedle money out of me."

"Couldn't you give it all away now, to the World Health Organisation or something, and then she might just as well leave you alone?"

"I've said that in my will, but I can't really do anything till I inherit. Even having it to give away puts one in a position of power. It's horrible."

"Most people long for power."

"Like old Loraine. Oh, you didn't know her, of course. All she really liked was organising people. She began by cleaning their houses and slowly took them over altogether. She was kind to me though. But she overreached herself in the end."

"How?"

"I suppose someone finally stood up to her and she couldn't stand it. So she took a lot of her asthma pills and sniffed up a canful of spray-cleaner."

Apparently wanting to get away from the subject, he looked at his watch and said, "Ought we to go back? James said he'd collect the dog between nine and ten."

"We've got hours of time yet," she said quickly. "Why did he leave the dog behind the second time? Wasn't that rather peculiar?"

"He said it hated car-rides."

"Gabriel," said Catriona, rolling over on her stomach to look at him.

"Umn?"

"If James *has* found this place—and it's all right for you to go there—can I come too?"

Her voice was very low, and she had become even paler than usual.

Gabriel made no answer for a moment. Then he said gently, "You did *promise* you wouldn't do this."

"I wouldn't be a bother. Truly." She swallowed. "I— I wouldn't even *speak*. I'd just stay somewhere quietly. Till it was over."

"Why? What possible difference could it make? Dying is something you have to do by yourself. It's a solitary affair."

"I could keep you company. I could die too."

"No you couldn't!" he said bluntly. "You don't really want to. You've got a hold on all sorts of things. Your job is music and staying alive. You'll make out all right once I'm gone. Don't you remember that story I used to love in the ghost book—about the woman whose dead husband came back and sat on the window sill and said to her, 'Jump!' and you always thought it was frightening, but it gave me a wonderful secure feeling. I've always been half in love with death."

"*Easeful* death." She smiled faintly.

"So you see I've got to go and you've got to stay."

She stared across the park, between the verticals of the trees, pressing her pale lips together, seeing the long, empty, dusty unbearable vista of life without him.

"I do hate it so. Just saying good-bye to you somewhere—in some place like *here*."

Looking at him, she thought in helpless pain, if only he'd call me his precious girl just *once* more, if only he'd put his arms round me, just to show he enters *at all* into how I'm feeling. He's gone some steps of the way already. He can only just hear my voice.

"It doesn't really make any difference where you say good-bye," he said, still in the same gentle, reasonable voice.

"It does, it does! And suppose something went wrong? He isn't going to stay with you, is he? James?"

"Oh no. He's going to Canada. He said he'd just take me there and leave me."

"Well suppose—suppose you needed help? Suppose you were in pain? Suppose you changed your mind?"

"I don't mind pain. It wouldn't last forever. And I shan't change my mind."

"Suppose you didn't die for ages? You'd just starve to death. It would be horrible."

"No it wouldn't. And all this is beside the point." Gabriel seemed so tranquil about it that for a moment she wondered if he had taken other measures—pills, razor?—for additional security, for a fail-safe. "You're starting to fuss and you promised, you promised faithfully, that you wouldn't. I want my mind free, don't you see? I have to concentrate. This takes all the energy I have. If you were sitting an exam—"

"I'm not making *much* of a fuss. But I'll try not to. I do know you hate it. . . . Can I tell you a story?"

"Yes; all right. One of your moral fables?" He gave her a brief smile. "Wait a minute—"

It was beginning to rain quite hard. He took the old umbrella, which they had rescued from a trash-can in Sixth Avenue, opened it, and tied the rope they had used for a dog-lead to its point, then suspended the open umbrella from a branch above their heads.

"Now we can sit under it. Go ahead."

She sat cross-legged under the umbrella, and he turned round and lay with his head on her knees.

"Like the Unicorn," she said. "Putting his head in her lap."

"She was really trapping him for the hunters. It's a horrible thought. That's why she's so sad."

"Your legs are going to get wet," Catriona said.

"Doesn't matter. They can do with a wash. Tell the story, then."

He lay relaxed, gazing up at the leafy ceiling, and she looked down at him with the Lady's expression of hopeless foreknowledge. Holding his face between her palms, she began:

"Once there was a princess called Savitri, daughter of King Asvapati, who was so extremely beautiful, good, clever, and perfect that she could find nobody willing to marry her. She had no suitors. I suppose they were all put off by her perfectness. So one of her father's wise counsellors said, 'She had better go out into the world and wander about and find a husband for herself.' So off she went."

"Did she find one?"

"Yes, she found a prince, Satyavan, who was good and kind and noble. Only he hadn't any money. He lived with his poor old parents, who had been driven from their kingdom by a usurper, and the father was blind, so they had nothing but a little hut in the forest, and Satyavan earned their living by cutting wood. Savitri went back to her father and said, 'Satyavan is a man I can love; I will marry him.' Well, her father didn't mind his being so poor, but the wise counsellor said, 'There is one great disadvantage about this prince, which is that he is doomed to die a year from today.'

"But Savitri said, 'That makes no difference to me. Live or dead, he's the only man I can love.'" Catriona's voice trembled, briefly, but she collected herself and went on. "So they were married, and she went to live with him and his parents in the forest. At the end of the year he went out to chop wood one day as usual, and she went with him. And he said, 'I feel a little drowsy, I think I'll have a nap.' He lay down to sleep with his head in her lap."

She looked down at the upside-down face of Gabriel

below hers. But his eyes were fixed on the distant trees and the lattice of falling rain.

"Savitri looked away through the forest, and she saw a tall, dark, stern-faced stranger in a yellow robe coming towards them. In his hand he held a noose. He was Yama, king of the dead. He said, 'I have come to take your husband's soul,' and, with his noose he drew the living essence out of Satyavan. Savitri put down her hand, and she felt his heart stop beating. Then Yama strode off, and Savitri gently laid her husband's head on the moss and began quickly running after him. Yama heard her, and said, 'Turn back, Princess, for I am going to places where you may not follow.' But she said, 'A wife's duty is to go wherever her husband goes,' and she spoke so earnestly and so movingly about the joys and duties of married life that Yama was touched, and granted her a wish: anything but the life of her husband. So she wished that her old blind father-in-law should get his sight back. And Yama granted her wish. Then he strode on, and in spite of his forbidding her to do so, she still followed. 'For,' she said, 'I am in the best of all company, and why should I leave it?' and she spoke so impressively about how the right way to live is to seek out good companions and remain faithful to them, that again Yama was touched and granted her any wish but her husband's life. She wished that her father-in-law should regain his lost kingdom, and that was granted. 'But now,' Yama said, 'you must turn back.' 'No,' she said, 'for it is a virtue to stay with my husband,' and she spoke about how goodness is first an avoidance of evil and second a clinging to what is excellent. And Yama was moved in spite of himself and granted her another wish, anything but her husband's life. She wished her own father should have a hundred sons, for she had been his only child. And her wish was granted. 'But now,' Yama said, 'Lady, you must turn back.' 'You can't make me,' she said, 'for it would be unjust to prevent my being with my husband, and everybody knows that Death's justice is absolute.' He was forced to acknowledge the strength of her reasoning, and he granted her another wish. She wished for a hundred sons for herself, to carry on Satyavan's name and race. And he granted this wish too. 'But now you must go to your own home,' he said, 'for I am going to the Kingdom of Death, far to the south, and that is no place for you.' But Savitri spoke so eloquently about the whole solar system, the sun, the moon, and the earth, each in its own orbit, and how the only possible home for her was with her husband, that finally Yama was conquered, and cried, 'Lady, your wisdom and virtue deserve any reward, even the greatest. Ask of me anything you like!' And she cried, 'Give me back Satyavan!' So he undid the noose and set free the spirit of Satyavan. And she ran till she came to the spot where his body still lay. And the spirit flew back into its nest, and Satyavan stirred and yawned and sat up and said, 'What a refreshing nap. Why, what a long time I have slept! It is quite dark. You should have woken me sooner. I feel as if I have been away on a journey.' And she said, 'Oh, my lord, you have been even farther than you thought.' And as they went back through the wood to his father's hut she told him the whole story. And when they got home they found that his father wasn't blind any more—"

Catriona's voice died away. She had come to the end of the story before she intended to. Surreptitiously she wiped a ribbon of wet from her cheek.

Gabriel's face smiled at her, upside-down. She saw creases running radially from his eyes into the freckles on his nose.

"Do you see yourself as Savitri?" he said. "Do you think you can make Yama change his mind?"

"It isn't Yama who has to change." She clenched her hands and drove the nails into the palms. "It's you."

"You know I never change, once my mind is made up."

She did know. But she drew a long, difficult, despairing breath, trying to summon strength for more argument.

"Look," he said, tipping his head forward. "The man with the dove is coming back."

He was far away still, but lurching along in their direction at his rapid, erratic pace. The dove still kept him company.

Despite the rain, more people were in the park now: boys jog-trotting along the paths, girls walking their dogs before going to work. A few children were playing baseball. A man wrapped in a raincoat lay asleep on a bench across the pond.

The madman with the dove came up to them and stood, as before, in speechless supplication. His jaws worked with the urgency of what he had to say, and finally he forced the message past the barrier of his unwilling tongue.

"Georgie took a pill. Georgie took a pill. There are too many fires."

"Yes there are too many," Catriona said. "Far too many."

Gabriel pushed himself to his feet in one swing and moved round behind the man to read the paper pinned on his back.

"It says, 'Please bring my brother home. 667 West Eighteenth Street. Maria Fernandez.' Don't you think we'd better do that? He may have been out all night."

"I don't think we have time. If we're to get home to meet James."

"Well, then, you take him, and I'll take the dog home."

Catriona bit her lip. Then she said, "All right. I'll take him. But—but you won't *go*—will you—till I get there?"

"I'd better not promise," he said quietly. "We don't know how James is fixed for time." He pulled down the umbrella from the tree and whistled to the dog.

A great surge of silent protest almost broke up her resolution. But at last she said, "All right," and, taking the arm of the man, who shied away nervously, she started in the direction of the park entrance.

Across on the other side of the little lake a voice cried, *"Gabriel!"*

Eleven

Bo 1974

Bo and James were having breakfast in a coffee shop. Weak sunlight when they first walked in had made the imitation captain's chairs and rustic tables covered with red-and-white checked paper cloths appear quite cosy and cheerful, but now the rain was falling steadily outside and the whole place was shrouded in grey dusk, particularly the corner where they sat.

202

Bo's breakfast consisted of black coffee and his dangling cigarette, but James was seriously working his way through juice, eggs, toast, bacon, waffles, and syrup.

"It's hardly the dream-place of his childhood," he was saying. "In fact, my God, what a dump! But I daresay it will do well enough as a retreat where he can peacefully glide into the great unknown, poor little beast. If that's what he wants."

He smiled at Bo. When James smiled, the outer ends of his very volatile eyebrows tilted down, while the inner ends shot up, and the corners of his mouth turned up, so that mouth and eyebrows together suddenly sketched a circle in his face; the effect was one of immense charm, but also disconcerting, as if he had drawn a lightning diagram in front of his face and labelled it "Fun."

"Is it what he wants?" Bo said slowly.

"Oh, very much so. We had a long talk. The girl had gone off to work at her restaurant. He bared his soul to me. He just wants to finish this opus he's at work on—apparently it's a meditation on death, all his reflections about it—and then he's going to sit back in the lotus position and wait for nirvana. All he wants is to be left alone, without interruption or fuss, to get on with it. From our point of view, couldn't be better."

"But what about the girl?"

"She's not to come. He wants to be completely alone. And she's accepted this, it seems."

"Suppose she hasn't accepted it? Suppose she tries to follow?"

"She has no idea where the place is. For all she can tell it's in the Arizona desert. *He* doesn't know where it is either. Just had these idyllic, romantic memories."

"So if he didn't know, how did *you* find it?"

"Oh, it was partly luck. A combination of that and local knowledge. After she'd gone off to her night-shift I questioned him very minutely about the place and he managed to recall that they went once for groceries to a place called Huguenot—the name had stuck in his mind because Gus was reading *The Three Musketeers* aloud to him every night at bed-time—pretty good for a six-year-old! And after a lot of digging he thought he remembered a river called the Kill River."

"Huguenot? Somewhere up in the Catskills?"

"No. And not the one near New Rochelle either," James said cheerfully. "Much closer to home."

Bo looked at him through half-closed eyes and slowly exhaled a fan of smoke, pushing out his lower lip to its full extent. He tapped on the red-and-white checked paper with long, beautiful, dirty, paint-spattered, nicotine-stained fingers.

"Don't be so bloody smug and pleased with yourself, sugarcookie," he drawled malevolently. "How did you come to know about this other Huguenot, then?"

"Because one of my students happened to have a grandparent who died there and went back for the funeral. Can't imagine any other reason for wanting to visit the place."

"Suppose you hadn't happened to have this piece of luck, what then?"

"Then I'd have found him another place, equally suitable," James said indifferently. He took two quick bites of bacon and munched briskly. With his shock of white hair and long, narrow, intelligent face, he looked, Bo thought, as so often before, like a clever badger; attractive, but in a not-quite-human way; there was something alert but removed in the expression of his rather close-set pale-grey eyes; they observed, they scrutinised, but then flicked quickly away; they failed to engage; he frequently gave the impression of looking at a mental watch, wondering if it was time to move on. As a matter of fact, James had the useful atavistic faculty of always knowing to the minute what time it was; he never wore a watch.

"So you went and poked about?"

"So I went and poked about. And I found the place—remarkably much as he had described it—again, pretty good after a ten-year gap—and allowing, of course, for the fact that it has been more or less devastated in the meantime, and subtracting the rosy glow of youthful impressions, et cetera. Instead of being in the middle of a vast untrodden wilderness it's—where it is."

"And it was actually vacant?"

"Vacant and slowly becoming derelict. The land's too swampy for building, so the real estate companies which are busy covering every other square yard with boxy little houses packed tight as tombstones—and performing much the same function—were obliged to leave that bit alone. And I gathered from the old man's granddaughter that the local historical society would quite like to acquire it, but can't raise the cash at present, since they're fully extended with their town reconstruction scheme. And nobody wants to live there because it hasn't any amenities like piped water or electricity—the old boy never bothered —and is in the middle of nowhere. She jumped at my offer to rent it for a couple of months."

"Where is the old man?"

"Slowly dying of cancer in Pleasant Plains nursing home."

Bo shivered, and dragged on his cigarette. "What about the granddaughter? Is she likely to remember you?"

"Not a chance, my dear. An avaricious, kinky-haired little bitch, only interested in making a quick dollar at no trouble to herself. I wore dark glasses and an auburn afro wig, she wouldn't know me from Ludwig van Beethoven."

"You paid in cash?"

"Of course. Got the keys, and permission to do what I like. There's an iron stove, and a woodpile, and basic furniture—table, chairs, bed."

"So what's the plan?"

"I went on into town and stocked up with a suitable supply of groceries, candles, matches, even loo-paper, all the luxuries. The complete castaway. Mrs. Swiss Family R. could have done no better. He won't need to stir a step outside the place."

"And the bonus?" Bo asked, speaking very quietly and looking down at his hands.

"And the bonus." James dropped his voice to match. "So now all the kind man has to do is go back and pick him up—without the girl—take him there by a roundabout route—and then we proceed to phase two. And sit back and wait for phase three."

Bo looked up. His eyes were full of grief. "I wish it didn't happen to be *him.*"

"My dear, what's the odds? He's not long for this world anyway. Any other world will suit him better. That boy has a real death wish if I ever saw one. Put him out of your mind. There's as good fish in the sea. Or at least, there's fish."

Sucking in his cheeks, drawing on his cigarette, Bo looked more than ever like a death's head. "He's all I've got left to remind me of Gus."

"Oh, Gus, Gus! You're all nuts about this wretched

Gus," James said. "What did he have that was so special?"

"He was special. I've often tried to pretend that he wasn't, but he was."

"You just need him to be special. He was dying like the rest of us. Hooked on life, trying to sink his claws into something—anything—before he was dragged off kicking. Anyway the boy's not his—there's no real link."

"Don't be so literal, Jem. Gus put a lot of himself into the boy. And no funny cracks, I beg. He loved Gabriel."

"All right, he loved him," James said patiently. "Sure he did. He seems a nice boy! A nice kid with a death wish. No good to you. So let him have his wish. Think of the benefits that are going to accrue. Freedom—security—independence at last from that god-awful Bella who's been draining out your guts like a vampire all your life long—*and* a sock in the eye for Thomas."

"You don't think there's any chance of him finding the boy—Thomas?"

"How could there be? You say he's all shot to bits with his rheumatism and the stuff he takes for it. And nobody else knows where the boy is, or will be. He told me he hadn't told his grandmother where he was—said he didn't want the old lady bothered. So *she* wouldn't be able to tell Thomas. And Thomas doesn't know the girl. Doesn't know she exists. And even if he did, Gabriel could be in Easter Island for all she knows. The boy's not going to tell her. I advised that, and he quite agreed. Just to be on the safe side."

Bo nodded several times, slowly. "Just the same I do wish blasted Bella hadn't fetched Thomas over," he said slowly. "He really bugs me. Every time I see him he reminds me of those pictures. I could kill him. I could with great pleasure put my hands round his neck and squeeze till his eyes popped out like peas. Six months' work! And the best work I ever did."

"Don't kid yourself. You'll do as good again."

"No I shan't. Not ever. That was my peak creative year. Now I can't be bothered. I don't have any ideas."

"You use up too much energy feeding your parasite sister. You're living under strain. When you can afford to get away—travel—see new places—"

"That's what people always say." Bo savagely ground out a stub and lit a new cigarette.

206

"Well, at least with financial security, you won't need to paint. Can do it or not, as the spirit moves. If you don't need to you probably will."

"And to think that miserable moron doesn't even *remember* about it," Bo muttered, slitting the extinguished stub with his long jagged thumbnail and scattering charred tobacco on the red-and-white checks.

"Well, you can remind him sometime."

"I intend to."

"Now look, take it easy, baby, will you? We don't want to ball up this enterprise on account of your nursing a petty grudge. If the truth be known, that business of the gramophone record was pretty childish and pointless. Suppose he had arrived early and found you there?"

"He couldn't have. I called Crusoe and Selkirk and checked the time of his plane. And then I watched from the window and saw him come wambling along the street like a zombie with his bags. There was plenty of time to start the record and lock up and leave by the fire stairs onto the roof before he came crawling up with his luggage."

"Well I hope it gave you a big lift," James said drily.

"Oh it did. It did. But not as big a lift as it will give me to tell him sometime all I know about Gabriel. *All* I know. Thomas has got that boy on his conscience like a —like an albatross. Thomas has got so much conscience he's wet all over—he drips with it. He's drowning in it. When Bella got shot of him he wanted to adopt Gabriel. But of course she wasn't having that."

"Who divorced whom?" James asked, pouring syrup on another waffle.

"Oh, she divorced him. Cruelty. Incompatibility. Instability. My pictures and so forth. He didn't contest. Didn't answer any letters. Seemed a bit stunned by it all."

"What about the boy? How did he react?"

"Got more and more withdrawn. I asked him once how he felt about Thomas offering to adopt him, and he looked miserable, the way he does, and said it would be for the wrong reasons. I think in a way he was fond of Thomas but he always felt there was a layer of deceit between them."

"What a little prig."

"Yes, he's that . . . I suppose any product of alternate

upbringing by Bella and Gus was bound to turn out pretty weird."

"Well, it's prigs who make the world go round. . . . What do you suppose will happen to Bella?" James asked after a pause, pouring his final cup of coffee.

"God knows. I don't give a shit."

"Are you *sure?*" James said, looking at him narrowly. "So many times you've said that—and then she's come wailing, and you've got all tangled up again."

"Once I'm independent, so far as I am concerned she can go to the devil in her own way. Maybe she'll go back to Arthur whosis. I've rescued her enough. I got her married to Gus and settled in life. Though he was wasted on her. Oh, why did he have to go and *die?*" Bo burst out in bitter rage. "Gus was the best thing that ever happened to me. Sometimes I think he was the only good thing."

"That's not very chummy of you," James observed, drinking his lukewarm coffee.

"Don't be lugubrious, Jem. The thing about Gus was," said Bo, pushing the tobacco grains into a pattern with his fingernail, "that he respected a person's individual integrity. Dignity. No matter who the person was. . . .For instance, he's the only person who ever called me by my real name."

"What's that?"

"Calvin."

"*Calvin?* You never told me that. I thought your name was Hugh and you didn't choose to have it used because it had unfortunate associations."

"Calvin is my middle name. Hugh Calvin Farragut. And Bella is Daphne Bella Farragut."

"I would have used Calvin any time you asked me to."

"Oh, sure. But Gus took the trouble to find out, and why I hated the name Bo."

"I didn't know you hated the name Bo as well. Why didn't you say? What a mass of hang-ups you are. What's wrong with Bo?"

"That was Uncle Hugh too. Dear Uncle Hugh's conversation was always full of euphemisms. Of a kind peculiar to himself. Sex was the old oompa-doompa. Whores were slot-machine sweeties. Various parts of the body had various whimsical aliases. Shit was curds and whey. Going to the bog was taking a trip to pango-pango. The male cock, don't ask me why, was a nasturtium. The

208

female equivalent was a cabbage salad. Breasts were itsy-bitsies. 'Oo, she's got a nice pair of itsy-bitsies!' he'd cry, watching television. I can't describe to you the inexpressible degraded coyness of Uncle Hugh's conversation. He dragged in these phrases all the time. By their hair, screaming. Having coined them, I suppose he wished to get the maximum usage out of them. Listening to him was like hearing *Portnoy's Complaint* rewritten by Enid Blyton."

"You poor little mite," said James, grinning. "Raped by a euphemist. Much worse than death. So?"

"So Hugh's word for ass was generally *derrière*. 'Get on with that job, boy,' he'd cry, 'or I'll be obliged to connect my *bottine* to your *derrière*.' He had a kind of snuffling giggle, a simper, that would come out with his more idiomatic usages; I can hear it still. Another word for ass, don't ask me the derivation of this one, was *bohu*. Maybe it came from the French *tohu-bohu*. He pronounced it bo-hew. And as I was called Beau by our asinine mother, and my name was Hugh, he got endless etymological fun from permutations and variations on my name. Our chum the bum. Our little chump. Our youthful rump. *Amo, amas,* I love an ass. For months he called me Bottom and Bella Titania."

"What were her reactions?"

"Oh, she loathed him too, of course, but not to the degree I did. He wasn't quite so sadistic with her. Though I daresay he accounts for her sado-masochistic gambols with Artie and Peter. Anyway, unfortunately she got to calling me Beau, and it followed me to school, and some journalist picked it up when I had my first show, and it's clung to me ever since."

"From now on I call you Calvin. And treat you accordingly. Why didn't you ever tell me this before?"

"Sunk in the sands of the subconscious. Never got washed up to the top. Gus had this theory—did I ever tell you about it?—that we ought to learn to hibernate. Hibernation is all to do with testosterone, it seems; if you inject people with the blood of hibernating bears, it's possible they might go into a state of suspended animation, body temperature right down and so forth."

"What's the good of that? I'd rather be awake, while I'm here. I don't get the connection."

"Why, for one thing, we could pass away long stretches

of boring time, space-flights or sea-voyages or absence from the beloved. Gus's main point was that death takes place most frequently at certain periods related to the sun—February in the northern hemisphere, July in the southern. Put yourself in a four-month sleep straddling the crucial period, you'll live twice as long."

"Better tell that to little Gabriel. Maybe hibernation would serve his turn."

"Hush," said Bo, glancing round the almost empty place.

"But I still don't exactly see its relevance to your hang-up about your name."

"A four-month moratorium on conscious activity—all that extra dream-time—would help the subconscious get that kind of bad experience properly digested. We'd all be calmer and more rational. I'd have dreamed it all out of my system by now."

"Melting down the past in retrospect."

"As no doubt Thomas wishes he could."

"Who doesn't? I thought you said he doesn't remember about your pictures."

"No he doesn't. Bella brought up the subject and he didn't know what she was talking about. I meant about Gabriel."

"Oh, that."

"The fatuous, complacent oaf! How he had the face to set himself up on such a moral pinnacle—he was always griping away about Bella's awful turpitude because she inveigled him into bed just after the accident. And all his stage-struck, adolescent, hero-worshiping, teen-age mawkish crush on Gus, whom he never even *met*. Pretending that, because he had wriggled his way into the family, he had a kind of *share* in Gus. The sentimental fool!"

"You're jealous," James said dispassionately. "Just as you were jealous of Bella's relationship with Gus."

"What if I am? At least I don't kid myself about my own emotions."

"Being jealous over a dead man is a pretty stupid waste of emotional energy."

"I've got plenty of *that* to spare."

"Well for Christ's sake," said James soberly, "Don't waste any more of it on Bella. When you've got clear of her this time, *leave her alone*. You say you keep rescuing her. *I* have to keep rescuing *you*. And I've done it as often as I'm prepared to. Any more fuck-ups, and I'll be the one to go into hibernation. My emotional energy isn't as inexhaustible as yours."

He stood up, and cupped a hand under Bo's elbow. "Come along, it's time I went back and reclaimed poor Rufus. And got the show on the road."

"Why did you leave Rufus behind the second time?"

"I said he hated long car-rides—a black lie, he adores them; he'd never forgive me if he knew how I had betrayed him. So I asked if Gabriel would be kind enough to continue looking after the dear dog till I'd got back from my excursion to hunt for the mill. Of course he said he'd be glad to."

"Why did you do that?"

"Just in case the boy took fright, had any impulse to go off on his own and vanish before I reappeared. He's such a conscientious little cuss, I knew that, having said he'd look after the dog, he'd feel bound to stay there till I got back."

Bo glanced at James under his heavy lids. "Dear fellow! such a shrewd judge of character. And what little job are you going to give me, to stop me from bolting till you get back?"

"Look after Bella," said James. "Keep her out of mischief, for the last time. And don't get into any yourself."

Twelve

Thomas 1974

Thomas was dreaming. He had gone to Bo's studio on an errand for Bella, who wanted some drawings of plants that he had promised to do for her.

The studio, part of the old Fynche Place stable block, was out in the middle of Wanborough Common, astonishingly secluded and rural for a spot only five miles from Westminster. Bo said that he heard owls at night, foxes, even badgers. He slept there, on an army cot in the corner, did his cooking on a Primus, washed in the cold-water sink. Six large glass panes in the roof let in a cold steady light. Heating there was none, but Bo never seemed to feel the cold. Nobody ever came past except golfers and little girls riding ponies. Bo was interested neither in golf nor in ponies, nor in little girls.

It was a beautiful spring day, balmy air with just a tiny tang of frost. Uncurling green leaves. The soil warm and crumbling to dryness. Birds trying out their spring songs. Thomas crunched along the narrow cinder path to the stable door and knocked. But there was no answer, so he pushed open the door, which had become so swelled with damp that it never properly closed, and walked in.

The air inside was thick and fetid with cigarette smoke. Days and days of solid smoke. The studio smelt like an old filthy railway carriage. Blinking eyes which had started to sting painfully, Thomas peered through the blue haze.

The room was a total mess. Tubes of paint, newspapers, magazines, and huge toppling piles of old 78-rpm discs lay all over the floor, interspersed with orange peel, cigarette butts, eggshells, and chocolate wrappers. Bo sat as usual in his kitchen chair in front of his work-table, which was piled to shoulder-height with more things— rolls of paper, bottles of oil or whisky, and objects which Bo had fancied and carried home—a dead bird, a chunk of driftwood, a red-and white triangular road-sign, some polystyrene packing components.

Looking through the murky smoky air past all this piled clutter. Thomas was disconcerted to see Loraine in the far corner of the room, quite at ease, leaning back in an old deckchair, with her fat legs and feet resting on a cardboard carton. She was wearing her dirty old mauve coat and a gaudy-patterned part-silk headscarf, she had her jewelled glasses and her rubber-soled canvas Marks & Spencer housewife's flatties. She was smoking too, a cigarette stuck sideways at a rakish angle from the corner of her traplike mouth.

"Why, Thomas!" she said. "We weren't expecting you for another hour. We thought you were going to visit your father. Didn't you go, after all? Poor old fellow, he will be disappointed."

"Won't do, Thomas," said Bo, shaking his head. "Unfilial. No respect for your elders. Won't do at all."

"Thomas," said Loraine, "we're disappointed in you. I'm afraid we shall be obliged to tell Gabriel that the night he was in hospital you spent making love to his mother—"

"Screwing nonstop on the chapel floor," added Bo in a

bored drawl, squeezing a long worm of violet paint from a tube on to a broken china dinner-plate.

"And Bella—and your father—they'll all have to know, I'm afraid, unless you—"

"Unless I what?" Thomas tried to shout, but his tongue stuck to the roof of his mouth.

"I don't like disagreeables, you see," Loraine announced in a high, hard voice, quite unlike her normal rather gruff, deep tones, which had been deliberately cultivated, Thomas was certain, in order to impress and alarm her subordinates and people she wanted to control. "No, I don't like secret grudges and underhandedness, I like everything open and above-board."

"But what possible good will it do anyone if you tell them now?" Thomas demanded. "And why did you tell Bo?"

"How do you know I did tell Bo?" Loraine said, looking at him with her head tilted enigmatically.

"Well he seems to know. Who else could have told him?"

Irritatingly, neither of them answered. Loraine got up and began moving things about; she found a broom and tried to sweep. A fog of dust rose, the air became even more chokingly mephitic.

"*Don't* do that, ducky," Bo said languidly.

"But I'm tidying your mess."

"I don't want you to. Kindly sustain your self-regard in some other way. I hate people doing things for me and pretending to themselves—they certainly don't fool *me*—that they are being tremendously useful. That's why I could never employ anyone to work for me; such a dreadful relationship. *Do* sit down, dear heart, you're making me quite nervous. Bring me one of your sudden-death gateaux whenever you feel inclined, but meddling with my possessions is quite another matter. So content yourself with looking after Bella and keeping *her* in order. You know you do have this little penchant for blackmail; I'd as soon not be one of your subjects; or I might end by having to murder you."

"What a strange notion you have of blackmail," Loraine answered calmly. "A blackmailer is someone who extorts money or concessions for himself. But what do I stand to gain?"

"You want to blackmail us into loving you, my angel," Bo replied, picking up a long brush and going over to the wall, where he began painting in large, broad strokes on top of the posters and newspaper clippings that were pinned there. No, it was not a brush that he used, it was a can of spray-paint. So much smoke in the atmosphere, it was really hard to see anything.

"But you can't kindle the tender passion by brute force, you know. The tender passion! What a truly Victorian piece of misstatement. If there is one thing passion is not, it's tender. However I digress. We were wondering, weren't we, what Thomas was going to do. What are you going to do, Thomas, when we tell your mother *all* about you?"

"My mother," Thomas began. "But she's dead. . . ."

Surely there was something wrong with this scene altogether. For one thing it had taken place, not in Bo's studio, but in the kitchen at Number Thirty-eight, and Bo had not been there . . . or rather, the scene in the studio had been on a totally different occasion.

With a jerk of fright, Thomas realised that he was awake, in pain: lying, damp, stiff, and uncomfortable, on a seat in Central Park. He had walked into the park after leaving Bella, with the intention of sitting in the sun for a few minutes. But that had been how long ago? Now the sun had disappeared, grey clouds covered the sky, and it was raining quite hard.

He raised himself with difficulty, cursing his stupid carelessness. To fall asleep in the rain—what a piece of folly. He would be lucky if he were not almost completely crippled for several days. And—what time was it? In a rush of anxiety he looked at his watch—would it be after bank-opening time already? But he was relieved to find that it was still well before nine—he could not have been asleep more than a couple of hours.

What a strange dream, though! It had bracketed together in his mind two completely different memories, separated by a span of several years. That horrible, uncomfortable interview with Loraine in the kitchen at Number Thirty-eight. And the time, not long after his marriage to Bella, when he had dropped in at Bo's studio and been startled to find Loraine there, so cosily at home in what seemed a totally inappropriate milieu and company. Why were Bo and she such friends? Thomas had never decided what unlikely affinity drew them together. Perhaps it was her need to admire, his to be admired? She had a kind of blind, snobbish veneration for any form of

214

creativity, which was one of the more naïve elements in her make-up; it lay behind her tireless pushing and nagging at Bella to make her brush up a mediocre talent and resume her not particularly rewarding career. Bo, in Loraine's regard, was the creative aristocracy, pure gold; she would have thrown down her best damask table-napkins in the mud for him to trample on. She performed endless services for him, when allowed to do so. And Bo, in spite of all his cynicism and his jibes to Bella about her "attendant elephant" her "devoted oaf" and "two-ton Lorry" for all his claim to hate having things done for him, nevertheless seemed to tolerate having meals and cakes brought to his studio, clothes taken away to be cleaned and mended, groceries fetched, letters posted. Did they converse, did they confide in each other? Thomas never discovered. She brought him gifts, which he sneered at behind her back.

For some reason Thomas suddenly remembered clearing out the house in Wansea after his father had finally died in 1968—those drawers and drawers full of the unused socks from countless past Christmases.

"They seemed to irritate him very much," the housekeeper said. "He never wore that kind, only cotton ones from Woolworths. But he wouldn't have me tell you that, and he wouldn't have me give them to the Women's Voluntary Service—just keep them there, like he kept all your mother's things."

Somewhere inside, buried deep, father must have had the capacity for love, to be able to miss Fanny so painfully for so long, to hate Harold Wilson so vigorously—why could I never call out that love, or feel any towards him, the sad, thin, dry stick of a man? Poor Samuel, six years dead, and poor Loraine, her work, her help and good offices all finally rejected. Had anyone, anywhere, in all her life, truly loved her? Or had every kind word she heard been bought with service, with sycophancy? Some lives, Thomas supposed, must pass in this way; love, mutual love, along with an independent income, a house and garden, enough to eat, a dignified death, these things are not yet common luxuries, not likely to be.

It's mad to sit here in the rain; wake up properly, pull yourself together, you fool. Get up, go and get the money from the bank, go down to the Stake-Out.

But he felt full of lassitude, as if the pull of gravity had

215

overnight grown twice as strong and his body had become heavy as lead, inert as lead.

If I find Gabriel, if ever I persuade him to come back and have the operation, perhaps I can also persuade him to come away afterwards to some warm African beach where we can lie day after day in the sun, talk and relax, and finally get everything straightened out, go right back to the beginning and start over.

He sat up, feeling with dread the first movement of the blood down his seized-up legs, uncurling his cramped, painful hands.

The seat he had chosen was not far from a small lake, a duck pond really, near the open-air theatre. On the opposite bank of the lake the ground had been landscaped into a tree-grown rise. While he still lay drowsily assembling his thoughts, struggling to throw off his dream and push his mind into full wakefulness, Thomas had half-consciously observed the actions of two children quite a long way off, sitting under the trees at the top of the slope beyond the lake. It was too far to distinguish their faces, and their clothes were much the same, but he guessed they were boy and girl from the rather touchingly thoughtful way in which the taller of the two had, when the rain came on harder, stood on tiptoe and carefully suspended an open umbrella from the tree above them; then he lay down with his head in the girl's lap. A dog lay stretched not far from them, apparently indifferent to the rain on his thick coat. Happy trio . . .

Thomas knew that he must move, he must urge his reluctant legs into a brisk walk, but he found it almost impossible to get started; he remained leaning back, taking a dreamy pleasure in the view before him. The trees, with their slender trunks and heavy late-summer foliage, seemed like a painter's device for framing small individual scenes, each between a different pair of trees: some coloured iron tables and chairs outside the theatre, a mother pushing a pram, two boys with a baseball bat, a running athlete in shorts, a girl on a bicycle, a strange plump man wearing a knitted cap, with an apparently tame pigeon flying round his head, who was taking an erratic, lunatic course round the pond.

Why did that pair of teen-agers affect him so strongly? The young things, deep in their dialogue, they were so free from care, so untroubled in their simplicity. Thomas felt a deep outgoing of envy towards them—not envy, pure empathy really, pure love. If he had been near them, and could have done it unobserved, he would have liked to touch some part of them, the boy's collar, the ragged fringe of the girl's denims, even the umbrella, or the dog's fur, as if some of their abundance of grace might magically be transferred to him.

This is the way Gabriel feels *all the time,* Thomas thought. I have seen him stirred to the heart by some passing encounter: the blind man in Oxford Street, we had walked twenty yards on when I saw that his eyes were full of tears. "Lend me half a crown, please, Uncle Tom?" he said, and took it and ran hastily back to drop it in the man's begging cup. The grossly fat man in St. Paul's, that time, and the imprisoned bird—Gabriel was so terribly distressed that we had to leave, he couldn't bear it: the contrast, or was it the affinity between the swallow, silently, endlessly, desperately, agonisingly circling up there in the dome, wheeling and wheeling, round and round—and the immense, grotesque man with his tiny ballerina's feet, pathetically slumped across four chairs down below. The man hadn't seen the bird, he was fully concerned with his own exhaustion. I know now just how he felt. But Gabriel knew *then,* I remember his saying afterwards, It seemed as if the bird were *inside* the man, he was so huge he would almost have fitted into the dome, and all that helpless exhausted struggling was the man's own imprisoned spirit, trapped in there. I wonder if Gabriel remembers that day still? He must have been ten or eleven; it was one of the first times we went out together after his leg mended. . . .

The madman with his attendant dove was now veeringly on his way towards the boy and girl under their umbrella. He tacked, he swerved, he bore off and came back; now he stood in front of them, addressing them, urgently waving his hands. Thomas could see his face as a faint blur, but not the faces of the pair, they had their backs turned to him. Suddenly the boy jumped up, with a peculiar sideways rocking swing, sparing his right leg; a very characteristic movement. Why do I keep thinking about Gabriel? That boy is so like him, he could be Gabriel's twin. . . .

Instinct is far speedier than intelligence. Thomas found himself on his feet, heard his voice shouting *"Gabriel!"*

before his mind had come to any conscious conclusion as to the boy's identity.

Could they hear, across the lake? The boy cast a brief glance in his direction—a hunted glance? He grabbed the umbrella and some blue item of clothing from the ground, and whistled up the dog. The girl took the madman's arm and urged him towards the southern end of the park; the dog sprang up and galloped in pursuit. All four disappeared with the speed of a dream over the slight rise in the ground.

Thomas moved hastily to his right a few steps, then changed his mind and ran the other way, clockwise round the lake. Agonising darts of pain shot up his legs; if he had been trying to run on two broken ankles, it could hardly have been more excruciating. The bent arms with which he tried to row himself through the moist, warm air were like the deformed, useless wings of some non-flying bird; he struggled, he pushed vainly, he felt the angry throb and swelling in wrists and ankles, he felt his whole suffering, protesting body grind and creak as if rust had invaded every hinge. It was a nightmare of long and recurrent familiarity, but this time it was real.

Of course by the time he had made the circuit of the lake and struggled up the little slope, they were far away in the distance; they crossed a road, and at once a bus, cars, taxis maddeningly swept between; the next time he saw the little figures they were tiny; another rocky slope lay ahead of them; they passed round and were lost behind it.

Doggedly Thomas limped on, at a wretched half-trot. Jesus, what a body to be cursed with; if I had bought it, I'd return it to the store and ask for my money back. I'd warn my friends, I'd write to consumer guides advising against this model, I'd sue the retailers, I'd write to *The Times* warning against the manufacturers; if I'd been given it I'd pass it on to a rummage sale and take pains never to meet the donor again.

Gabriel. Was it Gabriel? That boy had Gabriel's tiny limp. But if it was Gabriel, why did he run? But if it was Gabriel, why was he free? What about the kidnap message? Some crazy hoax, some mad mistake?

He came to the road. The traffic lights were against him, he had to wait. A taxi glided by.

Take it?

Abandon hope of catching up with that strange fleeing quartet—the boy, the girl, the dog, the man with the dove? No, he could not quite bear to do that.

WALK said the lights, and he toiled across, and up the slope on the far side. Rocks, plane trees, mothers with baby-carriages, children playing, squirrels nipping about with insouciant grace. No Gabriel, no man, no dove. Gone, vanished, totally vanished.

A disastrous thought penetrated like some hungry bacillus into his cortex. Hallucination. Vision. You dreamed the whole thing. You had been thinking about Gabriel, remembering the time in St. Paul's, the fat man and the swallow; you manufactured the whole scene. But could I have dreamed that boy, so carefully tying the umbrella to the branch, just the kind of thing Gabriel might do? Why not, your dreams take even more plausible forms that that. Remember how you dreamed that Jan called you up—after the divorce, after the court case—and said, Thomas, I feel bad about the past. It was all stupid. I shouldn't have taken the line I did. I'm a fanatic when my protective instincts are roused, I know sometimes I behave unreasonably. But now they're roused on your behalf, even if you got off I think you had a very bad deal. The case should never have been brought. Why don't we meet?" Intelligent, kind Jan. They were things she might have said. "Let's meet in front of the 'Battle of San Romano.' Uccello. In the National Gallery tomorrow at three."

So sure had he been it was not a dream he had even kept the rendezvous. But Jan had never turned up.

And there had been other dreams, equally convincing. Many about Gabriel. So probably this was just another in the sad, self-deceiving succession.

Futile Thomas, impotent, infantile, romantic, unpractical idealist.

Which court case had Jan meant?

He climbed the slope and through the gap in the wall, emerging onto Fifth Avenue. His legs were so bad now that he had to limp as best he could to the nearest bench and sit down. His feet lay like mangled lumps of flesh in front of him on the hexagonal paving stones. A woman passed by in a long plum-coloured skirt and raincoat cut like a pelisse. Hairstyle after Emily Dickinson. But she had four children with her, each carrying a balloon on a

219

stick. No spinster she. A few withered yellow leaves drifted among the discarded ice-cream cones. Soon autumn would be here: bonfire smoke and smell of burnt pretzels. Where would Gabriel be then? Oh, hurry, hurry; why are you sitting here on a grey wooden bench with your back to the wall when Gabriel is drifting nearer and nearer to the edge of the whirlpool? He used to talk a lot about whirlpools, they fascinated him: heavy objects go down fast, but light objects may spin for hours on the upper lip. Gabriel, dear Gabriel, go on spinning for a while yet, please wait until I catch up with you.

The bench was hard, sharp splinters pierced through his thin cotton trousers. The hexagonal stones bruised his feet. The roaring, flashing torrent of Fifth Avenue poured ceaselessly by. Presently another cab floated near and he mustered enough strength to wave to it.

"First to a bank. The British National and Mercantile in Park Avenue. Then I need to find a lunchroom called the Stake-Out down in the Village. Do you know it?"

"Never heard of it. What street?"

What street? Thomas wondered. What had Pattie Lloyd said? "Oh yes, West Fourth."

"Park first. Then down Fifth and along Ninth," said the driver. "We'll hunt around. We'll find it."

"Oh, and I want to buy a couple of suitcases," Thomas said. "Can you stop at a dime store?"

Sitting back, he let pain take over his body while his mind floated loose.

The Stake-Out was a narrow little place, round red-leather stools along the bar, a trio of tiny tables. The tables were occupied by teen-agers taking their first Cokes of the stifling day. Thomas levered himself onto one of the awkward little stools, and for a moment felt so bad that the whole room dissolved into a swimming, humming darkness. He rested his head in his hands, pressing the pain back, deep into the middle, rather like kneading dough; you push it in, but it bulges out again somewhere else.

". . . mister?" the voice was saying, over and over. "You all right, mister? You sick?"

A red-faced man in a white apron and chef's cap was looking down at him in friendly anxiety.

"I'll be all right in a minute," Thomas managed to

articulate. "If you'd be good enough to get me a glass of water."

"Sure. Of course. Right here. Ice in it?"

The water was sparkling clear, ice-cubes floated in it like cubes of moonstone. But to his acute embarrassment and humiliation he found that, after carrying the heavy cases, his hands were too painful and tremulous to pick up the glass. If he tried both together—but that meant taking elbows off the counter. Water spilt and slopped, tears of despairing weakness came into his eyes.

"Here, lemme help you—" The kindly, concerned red face came closer. The water was tilted towards his mouth.

"Thank. Thanks very much. Half a minute—I've a pill that I need to take. If you could just—"

Two hours too soon, but what the hell? He couldn't go on like this.

"I'll open it for you, shall I?"

He had taken to carrying three or four of the red capsules around with him in his breast pocket. The white-aproned man tipped one of them out of the Perspex tube, and he gulped it back. Cold water like nectar followed it down his throat.

"That's extremely kind of you. You must think I'm a dipso or something. It's not that—it's just that I have very painful arthritis—"

"Mister," said the man with emphasis, "I don't think *anything*. All I see is, I got a customer in bad pain who wants some help. You be okay now? Like anything else? Cup of coffee? Glass of milk?"

Thomas thought he would have a glass of lemon tea. When it came in a saucer, with its bag trailing a little tail like a kite, he said to the man:

"I wonder if you can help me? I'm looking for a girl, I believe she works here, called Catriona Vanaken."

"Trina. Sure she works here. Not in right now but she's due back at three. You want to wait?"

He was tempted. The Stake-Out seemed a peaceful, friendly haven. But it was only half-past eleven now; better go back to Tenth Street and stay by the phone.

"I'll come back later, then, thanks."

"Any message I can give her?"

"No. No thanks"—she might take fright—"I'll just rest a few minutes more if I may."

"Sure. Stay the whole day if you want. You're not in

221

anyone's way. Why don't you go sit in that corner. Then you can relax better."

The Coke drinkers had gone by now. A table was free. Leaving his counter, the proprietor helped Thomas across the five feet of floor and he sank with inexpressible gratitude onto a padded corner-seat, and rested his arms on the table. His head sank onto them.

"Drink your tea while it's hot. Do you good."

The tea had followed him.

"I suppose you don't know where Miss Vanaken lives?" it suddenly occurred to him to ask.

The white-capped head shook. "Nah. These kids—you know how they are. Always on the move. I don't keep track—"

He nodded in acceptance of another frustration, and drank the tea, gulping it thirstily. It was cool already. Then his awareness dissolved into a peaceful state that was half sleep, half trance. He could see the owner, back behind his counter, the hot-chocolate machine, the trays of tuna and potato salad, the bottles of beer and Danish pastries, but he could also see St. Paul's, the great columns and airy gilded wreaths, the white and dark-brown elaboration of the domes. Someone was playing the organ. And there was a soprano solo. No, it was a girl's voice talking: an unusually pure, clear voice, not loud, but seeming to hit the note exactly dead-on, like a tuning-fork, so that it carried.

"I'm terribly sorry, Mr. Vanucci, I hate to let you down," she was saying; "I just called in to explain why I can't come later; you see I'm so upset, I'm so worried about my friend—"

"That's okay, that's quite okay. I understand how it is. You run along, I'll call Tessie, guess she'll be able to come in later on. You don't usually let me down and you're never off sick; we'll manage all right, don't you worry. It was nice you bothered to come and tell me. Some wouldn't have. Now you go see after your friend and come in tomorrow night, right?"

"But I don't even know if I'll be able to do *that*," she said despairingly.

"Well then, just call me and tell me when you'll be back. Now run along. Hey, no, wait, there's a customer wanted to speak to you. Over there in the corner."

The girl turned and came towards Thomas. Her face

222

bore a polite expression of inquiry but it was nothing more than a mask, Thomas could see; the real essence of her was far away. And she was in a desperate hurry.

"Excuse me? What was it you wanted? I'm afraid I'm in rather a rush——"

"I just wanted to speak to you a moment."

Thomas struggled to his feet and picked up his heavy bags. "Perhaps we could talk outside? I could walk along with you if you don't mind waiting till I've paid my bill——"

Then they were out, in the thunderous heat and wet dust of Sixth Avenue. The girl bit her lip, obviously she wished Thomas at the world's end; she courteously restrained her pace to his but it was plain she longed to break away, to run, to fly on some errand of her own. She was a cool pale little creature, her silvery braids, the colour of well-polished doctors' name-plates, twisted together and up into a plume on top of her head. Her sad eyes reflected the rainy sky. In spite of her desperate private worry she had compassion on Thomas; she waited patiently for him to speak.

"You see," he said simply, "I'm looking for my son. I'm looking for Gabriel. I thought you might know where to find him."

"For Ga——" She stopped, clutching his lapel, staring at him in astonishment. "For *him*? You're looking for Gabriel? Then it—was that you, in the park, this morning?"

"By the lake? You were under the tree with the umbrella?"

"Yes, till this man came with a label saying to take him back to his sister. So I took him back and Gabriel went home with the dog because his owner was coming at ten. But who are you? You said your son—but his father's dead!"

She stared at Thomas accusingly.

"I'm sorry. I didn't mean to deceive you. I'm Tom—his stepfather."

Before that clear, measuring gaze, Thomas felt indicted, judged, found wanting.

"You're *Tom*. I've heard about you. . . . But you aren't his stepfather. You and Gabriel's mother were divorced. You're not connected to him any more."

"Look, Catriona." Stopping, he set the atrociously

223

heavy bags down on the sidewalk. He held onto her arm. "Do you know about love? Love is like weather. Once you feel love for a person it's always there. Weather doesn't stop, does it? *Some*thing's always happening— rain or sun or cloud or mist. I can't stop loving Gabriel just because his mother and I were divorced. Concern for him is part of me. I'll love him and worry about him as long as I'm alive."

"Yes. I see." There was a different quality in her looking at him now. She was receiving him as a person; she had ceased to regard him as just a nuisance to be dealt with politely and as fast as possible. "But that's your affair, isn't it? Just because you worry about Gabriel doesn't mean that you have any right to interfere in what he does."

"No, of course not," he agreed humbly. "But I would— *terribly*—like to have just one chance to put my point of view to Gabriel; just to *try* to persuade him to consider it for a few minutes. Don't you think that's fair? Gabriel is such a gentle, considerate person; I would have thought he'd agree to that if he knew I was here, if he knew how much—how desperately much—I wanted it? Don't you think he would?"

She looked down and kicked one of the heavy bags absently with her bare, sandalled toe. She was extremely pale.

"Perhaps—" she said. "But he's very busy, you see. He hasn't a lot of time. He doesn't want anybody bothering him." Her voice was so forlornly that of a child imitating parental authority—don't bother father just now— that Thomas could have laughed, if he had not been closer to tears.

"Just the same," he said gently, "my dear, don't you think you could stretch a point and tell me where he is?"

She looked up again. Her small face was all crumpled. He realised that he was not the only one to be on the brink of tears.

"But don't you see—" Her voice wavered; she swallowed and took resolute hold of herself. "That's what I can't do. He's left me already. He's gone. When I got back to the room I found that he'd gone off. I don't know where he is."

After another minute she added, "He left me this."

She pulled it from her jeans pocket. A sheet of paper

folded into eight. On one side was written in Gabriel's writing:

"Darling C. It was best this way. He's come back and is taking me in his car to where it is. Don't grieve for me. If I come back as a bird or a cloud, I'll always be with you. All my love. G."

Thirteen

Bo, Bella, Thomas 1974

The minute Bo came in the door, Bella flew at him like a tigress.

"Where have you *been* all day?"

"Went to some galleries. Hey, easy, easy, easy! What the hell's the matter?"

He was fending her off with one hand, with the other hand trying to take away the piece of paper she held.

"You bloody cheat! You lousy, deceiving, swindling crook! How are you going to explain *this?*"

"Oh, Christ, have you been at my things?"

"I should just about think I have! And this was what I found! James's little billet-doux! Written to you in England! How long have you and James been hatching this? You've got to ring him up—right away—and tell him to bring him back. *Right* away. You filthy pair of murderers!"

"Shut up, Bella," said Bo, now seriously roused. "Firstly you shouldn't have gone rummaging through my private papers—though I suppose I should have expected as much—"

"I always do. And a bloody good thing too."

"I suppose I'm a fool to have left it where your prying little paws could get at it—James was right—"

"Ring him up! Go and phone right off! He's to bring that boy back."

"Now, look, wait, ducky; *don't* fly off the handle. It doesn't help *any*body. For a start, Thomas will be here soon, and we don't want *him* beginning to smell a rat, do we? You don't want to find your dear little self landed in the middle of a prosecution for criminal conspiracy, extortion, kidnapping, and maybe murder? Right? Just keep your fur on; it's too hot for these histrionics."

"They are not histrionics! Gabriel has got to be brought back from wherever James has got him. You have to call James up and tell him so."

"No place to call him. Anyway they probably haven't got there yet," Bo said evasively.

"Where is this place?"

"*I* don't know. James didn't tell me. Some place where Gabriel once stayed with Gus, years and years ago, the time when you persuaded me to go to Cyprus and it was so awful. Gabriel took a great fancy to this place, apparently; wanted to go back there. So James took the trouble to find out where it was."

"Very kind. Very thoughtful of him," Bella said, curling her lip. "I read his letter, don't forget." She held up the page, furiously close to her short-sighted eyes. " 'If he really wants to go away and die by himself in the wilderness, why not give him a helping hand? Leave him in some rural spot with a supply of baked beans—and maybe a dose of pethidine in his dried milk, just to accelerate the course of nature—of course I will think of something more sophisticated than that if you think that some such catalyst might be advisable—if your bird-witted sister is really going in for all this advertising and publicity, the sooner the poor little tyke is well on his way the better, in case some well-meaning oaf accidentally stumbles across him'. . . . Oh, you beast!"

Bo, watching his chances, had grabbed her hair and jerked her head violently back; while she was distracted by the sudden pain, he twitched the letter from her hand, and set fire to it with his lighter. Bella jumped forward again, but he fended her off with his elbow until the written part was completely blackened, then dropped in on the floor and trod it into fragments.

"I'm going to the police!" Bella said, scarlet-faced.

"No you're not, my girl," he replied, watching her narrowly from under his heavy lids. "If you did any such thing I'd make sure you were pulled in too, so fast! It was your idea to get Thomas over here, after all; which made it so easy for him to persuade Crusoe and Selkirk to come through with the ransom money. And don't forget that I have some highly circumstantial hypotheses about Loraine's sad end."

"I got Thomas over because I thought he'd help to *find* Gabriel!"

"In his state of health? Do you think the cops will buy that?"

"Well at least he's been trying," said Bella bitterly.

"And why do you want Gabriel found? Just for your own selfish motives. Not because you love him. Not at all because you're interested in whether the poor little bastard lives, or is happy, but just because you want him to survive till he inherits, right? After that I daresay he can't die fast enough."

"I love him! I do!"

"I've seen remarkably few signs of it," Bo said, "over the last sixteen years. And he certainly doesn't seem to reciprocate. Maybe, way back there in his innocent young subconscious, he remembers how very casually he was once dumped. Maybe he owes you a tiny grudge over that."

"Oh, belt up. What's that got to do with anything? Well, what could I do at that time? Anyway," said Bella sulkily, "you would benefit just as much from anything I get out of the estate, you seem to be forgetting that. . . . Or you would have; I gather you and James are now planning to go off to some brave new world where family ties are of no account? What was that charming epithet he applied to me—Bella the bloodsucker? I always suspected James was a skunk but I hadn't realised quite how much of a skunk he was till now; just wait till he gets back—"

"Luckily," said Bo, "he is not coming back. He was going straight on to Newfoundland."

"*Newfoundland?* What—Anyway, tell him he's *got* to come back. He's got to. That boy has got to have that operation."

"How can I tell him to come back?" said Bo. "I haven't the remotest idea where he is. For all I know, this place where Gabriel once stayed with Gus *is* in Newfoundland. And, even if James brought Gabriel back—and how would he be able to do that? Gabriel is going with him of his free will—do you expect James to tie him up? He won't *want* to come back. Even if he brought Gabriel, I very much doubt if you can force the boy to have the operation. Doctors don't take kindly to that sort of thing, you know; there are plenty of patients who need operations without forcing surgery on the ones who prefer to manage without."

"Thomas will have to persuade him to have the operation."

"Bella dear," Bo said wearily, "do stop being so lunkheaded. Gabriel knows much too much about Thomas to have the least respect for his opinion. Gabriel, by some genetic eccentricity, is a far stronger character than *any* of us; he may not have Gus's genius—"

"How could he? He isn't Gus's child."

"Oh, don't be so boringly, pedantically literal, of course he isn't. He's no genius, but he does have a weird moral force of his own; even if Gus had no legitimate child, Gabriel is the child of his spirit. And if he wants to die, die he will. So why don't you just keep quiet and think about this: any minute now Thomas is going to turn up with a bloody great trunkful of cash and arrangements for dumping it somewhere. Are you going to run yelling to the police, or are you going to show a bit of sense, are you going to grow up at last, stop telling lies to yourself about yourself, and accept the kind of person you are? And accept a third of the cash? Even split three ways it'll make quite a comfortable supplement to your allowance—"

"How do you *mean,* stop telling lies to myself? And why should I have to share with that rat James? It's my husband's money!"

"Oh, Christ—women!" said Bo, and poured himself a full tumbler of whisky. "Will you, just for once in your life, stop trying to eat your cake and have it?"

"The money ought to be mine. I was married to Gus. That was a very unfair will."

"Indeed you were married to him. And clever old Gus, having taken your measure exactly, left you just as much money as would be good for you, doled out at regular intervals for the rest of your life, and not enough to, as he once tactfully put it to me, encourage fortune-hunters. He truly had your welfare at heart. He wanted you to grow up and end as a self-respecting, self-reliant individual."

"He might have taken into account that I'd have to support you as well," she said spitefully. "And he wasn't so clever, I often think. Leaving all that money to Gabriel was just plain ridiculous. A child of that age. And not even his own son."

"Gus didn't know he was going to die so soon."

"Anyway, how could he tell what sort of person Gabriel would turn out to be? As it is, look at him—dreamy, unpractical, just not interested—"

"Just the sort of person Gus would think might put the money to intelligent use, because he had no axe of his own to grind. And I expect," Bo said, "if Gabriel did live to adulthood, that is just the kind of use he might put it to. Gus had Gabriel fairly well sized up, even at ten. He had high hopes for Gabriel."

"It's outrageous that he should get all that money and I have no say in it. He's my son."

"Yours and whose, my angel? A child has two parents," Bo said gently. "Maybe his father should have some say in the matter as well."

Bella, who had been on the point of another angry interjection, checked it and remained silent; she set her lips together tightly. Her pink face became close and secretive.

"Never you mind who his father is—was," she said. "For all you know he's dead. That's strictly my affair. *You* were out in New Zealand, having it off with all those Maori girls."

"I must say you covered your tracks pretty thoroughly," ruminated Bo, "going off to Greece with that struck-off tubercular gynaecological friend of yours—what was her name—Alice Myers—and getting her to register him as hers, father unknown Greek—I managed to check as far as that. It was annoying of Alice to go and die of her silly disease. No one does nowadays. And she might have cleared up all these points."

"You'll never find out," said Bella looking at him steadily. "You're not getting any other handle to hold over me. So you might just as well stop fishing."

"The point is," said Bo, steadily looking back at her. "that if by any chance Gabriel were *my* son, I might feel differently about all this."

Into her stubborn silence came the sound of the doorbell.

She said, "Hadn't you better go and let Thomas in?"

Thomas came into the room looking stupid and dislocated, like a person who has survived shipwreck, but only just. He was very white, and limping badly. His hair and raincoat were wet. He carried nothing.

Bella ran up to him and took hold of his lapels...

"Did you get the money?" she asked in a low voice.

"Yes. And the people called again—"

"Where is it?"

"Somewhere to the north—up Route Seventeen—"

"No, the *money . . . ?*"

"In a safe place," he said impatiently. Bo scowled at Bella. He had strolled slowly back after letting in Thomas, and was leaning against the dusty mantelpiece, watching them both.

"You didn't leave the money in the flat at Tenth Street?"

"No. But it's a hell of a weight and my arms are very bad. The man rang again—"

"What did he say?" Bo asked.

"Drive across the Tappan Zee bridge, Route Seventeen to Rock Hill—I've got it all written down, there's about a page of instructions; anyway, I have to get to a motel called the Sleepy Hollow and at midnight they'll call there with more instructions; it's some lake, we have to put the money in a boat. But he'll tell me about that in the next call."

"Oh, Jesus, all this waiting around!" Bo suddenly exclaimed in a thin, exasperated voice.

"Did they call you?" Thomas asked Bella. "With the tape of Gabriel's voice?"

"Y-yes," she said nervously.

"Was it Gabriel? Did you recognise him? What did he say?"

"It was Gabriel all right." Dew of sweat sprang out on Bella's forehead; she looked from Thomas to Bo and back again. "He wasn't talking to *me;* or asking for help; he just seemed to be talking on about how he wanted to be alone, and how he doesn't like the way things are now, the way the world is run—"

"So it doesn't really prove they've got him; the tape might have been made at any time?"

"Oh, I don't know!" She plaited her fingers together nervously. "Have you got the car?" she said to Thomas. "When should we start?"

"Not for a couple of hours. No, I haven't got it yet."

"For heaven's sake. What have you been *doing?*"

That sounded like the old Bella. Thomas did not answer her. All of a sudden he had a deep longing for his comfortable, untidy office at Crusoe and Selkirk; the contracts waiting for his signature, the manuscripts waiting to be read, Miss Stanney with the day's mail and the day's appointments, John Voynitch wanting to argue about some new project—

"I thought you said we might borrow James's car?"

"Oh no, that's no good. He lent it to his brother."

"His brother?" Bella said. "I thought he was in Cal—"

"Get a Hertz car," Bo said, giving Bella a quick frown. "Anyway that would be more reliable than borrowing. There's a place in Thirty-eighth Street isn't there—why don't you call them from here?"

He found a telephone book and gave it to Thomas, who began leafing through and dialled a number. Bella caught Bo's eye and said:

"Come into the kitchen."

He jerked his head warningly towards Thomas, but she pulled him into the next room and muttered in his ear:

"What had you been planning to do with him? When you'd planted the cash? Were you going with him? Who was going to collect it?"

Bo made no verbal reply but she was silenced by the expression on his face. He gripped her wrist, digging the nails right in.

"Can you have it ready in half an hour?" Thomas was saying in the other room.

"Let go of me! I'm coming on this trip too," Bella said.

"No you are not. You are going to stay right here."

"I—am—coming—along. You're not going to get away—"

"Be quiet!"

"All right, that's fixed," said Thomas. He came through the doorway in time to see Bo let go of Bella's arm. A set of inky bruises blossomed immediately on her crepe-white skin, like fast-developing prints.

"Just a small disagreement," Bo explained airily. "Darling Bella's illogical little brain doesn't seem to have grasped that this isn't some kind of picnic—"

"I want to come with you in the car," Bella said doggedly.

"Look—sweetheart—" Bo began between his teeth. "Thomas wouldn't want this enlivening family dialogue all the way on the drive up, would he? Thomas is the only driver among us, and he has his little arthritic problem— he isn't looking too good and we don't want him upset,

231

do we? Because when Thomas gets upset, things really begin to blow apart, remember? Remember the Waterlow Gallery? We don't want anything in the nature of a recurrence of that, do we? We're relying on Thomas, just at present, see. Old reliable Thomas is our standby right now. He got the dough, he's driving the car, and everything's going to work out *quite excellently,* if you will just exercise the minimum common sense and discretion. Right?"

He smiled rather wildly at Thomas, whose expression was full of trouble and growing doubt.

"Don't mind us, Thomas, bach. Why don't you go and pick up the car, and we'll have this all resolved by the time you get back. How would that be?"

"Yes. All right." Without looking again at either of them, Thomas turned on his heel and walked back towards the front door.

"Tom—" Bella began, but Bo clapped his hand over her mouth. They watched Thomas go slowly past Bo's mural. He turned and stared at it in a troubled manner for a long minute; then walked on and out of the flat.

"Anyone but a total imbecile—" Bo began to say as the front door closed.

Fourteen

Thomas, Catriona 1974

Having signed all the papers and collected the rented car, Thomas drove it straight round to the house in Twelfth Street. He did not like to ring the front doorbell, and stood hesitating on the doorstep, but Catriona had been on the lookout for him; she waved from the front window and in a moment he heard a gentle creaking and grating as she cautiously undid the various locks and bolts.

"Hattie's upstairs," she said in a low voice when she had opened the door. "The doctor just left. He's coming back later on. Old Mrs. Baird's been in a coma for twenty-four hours now; he says nothing more can be done for her."

232

"I'm glad at least they didn't drag her off to the hospital."

"What would be the point?"

The house was ghost-quiet, expectant; it felt as if the entire living essence of the building were being drawn away with her by the dying woman.

Their voices, although very subdued, had been caught by the sharp ears of Hattie, who came to the head of the stairs and looked down. She was just as neat as usual, in her grey cotton dress and striped ticking apron, her hair in its usual tight mass of frizzy iron-grey curls, but she was white with fatigue.

"Come on, come up," she directed in a vigorous whisper. "It won't bother *her*." This was an order, not a suggestion; they climbed the stairs. Hattie gave Thomas a sharp little nod as he reached the top; she stood aside to let him pass. The corners of her pale old mouth worked briefly, twice, as she met his look of sympathy, but, with a long, sighing breath, she took impatient control of herself and followed him into the bedroom. Catriona, inaudible on sandalled feet, slipped in after them.

The blinds were drawn; the bedroom was in shadow. Covered almost up to her chin by an immense, weighty, carefully draped blue-and-white patchwork quilt, Mrs. Baird lay already like a figure on a tomb. Except for the faintest flutter of breath—far less than would be required to move one strand of cobweb—which faintly distended her nostrils every minute or so, she was completely motionless. There seemed only the barest distinction between her state and true death. The hooding lids were down over the deep grey eyes; the angular nose and chin, the firm mouth were at rest, fixed in a calm, almost triumphant severity. Her arms, thin as stair-rods, lay tidily at her sides, more as if somebody had arranged them there than as if she expected to use them again. The wrinkled freckled hands, motionless, seemed like strange marine creatures, cast up by the tide.

Moved and impressed by such monumental stillness, Thomas paused, then slowly approached the bed.

He gently laid his hand over the old freckled claw, which felt quite cold, quite unresponsive, yet alive—just; like some hibernating creature that had withdrawn into itself for the winter. August's theory about hibernation came briefly into his mind. Could it be used to postpone death? August had thought it might; would that be a good thing? And then he thought, There she lies: August's mother, the old, formidable self-sufficient being; she had a good life, a well-filled life, she reared a genius; she knew famous people, she had many friends, she kept her days occupied and her mind amused; she knew Einstein and Shaw, she talked to Schweitzer and Russell; *where is it all now?*

Were all her secrets, her memories, still in there, alive inside the brain that had folded itself in for sleep? Were they fired away in there, vainly waiting for the impulse that would call them into motion, like a computer standing idle with no attendant to press the button? Imprisoned within the cortex, behind the brow that so closely resembled the skull it would soon become, love, wisdom, humour were helpless, inoperative, null. What becomes of our emotions when we die?

Cockroaches, Thomas thought, his mind running off wildly, cockroaches can survive for thousands of years without food or water, without air, even; why should cockroaches be so superior in staying power to the human race? Is there no solitary part of us that can endure in that way, no residue apart from the external traces we leave of books or buildings or scratches on rock?

What remains of us when we go, beyond the torn fragments of love and learning that we pass from hand to hand? What do we take with us, if anything?

We leave nothing but messages. Legends. Tokens. The night is freezing fast, tomorrow comes December, and winterfalls of old are with me from the past, and mostly I remember how Dick would hate the cold. . . . At most we can say, Good-bye, remember me.

He felt a sad, trapped affection for the dying woman. He had known her so briefly; hardly at all. He had read the last page, the last line of her; now the book was closed. It was too late.

A truck passed outside in the street; it did not scratch the surface of the silence in the house. Hattie had immediately resumed what was obviously her day-long position, seated in a hard upright chair by the head of the bed, with her hands folded in her lap. Catriona came softly up beside her, facing Thomas. Then with silent care she knelt down by the bed, not in an attitude of prayer, but half crouching, as a child might by a parent's armchair, so as to be as near as possible to what was taking place, with her head bent a little forward, watching and listening intently. She, too, laid her thin young hand on the old thin one.

As he stood now, Thomas could see without moving his eyes the three faces, close together in a triangle; the two concentrated on the one, the two old and calm, the one young and observant, but all three wearing the same look, absorbed, mysterious; they were in some way knit together. I am alone here, he thought; the room does not hold four people waiting for a death; I am the only person here. They are the Norns. If I took my eyes off them for a moment, they would vanish.

The silence drew out like a thread from a silkworm; he was aware in a detached, third-party way of the pain in his body; his arms and legs were like fluorescent tubes of bright, cutting fire; must take another Najdolene; four hours since the last? Time was passing; Bo and Bella must be wondering where the hell he had got to, why he did not return. The telephone downstairs began to ring and then abruptly ceased, as if someone had reminded the caller that the process of death should not be interrupted by trivial inquiries.

A church clock not far off pealed out a short cheerful tune on its chime. Familiar hymn. Glory be to Jesus, Who in bitter pain, Poured for me the lifeblood, From his sacred vein. Haydn used the same tune in one of his symphonies, number fifty-three? Irritating habit playing tunes on bells; chimes are better. More dignified.

Suddenly Mrs. Baird's eyes opened. The lids flew up, exposing twin orbs, bright, full of life, luminous with meaning, with some message that must be imparted. They met the eyes of Catriona, who was poised, waiting. A long look was exchanged, pupil to pupil, an electrical impulse was transmitted. Light travelled across the immeasurable space between one world and another. Then, the signal having passed, the lids dropped again, definitively. The hands relaxed. The minimal flutter of breath was discontinued.

Like the end of a performance, Thomas thought: curtain, lights, doors, windows, finish.

Another silence began, as portentous, trivial, coincidental as the one in which the clock, listened to, stops ticking. The gap lengthened, became cosmic, and was broken by Catriona, who rose matter-of-factly to her feet and stepped back towards the door. Before doing so she

235

lightly laid a hand on Hattie's shoulder. Hattie neither moved nor raised her eyes.

"Come," Catriona mouthed silently to Thomas, and beckoned him downstairs. They went into the drawing-room where he had first interviewed Mrs. Baird. An untidy heap of papers lay on the small hard sofa.

Catriona said in a low voice, "We'll leave Hattie in peace, she told me she was up all night. The doctor will look after her by and by. Here—this was why she called you up. She asked me to show you these, all Gabriel's letters to his grandmother. She's been collecting them all week, she said. There was one in just about every book in the house. No dates, and not many addresses, but you can tell which are the later ones from the writing. And the last few are typed."

Thomas felt his heart leap, and then drop again. A feeling of hopeless disappointment took possession of him as he leafed through the heap of sheets, some scribbled, some printed, a few type-written—poems, pencil drawings, a few on school exercise paper, some on the green-headed paper from Wanborough Parkside.

"But these are no use now," he said. "I'd asked for them, it's true. But that was before I'd heard about you. I thought the latest ones might give some clue to where he was staying now. But none of these look that recent. And even if they were we know that now he's moved—"

"Wait," said Catriona. "Look." She dug right to the bottom of the pile and pulled out a big yellow sheet of squared graph paper with a child's drawing of a duck, and some anonymous four-legged animal with a long black-and-white tail.

The letter was printed in large staggering script.

Dear Grannie
> *Gus and i are staying in a luvly hous that belongs to a man caled Tom Thum. We went on a boat to get to it. The boat was caled Cornelys van der Bilt. The hous is in Zebra Street. There arnt any Zebras but lots of chipmuncs and a luvly pond were i can swim every nigt. Daddy sends lov. i.. do too.*

GABRIEL

Catriona said, "While I was waiting for you to come I phoned Central Reference Library and they found out

236

for me that one of the Staten Island ferryboats used to be called the *Cornelius Vanderbilt*. And Gabriel told me once that the beautiful mill he stayed in with Gus belonged to Tom Thum. And there is a road called Zebra Place right in the middle of Staten Island; the library confirmed that too."

So much had happened to Thomas in the last twelve hours, on top of a sleepless night, that it took him a minute to assimilate this. Zebra Place. Then he remembered where Staten Island was. Off the south tip of Manhattan. Where the Atlantic liners come in and turn right under the great Narrows Bridge. Staten Island. Surely not more than an hour's ride away.

"Where do the ferries go from?" he asked. "Are there still ferries?"

"Oh yes. Every twenty minutes or so. They go from Battery Park—right downtown, past Wall Street."

"Do they take cars?"

"Oh yes," she said again. "Did you get a car?"

"It's outside."

"Can I come too?"

"Of course."

Thomas telephoned Bo.

"Bo, it's me, Thomas."

"Thomas! Good jumping Christ, where the fuck have you *been?*"

He did not say, Waiting by Mrs. Baird's deathbed. Hattie had made it plain that she would refuse to admit Bella; would stand no nonsense from her. But he did not want Hattie bothered. He said, "Look, Bo, I've been considering very deeply. The more I think about those people's offer to produce Gabriel at the cardiac unit the minute we've paid over the money, the less I like it. That would be an outrage. Gabriel's not a child, or a criminal. He has a right to make his own decisions, not to be carted about like a—like a sheep."

"But if he's—"

"So I'm not going along with their proposals. Not immediately, anyway. I've got a lead, and I'm going to follow it."

"God almighty, are you *mad? Thomas*—" Bo's voice rose almost to a scream.

"I expect they'll be in touch again," Thomas said, assuming more calm than he felt. "Then, if my lead

237

proves to be wrong, we can always accept their terms. I haven't taken the money back yet."

"What have you done with it?"

"It's all right. It's safe."

Bo's distant, shrill voice ran off into a string of such bitter, obscene abuse that Thomas, with an instinctive gesture of fastidious affront, held the receiver away from his ear. He was in a pay booth near the ferry port; from where he stood he could see weathered wooden piles leaning against the sky in a ragged frieze, and a red-painted fireboat, its vermilion snouts pointing cockily upward.

"You stupid, weak, destructive shit—"

The angry words, pouring on and on into his ear, shook open one of the floodgates in his mind.

The deck had been so hot that it burnt one's feet even through rubber soles. Shade was not a luxury, it was a matter of life and death. The sea looked cool, but it was full of predatory fangs, and anyway, getting into it would have meant baring oneself to that murderous sun. He remembered one day when he and Bo had been put ashore in a little bay; from the ship the cliffs had appeared deceptively cool and green, covered with scrub, but the bay was really a broiling sun-trap, with only one patch of real shade, under a small fig-tree down on the beach, and there, willy-nilly, they had to spend the day, huddled together, waiting for the boat to come and fetch them off. Bo had done a little desultory sketching; Thomas had been able to do nothing at all.

"Should be good for your arthritis, anyway," Bo said morosely.

In those days they got on well enough. Or rather, paradoxically, they got on well enough so long as they did not talk too much. Any dialogue tended to outline the jagged areas of disagreements; in their mutual silences a kind of comfortable amity, almost an affection, had time to build up. Thomas felt that Bo was unhappy, that some struggle was going on inside him, but Bo was not communicative at any time. He spent most of his days in his cabin. Thomas avoided entering it as much as possible. It stank of five months' accumulated smoke and Bo's unwashed clothes; going in resembled entering a mummy's tomb, to find the occupant stretched out like a wrinkled corpse among his basic needs: cans of beer, paints, newspapers, the blue miasmic smoke. A couple of the crew used sometimes to visit him there; Thomas, passing the door and hearing wild laughter, abstained even more stringently from intrusion.

But in the sultry twilight, which lasted so short a time, Bo would wander up on deck in paint-stained khaki pants and sweaty shirt, hanging open to reveal the large heavy brown-metal cross, thick as a candlestick, which he wore on a chain round his neck.

Having frequently heard Bo's acid comments on religion of any kind, Thomas once asked, "Why do you wear that, Bo?"

"To keep off bullets and vampires of course." Bo added, rather stiffly, "James gave it to me."

"Oh I see." Thomas had never met James and did not in the least want to; he steered clear of Bo's friends. But he had frequently heard Bella comment on James.

"There's something horribly *creepy* about him. He's religious in a spooky way. When everybody's talking, you sometimes see his eyes go backward in his head and you know he's not there at all; he's gone off somewhere inside himself. He doesn't really need anybody. Sometimes he really does go off; he'll wander out because his car's on a parking meter and not come back for six months, and he'll say later that it was because God called him. And yet he isn't *good;* I think he's really bad. He says the conventional idea of goodness isn't in the least the same as being in touch with God. He's a *snob* about God." Bella's blue eyes were round with spite and dislike. "The worst of it is that he's got the most awful sort of hold over Bo. Bo doesn't really believe in all that mystical rubbish at all, but just the fact that James doesn't need him has got him hooked. Bo's a sucker for anything mysterious and out of reach. *I* think James is just *poison.*"

"No doubt you've been treated to plenty of Bella's views about James?" Bo raised an ironic eyebrow sideways—they were leaning on the rail, gazing at the swampy coastline. "She loathes him of course; she's jealous of him."

"Where is James now?" Thomas asked rather awkwardly. He was nervous about the Bella-James-Bo confluence; wanted to know as little about it as possible; and yet he could not help feeling a certain sympathy for Bo, who seemed so unhappy about his friend. Because of his long days below decks, even the tropics could not turn Bo brown; he was noticeably pale at the moment, his skull-face bent broodingly to look down at the water below, full of sharks no doubt.

"Went off to Prague for six months; he'll be there till after Christmas." Bo added irrelevantly, "Has it ever occurred to you that Christianity is a northern hemisphere religion? God's birth at the winter solstice and resurrection in spring just don't work south of the equator. Down there, Christmas ought to be in July."

"I suppose so," Thomas answered vaguely. "Didn't August write some piece about religion being affected by weather?"

"Oh, August, August—" Bo's tone was full of bitter impatience. "Sometimes I think the only reason you hang onto us is because of August. You want to suck the essence of him out of us like a *leech*. August's *dead*—can't you get that into your thick head? It's no use expecting that through union with Bella—or Gabriel—you're going to get into mystical contact with August because you bloody well aren't."

"Of course I know that." Thomas spoke with what he hoped was dignity but was afraid sounded merely peevish.

"August's a great big ghostly father-figure to you, isn't he, because your own father was such a washout. But I *loved* him. I *knew* him. He wasn't really like that. He had feet of clay like the rest of us."

"I daresay. Do you know, I'd much rather not talk about him?"

"Oh, Christ, Thomas. Sometimes you're such a fuddy-duddy you make me want to *puke*."

Two boys from the crew passed them; one of them aimed a friendly kick at Bo in passing and he called something after them in Arabic; Bo seemed to have acquired a working knowledge of Arabic with remarkable speed.

Ignoring this bit of byplay, Thomas turned his eyes to the beautiful grey-green entangled line of the coast. Large white birds were flying and diving among the reeds; their cries came faintly over the water. A warm, salty, muddy, brackish smell drifted from the land; he sniffed it hungrily, thinking, In six weeks I shall be back in London, all this will be like a dream, closed and unreal. But when I am on my deathbed these months will seem the only reality in my life. I wonder how many people manage to spend their lives in exactly the way they intend? But how can one be aware of one's intentions early enough?

"Thomas!" That was Bo's voice in his ear, exasperated,

dragging him out of solitude. "Will you *listen* to what I'm saying?"

"What? I'm sorry?"

"About you and Bella, for Christ's sake."

"What about me and Bella?" Thomas said with the utmost reluctance.

"Thomas. Look, marriage isn't a fucking Mozart *opera,* all bowing and curtsying and minuets. Anyone can see with half an eye that the girl isn't getting laid properly, and whose responsibility is that? We all know you've got arthritis, but you aren't paralysed; what's wrong?"

"I don't think this is any of your business, Bo." To his own surprise Thomas found that he was not in the least resentful of Bo's inquiry, but the whole problem, the thought of Bella, their relationship, made him feel so weary that he could have sagged down on the deck and put his hands over his ears, over his eyes. Their marriage seemed like some great unwieldy ship with steering broken, bound for the rocks; like a machine with slipped gears, out of control. What was to have been his redemption, her salvation, now threatened to crush them both.

"Of course it's my business!" Bo said furiously. "Who gets it in the neck when Bella's miserable? *I* do. She weighs on me like a bloody *dolmen.* She buggers up *my* emotional life. I can't work, I can't concentrate, and James gets mad and lights out for months together."

"Well I'm sorry," said Thomas, "but what can I do? It's a mutual thing, after all; Bella's bored with me, antagonistic—one can't just go riding in like young Lochinvar in those circumstances."

Bo grinned more amicably and said, "Yes, but it's no use expecting any help from Bella. *You're* the adult; she's permanently lodged at the oral stage. That's why she never cottoned onto Gabriel, poor little sod; *she's* the child. She always has to come first. You ought to know that by now. You took her on, and Gabriel; you can't just toss the responsibility overboard because it turned out tougher than you expected. For the love of pete, read a manual of sex, go to a marriage guidance counsellor, go to a shrink, do *something,* don't just sit dangling your bonnet and plume."

"It's all very well to talk," said Thomas slowly. He could not add, "The truth is that the more I learn about Bella, the more I find that disgusts me."

How could you feel affection for a person who seemed stimulated by two things only, food and pain? Without affection, how was it possible to make contact? Her exterior was a mirage, a façade; below lay something grotesque, a mass of twisted inclinations, of warped cupidities. He felt more genuine fondness for sad skull-faced Bo, leaning gloomily beside him, spitting grape pips into the water.

But it was true he had taken on the responsibility. And there was Gabriel too. First and foremost there was Gabriel. August's spiritual son. The fact that he had undertaken the whole relationship on a false premise made it more important, not less, that he should not relinquish it simply because it did not prosper.

But when they called at Lagos for supplies Bo found a letter from Bella waiting for him that put him into a black, silent rage.

"You ought never to have come on this stupid cruise. It was the most foolhardy piece of asinine, crass lunacy," he said after a while to Thomas, chopping out his words like sections of wood from a power saw.

"Why?"

Thomas was preoccupied with bothersome business mail from Crusoe and Selkirk; he was not giving Bo full attention.

"Oh, never mind!" Bo tore the letter in half and dropped it overboard. He hunched his shoulders and walked moodily away. After that day he refused to accompany Thomas ashore on specimen-hunts as he had done before, but stayed on the boat, drinking beer and making drawings of the crew. He was drunk every day from noon on, and, instead of being offhandedly friendly, seemed to go out of his way to provoke Thomas.

The climax came when Thomas burst angrily into Bo's cabin one morning to say, "Look here, Bo, you've got to stop keeping beer in my specimen-refrigerator. All that opening and shutting the door brings the temperature up every time. You've completely wrecked my last week's work, just because you're too lazy to go down a couple of flights. It's intolerable. Will you please keep your beer in the mess fridge, or in the kitchen!"

Bo lifted bloodshot eyes. He was sitting on his bunk with Juma, one of his friends from the crew; they had been giggling over some satirical portraits that Bo had done of the captain, and also, Thomas suspected, of himself.

"Piss off, Thomas," Bo said coldly. "I never invited you into my cabin. If the truth be told, I'd sooner have a six-weeks-dead sheep in here. If the truth be told, there is very little discernible *difference* between you and a six-weeks-dead sheep."

Juma laughed delightedly.

"All right, I'm going," said Thomas, white with anger but keeping his voice calm. "And if that beer isn't out of the refrigerator by lunch-time I shall throw it overboard."

"Oh, you will?" Bo raised his eyebrows. "Thomas the sheep is asserting himself, is he? What a bloody pity you can't assert yourself a little more with my idiot sister. Now *get out!*"

As he shut the door, trembling violently with a mixture of rage and horror at this powerful and suddenly unleashed emotion, Thomas heard Juma joyously repeating:

"Thomas the sheep! Thomas the sheep!"

War had been declared.

He heard quick footsteps, and Catriona's anxious little face came into view round the side of the phone-booth.

"Thomas! They're letting people on the ferry now. The line of cars has started to move."

"Okay," he said. "I'm right with you."

As he followed her, running, back to the hired Mustang, and drove through the tunnel and across the slipway into the car-deck of the ferry, he was thinking, How did I ever come to forget all that? What makes me forget these things? What else have I forgotten?

"Shall we go upstairs?" Catriona said, when the car was lodged in position. "There's no point staying down here, all the way across. And you get a very good view of Manhattan as we leave."

The ferry had three roomy passenger-decks as well as the car-hold. They climbed up to the top deck and walked outside through sliding doors.

As the day advanced, the morning's rain had moved eastwards over the Atlantic. Now, at five, the Hudson River mirrored a clear sky; the cranes and factory chimneys of the Jersey shoreline were faithfully reflected in blue water and the Statue of Liberty, catching the declining sun, shone copper-green as she waved her torch across a mile of water.

The ferry hooted and slid away from its semicircular berth.

"And yet," said Thomas, turning to study the profile of downtown Manhattan, which was now rising up behind them like some mad, majestic dream of monoliths all in black and stone-colour and pea-green, "the curious thing is that I still have a kind of fondness for Bo. Much more than I do for Bella. In spite of the terrible things that we did to one another."

How had he ever begun telling Catriona about the *Hetaira* cruise? He hardly knew. She listened so intently, with such acute, unprejudiced interest plainly expressed in her small calm face that he felt disburdened; the memory was cauterised as it was drawn out. She made no judgments, either on Bo or on Thomas. Perhaps she was assessing the effect of all this on Gabriel's later actions.

"What happened then?" she asked.

"Then I flew back to England. There wasn't any point in staying on, with six months' work down the drain. Bo had gone to the refrigerator and thrown all my specimens overboard. Every last one. My grant only just covered the expenses—there was no money left to begin again. And no time either. I suppose I took it for an omen that I was never meant to be a real scientist. And I couldn't bear the sight of Bo after what he'd done. I daresay he couldn't bear the sight of me either. Also there were problems at Crusoe and Selkirk. Oh, yes, and I'd had a queer letter from Loraine Hartshorn, who was a neighbour, a kind of friend—"

"I've heard about her from Gabriel—"

"Saying I'd better come back to Bella, dropping mysterious hints. That was just before Christmas."

"And then?"

What did her inquiring voice, her alert dispassionate curiosity, recall? Gabriel, of course—at age eleven still easily charmed by a story, or any long piece of explanation. "Well, and what happened then, Uncle Tom? And then? And then?"

"And then I arrived back at the house in Wanborough —Christmas Eve, snowing—everything bad happens to me at Christmas, or in snow—but this bit's not suitable for your ears."

"Oh, come *on*, Thomas, I'm not ten."

"You look it, however."

He had taken a cab from London airport straight to the house. Found Bella in bed, with not just one man, but two. A devastating scene. For him, anyway. He preferred not to dwell on its details. But he remembered saying to Bella with incredulous loathing:

"And you could do this with Gabriel in the house?"

"Of course he's not in the house, you *fool!* He left to catch the plane for Lagos. He was flying out on his birthday. Don't you remember anything? He's probably halfway there by now."

Thomas looked up the flight time, telephoned Heathrow, asked them to get a message to Gabriel Baird, passenger on the BOAC flight to Rome, Lagos, Cape Town; then he tried to start his car but failed; after six months the battery was defunct. Bella never bothered to drive, which she did very badly; she took taxis or asked friends. He got a radio cab back to the airport. But it was Christmas, and chaotic, with bad weather, and flights cancelled, and flights delayed, and extra, unscheduled flights; his message had failed to find Gabriel, who must have flown off half an hour before he reached Heathrow.

"I remember Gabriel telling me a bit about that trip," Catriona said. "He arrived to find Bo in a pretty disjointed and alcoholic state, and escorted him back. . . . So what did you do next?"

"Took yet another cab back to the house and found that Bella had gone. She'd left a note telling me to pack up my stuff and get out, as our marriage was through and the house was hers. Which it was of course. So I packed up my stuff and got out."

"Where did you go?"

Old Samuel had died three years before. The little house in Wansea had been sold. No point in going across there.

"Hotel first, and later I found a flat in the part of London where I'd lived before. The one where I am still."

"And then?"

"Then I have another gap," he said slowly. "I can't remember. Something bad happened, connected with Bo. What the hell can it have been?"

"Don't worry about it," said Catriona. "Maybe it'll come back later on. Maybe it's a protective mechanism in

245

your mind that only lets through as much as you can take." She smiled faintly. "Do you see that old pair ahead of us?"

They had moved inside, to one of the rows of seats in the top deck, and Thomas had fetched them cups of coffee from the sandwich bar. Catriona pointed to an elderly couple, the husband bald, the wife snowy-haired, who were sitting arm-in-arm two rows ahead of them.

"Yes, why?"

"While you were getting the coffee I heard the husband say, 'Ah, things aren't the same as they were in the good old days. Why, forty-five years ago there used to be shoeshine guys on these ferries who'd polish your shoes for a nickel, and there used to be men playing accordions and violins on the boats. You don't get things like that any more,' and his wife sighed and said, 'No, it's true, you don't get things like that any more.' "

"Well?"

"Well, the shoeshine guy had *just passed* them. Granted, he charges fifty-five cents now instead of a nickel, but he's *there*. And there's a trio playing music by Telemann up in the forward part of the boat this very minute, I can hear them from here. Shall we go and listen?"

"Okay." He drained his paper cup and followed her narrow, purposeful back.

When he caught up with her he asked, "Why didn't they notice the shoeshine man and the music?"

"Because they wanted to enjoy their nostalgia, of course! It wouldn't be any good if everything was just the *same* now as it was then."

"Or perhaps," he said, "*they* have changed so much, they can't bear for everything else to have stayed the same. But why do I forget? Do you suppose it has anything to do with my physical pain? Or this drug? Or have I got more basic reasons?"

She turned and looked at him thoughtfully. It was a long time, he thought, since anybody had taken him as seriously as this child was doing.

"I expect it has something to do with the pain, and the drugs," she said. "After all, practically nothing that happens has just *one* cause, has it? It's all different forces and currents and draughts pushing and pulling. And you've had a good deal of trouble one way or another. Your mind can only tackle one thing at a time, so it forgets the rest."

"I haven't had more trouble than other people," he said moodily. "I'm just weaker than other people."

Give way to impulses. He remembered Jan's letter, some time in the middle of his marriage to Bella. ". . . It was because of what you said to my mother, telling her she was like an octopus doing her best to strangle my whole life. The poor old girl never really got over it, you sowed the most terrible seeds of self-doubt and insecurity in her; after that she practically never dared phone me and suggest doing anything together. At the time I couldn't think how you could have been so cruel. . . . Now I see it was the result of that stuff. I don't blame you for it any more, but the thought of her death makes me so sad that whatever had happened to you, there would have been no future for us together, our relationship has been permanently affected. . . ."

"Hush!" Catriona laid a hand on his arm. "Listen to the music."

Two boys and a girl were playing a trio sonata for flute, oboe, and recorder, by the forward entrance to the cabin. They had their music on stands and a cap lay on the deck between them into which a few of the passengers, rather bashfully were dropping quarters and occasionally dollar bills. The players wore jeans and looked to be about Catriona's age; in fact he saw a nod of recognition pass between her and them; fellow-students perhaps. They played well, Thomas thought; it was cheerful music, but it could not cheer him. He felt intensely depressed.

Was he doing the right thing? Was this a mad, harebrained wild-goose chase, when all the time Gabriel was somewhere else entirely?

Crucially important time was being wasted, he had broken faith with the kidnappers, he had alienated Bo and Bella. . . . The things that Bo had said over the phone came back to him, unsweetened by the passage of time.

He hates me, he really hates me. What have I done to create such bitterness in him? Parting from Bella? Or something to him personally?

Another lurking question moved into view: Loraine's death. Why can't I remember anything about that? Did I have any hand in it?

The music wound to its gay and formal end. Catriona

was talking to the three players, commenting on their arrangement of the piece. Thomas was suddenly hit by an idea; a long shot but worth trying.

"Ask them—" he began.

Catriona had had it at the same moment. She turned to the eldest boy.

"Have you been playing on this boat all day?"

"Sure. We just go backward and forward. It's a great place to practise. Only costs a dime for as many trips as you care to make. And we've collected quite a bit."

She said, "Do you know my friend Gabriel? Did you ever meet him or see me with him? I don't suppose you'd have happened to notice if he went over on the ferry any time today?"

The boys looked blank but the girl said, "Gabriel? That dark-haired English kid who used to be with you on the Morton Street pier sometimes? I think I did see someone this morning who might have been him. Quite early. There weren't many people about then, that was how I came to notice him."

"Was he with anybody? Thomas asked.

"He could have been. There was a white-haired guy— looked like a professor. I noticed him say something to the boy. But I don't know if they were together."

The ferry was awkwardly, bumpily working its way into its berth, nudging along the wooden piles until the semicircular lip of the lowest deck fitted into the semi-circular dock. Thomas suddenly recalled the car, and ran below, calling to Catriona:

"Ask them which way they went—if they saw—I'll meet you on shore."

But the three musicians had not noticed where Gabriel and his possible companion had gone, once the ship docked. She thanked them, and they instantly began on another piece of music.

Catriona waited on the main deck, from which the foot-passengers went ashore. The boat was the same shape at either end, without bow or stern, and so had no need to turn round, merely reversed direction on each trip. The main deck ended in a horseshoe consisting of two footways, each protected by a guard-rail, with a curved bite between them, down below which could be seen the car-deck. The instant the ship had docked, two massive metal ramps, at present ten feet over-head, were rapidly lowered from a gantry until they rested on the

248

twin footways; attendants whisked back the guard-chains, and the passengers hurried up the ramps. Catriona, glancing up, admired the six pigeons perched on the gantry, and two more seated nonchalantly on the ramp itself. They waited till the last possible minute before leisurely taking off as the metal jaw snapped down onto the deck. I'd hate to be caught under that, Catriona thought, and then, looking down, saw Thomas's hired Mustang below, inching its way in the queue along the car-deck; she ran up the footway and through the terminal building to join him in the approach road outside.

"Where now?"

"Well I got a map of the island but it's not very large-scale, it doesn't show Zebra Place. But the library told me it turned off a bigger one called Arthur Kill Road, which is marked here, so we'd better go along that and keep looking out. Drive up here and turn left."

Ahead of them the wide roadway sloped up to a row of modern municipal and mercantile-type buildings. To the left lay a public square with bus stops and a fenced-in patch of brown grass. They drove on and passed older shabbier buildings, stores, frame houses, and supermarkets. Up on their right rose a wooded height of land, dotted over with more houses.

"I suppose, being so close to New York, Staten Island is pretty well covered with building," Thomas said. "Can there really be a spot remote enough for—"

His voice trailed off. Any spot, he thought, is remote enough to die in. My mind isn't working so well.

. A blanketing fog of weariness was beginning to invade him; even the pain in his arms and legs had retreated, or was dulled by fatigue. He yawned, twice, lengthily, and shook his head to clear it.

"I think there are just a few bits of farmland left in the middle," Catriona said. "In the nineteenth century the island was quite rural, there were a lot of orchards."

"Not much sign of that now."

They drove on for five or six miles past more urban development: small town-centers linked by a continuous ribbon of building, with the wooded height still rising on their right, and, down to the left, beyond a mile or so of more closely packed housing, a view of the ocean. Then they passed a village green, with some older-looking frame houses, neat and pretty.

"I'm sorry," said Thomas. "What did you say?"

He yawned again until his ears crackled. The fog was creeping closer.

"That's Richmond Town reconstruction. They're collecting all the oldest houses on the island and moving them there; making a kind of museum village."

"Do people live in them?"

"I don't know."

He yawned again, and with difficulty avoided a swerve. It was becoming harder to remember to drive on the right-hand side. Careful, for god's sake, he warned himself.

Now the land began to rise on the left, bushily wooded; they had turned away from the Atlantic, towards the centre of the island. Brand-new dirt roads and new patches of housing development still under construction gouged here and there into the woods, but less frequently now, with larger stretches of the scrubby trees in between. The leaves were the tarnished yellow of late summer. On the right were banks of great fawn-coloured rushes, patches of swampy water, brown marshland beyond; and beyond again, factory chimneys and wide stretches of industrial waste.

"That's New Jersey we can see over there," Catriona said.

Thomas thought Staten Island was a forlorn region. He wished it were greener. Hard to imagine it as it must have been once, covered with orchards. But you don't need a green place to die in. . . .

"Watch it!" said Catriona, and grabbed the wheel.

"Catriona, I'm terribly sorry." Temporarily Thomas was startled wide awake. "I didn't get much sleep last night—except on a park bench."

"Shall I drive for a bit?" said Catriona, who had had none at all.

"Can you?"

"Sure."

He got out and walked round; she wriggled across. They drove on. Thomas battled against sleep, which assailed him sometimes in slow, nibbling, shallow waves, sometimes in large engulfing breakers.

The channel on their right lay quite close now; they had come clean across the island. They passed a small waterside settlement, notable chiefly for the most monumental pile of rusting industrial junk that Thomas had ever seen.

"No sign of Zebra Road," Catriona was saying, anxiously. "I'm sure I haven't missed any signs; I should think it must be on the left, because on the right it would just run into the channel. But you will keep a lookout, won't you?"

All very well to say keep a lookout. Eyes won't stay open. Oh god, I just let everybody down.

"Please don't go to sleep, Thomas! It's too hard watching both sides at once."

She'll start despising me too. Perhaps she does already.

But a few minutes later she was gripping his arm excitedly. *There it is! We passed it! I saw it.*

"Wonderful. Clever girl."

She went on a short way, reversed in the first opening, and drove back. Presently he felt the car make a right turn.

"Now you really must wake up, Thomas, because we'll have to keep a lookout on both sides. Specially as we don't know what it is we're looking for; do you think we had better stop and ask somebody?"

"Good idea," he mumbled. "Stop and ask—"

"Oh!" She brought the car to a stop. Even through his enveloping quilt of sleep, Thomas picked up the dismay in her voice.

"What's trouble, Catriona?"

"Zebra Place. It's only a quarter of a mile long. It's just a link road, crossing over the highway."

With an effort that felt like pulling himself out of his grave, Thomas sat up and looked about him. They had driven up a slight rise and crossed a bridge that spanned a six-lane expressway. Behind them lay the narrow channel and a depressing vista of factory chimneys and cranes on the New Jersey shoreline. Ahead, the road, much narrower, with a cracked and pitted tarmac surface that suggested it was not used a great deal, ran off into the scrubby woodland. But it was now, according to the yellow road sign, called Bloomingdale Road.

"D'you think we should go along it, or d'you think we should ask somebody?"

"Ask might be best. Find somebody—ask for mill belonging to Tom Thum."

"Not a soul in sight. Should we go back to the main road?"

"Catriona," said Thomas, "terribly sorry but must have short sleep. Too tired—"

He sank into his corner and let his head loll against the seatback. A moment later he was fathoms deep. Just be-

251

fore total blankness a single piercing reproach: But you are hunting for Gabriel. For Gabriel. Suppose he is dying *now?* At this minute.

He took the thought with him into the dark, like a wire twisted round his brain.

Fifteen

Gabriel 1974

Gabriel sat in the attic and methodically listed its contents in his mind. I am sitting at a small round dusty table on which are masses of old ten-inch 78-rpm records, many cracked, a pile of old agricultural journals, a Baedecker map of Paris, 1910, and a heap of old letters. More letters in a dog-basket at my feet. In front of me a large twenty-paned saltbox-type dormer window, flanked by two smaller ones, and two more at right-angles, triangular, those. The whole window is about twelve feet wide, constructed of old, solid, salt-encrusted pine; the window sill is made from logs, and the diagonal beams on either side are pine also, a rough red-gold. On the sill are a gallon stone jug and a large pair of stone breasts, lower part of a bust presumably; cobwebs everywhere. Old bit of brown carpet underneath me. Outside the window nothing to be seen but the tops of trees; down below, the ground slopes, gradually at first then quite steeply down to the swamp. Small grey wooden roof of outside loo can just be seen. The nearest tree is a big cedar, then there are locust, wild plum, black walnut. . . . The rain is pouring down and the wind is tossing the branches; it makes me think of the cedar back at home. Beyond the marsh one can just see the trees on the hillside opposite. Beyond the hill is a road, but you wouldn't know it from here. Inside, to the right, under the sloping roof, a dusty staircase, a wooden chest, cardboard cartons, a kind of metal safe, a large glass jar, a lobster pan, a basket full of old lampshades. A moth-eaten bearskin on the floor behind me. Huge wide floor timbers. Large old rough brick chimney, black and red, comes up through the floor and out through the roof. Distant view through side window of spruce trees. Rough planks on walls may once have been painted white; now it's all peeling off. Old flour-sacks. To my left, stove-in cane chair; planks arranged to form shelves with bricks in between, holding stacks of magazines, shoe-boxes, rat-poison containers. Bursting chaise-longue with missing head of bust, and saucepan lid. Truckle-bed with suitcases and folded curtains. Ironing-board stacked with old New York *Times*es, very yellow. Beams cross the angle of the roof, about ten feet above the floor. Back and front, the roof slopes right to floor level, except for the dormer. Windows at each end, stuck shut with layers of paint, cobwebbed over. Up in the peak of the roof it is dark. I am sitting on an enormous Bible, rather mouse-eaten. If I stand, I can see the whole of the outhouse, a rather absurd elongated sentry-box with peaked roof and small window in door. Behind it the slope runs down to the swamp and there is a wild plum with six black branches reaching up like fingers. Wild periwinkle growing against the walls. I can hear rain pattering all the time on the wooden shingled roof and a wood-dove's mournful coo. Great drops of rain dripping past the window from a leaky gutter. The wood-dove's cry is the same as the cuckoo's, a minor third, two notes, but with the second repeated in a different rhythm, very slow and sad.

This is a good room to die in, even better than the one in the Bowery.

He had spent the first few hours methodically exploring the outside terrain. The millstream, which he had remembered as a clear, rushing, rocky brook, was now choked with mud and weeds; only the barest trickle crawled through tussocks of moss and bog weed and reddish mud covered with a bluish oily stagnant film. And the millpond where he had swum was now an oozy swamp, round the edge of which grew great blond rushes, seven feet tall, with feathery plumy heads. The grass slope had gone. Waist-high thorn bushes grew all around, within six feet of the house in some places. And the mill machinery was rotted, derelict, hidden in a tangle of growth; creeper, trumpet-vine, poison ivy probably. Even during our visit the machinery wasn't actually working. But you could still see the great wooden wheel and the sluice-gates, which now seem to have collapsed entirely.

Sad that the bright brook had gone, and the grassy lawn. But still, what had they to do with me? They belonged to another time.

But it was a pity, he thought, that the remote island he imagined he remembered, the huge territory, was now shrunk to this forlorn patch, half a mile of overgrown swampy woodland, with the old grey-shingled house huddled in the midmost thicket.

Five cents' ride from the Empire State Building.

"Like the Sleeping Beauty's palace," he said aloud, and the half-wild tabby cat, which came and went through a square hole in the floor, rose up from its nest among the flour-sacks and rubbed against his leg. If one had the rest of life to spend, it might be a salutary thing to learn that childhood memories are so untrustworthy? But with such a short future ahead it would have been pleasant to keep those falsities intact?

No! No! cried an inner voice, the inmost voice, let us all die together with our eyes open, none of us deceiving the others. The brook, at least, was really there then, and the lawn, I am sure of that; and if the railway ran half a mile away to the south, and the Jersey factories stood within view from the top of the hill, as they must have then, what essential difference did it, does it, make? If the woods round about are strewn with garbage thick as dandruff, and the oyster-beds along the shore choked with effluent, and the trees broken and diseased in the scrubby woods, isn't that the very proof and justification of what I am doing?

At least the old house, huddled with dignity in its thicket, is just the same, strangely the same; I can remember every creak in the floorboards, every knothole, the height of each step in the steep narrow stair, and the exact smell of weathered, resinous hot wood, fragrant and mysterious as incense.

And up here, where Gus used to sit—almost certainly at this very table—yes, this is a good room. One doesn't need to go to the north pole. I used to envy Frankenstein, after seeing that film; I used to long for such a terrific conclusion, far off in the arctic wastes, under a cataclysmic avalanche, trapped in a cave of ice with my mournful monster. Now my requirements aren't so grand. This will do just as well—no, far, far better. A place where Gus sat, and thought, and wrote, and looked out, and wrote again; this will do best of all.

What a strange, sad, kind man, that James. As if my dying made him sorry, even though we'd only just met; but as if he fully respected my rights in the matter. Like

Catriona. But she was beginning to mind too much. It was mean to go off; but I had to get away. Poor Thomas will hate my dying too; I wish I could have talked to him, explained why. But grannie will do that, she'll do it better than I could. Or Gus will. James just intended to do me a disinterested kindness; but he'll never know how great a kindness. He didn't come up into this attic; he didn't look in the tin safe. He didn't know what was there; still there after ten years.

He left me tins of baked beans and eggs and loo paper and matches and a hatchet. "Keep warm in the evenings," he said, "there's plenty of dry wood and a fire is company. You might as well be comfortable while you wait."

He doesn't know that I'm never cold. And that I like it better up here than down in the kitchen; fireplace or no, it's too dark down there, with the walnut and cedar and the syringa pressing so close against the windows. This is the best room in the house.

I'll stay up here, like St. Simeon Stylites. I wonder how he managed about his toilet arrangements? It must have been rather tough on his worshippers down below. But I haven't any admirers down below and I have the handsome pansy-bordered chamber pot and if I empty it out of the window onto the thickety slope running down to the swamp, that isn't going to be an offence to anyone. And with luck nobody will come here till the winter, or later, and what's left of me by then will be simply a mummy, and if somebody does find it sooner they'll just have to get in touch with Harvard, which will do whatever they do with bodies. So that's taken care of.

He pulled a piece of paper towards him and wrote:

Death is friendly
but dying is no joke
death is easy
but dying is hard work
death is severance
dying is the point of the knife
death is a moment
but dying is the whole of life.

That was a strange dream that I had, sleeping on the truckle-bed. This must be a good place for dreams? I hope so. I'd like to go off in one last terrific dream, sailing into death with canvas spread and flags flying. And music playing.

I was dreaming about this angelic little boy—and his name was Gabriel too—who at six, not sixteen, was due to die of heart trouble; an operation might save him, might not. The dream was not so much about him as about the people concerned: the old priest who had taught him—the family were Catholics—who was so distressed by the thought of his death, and ashamed of his distress because obviously it would be better for Gabriel to be in heaven, with God, but he kept saying, "There are plenty of angels up there already, why couldn't God leave him here?" Accompanying his words in my dream was a visualisation of a sequence of angels in height order with little Gabriel right at the bottom. Gabriel had hundreds of friends—there was a road-mender, a lift-attendant, there was a shabby, eccentric homosexual teacher who loved him, which made Gabriel's father very angry; the main scene in my dream (while the doctors were discussing Gabriel and he was talking to the priest) was a conversation that took place between the parents. The father, a thickset, bull-necked sort of Tory squire, was in a rage with the mother; she had wandered off into an empty lecture hall in the hospital and he followed, storming at her, saying that it was all her fault, because of the insanely careless way she had brought up Gabriel; his illness, his unsavoury friends, everything; while he raged, she lay down along a row of seats in the auditorium—like the man in St. Paul's; she had gone in there because the place was dark and empty; she was in a silent agony of tears.

Why did I call the boy Gabriel in my dream? Is that how I think of myself? As a little six-year-old saint? How old is one in dreams, anyway? The age of *now*, or some happy age from a long time back, the best time? The age that I was when I stayed here with Gus? Who was the squire father? Gus was never like that. And Bella is not the mother; I do not think that Bella will weep when I am dead. I remember when *her* mother died— Grannie Sadie—Bella had just been dyeing her lashes, brushing on the stuff that she mixed in a little dish with peroxide. The phone rang and she said, "Get it will you, honey?" and a voice said, "This is a telegram: Mrs. Sadie Farragut passed away last night please phone Eva Trouton, Matron, Sunnyside Home, Worthing," and Bella just sat there, wide-eyed, staring; she said, "I can't cry or I'll wash off this stuff and it's ten bob a tube, besides it stings like the devil."

My thesis: my *Dissertation on Death*. Did I *know* that Gus had already written it? Could he have read bits to me, discussed it with me? Could I have remembered it? Could I have known, deep down inside, that it would be here waiting in the tin case, sparing me the trouble of doing it myself? Was that why I came here?

What was the point of my being alive at all? Gus had done it all before.

All I want now is to be free; to forget all the secrets I ever knew. Root up the infernal grove. Forget about Thomas. Forget about Bo and Bella—the stiff studio door, opening onto that smoky scene. Forget about that, blot it out. There isn't room for all three of us in the same world. Go blank, forget. Not easy, right away; here I am with nothing but my mind for company; but I can go on pulling things out of it for a long time yet. Catriona says I'm a poet; poets don't belong anywhere. They haven't any place. Slow. Slow down. Hushabye, baby, in the tree top; simply let everything come to a stop.

He wrote:

Scientists tell us that, for quite long periods, time runs backwards
Scientists can prove this from the fossilised rings of trees
Time turns in its tracks and runs in the opposite direction
Scientists can tell this from fossilised rings in the human mind
Time reverses and goes the opposite way, at the same pace
During these periods of reversal (do you suppose we are in one now?)
Birds sing their songs back to front, trees grow upside down
My true love hath my heart and I have his. . . .

Sixteen

Bo, Bella 1974

The room was dark, except for the orange-shaded lamp, and silent, except for the regular clink of the whisky bottle on Bo's tumbler. Rain poured down outside, cascading over the windows like a portcullis, barring them away from the street, which was empty; the terrible weather had discouraged late-night traffic. Only an occasional police car shot by giving off its banshee wail.

On the wall Bo's little painted people silently writhed and screamed.

When the telephone rang, Bo got there first. Bella softly darted into the other room.

"Bo? Are you there? What the hell happened? He never came. Why are you still in New York?"

"It got fucked up," Bo said. "Thomas went off to pick up the Hertz car and didn't come back. He called up from god knows where to say he wasn't going to deliver the cash; he'd got a lead and wanted to follow it."

"Follow it *where?*"

"Didn't say."

"Is there any possibility that he might be going *there?* To the mill?"

"How should I be expected to know?" said Bo sourly. He heard a click, and the sound of breathing. Bella had picked up the extension in the kitchen.

"What about the money? Did he get it? What did he do with it? Where is it?"

"He said he had got it, but he didn't bring it here and I don't know where it is. For all I know he left it in a trash bin somewhere."

"Did you look in the flat in Tenth Street?"

"Of course. It wasn't there."

"My poor Bo. You've properly blown it this time, haven't you?"

Bella, who must have been listening with growing impatience, now screamed into the phone:

258

"You bloody murderer, where have you got that boy? Tell me where he is! I know all about your plans—I found your letter to Bo, you *swine!*"

"Oh, be quiet, Bella, will you," Bo said. "Stop acting like a madwoman and get off the line."

"Bo?" That was James. "You let Bella *read my letter?*"

"Of course I didn't let her, you fool; she found it, grubbing around among my things."

"I am not a madwoman! It's you two who are the most unnatural, monstrous, outrageous—will you tell me where that boy is?"

"Gabriel isn't the only one with a death wish then," said James's calm voice. "You really have a will to destruction, haven't you, Bo? You know what she's like. Why did you leave it where she could find it?"

"Where is he?"

"Oh, cool it, Bella. Cut out the hysterics."

"Don't you tell me to cool it, you murdering skunk."

"Have you done?" James inquired. "Well you can both be sure that I won't get involved in any more of your family affairs. This is positively the last time that I make any attempt to help you out of the messy situations that you two continually cook up between you. I'm going north now. I'm quitting. Bo knows where the boy is, Bella. And you'd better get out there fast if you think that Thomas really has a clue; you may be too late already.

"Good-bye, Bo."

There was a click as he hung up, in some distant telephone booth, in the dark, a long way off in the Catskills.

"He's gone." Bo stared down blankly at the dead instrument in his hand.

"And he won't come back. And a good riddance too."

Bella pulled on a shiny white raincoat and tied a scarf over her hair. "Hurry up, get your anorak, we're going."

"Going where?"

"To Gabriel. He said you know where it is. You're such a liar, I might have guessed you'd been lying about that too," she said bitterly.

He was still standing motionless, with a dazed expression. Impatiently she snatched up his old green anorak from the floor, found her purse, and said:

"Come on. You have to come, to show me the way. Where is it, anyway?"

"Staten Island," he said mechanically. He picked up

259

the whisky bottle. "How do you propose to get there, may I ask?"

"While you were sleeping I phoned Angie Wasserman's garage and asked them to get her car out. It's down below; I fetched it."

"But you can't drive. You never drive. You haven't even got a licence."

"I can drive if I have to, I suppose. And I have to now, don't I?"

"Christ," Bo muttered with foreboding. He dragged on the anorak and followed her down the stairs like a sleepwalker.

The car had already acquired a ticket. Bella waited until Bo had got in, then started it with a savage jerk.

"Lucky there's no traffic at this time of night," she said.

"Bella," he muttered. "Why are you really doing this?"

She answered between her teeth, gripping the steering wheel much too hard:

"Because he's my son. Because I didn't make all the arrangements at the cardiac unit and persuade Manresa to fly over here just to have the boy demolished by some poison that James has stuck in his oatmeal. He's *mine;* I had him. *You* weren't there; you were off in New Zealand."

"He's not yours. He's cut the connection. He isn't your property," Bo said obstinately. "James had far more real sympathy for him. James wouldn't drag him off to a cardiac unit if he didn't want to go. James arranged a painless exit for him."

"We aren't going to discuss James! I hope he goes to the north pole and freezes to death. If he's finally decided to stop meddling in your affairs, it's a bloody good thing."

She crossed a red light, raising a barrage of furious hoots from a taxi that had to make a violent swerve to avoid her.

"Jesus, sweetie, do take care." Bo gripped the door handle. He was sweating liberally, but the haunted, sightless look never left his face.

"What *was* this delightfully painless end that James had so thoughtfully planned for him?"

"I don't know."

"I don't believe you."

"It's the truth. It doesn't matter whether you believe me or not," he said dully.

"If you and James love Gabriel so much, why do you want to push him over the edge? Why not just take the money and run; leave nature to take its course? I should have thought that would be more your line."

She swung out widely to make a right turn and just missed a truck which was trying to overtake on her left.

"We probably would have done that if *you* hadn't arrived on the scene, advertising and stirring things up. James wanted to help him. Get this into your head. Gabriel wants to *die*. Which is probably due to you as much as to anything else that has happened in the course of his short life."

"Oh?" She shot a glance sideways before swooping out round a stopping bus. "And I suppose you've been nothing but sunshine and help to him?"

There was a shriek of brakes from behind them.

"Bella for god's sake look what you're doing. Look in the mirror sometimes."

"*You* can't drive, so shut up!"

Rain-blurred lights lurched past them. Neon signs. Zenith. Pizza. Brew 'n Burger. *Te Amo, amas*, thought Bo, I love an ass. James. Please come back. He never will. He's gone forever this time, into the frozen north. Gone like August. Gone like the taste of strawberries and the scent of a blossoming bean-field. Gone like Gabriel, out of reach.

"I'm sorry, Uncle Bo, I'd really rather not see you any more. Ever again."

"Why, Gabriel?"

"You know why."

They had arrived, by a series of miracles, at the ferry port. The port building was empty and echoing at this hour of night. Bo waited vacantly while Bella paid for the car; he took a couple more drinks from his bottle.

"All this trouble to rescue someone who doesn't want to be rescued," he said, when they were driving down the slope into the boat. "Perhaps now you're sorry you had that hysterectomy after he was born. How long were you and August married—ten years? You could have had half a dozen little Bairds, all alive-o. Plenty of eggs in plenty of baskets."

"Be quiet."

I could just knock myself out with scotch, Bo thought. Then how'd she ever, ever find the place?

But a sneaking hope was beginning to uncurl in him, a sneaking wish to have just one more try at explaining, at justifying—

"What's the name of the place where he is?"

But if Thomas has got to him—*how? how?*—how could Thomas have done that?—but if he has, suppose he told Gabriel that I arranged all this and then betrayed him?

That I could not bear. I have to explain to him that it really isn't my fault. I never, ever intended things to turn out this way. Poor little Gabriel. Poor little lonely boy standing in the park staring at his ice-cream cone. I can't taste ice-cream any more since Thomas knocked me backwards into the refrigerator and busted all my teeth. Who would have thought Thomas packed such a punch.

I have to explain everything to Gabriel. So that at least, if he goes, he goes understanding I never meant to harm him.

Maybe when we get across I can somehow give her the slip.

They remained in the car during the twenty-minute crossing, sitting inertly side by side, without speaking to each other, like two very old people who have no more ideas to exchange and no energy to find new ones.

The wide street on the far side was deserted, and so was the town square. But Bella spotted a man standing on a corner, and pulled up to ask the way.

While the man was explaining, with many gestures, Bo slipped quietly out on his side of the car.

He had noticed a bus pulling up twenty feet behind them. The illuminated sign on its front said TOTTENVILLE. Silent as an Iroquois in his sneakers, he walked with immense strides back to the bus, reached it just before the doors closed, and swung himself aboard.

"Go anywhere near Zebra Road?" he asked the driver, who nodded.

"I'll tell you when."

By the time Bella looked round and realised that Bo was not in the car, the bus had pulled past, and was speeding out of sight round the next bend. She stared about in a panic. The man of whom she had asked the way had walked off; no other person was in view. She

262

had pulled up beside a deserted, empty store; the street-lights shining into its window displayed a mournful collection of aged cardboard ice-cream sundaes, painted pink and brown, covered with dust.

Seventeen

Catriona 1974

When Catriona let the car roll to a stop, Thomas was still sleeping. She dared not drive any farther in the dark along this dirt road between stretches of dense, inky boggy woodland. The road, which had been posted as a DEAD END, was steadily becoming narrower and threatened to dwindle into a footpath; she did not fancy having to back up and risk running off the track into swamp. Also, supposing this was the right road and led to Dongan Mill, she was reluctant to drive too close and disturb Gabriel, if he was there, with headlights and the noise of the car.

She decided to explore on foot. If it was not the right road, no doubt she would presently discover her mistake.

Switching off the engine and lights, she got out. Thomas did not stir. She pushed the door until it clicked shut, then stood still in the dark, waiting for her eyes to become accustomed. The rain had settled in again, quite hard. She wished that she had a jacket, and that they had had the foresight to provide themselves with a flashlight. The woods were so very dark.

Catriona, city-bred, found herself, to her own surprise, overwhelmed suddenly by a simple primitive dread of this unknown, dark, bushy, silent, mysterious territory. It was not a fear of being raped or mugged; like any sensible person she stayed out of Central Park after dark, but it did not seem particularly likely that potential muggers or rapists would be roaming about this unpopulated stretch of woodland on such a very inclement night. But there was a much deeper, more basic and atavistic fear of nothing that she was able to classify. She remembered a hair-raising story that Gabriel had read her once about a creature called the Wendigo, which flies wailing through

263

the vaster woods of North America, compelling all who hear it to follow its huge, spaced-out footprints until they die of starvation and exhaustion. Granted it would be difficult to die of starvation on Staten Island, she thought, or even of exhaustion, since it was only about thirteen miles long by six or seven wide; but these woods were so very dark and silent and wet.

She began to move nervously along the dirt road, prospecting ahead with each foot before setting it down. For the first few minutes she kept blundering into the bushes at the side of the track. They were covered in tiny, needle-sharp thorns; soon her legs and arms, even her face, were scratched and bleeding. When a roosting pheasant exploded from the bushes right beside her with an expostulatory crescendo of aggrieved shrieks, she thought she would die of fright; she stood still, getting her breath in silent gasps, with her hands jammed against her breastbone, until the pneumatic-drill thudding of her heart had slowed down.

And then, when she walked on, she began to notice other sounds, farther off in the brush: rustles and thumps —deer? racoons? She felt it was foolish to be scared; very likely it was no more than a rabbit, but it could equally well have been a mammoth or some sinister watcher stalking her.

She had expected that the path would quickly bring her to a conclusion one way or the other, but instead it led on and on, up over a slight rise. Catriona began to worry about Thomas sleeping there in the dark. Suppose he woke and found her gone, what would he do?

He had looked utterly exhausted and ill, though; she did not think it likely that he would wake.

After a while the path began going downhill (by now her eyes were becoming more accustomed to the dark) and she saw what seemed to be two short stretches of dry-stone wall on either side of the track. Standing by one of them she was just able, above the patter of the rain, to catch the faint murmur of a brook down below.

At the Rip Van Winkle Inn, where a surprised woman had given her directions—"But nobody lives there now, my dear, since old Tom went into the hospital, I'm sure you must be making a mistake"—someone had mentioned a bridge. "Along the dirt road, over the bridge, and it's about two hundred yards farther on. You'll see it over to the left among a lot of old trees."

After more walking she did begin to think that she might be able to see a block that was slightly darker than the rest of the thickety dimness ahead and to the left. She increased her pace, treading softly on the wet sandy track.

But shouldn't there be a light? Hadn't the man said he would equip Gabriel with matches, candles, lanterns, oil, if necessary—for there had been no power in the place when Gabriel stayed there long ago with Gus.

Now, for the first time, Catriona, who was not normally given to suspicious or analytical ponderings over other people's motives, found herself wondering why all this had been arranged with such goodwill for Gabriel? Why had this stranger been so helpful? Of course everyone always *did* want to help Gabriel, that was the effect he had on people, but why had this man gone so particularly far out of his way to do it?

Could he, after all, be connected with that extraordinary kidnap business, about which Thomas had told Catriona? Like her friends, who never listened to newscasts or read the papers, she had not even been aware that Bella had been advertising for Gabriel. Could the stranger *be* the kidnapper? But he had not kidnapped Gabriel after all—merely helped him to leave of his own free will. But had he done this out of pure kindness or for his own advantage?

According to Thomas the kidnapper had said that he would either kill Gabriel or, if the money was paid, would deliver him straight to the cardiac unit for his heart surgery. How did the kidnapper know about Gabriel's condition? Well, he might have heard the broadcasts.

Anyway, the money had not been paid. It was still sitting in the cases, under Hattie's bed. No one was likely to find it there. When Thomas told Catriona about the offer, she had cried out that it was the most horrible bargain she had ever heard of, worse than selling someone into slavery.

"But if it's for his good, Catriona?"

"What right have you to do that to him when he didn't choose it for himself? If Bella wanted that, I'm not surprised Gabriel feels about her the way he does."

"How does he feel about her?"

"He can't bear her," Catriona said briefly.

Since the ransom money had not been paid, would the alternative threat have been put into execution? Somehow the ideas seemed pitifully unnecessary, since Gabriel was due to die anyway. Not that he'd mind much, perhaps. . . .

Or had the mention of this mill been a complete blind? Was Gabriel somewhere else entirely?

If he was inside it, why was the place so dark?

No longer making any attempt to conceal from herself how thirstily, painfully, consumingly she needed to see Gabriel again—just once, if that was all he would allow, just for a moment, just to say a proper good-bye, which had been denied her, just to say she would love him till the day of her own death whenever that should fall—Catriona moved on towards the dark oblong outline of the building.

She was certain now that it must be the mill. It stood above what seemed to be a considerable drop of land. It consisted of two sections, the dwelling, presumably, long and low, and the mill proper, a square high tower.

Gabriel would be occupying the dwelling-house. But where was the entrance, and why was there no light?

She seemed to have lost the path—or else it had lost itself and been overgrown by a tangle of ankle-high bramble. Struggling through this with difficulty, she slowly worked her way forward. The sudden beginning of a much heavier downpour at least drowned any noise of her approach, but made it even more desirable to get under cover quickly.

Thrusting past a bush, she arrived, more abruptly than she had expected to, against the wall of the house. She groped with her hands, felt wooden shingles overgrown with creeper; then found the slats of a shutter. She moved along sideways, counter-clockwise, away from the mill end of the building, and found another window, unshuttered but much grown over by what might be a grapevine. Now round a corner. The ground was clearer; she realised that this might be the main approach to the house: a patch of tussocky grass and a gap in the surrounding bushes suggested so. Another window—screened, this one—and at last a door. A flat, solid wooden door, with a handle but no knocker or bell that she was able to discover.

The handle turned but the door failed to open. It

seemed immovable. Locked, all too probably. Catriona banged with her knuckles till they were sore, and then stopped, suddenly prey once more to the irrational deep fright that had assailed her when she first left the car.

Suppose somebody—or some *thing*—were to open the door very quickly and put out a hand—or claw—and grab her?

But common sense reasserted itself. The rain was cascading down, she was drenched; if the door wouldn't open, the best thing would be to return to the car and drive along. The track seemed adequate if she went slowly.

She gave the door a last rattle, shove, and tug before turning away, and it moved, opening outward. It had simply been stuck with damp, and she had been trying to push, not pull. There was a screen door inside —which she could feel with her hands—but though the screen was latched, she found a hole; she was able to reach through and undo a hook.

Breathless again, she walked inside, and then stood completely still, listening intently, sniffing the musty smell of old unpolished wood, trying to pierce with her eyes the dense bleakness that now surrounded her. After a minute she gingerly felt around with her hands. Nothing. She moved forward a couple of paces and felt again. Still nothing. Now a square of dimness in the otherwise opaque dark declared itself as a window. Oriented by this and rendered slightly more confident, she moved forward once more and encountered a sink—a massive deep wide sink made from what felt like granite.

Running her hand along its outer edge to a solid wooden draining-board, rough and furred with years of scrubbing, she went on exploring, found a shelf on which lay a clutter of small, perplexing objects—stone with a hole? cotton bobbin? pine cone? fishing-float?—and presently to her delight discovered an unmistakable box of matches.

Trembling but resolute, she struck a match and looked about.

As she had guessed, she was in a roomy kitchen. It was barely furnished by a round table, a single chair, a large black potbellied stove, and the sink. There were also some shelves but the match had burnt down to her fingers by the time she discovered them. She just had time

267

to notice a candle in a bottle before the match burnt her and she blew it out.

Lighting another, she made her way over to the candle and lit it, then gazed around, in the mild hazy light that it gave. She felt a small but growing hope.

In a corner she noticed a cardboard carton of groceries—eggs, a jar of instant coffee, tins of stuff. It had not been unpacked. A large washbasket beside it contained kindling wood and a hatchet. But the black iron stove was badly cracked; it seemed unlikely that anyone would be able to build a fire in that.

A door in the opposite wall led to another room; Catriona went through, treading softly on wide, aged painted boards which had no covering but dust.

The next room, a good deal smaller, was panelled in dark old pine and contained nothing but a bed with a thin palliasse and two tidily folded blankets. There was a brick hearth. In one corner a narrow flight of stairs led upward, shut off by a latched door across the third step.

Catriona hesitated. More courage was required to go up the stairs than it had taken to enter the house. If Gabriel were up there—all of a sudden she was overwhelmed by an awesome sense of the dignity and weight of his self-imposed isolation; it seemed to surround him like an impenetrable cloud, like the Heaviside layer, deflecting all waves of communication. Since he had gone away of his own choice, what possible right had she, really, to follow and break in on his seclusion?

And even if the upper floor held nobody, exploration of it seemed more hazardous than entering the downstairs part of the house had been. Once up those stairs, her line of retreat would be cut off.

If Gabriel were not up there—her imagination shied away nervously from the thought of the dark empty rooms above.

But while she was standing motionless, undecided, she heard a faint sound above, a gentle creak. All her blood paused in its flow; her breath checked; warm wax from the candle spilled down her shaking hand. The creak came again. Somebody was certainly up there.

At this moment, as she glanced rather wildly back to the door through which she had entered, her eye was caught by a small patch of blue on the floor: it was a little string of blue beads. In an almost dizzying rush of relief she recognised a set of wooden Greek worry-beads that she had given Gabriel for his birthday; she had bought them in a shop in the Village.

She called softly, "Gabriel? Are you up there? It's me —Catriona," and moving over to the stair-door, tried it. But it did not budge; was apparently fastened on the inside.

"Gabriel?" she called again.

"What do you want?" replied a voice—his voice. It came from overhead but seemed faint and distant, distant not only in position but in quality too, as if he were far withdrawn inside himself, almost out of reach. Perhaps completely out of reach? Her heart sank miserably. Could he have taken something—be on a trip? He never did, because he said he needed all his time for his writing —but maybe here he felt differently— Or maybe the man had given him something?

"Where are you?" she said, trying to make her voice normal and friendly, and thinking at the same time how wretchedly strange it was that she should have to try to be normal towards Gabriel, her dear friend and playmate, whom she loved with all her heart.

"I'm here," said the voice, startling her because it had changed its position.

Looking up she noticed a small square hole in the ceiling where evidently there had once been a trapdoor, before the stairs were built. It had been partly boarded over and only a book-sized opening remained.

Through this she could see the upper part of Gabriel's face and his eyes, steadily regarding her.

She gasped with fright. To see just his eyes staring at her through the hole, as if through a mask, made him into a different person; hostile perhaps, formidable, certainly.

His voice, when he next spoke, was not hostile, but it was calm and severe.

"Why did you come here? You know I wanted to be alone. I wish you'd go away."

She felt pierced with anguish; marooned in desolation. The eyes looking down at her were those of a stranger. The only person who could comfort her in this bereavement was Gabriel; and he was not here.

"I'm sorry," she said humbly. "I didn't *want* to bother you but—"

"Why did you then?"

"No, I did want to," she corrected herself in truth, "but that wasn't the main reason why I came. Something strange has happened."

"Well?"

He did not seem at all interested; nor did he ask how she had found her way there.

"Did you know that you've been kidnapped, Gabriel?"

"What do you mean?"

"Somebody telephoned your mother—and Thomas—and said that unless they paid three-quarters of a million dollars you would be killed; and if they did pay you would be handed over to some hospital for your heart operation."

"But that's rubbish," he said, in his perplexity sounding more like himself. "I'm not kidnapped—I'm perfectly free. I'm all alone here—I can go out if I want. They didn't believe that, surely? They didn't pay the money? Where would they get all that, anyway?"

"From your father's estate. Thomas *did* get it, as a matter of fact. But then I told him it was wrong."

"You've met *Thomas*? He's over here?"

"He and Bella are both over here. And her brother."

"Do they know where I am?"

"I don't think so. Thomas and I have been looking for you."

He was silent for a while, turning all this over in his mind. At length he muttered, "Was James not to be trusted then? He *seemed* sincere." And after a minute he added, "Who would have got the money?"

"Perhaps," Catriona suggested diffidently, "James just intended to take the money, but not do anything about you—just leave you here peacefully."

After another long pause he said, "I wish you hadn't told me all this. It doesn't make any difference. It's just disturbing. I wish you'd go away."

The words were like his knuckles in her face.

"But Gabriel—"

"Well, what?"

"Aren't you going to eat anything—or, or make a fire —or anything? What are you doing up there?"

270

He said calmly, "I'm just going to stay up here from now on. I've nailed a bit of board across the door."

Her heart had been aching so badly already that she was quite surprised to find the pain could become worse. It's *real* pain she thought wonderingly; a real, physical pain. When they say, My heart is broken, this is the pain they mean.

She moved, slowly, like somebody who has just risen from bed after a long, severe illness, to the bottom step of the stair, and sat on it, leaning her cheek against the door, touching the edge of it with her fingers, gently, as if it were Gabriel himself that she touched.

After a while, she said, "Gabriel?"

"What?"

"I'm cold and wet; I've been walking in the rain and got soaked. Would you mind very much if I made a fire and dried myself?"

"Suit yourself," he said.

"And another thing."

"Well?"

"Thomas is outside in the car. He's very unhappy about you. I think he badly wants to speak to you. Will you let him? Just for a little?"

"He'd only try to argue with me. It's so useless. It's just a waste of time and energy. And I haven't got much."

"Please let him come."

"Oh, very well," he said reluctantly. "This was just what I didn't want. Tell him, only for a short time."

Catriona felt so tired that it was difficult to come to a decision. Should she fetch Thomas first, or build the fire first? I'll make a fire, she decided finally; that will be better for Thomas to come to. And if I make a fire in this room, at least a little, a very little, warmth and light must find their way up through that hole to where he is.

She brought the basket of wood from the kitchen and kindled a fire. The wood was bone-dry and caught easily; it burnt well in the brick hearth.

Catriona would have liked to sit on the bottom stair again when the fire had burnt up, to sit with her cheek pressed against the door and just *be* with Gabriel; to be alone with him in this way would be something; though her arms, even her fingers, ached with the longing to stroke his dark soft hair, just once more; to cup her fingers round his obstinate jaw; to press her face against the much-mended blue pullover and put her arms around him and hug him. The unused, inflamed love inside her felt painful enough to kill her.

Perhaps it'll go critical, she thought. Or burst and give me peritonitis. . . . She had better go and fetch Thomas.

"I'm going now, Gabriel," she called steadily. "I'll be back in a little while."

No answer from up above.

She wondered where he was sitting, what he was doing up there. The eyes had gone from the hole in the floor.

Having made sure of the whereabouts of more candles, she left one burning on the draining-board, to light their way back, and went out, pulling the screen door to behind her and latching it.

She left the outer door slightly open, so as to let out a guiding crack of light.

Then she started making her careful way back through the dark towards the car and Thomas. Rain and tears poured down her face.

Eighteen

Thomas, Catriona, Bo, Gabriel 1974

He came to with a terrified start, feeling as if all his organs had been violently wrenched out of and then shoved back into place. Where the hell was he, anyway? He was in a crouched position, stiff with pain, in the pitch dark. I'm the sort of person, he thought, who constantly gets into these appalling situations. This is all so familiar. If it's happened once, it's happened a dozen times. And that's no help at all. Because, because—

I wish I was back in my office. What office?

His mind rattled feverishly. Words poured along the top of it in a loose, jolting cascade. My name is legion, for we are many. My name is Norval, on the Grampian Hills. Oh, breathe not his name where cold and dishonoured his relics are laid. Their name liveth for evermore. Runs away to the name of Fido. That was

272

somebody's family joke, an advertisement for a lost dog. Holla your name to the reverberate hills. Hector and Lysander, and such great names as these. I used to think that was pronounced Lysonnder, and I always called the aircraft that, too; it was the only one I could ever recognise because of the peculiar shape of its wings. I was born in 1933. Good: date of birth comes pat as butter. National insurance number, BKEH 173 2. That's very good too. I'm sorry, the face is perfectly familiar, it's just my name that escapes me. An age without a name. That's what I shall be. Who's that white-haired old scarecrow in the corner of the ward? Oh, he's been here a long time but we don't know his name.

Now, the thing is, the thing is, I know I'm supposed to be going somewhere and doing something, urgently. That's perfectly clear. It's just a case of remembering what.

I seem to be sitting in a car. Shall we start driving? Where shall we go?

He fingered along the dashboard gadgets, unloosed a blast of radio music, washed the windscreen several times, found the horn, the indicators, and finally the headlights.

Good. We appear to be in a wood. Where are we bound for? State your destination and tender exact fare. Tender the fare and swift the journey, swift the journey and speedy the route, down the passage that has no turning, straight to the arms of the absolute.

See? No hands.

He found the ignition and started up; drove a yard or two. The door, not properly closed, flapped open. Funny. I wouldn't ever leave a door like that. Was somebody with me? Was—somebody—with me? Who?

He stopped the car again and was reaching across to shut the door when a man walked blinking into the lights, coming from the side of the track.

"Excuse me, I wonder if you'd mind telling me if I'm on the right road to Dongan Mill—"

Then he came closer still, looked inside the car, and said, "Good Christ, it's Thomas. Well, I suppose I might have expected that you'd turn up."

"I beg your pardon? I'm afraid I can't help you. I seem to have forgotten my name temporarily. Who did you say I was?"

273

"Oh come off it, Thomas. That's not funny in the slightest degree."

"It isn't meant to be. I've forgotten my identity."

"Cut it out. You're Thomas Cook and I'm your brother-in-law. Ex-brother-in-law I should say."

"Well I'll believe you if you say so but I haven't the slightest recollection of it."

Bo peered closely into his eyes and said, "You do look ill I must say. I wonder what the plague we ought to do now."

"Do you know where I'm supposed to be going?"

"Sure I know. We're both going to find Gabriel."

Gabriel. The name gave him an obscure but deep pang. It seemed to be associated with two separate but equally piercing sets of feelings—old, deep-buried hurts, and unhappy forbodings for the future.

He said, at a venture:

> Gabriel, to thee thy course by lot hath given
> Charge and strict watch that to this happy place
> No evil thing approach or enter in.

"Good grief, and you don't know your own name? Not that Gabriel, old dear, not the archangel; your stepson. My nephew. It would certainly seem," Bo said thoughtfully, "that Bella picked badly. You were the worst possible choice for this quest. Don't you remember anything? Don't you remember Bella?"

"Bella?"

"Well, never mind. You're better remaining oblivious to her, I daresay. She gave you nothing but trouble. Poor old cuss."

"Should I drive on? Is it urgent?"

"Yes, drive on. But go carefully, will you? Are you sure you're fit? . . . Well, I can't drive, so you'll just have to. This is a very weird do," said Bo, slouching back with arms folded and looking thoughtfully at Thomas's profile in the reflection from the headlights. "Can you really remember nothing?"

"It probably won't last very long," said Thomas uncertainly. "I believe I have these things quite often. And generally come out of them in about twenty minutes or half an hour I think."

"Very spooky. And it's set off by that stuff you take for your arthritis?"

"Najdolene. That's what my doctor says. They've had some other cases but not so bad."

"That came clear enough. But you don't—you really don't, for instance, remember our little fracas? Yours and mine? You don't remember punching me? . . . Do you know, ever since that day I've completely lost my sense of taste and smell. Can't even taste scotch. I just have to drink it for the lift, and the lift's not the same without the flavour."

"I punched you? Why did I do that?"

"Oh, you had plenty of provocation. Don't worry. But then you went further, and squirted corrosive cleaning foam over what's almost certainly the best set of drawings I'll ever do. I was very annoyed about that, I must admit. Yes, I guess you came out one up from that little tiff. But the funny thing is," said Bo, sounding really surprised, "that I don't seem to hate you for it any more. I suppose it just wore itself out. Do all emotions wear out in time? Even hate? Perhaps when I'm old I'll even feel quite calm about Bella. Will you feel calm about Bella, I wonder?"

"Bella. What does that—"

"Now *don't* produce any more quotations from English literature, I beg. Anyone would think you were an English don— Whoa, slow down, what's that?"

A figure had stepped in front of the car, waving. Thomas, who had in any case been driving at about five miles an hour, came to a stop.

Catriona walked round to the passenger side and opened the door. She was greatly startled to find Bo already sitting there.

"Hullo?" said Bo. "Where did you spring from?" Then he looked at her keenly and said, "Wait a minute, I recognise you. I never forget a face—"

Catriona said to Thomas with bitter reproach, "Did you *plan* this? Had you arranged to pick him up?"

"No, he didn't plan anything. But it's no use asking Thomas questions at the moment, I'm afraid," Bo said. "He's suffering from a slight touch of amnesia."

"How do you mean? Are you joking? This isn't exactly the time for kidding around."

She looked angrily from one man to the other. She was very pale. There were tears in her eyes.

"Here, get into the car, do," Bo said. "You're drenched; don't stay out there in the rain. There's room in the front if we all huddle together."

Catriona preferred to get into the back. Bo switched on the overhead light and swivelled round to look at her.

"Vermeer's girl reading a letter," he said. "No; I know who you are. Little Catriona, who used to play with Gabriel. Have you come from him now, by any lucky chance? Do you know where he is?"

"Yes, I've come from him," she said. "And he doesn't want to be bothered by *anyone*. He wants to be left in peace. And I think you should do that. If he wants to die he should be allowed to."

"Christ, yes," Bo said. "I wouldn't want to stop him, poor little sod. If he thinks he's got reasonable justification. Live and let die, as someone has already observed. If he wants to die, that's his affair."

He pulled a tin of cigarettes out of his anorak pocket and lit one.

"Well, then, what are you doing here, hanging around?" Catriona demanded.

"Things got a bit out of hand, my dear. . . . *I* know who you really look like," Bo broke off to say. "The lady holding up the mirror—"

"That's what Gabriel says— *Oh*," exclaimed Catriona wretchedly, pressing her fingers to her forehead, "I wish you hadn't come! Now I don't know what to do. If we all go back there—like a sort of picnic—it takes away all his dignity; it makes it into some horrible farce. He wants to be alone, he *should* be alone."

"Wait: let's think about this calmly," said Bo. "First, nobody is going to take away Gabriel's dignity. Whatever is taken from him, that he'll always have. Are you his friend?"

"Of course I am! I love him!"

"Of course you do," said Bo, looking at her with irony and tenderness. The cigarette dropped sideways from his lip. "Of course you love him. We all do. And we've all betrayed him and buggered him up. Even old Thomas here. We've done it with the best intentions, naturally. Speaking for some of us, that is. My own intentions were purely selfish; I'm not a saint like Thomas. But, as I was saying, if you love him, you ought to know that no one and nothing is going to take away Gabriel's dignity. Right?"

"Perhaps," she said slowly. "But he's got a lot of thinking to do. He'd so much rather be left in peace."

"Oh I know. So would we all. But the trouble is we come up against conflicting rights there. He has a right to die in peace, we have a right to try and dissuade him—"

"But you said—"

"Or," continued Bo, gesturing at her with a wave of his cigarette, "to ask his forgiveness for our various betrayals. And there's another complication—"

"His mother—"

"*She* certainly wants him alive—"

"He can't stand her—"

"Yes, well, that's regrettable, but not surprising. Anyway, luckily I've managed to shed her, and she's so hopelessly inefficient without anybody else along to hold her hand that very likely she'll drive across some bridge or other and end up in Brooklyn or New Jersey. Bella has absolutely no sense of direction, in *any* way. No, the complication I had in mind is that my friend James, well-meaning but perhaps exceeding his brief, had proposed to accelerate Gabriel's end by putting a dose of pethidine in his instant coffee—or methanol in his grapefruit juice—or something of the kind.

"Now that I cannot approve. So I think we should get along quite fast to this refuge and discourage him from using the stores that were left him."

Catriona was so appalled at this piece of information that she sat staring at Bo in silence for a couple of minutes.

Then she said, "He was going to *poison* him? And you knew this? Your own nephew? But that's *horrible*."

"Oh come," said Bo, "where's your sense of proportion? A little callous, perhaps, but after all he had cast us off pretty completely. And he was going to die in any case. It would just reduce the possibility of his being found while there was still time to drag him back—"

"You," she said slowly, "you wanted him dead?"

"Didn't you?" he asked with genuine interest.

"Never! If he wants to die, that's absolutely his affair. But of *course* I'd be happier if he decided to stay alive."

277

"Suppose he was alive but wouldn't see you or speak to you? What then?"

She thought about this carefully and said, "Even then."

"Then you're a better man than I am," he said flippantly. "If he be not so to me, what care I how kind he be?"

Thomas, who had been listening to this exchange with slow, frowning concentration, suddenly said, "Shouldn't we go on?"

"Oh, hullo, old mole!" Bo patted him on the shoulder. "Coming up to the surface again, are you? Have you remembered who you are?"

"Yes, I've remembered," Thomas said. His expression was bleak and sad; he started up and drove on without saying anything more.

Catriona said to Bo, "I don't understand you at all."

"Well, there's really no need for you to, is there," said Bo agreeably. "Don't trouble your pretty little head."

"It was you who arranged that fake kidnap message?"

"I didn't exactly *plan* it," he said carefully. "My friend James had the executive part. But I was involved in it, yes."

"How did you know about Gabriel's intentions? And where to find him?"

"He wrote a letter to his mother in England. She showed it to me. So I asked James, who was in New York, to try to locate Gabriel. Which he very efficiently did."

"And so you both planned to make a bit out of Gabriel's death," said Thomas neutrally.

"Only our plan was defeated by Thomas's failure to produce the cash. Of course we could still— What *did* you do with it, Thomas dear? It's not here in the car, is it?" said Bo with momentary hope. "I could put it to far better use than the World Health Organisation or whoever stands to get it ultimately."

"I doubt that. No, it's not here."

"So why are you here now?" Catriona asked Bo.

"Well, the plan's all fucked up, isn't it? And James is angry with me. Tomorrow to fresh woods and pastures new. I thought I'd just like to leave things tidy before I move on. I don't want to argue with Gabriel; nothing of that sort; just tell him a couple of things."

"This is as far as you can take the car," Catriona said to Thomas. "That's the house over there." She spoke jerkily, reluctantly. She added, "Gabriel has gone up into the attic and nailed the door shut."

Then she got out of the car and walked away quickly, stumbling, without choosing to look back and see whether they followed her or not. They did so, in silence; she found them close behind her when she pulled open the front door.

Thomas entered the house with a profound sense of *déjá vu*; coming into a strange house at night, the smell of old pine panelling and woodsmoke. . . .

I don't remember everything, he thought, I had no recollection of those things Bo mentioned in the car; but, my god, some things I do remember; surely I remember enough?

"Where is he?" Bo murmured to Catriona. She indicated the second room with a jerk of her head; she was feeling so deeply wretched, traitor to all her own feelings and beliefs, that she could hardly bear to be in the house with the two men. She had an impulse to walk off again, into the rain. But no, if they were going to stay, she would also; maybe she could find some means of defending Gabriel from them. If it was necessary.

They all went through into the next room, treading softly, as if they were in a hospital ward. The fire had died down to a glow of embers; Catriona built it up again, and then, wrapping herself in one of the blankets from the bed, sat down on the bottom stair and leaned against the door.

"Gabriel," she called in a clear cold voice. "Thomas and your Uncle Bo are here. They have things they want to say to you. I couldn't stop them from coming."

There was a long and what felt like a hostile silence from up above. Catriona shrugged herself farther into her blanket in her shadowy corner.

Thomas took the initiative. He called up:

"Gabriel? Are you there? I wish you'd come down here and talk."

Silence from above. Catriona plaited her fingers together under the blanket.

Bo called, "Gabriel? It's Bo. Can you hear me? I'm not asking you to come down. I just came here—I want to tell you that I'm sorry for any harm I may have done you. Deeply, deeply sorry. I daresay I may have harmed a lot of people for whom I don't give a crap, but for you I do care. You're the person I care for most in the world, after

279

Gus, and I'm sorry if I hurt you; I don't ask you to forgive me, I just wanted to say it."

After a pause he added, "Also I wanted to warn you not to eat any of the food that James left. Unless you want to accelerate your end."

Catriona said softly, "He wasn't planning to use the stuff. He wasn't planning to eat."

Oh, these youthful dramatics, thought Bo, with a touch of irritation. Everything they do has to be so consciously thought out and executed; it's as if they didn't trust themselves to live by instinct.

Then he thought, It's a wonder that James didn't anticipate *that.*

Thomas called, "Gabriel, please don't do this! I shall be so sad if you are dead. I just shan't be able to bear it."

I'm a fool, he thought. All the intelligent arguments he had planned to use had gone clean out of his head. He seemed to have no grammar, no vocabulary, to express the troubled love he felt, the deep, anxious, guilty tender sense of attachment, the apprehension that his own identity and Gabriel's had at some point become irrevocably entangled.

Also, with bitter self-reproach, he remembered old Hannah saying, "He has a right to his death."

"Oh, this is silly," Gabriel's voice remarked suddenly, just over their heads.

The voice coming from the shadowy ceiling was so clear and so much louder than they had expected that both men jumped. Bo dropped his cigarette and trod on it. Thomas, starting nervously sideways, bumped into the bed and sat down.

Bo stooped and lit another cigarette with a twig from the fire, which had blazed up. The leaping flames, yellow and salt-green, illuminated the room with a fitful but much brighter light than that from the candle, which Catriona had set on the mantelpiece.

Gabriel's voice went on, "I don't exactly know how much time I have left. Two or three days, perhaps. Not long. So I wish you'd stop wasting it and leave me in peace."

Thomas said, "Gabriel, surely you don't think Gus would have wanted you to do this? Don't you think he would have been bitterly disappointed?"

"Gus thought one of the main functions of life was preparation for death."

280

"That was only one among all the thousands of other things Gus said."

"Yes, but it's the one that's most relevant to me now. Besides," said Gabriel, and he could not keep a certain triumph out of his voice, "I found a confirmation of it right here. I found some old notes that Gus must have accidentally left behind that time he and I stayed here; they'd been stuffed away in a tin cabinet and I suppose nobody ever looked inside it since. Notes for a 'Dissertation on Death.' "

"You found some notes here by *Gus?*" Thomas said blankly. He got up and moved directly under the trap-door.

"In his handwriting."

"You hadn't known they were there?"

"No."

Thomas had an awe-struck sense of the workings of fate, or irrevocability. He stood in silence. Could this be defeat? Must it be accepted? But Bo exclaimed impatiently:

"Oh, for the love of mud. Now I suppose you feel that Gus was sending you some mystical message? That a divine finger has made a memorandum of the spot where Gus wrote those lines, and then it beckoned you here?"

"I hadn't said that," Gabriel's voice remarked dispassionately.

"No, but I bet you thought it! Let me tell you, Gus was highly preoccupied with death for the last four years of his life, and for a very good reason: he knew he was dying. He'd got leukemia. He knew his number was up. That was why he went dashing around the world so hectically, packing in as much as he possibly could. And that was why he packed so much into you, you poor little Strasbourg gosling, don't you see? He was trying to pack the whole of the rest of his life into you. Only," Bo ended sombrely, "all he really succeeded in doing was packing his death into you."

There was a long silence after Bo had spoken.

Then Thomas said in a low voice, "Was that really so?"

"Of course it was so. Do you think I'd make up a thing like that? He told me about it. He didn't tell many people. Of course he didn't know how long it would take; you can't tell with leukemia; it might have taken up to ten years; I think he hoped to live till Gabriel grew up. He

281

didn't reckon on the air-crash; that was a little extra bit of mischance. But maybe he wouldn't have minded. He'd made his provision, don't you see. Gabriel was his *investment;* his legacy. He had this notion that you could pack a child full of goodies like a—like a space-ship, and sent it off into the unknown. Only with Gabriel the plan seems to have misfired. Gabriel isn't going anywhere."

"Except into the unknown," said Thomas.

"I wonder if people like Gus don't do as much harm as they do good? A guy like that, who concentrates those exceptional forces of mind and personality on one target, whose whole existence is in focus like a laser beam, certainly plays old hob with ordinary people's random everyday life. Don't you think, Thomas, that he did *you* a certain amount of harm?"

"I can't blame him for it," said Thomas after some thought. "Any damage that has been done to me is my own fault."

But he did have a swift, appalling vision of the collision course along which his veneration for Gus had shot him.

Bo said tartly, "Oh, you're just eaten up with self-denigration. I don't know which is more boring, your assumption of superiority or your feelings of inferiority. Why can't you just be equal, like the rest of us?"

Because my sins are as scarlet, thought Thomas. But perhaps everybody's are? An echo came back to him of that scene in the kitchen at No. 38, his saying to Bella, "Everybody has some guilty secret," and her replying angrily, "Speak for yourself! I certainly haven't!"

Loraine had been there, and Bo.

With his mind still half-entangled in the past, Thomas suddenly broke out:

"Gabriel? What is your *real* reason for not wanting to live? For not wanting to grow up? Can you just *explain* to us?"

"I should have thought it was plain enough. I just don't like the way things are. What you call civilisation—the adult world that you and your fellow-grown-ups have created—is just a false degrading sham; humans aren't civilised at all; they are naked, hairy, dirty predators."

"*All* of them? What about Gus? And Shakespeare? And Thomas Paine?"

"There aren't many of those," Gabriel said. "And the rest is just a mess. I don't want to belong to it."

"But even ordinary people have their moments? They love their children and friends. They do disinterested acts of goodness. Can't you look back on *any* worthwhile things in your own life? Friends? People?"

Gabriel said slowly and bitterly, "Are you thinking of my mother? Or yourself, our relationship? Which was all built on deception from the very beginning, wasn't it? Did you think I didn't *know* that it was you who ran over me, that first night? And then took such pains to conceal the fact by driving round the block and pretending to arrive on the scene as a kind rescuer? Did you really believe I didn't know that?"

Thomas's heart shrank inside him to the size of a grain of salt. Sorrow and shame engulfed him. And yet this moment's arrival had been foreseen so long in advance that when it came at last it brought a kind of relief.

"When did you know about that?" he asked after a while.

"All along. Right from the very beginning. Loraine told me. She was up by the pillar-box, posting a letter. She'd seen your car swerve and drive on. She saw the number and the broken rear light. She said there'd be no point in telling the police—or Bella—because you were punished enough by guilt about it. I expect that was true. I used to wonder, often, why you wouldn't ever admit it to me. Why didn't you? It falsified everything we ever said or did together."

Even the chess-walks? wondered Thomas.

"I couldn't," he said. "Once having been committed—and there was Bella too—"

His voice trailed off. He was thinking, all the time Loraine was putting pressure on me by threatening to tell Gabriel, she had *already told him*. What a strange woman. And he thought; all that hideous load of guilt and concealment which I allowed to cripple me and weigh me down and wreck my marriage to Bella—all that time it was crippling Gabriel as well? How could I have been stupid enough not to see that?

He thought of various occasions on which he had considered confessing: "And by the way, my poor child, in addition to seducing your mother, it was I who knocked you down last night and broke your leg." "Oh, Gabriel, there was something that I forgot to mention when we first met . . ." "Incidentally, Gabriel . . ." Each opportunity had shot by, faster, faster still, accelerating like a series of rail-coaches; almost from the start, it had been too late.

His difficulty had been that every instinct urged him to reject the whole experience; disown it; dissociate himself from it. Even on the morning after, he had felt separated from it; to confess would be returning to an existence he felt he had already left behind him. Besides, how could one make such a revelation to an eleven-year-old in hospital? To one's dearly-loved stepson? To Gabriel?

I could do it now, Thomas thought. Too late. I learn too slowly.

Bo said to Gabriel, "He didn't confess because he was afraid of losing everything he had."

"You knew too?" Thomas said to Bo.

"Loraine told me. Devious old girl—she loved these little bits of knowledge and power, she used them like wedges. Not a very successful technique to get love out of people but it was the only way she knew."

Thomas said to Gabriel, "You feel that our relationship was falsified? All of it? Every word, every minute?"

"I would have thought so," Gabriel said after a pause.

"But, look, ducky," exclaimed Bo, "no one, *no* one tells everything to any other person—ever; people's relationships just aren't built in that way."

Catriona spoke for the first time since they had come in:

"Ours was. Gabriel's and mine. We told each other everything."

"It's just not possible," Bo said with conviction. "And even if it was—if you thought it was—you couldn't sustain it for more than a few months."

"Perhaps," Gabriel said.

It was plain that the argument seemed unimportant to him; the balance of his attention was not engaged.

It's like a cold-weather front, Bo thought; you can practically feel it: the warmth of our affection and concern rising to the ceiling and hitting that stone-cold shield of nonreceptivity and sinking down again defeated.

He said, "It's true we're all corrupt and a mess and have done atrocious things to each other. Like Thomas and me. But still, we're the only *us* we've got. We might as well make the best of it, don't you think? There really isn't any point in our hating ourselves, because very likely the things that we regard as our worst actions aren't the

284

ones that have actually done the most harm. Look at Thomas there—he can't even remember the worst thing he did to me. So what's the point of my bearing a grudge about it? We might as well try to like each other."

Gabriel remarked tonelessly, "How can you love somebody who's completely false, through and through, completely self-centred, like Bella?"

"Oh, you're such a child!" Bo said with impatience. "I keep forgetting you're only sixteen. Why did I let myself get involved in this argument? I came here with the intention of saying my piece and asking you to forgive me—or forgiving *you,* perhaps, for the pain you've given me—and then leaving. And I wanted to say, try to think less harshly of Bella. All she can do is play one part or another, she really has no core; it's no use blaming her, poor girl."

Gabriel said, and it was plain that this was where his thoughts had really been for the last ten minutes:

"Was Gus truly dying?"

"He was. I wouldn't lie to you about that. When he came to stay here, he'd just had the confirmation. I have a letter from him dated around then, telling me."

"You have it *on* you?"

"Of course not. Back in England. But part of it," said Bo, "I know by heart. Long before anyone else would have had any inkling that he was beginning to fail, he had guessed it himself. He wrote, 'This feeling of despair at being so consciously on the downhill run demoralises me . . . . So much that I would like to do, and know I can't; roads, oceans, endeavours, all closed to me; not, without pain, to be thought of.' "

Another long silence fell; during it, Catriona silently fetched some more wood and put it on the fire.

After a while Bo said, "Thomas would understand that too. You know, Gabriel, that Thomas is in severe permanent pain? At this very moment it's probably almost unbearable. He's an extremely sick man, and yet when Bella asked him to, he came over here and started clambering about New York looking for you which has no doubt made his condition considerably worse. And what is more, he is aware that soon—in a year or two—it will almost certainly get so very much more acute that he will be in *unbearable* pain *all* the time. You know that, don't you, Thomas?"

Almost inaudibly Thomas said, "Yes."

Catriona turned her head in the folds of the blanket and silently looked at him.

Gabriel said nothing.

"But Thomas isn't planning on putting an end to himself," Bo went on brutally. "No, he intends to stay alive. Why, I wonder? Because he's got courage—curiosity— a little bit of hope—a lot of love, distributed about in unlikely places? . . . You're such an authority on life, up there in your ivory tower, Gabriel—have you any useful suggestions as to how Thomas can make the most of his latter years?"

He waited, looking up at the square dark hole in the ceiling. Thomas and Catriona said nothing. From above came a short indeterminate sound, as if Gabriel had slightly shifted, or coughed, or begun to clear his throat.

Thomas opened his mouth to speak; he wanted to make some protest, say that his illness was strictly his own affair, in no way related to the argument, had been unfairly made use of by Bo.

But Gabriel cleared his throat again, then said, "Uncle Tom?" in a voice that swiftly took Thomas back five years to some frosty afternoon on Wanborough Common with tea waiting back at home. "Uncle Tom, maybe you could leave yourself messages? From now to then? Like polar explorers, leaving little caches to find on the way back?"

Thomas said, "You're thinking of Gus's message to you? Or perhaps the message was to himself; perhaps he hoped to come back here someday."

Gabriel was heard to move again. Thomas, remembering some of the things that had come into his mind while he stood by Mrs. Baird's deathbed—when? could that really have been today?—went on:

"Have you ever imagined yourself at the age of eighty, Gabriel? Old, and stuffed full of knowledge and learning, like Gus, with hundreds of friends—colleagues —children, maybe grandchildren, people you can't even *imagine* now; and all your memories, of us, of this time, of Catriona, packed away like a huge trunk full of experience? If you could leave a message for that person, Gabriel, what would you say? Or if he could leave a message for you, what do you think he would say?"

He could feel his heart was beating so hard that he had

to stop speaking. He pressed a hand against his chest and was vaguely surprised to find that his jacket was wet. Perhaps his heart had bled a little? But then he remembered the rain.

The interval after his question lasted so long that he began to wonder in terror if Gabriel was ever going to speak again. And when the silence was broken at last, it was not by Gabriel, but by a knock at the door.

"Sweet, vernal Christ," Bo muttered under his breath. "If that's Bella—"

He took four strides through the kitchen to the outer door, snatched open the screen, and disappeared outside. Thomas and Catriona heard the low murmur of voices—then a higher one, unmistakably Bella's, protesting:

"I certainly can come in! It's pouring! Are you crazy?"

Thomas quickly followed Bo through the door. He was in a state of confusion—exhaustion, exaltation; he thought, I'm played out, can't do any more, I've probably done too much already. How can one tell? The only thing we can do now is leave him in peace. Did anything we said have any effect?

Hannah's voice rang in his ears again: the boy has a right to his own death.

But Bo was right about Bella; her intrusion could bring nothing but disaster. Thomas wondered if he should drive her to some inn or motel? Both of them, perhaps? Leave Catriona with the boy?

It took a moment for his eyes to adjust to the dark. But at least the rain had nearly stopped. Then he saw Bo and Bella, outlined in the headlights of a second car beyond the patch of tussocky grass, evidently engaged in a furious argument.

He went towards them.

Bo was saying, "There isn't the slightest chance that anything you could say would influence him. He's upstairs, he's locked himself in. Thomas has spoken to him. I've spoken to him. No, Bella. It just wouldn't be the least use."

"Are you out of your mind? Are you planning just to leave him there?" she cried out in a high, furious voice. Then over Bo's shoulder she saw Thomas. "Is there a phone here?" she demanded. "Thomas, call up Dr. Redford Moberley at the Cambridge Clinic. Tell him Gabriel's here and he'd better send a psychiatrist as well as an ambulance. At top speed! And tell him to call Manresa. There's abolutely no time to lose!"

"No, Bella," Thomas said firmly. "That's not the way to solve Gabriel's problem."

He didn't even bother to tell her there was no phone. He put an arm around her shoulders and turned her. "Is this your car? Please go! I do absolutely promise you, the only thing for you to do is to go back to New York and get a bit of sleep. Bo, why don't you take her?"

"You're just beasts, you're beasts!"

Bella burst into loud, childish sobs, tears jerking from her eyes, her mouth drawn into an ugly square. "I've been lost for *hours,* driving all over this stinking island in the dark, on my own, while you've been here all the time conspiring behind my back, and when I do get here all you can tell me to do is to go away——"

"Don't talk balls, ducky," Bo said, "Thomas is perfectly right. The best thing for us all is to split—*Jesus*—what was that?"

Behind them they heard a sudden loud, rough, roaring thump, like a gulp of a gas jet, several thousand times amplified. Thomas whirled round just in time to see the roof-ridge burst apart, upwards, on the circumference of a great fan of ginger-coloured flame.

"Oh, my god!" he said, and started back towards the house.

Bella screamed, and stumbled towards the bushes.

"Thomas, you fool, *stop!*" Bo shouted. In three strides he overtook Thomas and flung him down into the wet grass. Then he raced through the door. The kitchen was still dark but the room beyond was already lit from within by red pulsing light. And the upper storey was roaring scarlet, sending out showers of sparks like a petrol-fed fire.

He can't be alive in that, thought Thomas, staggering to his feet. Not a shadow of a hope. Was *that* what James had arranged?

Bella ran up behind him, sobbing, and grabbed his arm. "What *happened?* Where's Bo?"

Bo reappeared in the doorway with Catriona, whom he half carried, half dragged.

"You okay?" he said, setting her down. She nodded, speechless. "Lucky for you your clothes were so wet——" And he vanished inside again.

288

"Bo, come back!" Bella wailed.

"Bo, it's hopeless!" Thomas shouted. He ran after Bo, through the door, but met a black stifling wave of chemical smoke, and paused; as he did so, Bo bumped into him coming out fast. He was gasping from the fumes.

"You're right: hopeless. One thing; it must have been a quick one," Bo said. "Poor Gabriel. Poor little lad."

"What do you mean, what do you *mean?*"

Bella stared from one of them to the other. "He can't be dead—you can't just give up like that?"

"Use your loaf, girl," Bo said, and turned her round to look at the flamboyant gold fountaining nest of fire which was already all that remained of the upper storey. The wooden walls had burned like paper. They could see half the central brick chimney sticking up, a black finger in the red fire; as they watched, it twisted and crumpled and fell. The mill building at the farther end was already beginning to catch; flames ran up the shingled wall and a shower of sparks flew from a lower window.

"Even a salamander couldn't keep alive in that," Bo said flatly.

"But what could have happened? What began it?"

Bo said, "God knows. But whatever it was we'd better go and get the fire squad or they'll have a bush fire on their hands next. Come on, Bella—you'll have to drive. You're not wanted here anyhow and will only be in the way. Thomas, keep an eye on the girl, will you? . . . We'll be back soon—"

Keeping tight hold of Bella's arm, he made her run to the car.

"Now, drive it *fast*—get going!"

Nineteen

Gabriel

Gabriel had left the trapdoor hole, and returned to the sill of the big dormer, where he was sitting with his arms round his knees. And he had withdrawn his attention from the group below into the very centre of his being. If they would only go right away, he thought, so that I could expand into the silence.

The tabby cat had jumped up beside him. Absently he rubbed its head, thinking, If Gus had lived a few years longer . . .

When the sudden, overwhelming, simultaneous fury of noise and red-hot wind flung him on his back, he felt an active outrage; he thought, I wasn't ready for this yet, what have they done to me? He felt his breath dragged away as if by a noose; flailing his arms, he struggled up, then fell forward again onto his knees. . . .

Twenty

Bo and Bella

Startled into compliance by Bo's voice and manner and the speed of his actions, Bella did as he told her, reversed the car, and drove back along the sand road. When they came to the highway he said, "Turn right." She did so. After she had driven about a mile they passed a house.

"Stop. Wait here," Bo said, "while I use their phone. Just wait. Don't get out."

She was still shocked and docile; she sat huddled in the car, giving an occasional sob, like a child that has almost cried itself to a standstill, until he came back.

"Very obliging people in that house," he remarked. "Mr. and Mrs. Moss. They were impressed by my English accent and civil thanks for the use of their phone. They even exercised admirable self-restraint and didn't listen. Now drive on."

"This way? Shouldn't we turn round?"

"No, I asked them the way. Keep going."

After a while she said, puzzled, "It seems so much farther than the way we came. Are you sure this is right?"

"It's okay. Keep going."

After another long interval she said, "But Boney—this is the town? St. George—isn't it?"

"That's right."

"But I thought we were going back to the house?"

"No, what would be the point? We can't help Thomas; and the girl may be a bit burned but she'll be all right. And there's nothing we can do for Gabriel. The fire squad will get there soon—the guy I spoke to knew the place, they're very likely on the spot already; though I daresay they won't be able to save much. No, you and I will just go quietly on our way."

When she began to protest, he said, "Just attend to your driving, sweetie, for Christ's sake, will you? It would be too boring for words to be picked up *now* for flagrant traffic violations. So shut your mouth and keep your eyes on the road. Look, there's the way to the ferry, down there on the right."

When she had safely driven them on board the boat, he said,

"Well done, ducky; clever girl," and gave her a light kiss.

There were few cars crossing over to Manhattan at that time of night. The roomy car-deck was two-thirds empty.

"Let's go up above," Bo suggested. "The car won't run away."

They climbed the stairs to the main deck, and on up to the top.

"Might as well go right up while we're at it," said Bo, "and gaze at all the pretty lights." He led her forward and through the sliding doors on to the outer promenade. "Now look: did you ever see anything to beat that?"

Across the black water sparkled all the lights from New Jersey, and from Brooklyn, and from Governors Island. Directly ahead of them the illuminated towers of Manhattan floated and glittered.

"Just like lit-up cheese-graters," Bo said. "I'm glad to have had that for my last eyeful."

Bella had begun to shiver, and was not heeding him. She said, "I'd really rather have stayed there at the house, Boney. There might have been just a chance—"

"Sweetie, there was no chance. It was hopeless. All we can hope is that old Tom Thum or his granddaughter are insured."

"I can't get that awful sight out of my mind," she wept. "That great awful yellow flame— Boney: why did the fire spread so terribly *fast?* Do you think it was something that James had done?"

He replied in a colourless tone, "Possibly; who can say? Maybe he stuck a bomb in the chimney. It could have been activated by heat; designed to go off when the fire down below had burned for a certain length of time; we'll never know."

"Well, if it was," she said vehemently, "I think it was the most horrible, murderous thing that I've ever heard. He deserves to be *shot.*"

"Oh come on," said Bo. "Things like that do get done. Let's not add hypocrisy to the list of our sins."

"It was murder."

"You can hardly talk, sweetie. What about poor old Loraine? Doesn't her death lie at your door?"

"I never touched her," said Bella fretfully. "Just told her I didn't want to see her again, after she wrote that tattletale letter to Thomas. Stupid old busybody."

"You were so savage to her that she went straight home and took an overdose."

"Well, who cared? No one gave a damn whether she was alive or dead."

"You miss her."

"Yes I do," she admitted. "But that's not like Gabriel—"

"There's no use going on about it," said Bo roughly. "We messed him up, one way and another, and he's done for."

"He wouldn't have been if it hadn't been for that

292

bloody James. . . . Anyway, let that be a lesson to you. I hope you'll never see him again."

"James, James, Morrison, Morrison, Weatherby George Dupree . . . No, well, don't worry. I never shall."

"Can't we go inside, Boney?" She had begun to cry again, as well as shiver. "It's *too* cold out here and I do feel so miserable. Perhaps we could get a drink at that bar."

"Let's just wait till the boat begins to move. Look at the pretty lights and have a swig of this."

He pulled the whisky bottle out of his anorak pocket and passed it to her.

"Leave some for me, though—That's the girl. Better?"

"A little."

He took a drink himself, then put his arm around her.

Bella leaned against him and said, hiccupping with sobs, "I just feel so sad about Gabriel. Poor little boy. Perhaps if I hadn't had him adopted right at the start, things might have worked out."

"Perhaps. But I rather doubt it. You weren't cut out to be a mum. You hadn't had a very good example in old Sadie, I daresay."

"Somehow, after I married Gus and got Gabriel back, it was all different. He wasn't the same dear little baby and I couldn't take to him. It was too late."

"Yes, too late," said Bo. "A lot of things have happened too late for us, Sarsaparilla. We can hardly be regarded as models of how to be successful and win friends."

"If Gus hadn't died—"

"If wishes were Volkswagens— Never mind. We've got each other, haven't we? When all else has failed we can keep each other company; at least you and I are in the same boat, my love, even if it's chugging across the Styx." He murmured absently, "Five, six, pick up sticks; seven, eight, lay them straight . . ."

"In the same boat?" Bella picked up the phrase, only half catching his drift. Her eyes were still on the lights ahead. "You mean we might go on a trip together—a cruise? I'd love that, Boney. —Maybe we should take Thomas along? Do you think that would be good for his arthritis?"

"*No*, my angel. It would not. There's only one thing we can do for Thomas: and that's a far, far better thing.

Just leave him in peace. Let him find his own way out. —Look we're moving. Want another swig, the last?"

"Yes, please, Boney," she said gratefully.

Tht siren sounded and the ferry slid out into the black rippling water over which the lights of New York danced and glanced.

"Shall we go inside now?"

"Yes, please, Boney," she said again. "It's too cold out here."

"Okay. That way. Along to the end. Through the little gate."

"This isn't the way we came," she said, as she had in the car.

"No, but it's the way we're going. It's quicker."

He guided her with a hand on her arm. "I'll unhook that chain; right; now turn left, round the corner."

First looking quickly behind him, he gave her a sharp, determined push that sent her hurtling outwards from the side of the boat. She let out one short, gasping cry as she fell, turning in mid-air so that he saw her face, white in the light from the main deck, staring at him in astonishment with her mouth open; then she was gone.

"I'm coming too, lovey," called Bo, and jumped outwards after her.

Nobody had seen them fall.

The ferry rumbled on its way.

Twenty-One

Thomas, Catriona

The fire-engines arrived with a crescendo of gibbering wails. Uniformed men came crashing through the bushes.

"You'll have to shift that car," one of them called to Thomas. "It's in our way there. Can't get close enough."

When Thomas returned from doing this, he looked around for Catriona. She had been standing by the walnut tree, staring numbly at the roaring mass of flame. But now she was gone.

"Have you seen a girl?" he asked one of the firemen.

Nobody heard him. Falling into a panic, Thomas began to hunt desperately about in the lurid half-dark. He tripped over tussocks of swampy grass. He blundered into trees. His arms and face were lacerated by thorns.

"Catriona!" he yelled. "Catriona. Where are you?"

Then he heard her voice, unexpectedly close behind him, and felt her hands grab at his arm.

"Thomas! Quick—come quickly—*I've found him!*"

"Found him? How do you mean, found him? Found whom?"

But already she was pulling him down the slope on the far side of the house and he was following her eager tug; they slid and stumbled, almost falling several times, for the reedy grass and mare's-tails covering the bank had been flattened by rain into a steep and slippery surface with no footholds.

Farther out, the puckered hummocky surface of the marsh was illuminated by the flames, but at the bottom of the slope there was a patch of shade. Tall pale crested rushes grew here, eight or nine feet high. And in the shadow, sprawled among the rushes, lay something that could have been a log. But it was not a log, for one of its outflung branchlike extremities terminated in a whitish blob, which, when illuminated by an extra-high tongue of fire leaping up behind them, Thomas saw to be a human hand.

For a moment he pulled back, overwhelmed by terror of what he might have to face, but Catriona said:

"It's all right—he's *all right*. At least—he's not burned. He's a bit cut about. He must have been blown right out of the window by that first explosion. . . . Do you think he's very badly hurt?" And she repeated in a lower voice, "Do you think he's very badly hurt?"

Thomas knelt in two inches of mud and water. He took the outflung hand, feeling for a pulse. It was there. Gabriel lay on his back, in a soft hammock of ooze and mare's-tails and broken rushes. One arm was doubled under him. His eyes were closed. But he was breathing.

"Catriona. Run up and collar one of the firemen. They have radio. Tell them to get an ambulance here *fast*. We daren't move him without expert help—he may have internal injuries."

What was that name Bella had been brandishing about

295

—something to do with Versailles. "Yes. . . . Say he's a patient of Dr. Moberley at the Cambridge Heart Clinic and may need urgent surgery—tell them to let Moberley know—"

She nodded, and was gone.

He has been betrayed again, thought Thomas, kneeling in the water. This time by a trick of fate. If we can get help in time—if he isn't too badly hurt—if it's not too late for the operation—is there a chance that we might persuade him to see a kind of comedy in it all?

He didn't want to live, he locked himself in, but providence, or God, just threw him out to start again.

Well, what can we do? We must go on living, Uncle Vanya.

Poor Bella. Perhaps I can somehow get to see her as comic too; as a kind of sad, awful joke—perhaps ultimately I can learn to love her by some such roundabout means? She needs looking after. I ought to do that. It's my job. I felt really bad about having to hustle her off with Bo.

He went on kneeling by the motionless figure. There should be snow, he thought. Black-and-white stripes on the road. Big dark trees tossing their branches. This has happened once already. But if we come out of this one, perhaps we can persuade him to turn in the other direction; hope for some change of viewpoint that'll make him devote his energy to life, not death.

Catriona came back, running.

"They've sent the message," she said, and, dropping down by Gabriel, she began wiping his forehead and face clear of mud and blood with her wet handerchief. His eyes remained closed. Thomas tried to stifle the foolish growth of hope. After all, what chance would there be? One in fifty? In a hundred?

Just the same, hope would grow.

Aftr a while, Catriona collected some armfuls of rushes.

"Here," she said. "Sit on these. They aren't dry, but at least it's better than sitting right in the *water*."

"Thank you, my dear."

She fetched another armful for herself and settled down to wait beside him.

Keep Up With The BESTSELLERS!